# Also by Antoine Vanner

*Britannia's Wolf*
The Dawlish Chronicles, Volume 1
September 1877 - February 1878

*Britannia's Reach*
The Dawlish Chronicles, Volume 2
November 1879 - April 1880

*Britannia's Shark*
The Dawlish Chronicles, Volume 3
April – September 1881

*Britannia's Spartan*
The Dawlish Chronicles, Volume 4
June 1859 and April - August 1882

*Britannia's Amazon*
The Dawlish Chronicles Volume 5
April – August 1882
(Includes bonus short story *Britannia's Eye*)

*Britannia's Gamble*
The Dawlish Chronicles Volume 6
March 1884 – February 1885

Being accounts of episodes in the lives of

Nicholas Dawlish R.N.
Born: Shrewsbury 16.12.1845
Died: Zeebrugge 23.04.1918

and

Florence Dawlish, née Morton
Born: Northampton 17.06.1855
Died: Portsmouth 12.05.1946

# Britannia's Mission

## The Dawlish Chronicles

## August 1883 – February 1884

By

# Antoine Vanner

Library of Congress Cataloguing-in-Publication Data:

Antoine Vanner 1945 -

Britannia's Mission / Antoine Vanner.

ISBN-13: 978-1-943404-23-0 ISBN-10: 1943404232

(The Dawlish Chronicles Volume 7)

Cover design by Sara Lee Paterson

Published by Old Salt Press

Old Salt Press, LLC is based in Jersey City, New Jersey with an affiliate in New Zealand

For more information about our titles go to www.oldsaltpress.com

To learn more about the Dawlish Chronicles go to:
www.dawlishchronicles.com

# Britannia's Mission

## Author's Note:

Though published as the seventh volume of the Dawlish Chronicles series, the action in *Britannia's Mission* falls chronologically between that in *Britannia's Spartan* and *Britannia's Amazon* (both: April – August 1883) and the beginning of *Britannia's Gamble* (March 1884 – February 1885).

# Prologue

## 1883, Congo Basin, South West of Lake Mweru

None of them had heard of Hell, but now it had come to them.

Noises like short thunderclaps had woken them just before dawn. The first screaming had followed, then shouting in some tongue strange to them. Half-befuddled by sleep, men had blundered from the huts, alarmed but not yet terrified, leaving the women and children cowering within. Brief stabs of flame flashed in the lessening darkness and several men cried out as they were smashed down by an unseen force. By now several huts were ablaze and the burning thatch cast flickering light and darting shadows through which the attackers advanced.

Nobody had seen anybody like them before, nor had any been further than a day's hunting from this village. The people known to be beyond that limit looked like themselves, their language different but a few words comprehensible, enough to know, and to accept, that they should not intrude upon each other without bloodshed. But these newcomers – men, all of them – who rampaged between the flame-lit huts were lighter skinned than they could have imagined. Loose clothing flapped about them and their heads were swathed in cloth. Others followed, dark and all but naked like the villagers themselves, but with tattoo marks or scar-patterns on their cheeks, merciless as they chopped down or speared any who resisted.

But that resistance was brief, shock and terror paralysing even the youngest and strongest of the men, and it seemed as if the attackers' objective was capture, not slaughter. As the sky lightened the greater part of the villagers had been herded together and ringed by spearmen, the men too bewildered and too numbed to speak, the women wailing, or shaking in silent fright, crying babies held close, terrified children clutching their knees. Around them, burning thatch was collapsing in showers of sparks and the stench carried by the drifting smoke told that some had not emerged from their huts in time. Others who had fled into the forest that pressed close on the vegetable patches beyond the huts had been tracked down. Wounded and blood-streaked, they came stumbling back before the blows of their hunters to join the knot of misery.

The clothed men had no eyes for the captives yet. They hurried from one unburned hut to the next, searching, not finding what they sought,

7

rushing on to the next. They came at last to the hut, larger than the rest, that was the place of awe to which the most sacred trophies had been carried for generation after generation. It had filled slowly – the killing of one of the great forest beasts was an infrequent and memorable event and whole years sometimes passed before more evidence of skill and courage joined the hoard. The searchers were crying out in delight at their find and summoning their companions to admire it. Now the long tusks were being dragged out, the first a still-bright reminder of a triumph a year before. Those that followed were older, yellower, the deeper-hued stored here since before any in the village could remember. The pile grew, and then at last the darkest ones of all, dull brown, a few wholly black. Yet even these most ancient showed creamy white streaks when blades were scraped along them.

It was mid-morning now, the heat intense, the captives crouched, hungry and thirsty and without shade in sun's full blaze. The women's wails were whimpers, the children silent, the men engulfed in a stupor, their minds stunned by incomprehension as much as by terror.

One young man – he had been of the party that had carried the brightest of the tusks back to the village a year since – tried to break from the group but a spear-shaft thrust between his running legs tripped him. The black men surrounding him were poised to plunge their weapons into him when a bellow from one of the light-skinned, clothed, men stayed their hands. He strode forward, loosening the long coil that hung at his waist, and at his command they threw the prisoner down on his face. His arms and legs were spread, then weighed down by a man apiece. The clothed man stepped back, measuring the distance, and then the coil was sweeping back across his shoulder, cracking as it straightened, then lashing forward to lay a bloody gash across the captive's back. He screamed, chest and stomach arching from the ground, his writhing almost enough to drag his limbs free before he was pushed flat again. And then the next lash, and the next, and the next again, the yielder of the whip stepping to one side or the other so as to lay each new stripe at an angle to the last. So it continued, the screams rising in pitch, the young man's back by now a bloody pulp, until at last there were groans only. And soon afterwards a silence, and a stillness. There were no further attempts to break free.

The captive villagers were now all but ignored by any but the guarding spearmen. There was no language in common but the price of attempting to escape had been made so clear that even the strongest shrank from risking it. The attackers were resting in shade, some asleep, some sharing food. Others like them arrived and they gathered around the heaped tusks, nodding, laughing, clearly satisfied. More of their black helpers had come with them and they were sent out into the forest, returning with newly-hacked branches. These seemed to have been selected carefully, all a generally similar length, all with a single stem that forked at one end, their purpose unclear.

A commotion just before noon announced the coming of yet more like the attackers, all carrying on their shoulders those long dark tubes set in polished wood that inflicted death and wounds with sharp barks and smoke-enshrouded flame. Behind them came the strangest apparition of all, a light-skinned, sharp-featured man – old, for his hair and beard were white – who wore loose garments of colours brighter than ever seen here before. He was sitting on a strange grey animal, one that nobody could have conceived of, four legged like a forest antelope, but stockier, less graceful, no horns upon its head, two long ears in their place. The plodding beast was being led and another man was following close behind and holding a circular shade above the old man's head. The procession passed the prisoners with hardly a glance and headed to the pile of tusks. The old man was helped from the animal when he reached the heap – his satisfaction obvious, his greeting of the finders jovial. Under his direction the tusks were examined and laid out in rows.

Only afterwards did the other sorting begin. First the old men and women, and the obviously badly wounded, all dragged from the cringing mass, herded to the vegetable patches and clubbed or speared there. Then, the turn of women who looked close to childbirth, and afterwards infants dragged from screaming mothers, their heads smashed on to the ground before them. The older children were driven to where the elderly had died, killed there no less brutally for all their piteous cries. What remained were the able-bodied.

The binding and the shackling commenced, the purpose of those forked sticks now revealed, submission enforced by lash. By mid-afternoon they were stumbling away from the devastated homes, a thin column of misery trudging into an unknown world.

They did not know it yet, but their village had been the first of many. The column would grow as it trailed from one to the next even though many in it would collapse by the wayside and be finished by a club or spear thrust. And all the while the number of tusks swinging from the poles resting on two men's shoulders would grow and with it the satisfaction of the old man on the tireless long-eared animal.

None of them understood why this had befallen them, where they were going, what would become of them. They had lost all count of days, lived in a present of minutes only. Existence was no more than endurance of the next step, of the day's thirst, of the night's hunger, of the dreaded lash, of festering weals, of flesh rubbed raw by wood and metal.

And then a last attack on a village, the one that yielded the greatest spoils of all. Afterwards the column had a new line of march.

Towards the direction from which the sun rises.

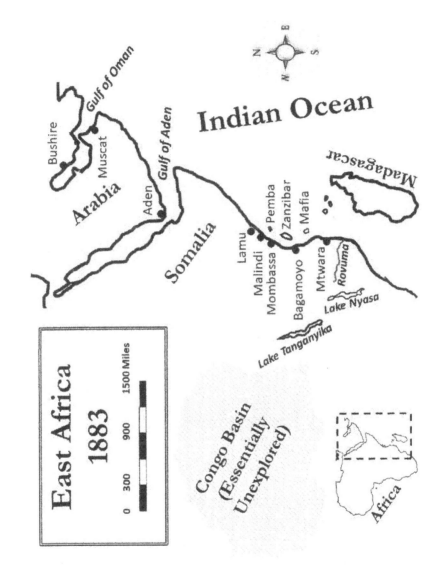

East Africa 1883

0    300    900    1500 Miles

Indian Ocean

Gulf of Oman

Gulf of Aden

Bushire

Muscat

Arabia

Aden

Somalia

Lamu
Malindi
Mombassa
Bagamoyo
Mtwara

Pemba
Zanzibar
Mafia

Madagascar

Rovuma

Lake Nyasa

Lake Tanganyika

Congo Basin
(Essentially
Unexplored)

Africa

Dawlish had left her in the tea salon of the Harte and Garter, where they had lodged the night before. Florence had seated herself by the window, looking out across Thames Street towards the green slope that led up to the massive wall of Windsor Castle. He knew that she would have given years of her life to have accompanied him there, though she had assured him that it was proper that he should be invited only by himself.

"It's your day, Nick," she had said. "It's you who earned it."

"Not just me, Florence. The entire crew."

And most of all those humble seamen and marines of HMS *Leonidas* who had been left behind forever in Korean soil. It was because the business there had been so diplomatically embarrassing, even if so essential, that there could be no official recognition, no awards of medals, no mentions in the *London Gazette*. Her poles bare, her discarded yards perhaps still drifting somewhere in the Yellow Sea, her battle-damage patched, but with her engines beating as smoothly after ten-thousand miles as when she had left the Orient, *Leonidas* had slid into the harbour at Portsmouth just after Christmas 1882 with as little ceremony as if she had returned from a training cruise off the Irish coast. In the eight months since then the cruiser, after drydocking and refitting, had served in the Channel Fleet.

Florence had handled the heavy vellum paper of the invitation – the summons, rather – with the reverence she might have owed a sacred text. The language was formal – Dawlish was addressed as trusty and well-beloved – and left no doubt that the audience would be no less so. A letter that accompanied it, signed by Her Majesty's secretary but probably drafted by some lesser functionary, specified that Captain Dawlish should not attend in uniform. Court-dress was not required for this afternoon meeting. He was to present himself at the castle the previous day to be instructed in the necessary protocol. The audience was to last ten minutes.

That letter had delighted Florence no less than the invitation and Dawlish guessed that she would preserve both to her dying day. She had insisted that he must have new clothes for the occasion, had accompanied him to a tailor whom he had considered too expensive – though he could not refuse, for the joy it gave her – and she had fussed over every detail of the fittings that followed.

She rose to her feet as he returned an hour later. Her face was flushed with love and pride.

"Was she as gracious as they say?" She asked when they sat. "Were any of the princesses there? Helena or Beatrice or Louise?"

"Gracious? As you might expect." He was happy in her pleasure. "But are you not going to offer me some tea, Florence?"

"You're going to make me drag it out of you, Nicholas. Aren't you?"

"There's not much to tell. I was told that the lady with her would be Princess Helena, and she was. And her secretary was there, and another gentleman." He did not say that it was Admiral Sir Richard Topcliffe. As ever, in severely elegant civilian garb. "Nobody else."

"The room must have been so splendid."

"Magnificent, Florence."

It had in fact been small, slightly shabby, as comfortably cluttered as any unassuming middle-class drawing room. It had seemed strange to enter it with such formality, to bow, to wait respectfully until a slight nod from the secretary indicated that he should respond to the small black-clad lady's thanks. She was more unimpressive than he could ever have imagined, a woman who radiated neither intelligence nor warmth. And yet for her he had seen men die and for her he had put his own life at risk.

"Did she ask about Korea, Nicholas? About Queen Min?"

There had been no mention of either. The British and Japanese governments, intent on forging an alliance, had both decided that what had happened the previous year had never in fact occurred.

"Nothing about that, Florence. She just asked about how long I had served in the Navy and she thanked me for it." He reached into his pocket. "She asked me to accept this." He laid a small leather-covered box on the table.

Florence took it up, flipped it open.

13

"It's emerald, Nick!" The faceted stone at the centre of the golden tie-pin sparkled green. "So beautiful! Oh, Nicholas! You must be so proud!"

"She mentioned you too, Florence. She'd been told about your care for seamen's families. And about the Sailor's Rest, all the good it does."

Topcliffe must have mentioned it. For one bitter instant Dawlish wondered if Florence too might have been included in the invitation had she had not once been a servant.

"She asked me to give you this. As a small compensation for the separations an officer's wife must endure, she said."

"Oh Nicholas!"

He took the book from his inside pocket. It was covered in tooled red leather, golden lettering on the cover and spine.

*Leaves from the Journal of Our Life in the Highlands.*

"Her own book!" Florence had opened it, had seen the handwriting on the fly-leaf.

*To Mrs. Florence Dawlish, in appreciation.*

And the signature.

*Victoria R.*

Florence was turning the pages in delight, pausing at engravings, closing it and running her fingers over the cover, opening it again.

"I could never have dreamt, Nicholas, never that…"

"I'm not sure that it's the sort of literature that a respectable married woman should be exposed to." He was frowning in mock severity. "There might be some subjects best not alluded to, some episodes that might outrage decent feeling. I think that as a husband I must protect your delicacy and …"

She began to laugh and her face was as he loved it most, as he always remembered it in time of absence.

"I love you, Nicholas Dawlish," she said.

They sat there for another hour, and had tea, and he told her more of the audience – though there was little enough to tell – and they were happy.

But he did not tell her that Topcliffe had followed him after he had backed, bowing, from the room.

"I'd like to see you at the club, Dawlish," he had said. "You know the place. Tomorrow, eleven o'clock, in the library. There's something you'll find interesting."

Dawlish had met Topcliffe in that Pall Mall club before.

And what it had led to had almost killed him.

*

There was no bait this time, no hint about command of some new ship, only the unspoken understanding that continued career-advancement would depend on absolute acquiescence.

They might have been two men, civilians, engaged in discussion of some shared cultural or scientific interest, a half-dozen volumes plucked from the shelves and lying on a low table by Topcliffe's wing-chair, one open. He rose when Dawlish entered, shook hands, asked the club servant who had ushered him in to bring coffee. Then the usual small talk while waiting, enquiries about Mrs. Dawlish's health and praise for her welfare activities. An admirable woman, an ideal naval wife, an example to others.

And as he listened Dawlish realised that he knew nothing of this man's own family, if there was one. An admiral Topcliffe might be, but one seldom seen at the Admiralty. He was unknown to the majority of serving officers, was remembered by his contemporaries as a man who had once been tipped for greatness but who had slipped into some obscure and nominal role. Even Dawlish himself had little understanding of what that role might be, other than that Topcliffe's concerns went far beyond naval matters alone and that he answered to authorities more senior than the Lords of the Admiralty. What others did for Topcliffe – Dawlish suspected that he himself was not the only one who served him – seldom came to wider notice but the consequences of their success or failure might well result in the making or breaking of nations.

All the while, unmentioned but recognised by both as they exchanged platitudes, lay the brutal fact that the older officer held the younger's career in his hands. Acceptance of certain missions had earned rapid promotion, command of a crack warship, unobtrusive patronage and a vague promise of further advancement. But a single refusal of a suggestion – never as direct as a request, or as stark as an order – would end that support instantly. No more desirable ship-commands, no prospect of an eventual admiral's flag and knighthood, nothing better than long stultifying years in an administrative position at some naval dockyard.

Now a brief discussion, enquiries and answers about the Channel Fleet exercises in which *Leonidas* had recently participated, about the remarkable accuracy of her six-inch breech-loaders, weapons that were now entering more general service. Her sisters were being commissioned – she was the first of her class – and the insights gained about boiler and machinery performance on her voyage to the Orient and back had resulted in various improvements in the new ships. No reference to what had happened in Korea, nor to the days of searching enquiry about it to which Topcliffe had subjected Dawlish on his return.

The library was otherwise deserted and Topcliffe asked the waiter who brought the coffee to ensure that that they would not be disturbed.

"You have extensive experience of anti-slavery work, Dawlish?"

Dawlish nodded. It was a statement rather than a question. Topcliffe knew that he had. The first time as a young midshipman off Brazil. And later participation in an operation at Pemba, the island north of Zanzibar, that had first brought Dawlish to Topcliffe's attention. Seven years before. An aeon.

"You understand the complexities and legalities and sensitivities."

He did, and they were more difficult than the simple act of running down dhows carrying human freight to Arabia. Slavery was still internationally recognised as legal within the territories of the Sultan of Zanzibar, the narrow strip of ill-defined Arab-governed possessions that straggled northwards toward Somalia along the East African coast. It was also recognised as legal in the smaller holdings of the Sultan of Mtwara further south. It was trading outside these dominions that was illegal.

"Anti-slaving's a good schooling for young officers, sir," Dawlish said. A neutral answer. "Hard lessons and fast learning. But it'll never be enough to stop the trade. Most of the dhows will always get through. It

16

would take half the navy if we were to stop them even if the lawyers were kept out of it."

For dhow-captains often argued that the slaves they carried were legally-held domestic slaves carried as passengers. Blindly-legalistic courts often upheld such claims. Lawyers prospered, junior naval officers were often condemned for naïve over-zealousness, careers were ruined and the slaves themselves were no more than pawns.

"We must live in the world as we find it, Dawlish, not as we'd like it to be." Topcliffe's smile was cold. "The solution's onshore, not at sea, and we'd need to occupy most of East Africa to stop the trade. There's no appetite in government for that. The area's rotten with fever. Little commercial potential either. And Egypt's enough to keep us busy for the time being."

A crisis the previous year had forced a reluctant Liberal prime minister to order Egypt's occupation so as to guarantee control of the Suez Canal. But it brought other responsibilities, not least the vast, restive territory of the Sudan, where Egyptian control had been nominal at best.

"Larger considerations might someday demand that we take East Africa," Topcliffe said. "But not just yet. At present it's enough for us that nobody else does. Nobody whoever."

So still the Arab slaver columns would strike deep inland, Dawlish thought, to the great lakes and beyond, even into the Congo basin, leaving a trail of death to mark the trudge of ever-diminishing groups of bewildered captives driven to the coast. They might spend weeks, months even, in squalid captivity there, waiting for the annual monsoon that would carry the crammed dhows northwards. A fraction would survive to reach Oman and small ports on the Persian Gulf. He would never forget the packed bodies, the corpses among them, the stench, when he had himself boarded slavers' dhows.

A pause. They sipped their coffee. Dawlish kept his face impassive. Something was coming.

"There are a few concerns nearer home," Topcliffe sounded as if wearied with some trivial but time-consuming obligation he could not avoid. "A certain gentleman in Downing Street is sensitive about unease

17

among a section of his supporters. The Anti-Slavery Society, Evangelicals, Methodists. Well-meaning but naïve people who gather in Exeter Hall to decry abuses and demand reforms."

A surge of support from such groups had brought William Gladstone out of retirement when he had denounced Turkish atrocities in Bulgaria seven years before. Now he headed a government that had been drawn into the sort of commitments in Egypt of which he had been so critical when his Tory adversaries had been in power. Commitments that many of his supporters did not like.

"What sort of concerns, sir?" Dawlish kept his tone neutral.

"The old refrain. The slave trade. Inadequate efforts to suppress it. Unwillingness to hold the sultans of Zanzibar and Mtwara to account. Reluctance to shoulder moral obligations that will invite divine retribution if we don't act. You know the sort of thing."

No different than when Dawlish had been hunting slave-laden dhows off Pemba and Lamu.

"You've possibly heard of Joshua Horne?" Topcliffe said. "The Reverend Joshua Horne?"

"The name's vaguely familiar, but I can't place it."

"Of the Bethel Missionary Society. He gets a lot of admiration in certain publications. Not quite my type of man, or yours, Dawlish, but admirable in his way. He's been maintaining a mission on the lower Rovuma river for six years now – holding out's the better term since half his people, and his wife, have died of fever there. He's been barely tolerated by Sultan Saif of Mtwara whose writ along the Rovuma is anyway nominal. The Portuguese further south resent Horne because he's not Roman Catholic. He's hated by the Arab slavers who're still active in that area – he's been rather heroic but also rather stupid in opposing them."

Bad enemies, Dawlish thought. Horne must be a braver man than me if he had exposed himself like this for so long.

"News has arrived that his place was raided a few weeks ago," Topcliffe said. "People he'd given sanctuary to were seized by a slaver column. Two of his local converts were killed and one of his English helpers wounded. There's a growing outcry in certain quarters here that something must be done for him. And Downing Street can't afford to ignore it."

"Am I that something, sir?" A sudden hollow feeling, of neither fear nor pleasure, rather one that mixed uncertainty and hope.

"I did think about you, Dawlish. We know so little of the area that we'd need a man who's prepared to take decisions on the spot that would be appropriate to the circumstances."

Decisions that could be disowned, Dawlish thought, disowned if they were later deemed inappropriate for reasons that might have nothing to do with the actual situation. Decisions that an officer could be blamed for, decisions that could end careers. He had no illusions. He had been lucky so far, but only just.

"I'm honoured to be considered, sir."

No other answer possible.

"You'd have *Leonidas* of course. The Channel Fleet will release her, I'll see to that. Probably more valuable for her crew than for her guns on this occasion. They did well onshore with you before and for this business you'd need them to form a small landing brigade. And you'd have a gunvessel too, good for work close inshore. A squadron of two ships, yourself as commodore, independent of the local station. Answerable to the Admiralty only."

"So, this man Horne needs to be rescued?"

"I doubt if he wants that," Topcliffe said. "I think he's got no intention of leaving. He has stated often enough that he wishes only to leave his bones in Africa. But not immediately, however. He wants the local slavers put under notice that his mission will be sacrosanct. And meetings of his admirers across the nation – Birmingham, Manchester, Preston, Leeds, and two-thousand of them at Exeter Hall last week – are calling on Gladstone to act accordingly. And he can't ignore them. They're the bedrock of his electoral support."

"A punitive expedition, sir?" Dawlish's mind was recoiling from the idea. Swamps, malaria, heat-exhaustion, insects, skin eruptions, dysentery. Human enemies the least of it.

"Let's rather say protective, Dawlish. Certain tender consciences would never countenance anything stronger. Even if that's what they really want."

"I take it that departure would need to be immediate?"

"As soon as humanly possible, captain."

"*Leonidas* could be ready in ten days, sir." She had been dry-docked recently, her machinery had been overhauled. The stores needed could be loaded in a week.

"I think that would be satisfactory." Topcliffe said. "The necessary orders and authorisations will be drawn up. I've already had a word with the First Lord. You'll have priority for any support you'll need at Portsmouth."

"And the second vessel, sir?"

"*Ibis*, Dawlish. A useful little craft, *Condor* Class. She's been on station off Borneo recently but a signal has already gone to Singapore to divert her to Zanzibar."

"Thank you, sir." Dawlish admired these small but heavily armed gunvessels. And shallow draught could only be an advantage.

"It's likely that *Leonidas* will be joining the Mediterranean Fleet afterwards," Topcliffe said.

"And she'll remain under my command there, sir?"

"I think not. But something interesting will turn up, Dawlish. I've no doubt that something will turn up."

No sense in pressing. The *something* would depend upon success.

"Downing Street wanted to give immediate notice to the press about this venture," Topcliffe said. "I convinced a certain gentleman there to wait until we have concrete results. You'll understand of course that he wants them quickly." He drained his coffee and stood up. The interview was very obviously over.

"I'll arrange for whatever maps there are of the area to be sent to you, Dawlish, and any books or reports that might be of value. We'll need another word once you've got preparations in hand. A few more details, but they can wait. You can see me in two days perhaps? Good! And better to meet here again. At midday. You'll have time to get up from Portsmouth."

As Dawlish himself left he realised that even though the Navy's formal administrative machinery had already been put into action there were still matters – a few more details – that Topcliffe would prefer to discuss not at the Admiralty but only in the privacy in this club library.

The Reverend Joshua Horne was likely to be the least of them.

\*

Florence thought the same.

"There's more to it than just this missionary, isn't there, Nick?"

It was late evening and they were sitting in the garden at the rear of their villa in Albert Grove in the Portsmouth suburb of Southsea. Scent from the flowers hung heavily in air still warm from the August day's sun. It had been after eleven when Dawlish had arrived home and this would be the last night he could permit himself to sleep ashore. Since parting from Topcliffe he had been swept up in a succession of meetings at the Admiralty and afterwards at the Portsmouth dockyard. Early tomorrow his officers and men must be told of what was intended so that the frenzy of preparation could commence.

"That old humbug in Downing Street does nothing without a reason." Florence, a convinced Tory, would never think good of Gladstone. "Handwringing and crocodile tears and some token assistance for Mr. Horne would be enough to keep the Exeter Hall people quiet. For that he doesn't really need to send anything as big as the *Leonidas*, and he doesn't need to bring another vessel from the East Indies, and he doesn't need to send you, Nicholas. So there's more to it, isn't there?"

"It doesn't matter if there is, Florence. I've been given a task and I'll do it."

"Like always, Nick, isn't it? And it's that wicked old man, I've no doubt?" She spoke with surprising vehemence. "That admiral, that Topcliffe. I loathe him."

"But you've only met him the once, Florence," Dawlish said. On a wet November night three years before when Topcliffe had come to the villa.

21

"It was enough," she said. "You went to South America afterwards and you're still unwilling to tell me what happened there even if you still get nightmares about it once a month or more. And then those telegrams that sent us to Cuba! I've no doubt they came from him even if you wouldn't say so."

"You don't understand him, Florence. Or what he is to me."

"I never wanted to see him again but when —" She stopped.

Dawlish sensed that she had already regretted saying so much. And that she had been on the verge of saying more.

"Let's change the subject, Nicholas." She rose, wrapping her shawl tighter around her. "It's late."

As she went in ahead of him in silence, he told himself that she was disappointed that they could not now make the European tour that he had promised her. He had leave outstanding, five or six weeks, but it must be deferred. Florence must instead occupy long months alone once again in worthy, often tedious, work at the Sailors' Rest and for his crew's families' welfare. The longed-for tour must wait another year.

At worst, perhaps forever.

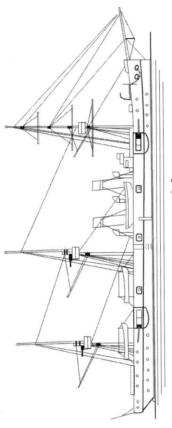

# HMS *Leonidas*

Builder: Pembroke Dockyard
Launched: February 1881
Completed: September 1881
Displacement: 4300 tons
Length: 315 feet overall
Beam: 46 feet
Draught: 20 feet
Armour: 1.5" deck, 1.5" gunshields

Machinery: Compound Engines, Twin Screw
5500 Horsepower
Speed: 17 Knot (Max.)
11 Knots (Cruising)
Armament: 10 X 6" Breechloaders
4 X 14" Torpedo-launchers
.45" Gatlings in Fighting Tops
Complement: 280

# Chapter 2

While *Leonidas* had sped south-eastwards through the Red Sea her forward motion had created her own wind above the glasslike calm. It had given a measure of relief from the heat. Now, swinging at anchor at Aden, only the whiteness of the hull that had been so hurriedly painted before departure from Portsmouth, and the awnings strung above her deck, offered a modicum of protection against the broiling sunshine.

Dawlish loathed this place, its furnace warmth that made metal painful to touch, its humidity that sapped all energy, its sense of the vast dead aridity that lay behind it. He wished only to be gone. *Leonidas's* bunkers had been topped up – Britain held Aden only for its value as a coaling station – and she was ready for sea. All that kept her here now was waiting for a reply from Zanzibar. The seabed telegraph cable laid three years before was a step in the link between Aden and Durban, and it now connected the Zanzibari Sultanate to the wider world.

The previous day's message had confirmed that the promised gunvessel, the *Ibis*, had already arrived at Zanzibar. Dawlish had responded immediately – his compliments to her captain, Commander Daniel Jarvis, whom he had never previously met and whom he ordered to proceed immediately to sea again. *Ibis* was to cruise slowly up the African east coast, past the sultanate's settlements at Mombasa and Malindi, as far as the most northerly, Lamu. Dhows sighted were to be investigated, boarded if suspect, burned if slaves were found and taken off. Liberated captives would be brought to Zanzibar. Dawlish expected to join *Ibis* there in ten days. He could imagine Jarvis chafing under these orders – it must seem ludicrous to him to be brought at such short notice from the East Indies only to undertake such a routine patrol. Only when they met would Dawlish explain why he had wanted no activity south of Zanzibar.

Not yet.

It was September already, the close of the summer monsoon season, bringing an end to the south-westerly winds that carried dhows from Africa across to Oman and to the slave markets of Muscat and beyond. The last of them had probably departed by now, and in a month or so the winter monsoon would begin to blow in reverse, stopping the dhow traffic between Africa and Arabia for the next seven months. The slave trade had always been heavily seasonal.

Until now.

Dawlish fretted. Another day without a message, another day eaten into the ten he had allowed himself for getting to Zanzibar, another day when the crew must endure – and resent – their inactivity in this oven. The greater part were men who had been to Korea and back with him. In fighting ashore and afloat there they had not disappointed. His officers he trusted no less, though he missed his previous navigator. The replacement, Lieutenant George Foxley, was competent but he had none of the brilliance of Takenaka Katamori, the secondee who had now returned to the Japanese Navy.

Another day passed. It was hard to maintain a cheerful demeanour, to feign active interest as he made inspections which he knew would find nothing remiss.

The longed-for message came at last, carried out in the warm darkness of early evening from the telegraph in the office of the port's Senior Naval Officer. The message was in cipher – a Playfair, its key one of a pre-agreed sequence that would be used once only. It was from the consul in Zanzibar.

Dawlish had known Doctor John Kirk seven years before. Though deputy-consul that time he had carried the full weight of the post since a succession of consuls had left, laid low by Zanzibar's killing climate. A survivor of Livingstone's fever-ridden expeditions, himself a medical doctor and a botanist, the intense and dedicated Scot had endured. Now he was consul in his own right.

"I can't say that Kirk's the power behind the throne at Zanzibar, but he's close to it," Topcliffe had said in London. "Sultan Barghash is still his own man. But he respects Kirk, relies on his advice, has been persuaded by him to be more cooperative on the slavery issue – he knows that outright abolition must come eventually – and he's doing his best to carry his chief people with him."

"Barghash is sincere?"

"Probably. But he knows that if he moves too fast on liberation then some less sympathetic relative will usurp him. It'll take time and I only wish that the Reverend Joshua Horne and his ilk could recognise that."

"We can rely on Kirk's reports for accuracy, sir?"

"His intelligence system is impressive. If he wasn't so valuable in Zanzibar there would be ample scope for using him elsewhere."

And afterwards Topcliffe had said more. Much more.

Sweat dropped down to soak the paper as Dawlish decrypted in his cabin. The message was short and he had the sense of it before he was half-finished. It had taken six days for Kirk's informant to get his information through to Zanzibar from Mtwara, the independent sultanate three hundred miles further south. It had most likely been carried on some trading dhow.

Six days. If weather permitted, enough time for the vessel referred to in the telegram to have covered between eight and twelve-hundred miles, half-way perhaps to where she was most likely heading. Given the difference in speed, *Leonidas* could be there ahead of her. But there could be no complacency. An overheated bearing, a boiler leak, a single sheared rivet, could mean delay. It was essential now to be at sea by morning.

A chart was spread on Dawlish's table, one he had pored long over in recent days. Now he studied it again, worked off distances – they could only be approximate since there was so much uncertainty, so many assumptions – and calculated steaming times, strove to put himself in the other captain's position. And at last a decision, little more than an informed guess, a mark upon the chart, an X drawn on open ocean.

The message provided a ship's name. Consultation of *Lloyd's List* – Aden's Senior Naval Officer must have a recent copy – might reveal more about her.

Dawlish spoke to the marine sentry outside his door. His compliments to Commander Edgerton, his first officer, and to Lieutenant Foxley. Both to repair immediately to his quarters.

Ponderously capable, reliable for anything other than being called upon for an independent decision, Edgerton never found change easy.

"I understood that we were headed for Zanzibar, sir."

26

"We are," Dawlish said. "But not immediately. And in the meantime, I want steam raised, awnings struck down, boats stowed." He looked at his watch. Almost ten-thirty. "Is there any reason we can't leave port at first light?"

Edgerton shook his head. "The men will be happy. They dislike it here. They'll put their backs into it to get away."

"Mr. Foxley," Dawlish addressed the navigator. "I'll need a course. To 22 north, 61 east."

He saw that Foxley was trying mentally to place it. Takenaka would have done so already. Edgerton had clearly recognised the approximate location but looked perplexed by it.

"Here." Dawlish's finger stabbed the chart.

At the mouth of the Gulf of Oman.

Where he hoped to run down an unsuspecting quarry a week from now.

*

Dawlish had given *Leonidas* her head. Her pistons beating a steady rhythm, her twin screws churning a foaming wake, a broad vee streaming out from her bows, she was running east north-east some twenty miles off the Arabian coast over a sea that was barely ruffled by the dying monsoon winds. Bare brown mountains shimmered on the northern horizon and the only signs of life were the flapping lateen sails of the occasional, all but becalmed, dhow. *Leonidas* disregarded them, rushing on by day and by night at a steady fourteen knots, three lower than her maximum but providing a better balance between speed and coal consumption. Four and a half days would bring her to that patch of ocean marked by an X.

The spirit of the crew was better now that they were at sea again, even when occupied in such mundane but unavoidable tasks as swabbing and holystoning decks. The burden of the heat fell heaviest on the stokers and trimmers and engine-room crew. Their work was exhausting at any time, but in this climate it was all but unbearable. Strict rotation was essential, even within individual watches, to ensure that they spent adequate time on deck.

Despite the oppressive still-humid warmth, training would make no concession to discomfort. Dawlish himself had practiced with cutlass and bayonet since boyhood, had owed his life to proficiency in their use, but now, at thirty-eight, he noticed a slowing in his reactions. That awareness made him all the more determined not to spare himself in the daily drill. It was good too that the crew should see him willing to confront experienced instructors in man-to-man mock combat and to rise to his feet and commend his opponent when he had been knocked down by a padded rifle butt. In the coming time such skills would count for more than *Leonidas's* ten magnificent six-inch Armstrong breech-loaders. It was the smaller, more mobile, weapons that were likely to be of greater value when brought ashore – the humble seven-pounder on its field carriage and the Hales rockets that had proved so effective in Korea, the Gatlings in the cruiser's fighting tops. He had secured a wheeled mounting for one of the six-barrelled weapons. In trained hands it would be worth a company of marksmen.

For there would be action ashore.

However much politicians might describe the mission as protective, it might well demand aggression in practice. The reports from Zanzibar that Topcliffe had provided in London all indicated that the area north of the Rovuma river, where the Reverend Joshua Horne had so unfortunately located his mission, was a no-man's land crossed and recrossed by heavily-armed columns of Arab slavers and their mercenaries. Local tribes cowered within their own territories, buying freedom from massacre by provision of porters. For the goal of the plunderers was no longer human alone, nor was it confined to the territories near the coast. A few ambitious slavers were thrusting westwards with what were almost small armies, their supplies carried on the heads of hundreds of porters, little better than chattels themselves.

The long narrow lakes Tanganyika and Nyasa were no obstacle. Small dhows had been constructed on their shores to carry the columns across to advance towards the Congo basin. There, where isolation had previously been a protection, there was ivory in quantities hitherto undreamed of. And there was labour to be had there for the taking, human beasts of burden who could stagger beneath the great tusks back to the coast, a trail of corpses marking their progress, the survivors themselves a commodity to be traded. The billiard balls that clicked and glided over green tables across the world, the piano keys that tinkled in thousands of prim parlours, all commenced their journeys amid blood and terror.

"Sultan Saif of Mtwara is up to his neck in it," Topcliffe had said. "His authority doesn't extend more than a score of miles from the coast, but that doesn't matter. Not when he controls a fine anchorage like Mtwara. The ivory can be shipped quite legally from there. He gets his share of that and he disclaims all knowledge about slaves going out too. And now that our patrols along the coast are starting to bite, slave prices are rising in Arabia, enough to make other ways of conducting the trade profitable."

"Have we a man in Mtwara?" Dawlish had asked.

"No consul appointed there has lasted more than a few months. The climate's deadly. We'd need another Kirk for that and men like Kirk are few and far between. Kirk maintains formal contact from Zanzibar with the Mtwara sultan but there's no desire from that side for any warmer relations."

"Is there some power behind the throne, like Kirk, there?"

"There may be. Some very strange people have turned up in East Africa recently."

"And Kirk knows about them?"

"Not enough. But he has somebody who does business in Mtwara occasionally, and they're invaluable."

And it was because of just such an informant that *Leonidas* was now ploughing towards that X upon the chart.

\*

When command of *Leonidas* had first come to him, Dawlish had found the solitude hard to bear. Surrounded by almost three-hundred men, disciplinary necessity demanded that he could have no friend on board. It sat easier with him now. Success in battle had proved the worth of the

29

style he had adopted as captain and it satisfied him that men were proud to have followed him. But the warmth he felt for so many of them – the gunnery officer Purdon, Egdean the boatswain, the marine lieutenant Ross, Latham the commissioned engineer and others too – must never be shown. He had determined that his relations with them, with the entire crew, must be formally courteous, that even when he was invited to dine in the wardroom – occasions he relished more than he ever openly admitted – there must be a barrier of reserve that must not be crossed. Officers and lower deck alike must know his intolerance of slackness, but know also that he demanded no effort from them greater than he demanded from himself. On the bridge, on his rounds, he never hesitated to praise when it was merited, for it made fair reproof easier to accept.

And always he was aware that his power over these men could, when demanded, verge on the absolute. Under his command *Leonidas* had lost men before, might well do so again before this mission was completed, and he would carry that responsibility to the grave. Sitting alone, reading in his deliberately Spartan quarters, or beneath a lamp on the quarterdeck to catch the marginal cool of evening, the thought of what lay ahead disturbed him.

Action ashore.

The men he would land would be well capable in any encounter with slavers. The greater danger was disease hanging in the humid air of swamps and mangrove and savannah. He had seen it kill unexpectedly, randomly, otherwise healthy men struck down and dead in days, others, who had barely survived, never again more than shadows of their former selves. Malaria had almost killed him in Ashanti and he still carried it within him. It had struck three times since, each attack a blurred nightmare of burning fever, shuddering chills and fire blazing in his head. He always carried quinine with him – it was the only remedy and seemingly the only protection. He had indented for four months' supply of quinine wine before *Leonidas* left Portsmouth.

"Everybody's going to take it daily," he had told Tadley, the surgeon. "You, me, every man on board. No ifs, buts or maybes."

"They won't like it," Tadley said. "They believe the old wives' tales. That if it doesn't make you blind or impotent it'll make you deaf."

"They'll swallow it anyway," Dawlish said. "Each man to call out his name after he's drained his glass and to hold it up to show it's empty."

"They'll like it even less."

"They'll see me take the first tot each day. And you the second."

Yet even then, he knew, it might not be enough to protect against this insidious enemy.

There was another concern, raised by what the Reverend Joshua Horne himself had written.

*With Cross and Bible among the Heathen – Five Years on the Rovuma* was a compilation of letters and articles Horne had sent back to supporters in Britain. The fifty-page booklet provided by Topcliffe was a seventh edition and it mentioned that 90,000 copies had been sold previously. Horne could write, and write vividly, Dawlish conceded. His prose was spare when it unflinchingly detailed atrocity, gathering pace as it rose to a pitch of righteous outrage, falling back to sad but never maudlin reflection on the sacrifices made by so many of those whom he called his fellow labourers in the vineyard. It was impossible not to be moved when he described his wife's grave, a dusty hummock alongside five others who had also succumbed to fever. It was easy to imagine these letters being read out in meeting halls and chapels, audiences shedding tears, widow's mites and rich men's guineas flowing willingly to fund the Bethel Mission's continuing work. That Horne had not returned to Britain in the last six years was a masterstroke that made his appeal stronger still. A living martyr, he was beyond criticism, a lonely voice in the hostile wilderness that could not be ignored – not even by Prime Minister Gladstone himself.

And failing Gladstone – or even not satisfying him – could be as fatal to Dawlish's prospects as if he were to lose *Leonidas* herself.

*

The parched island of Masirah had slipped past to port – bringing back memories of once lurking in its lee to surprise slaver dhows – and

31

another fifteen hours' steaming brought *Leonidas* to her destination. It was a calm open expanse, sunlight reflected blindingly from the waters stretching endlessly to the south. Arabia's eastmost tip was sixty miles westwards, the bare coast of Persia two hundred to the north, India five-hundred to the east. Shipping heading towards the Gulf of Oman and up into the Persian Gulf itself passed between this patch of featureless sea and the Omani coast, steamers standing well out, dhows hugging the coastline, all swinging north when the promontory of Al Hadd lay off the port beam.

Now the patrolling commenced, a long slow sweep westwards for forty miles, back eastwards for sixty, then reversing course again to retrace the track. Then again. And again. Speed had been reduced – seven knots now – and training had been suspended temporarily. Double-strength lookouts scanned the horizon continuously, the most agile young seamen taking turns with telescopes at the main-masthead. There was little traffic to be expected – the busy lanes between Aden and India lay far to the south and the small and squalid ports dotted along the coasts of the Persian Gulf drew little trade.

By the end of the second day Dawlish felt the monotony depressing, made worse still by awareness that this might well be a fool's errand. He might have relied too much on the message passed by Kirk's informant in Mtwara, might have made too sweeping an assumption on such a flimsy basis.

Twice during the first day's patrol a smudge of smoke on the southern horizon had sent a thrill of excitement through *Leonidas's* crew, a surge of relief through Dawlish himself, as the bows swung southwards to meet the advancing strangers. His hopes had remained high when they revealed themselves in his telescope's disc as thousand or twelve-hundred ton vessels, typical of the tramps that were the backbone of international trade. Smoke rolled from spindly funnels amidships and the yards of their sailing rigs were bare as they crawled slowly northwards at five or six knots. But Dawlish's hope had died as they made no effort to change course or increase speed as *Leonidas* approached. Flag signalling gained no response in either case and only when the cruiser swung over to plough alongside at fifty yards separation were there sullen responses to her hails.

The *Annie Bowles* of Liverpool and the *Sweet Afton* of Glasgow were about their lawful occasions, one heading to Muscat with a cargo of tobacco and cottons, the other to Bushire with ironmongery. Many merchant officers resented the airs of their naval counterparts and the *Annie's* unkempt master in a filthy collarless shirt, who spat over the side as *Leonidas* approached, was a fair example of the type. The replies he shouted through a speaking trumpet might be truculent but there was no doubting that he had reached here through Suez and Aden. The second vessel had followed a similar course. There was no need in either case to send a boarding party and *Leonidas* swept back at increased revolutions to resume her steady east-west plod.

Night fell. There was no moon and the million stars above did nothing to illuminate the soft darkness. Midnight brought a call of "Deck there!" from the masthead. A pinprick of red light had been sighted to the east. *Leonidas* swung over to intercept, her arc-light lancing a cold white beam towards the newcomer as she grew closer. Dawlish, hope rising but unwilling to show it lest it be dashed, sensed the excitement running through the ship, the men on the bridge around him, the boarding party standing by the whaler that was swung out, ready for dropping, the ready response from the engine room for increased revolutions. There was an awareness of shared but unspoken delight as the cruiser heeled slightly as she swung over into her new course and gathered speed.

But hope was once more dashed.

Another thousand tonner, a poor thing from Liverpool that seemed barely seaworthy, her captain terrified by the blinding light bearing down from the darkness. She had cut all forward speed and lay wallowing as *Leonidas* drew close. Shouted enquiries, answers about sugar loaded at Mauritius for delivery at Bushire that left no room for suspicion.

And above all, no smell, Dawlish thought.

Then the merchant captain's shock wearing off, his resentment and anger growing. Trade was supposed to be free, was it not? And the navy was costing the country too damn much already. At last, reassurances, no offence taken, apologies, best wishes for a safe onward journey, and then *Leonidas* shearing away once more into the darkness.

The possibility of failure lay on Dawlish as he returned to his quarters. He could not sleep, tortured by knowledge that any one of the dozen assumptions that had brought *Leonidas* here could be wrong.

The next day proved no better, a single British sailing barque heading north, two steamers heading south, nothing resembling what was sought, nothing in the night that followed.

And at last, in the next dawn, smoke dark against the brightening eastern sky.

Please, God, let this be it.

## Chapter 3

Since his first encounter with slavers years before, Dawlish had carried the memory of the stench with him as something almost palpable, something that hinted at a depth of evil so terrible that he wished he had never known of it. Now it drifted from the other ship, a miasma that was foul at even a half-cable's separation, telling of yet greater horror behind the black flank streaked by the human waste that had fanned down from the loading port in the bulwark. She looked otherwise no different from the steamers investigated in previous days but she had chosen to run when challenged. A single shot across her bows had brought her to a standstill. Now she lay wallowing in the slow smooth swell as *Leonidas* circled her slowly. A tattered red and white ensign drooped at counter.

"What flag?" Dawlish asked.

"It's not familiar, sir." Foxley had the watch but the other officers had come to the bridge also. "It could be…"

"Peruvian," Edgerton said. "I'm not sure, but yes, I think it is. I've seen that flag before. At Callao."

Black paint had flaked away from the name on the bows that it had clearly been meant to obliterate.

"*Lady Em…*" Edgerton's telescope was focussed on it. "I can't make out any more. It could be *Emma*, I suppose."

"It's *Emmeline*," Dawlish said. His assumptions and guesses had paid off. "It's the *Lady Emmeline*."

She had been British-registered when Kirk's informant had seen her steam from Mtwara with her cargo of shame. The Peruvian ensign and the painting out of the name were feeble attempts at disguise.

Edgerton and the rest were looking at Dawlish in surprise. He had told them nothing of what he sought other than that it was an average tramp, nor had he said anything about why it should be found. Not even Edgerton had questioned further. A captain was not to be pressed.

"Should we hail them, sir?" Foxley said.

Dawlish had ordered an approach in absolute silence.

"No," he said. "Not yet."

The men at the steamer's bulwarks, the few slovenly figures on the bridge who must be the officers, were all staring at *Leonidas* in transfixed dismay. As well they might. Purdon, the gunnery lieutenant, was personally directing the crew of the forward six-inch on the port side. Sponsonned out to allow fire directly ahead, and all but directly astern, the gun was edging around slowly to hold the *Lady Emmeline* firmly in its sights as the cruiser circled her. The Gatlings in the fighting tops were following suit.

"No hail," Dawlish said. Let them suffer a little longer, he thought, and then longer again.

*For ever and beyond if I could have my way.*

He turned to Edgerton. "Send the boarding party across. And tell Lieutenant Ross that I want no chances taken. He's got my approval to shoot the first man who offers resistance."

The whaler dropped and stroked towards the steamer. Ross's marines – eight of them – stood between the seamen straining on the oars. Somebody was coming down from the bridge to supervise opening of the loading port. It swung open. Two men there and three more behind dragging a rolled-up pilot ladder. Ross was calling up, his words inaudible, and a man at the port above was nodding obsequious compliance. It was obvious that there would be no resistance. A line snaked up from the whaler's bow, was caught above. The pilot's ladder dropped, the boat was drawn in and Ross was first up. His men followed.

35

*Leonidas* lay stationary now, fifty yards of blue water separating her from the *Lady Emmeline*. The smell drifting from her was revolting but must be worse still for Ross's marines. Half were driving the crew on deck back against the opposite bulwark, arms uplifted, flinching before the levelled bayonets. Two more men emerged from the forward deckhouse – one, by his stained apron, probably the cook – and were shoved over to cower with the others. Ross and his remaining men had reached the bridge. No resistance there either, though one man there – presumably the captain – seemed to be protesting volubly. He and those with him were driven down to join the rest of the crew.

"Neatly done," Dawlish said.

Anger mixed with disgust was rising within him and he knew he must not show it, nor be governed by it. He could sense something like shock in the officers around him on his bridge. Unlike him, none had seen service that had prepared them for this. Accounts in print could never convey the foulness of the stench or what it signified.

Ross disappeared down a companionway with two of his men. Soon after came a low sound, a remote but sustained moan that rose and fell and seemed to reverberate through the deck as if from a drumhead. It might have been the despairing protest of damned souls realising that their torment was eternal. Minutes passed, then Ross emerged again, ashen-faced, his men following. One of them lurched towards the scuppers and vomited. Ross headed for the bridge, picked up a speaking trumpet there and called. His words confirmed what Dawlish had expected.

"Slaves, sir! Hundreds of them!"

The message from Mtwara had been proved true. Time now to go across to confront the full horror.

*

Dawlish had often before now boarded dhows packed with slaves, but never more than a few dozen, all crouching in a space too low to stand up in, too packed to stretch out fully. They lay for weeks in their own ordure as the vessels were urged slowly up the coast by their billowing lateens. Some, the lucky ones perhaps, died quickly, slumped lifeless among their fellows until finally cast overboard. Manacled, tortured by hunger and by thirst, shut off from air and light, the strongest somehow survived.

But nothing had been as bad as this.

It was not the numbers alone that shocked, but the efficiency – the industrial efficiency – with which the vessel's holds, one ahead of the boiler and engine rooms, one aft, had been fitted out. Now, in the near-darkness of the forward hold, the flame of the lantern that Ross carried flickered and almost died in the foetid air. The feeble light illuminated only a few yards of what seemed a triple row of wooden shelves down either side of the hold, leaving only the narrowest of passages between. And the floor of that passage, far below, was covered by bodies that seemed to stretch out under the lowest shelves, just as they lay three or four side by side on those above. They were stirring, shifting rather, for they could do no more than jostle within the confines of their own constricted spaces. Their moans told that they were aware of the light and fearful of it.

Dawlish had been here for minutes only – he had come across with Edgerton and the surgeon, Tadley – but he was already on the point of nausea, for the handkerchief he held to his face did nothing to lessen the stench. It was not of human waste only but of a corpse, maybe more than one, rotting somewhere among the still-living. He longed to turn away, to rush back to the open deck and yet a feeling of shame held him here. These people did not deserve revulsion.

He reached out, touched the nearest body. He felt it shrink from him, saw the whites of terror-stricken eyes, heard a gasp that must be an appeal for pity.

"There," he said. "There, there." The words were useless yet spontaneous. "We're going to help you, my friend."

He felt hopeless in the face of such misery, knew that anything he could say would be incomprehensible. He ran his hands along the man's arm and it jerked, and a chain clinked as he touched it. There was wet ooze beneath his fingers as they reached the manacle around the wrist.

A memory of a medallion, one reproduced by the ten-thousands in Britain a century before. A slave kneeling, begging, arms outstretched, words encircling on the rim. *"Am I not a man and a brother?"* But it was essential to put a barrier between emotion and stark necessity. Action was needed, not tears.

"What do you recommend?" Dawlish forced coldness into his voice as he turned to Tadley. The enormity of what was must now be done weighed upon him.

"I don't know, I've never..."

"We need to get the hatch opened," Edgerton said. "They need air. They're suffocating here."

"Open it, but not wholly," Tadley said. "They won't be able to stand the light. Not at once. And then we need to get them on deck. Get them washed, get them fed, get this place fumigated and..." His voice trailed off. He too was recognising the enormity of the task.

"We need more men across," Dawlish said to Edgerton. "Twenty – no, make that thirty. Reliable men, ask Egdean's advice and have him come with them." *Leonidas's* boatswain could be relied on for practicality as well as rough kindness. "And Tadley, I've no doubt you'll need medical supplies. Once you've examined a few of these people, and understand the state they're in, I'll need your advice on how to feed them."

"We'll kill some if we give them too much, too soon," Tadley said.

"Do you know what too much, too soon would be?"

"I don't know. We'll just have to be careful. A little at first. They can all have water, but food... I don't know."

"Your best judgement, Tadley. That's all you can offer." Dawlish turned again to Edgerton. "And my compliments to Mr. Latham. I'd like to see him here." The commissioned engineer would find a way to get water distilled. Clean water would be needed in quantity.

Back on deck. By now Ross's marines had penned the entire crew against the bulwark with levelled bayonets. As Dawlish approached, the only man wearing an officer's jacket – presumably the captain – pushed forward and began to protest. At a nod from Ross the nearest marine swung his rifle up to the horizontal and struck the man squarely across the chest. He went sprawling on the deck behind and when he rose his clothing was streaked with filth.

"Any trouble, Mr. Ross?" Dawlish was surveying the sullen group. Forty, forty-five maybe, far more than needed to man a ship of this size, but probably just enough to keep the captives under control.

"Just that gentleman, sir. He's got a lot to say for himself."

"He'll have his say with me, soon enough," Dawlish said. "But first, which of them looks after the manacling and the chains? Find them."

They were a surly, frightened group now but it was easy to imagine any one of them glorying in the power they had wielded. Europeans or Americans, most of them, the sort of random mix that would be signed up by any tramp for a single voyage. But there were also three black Africans and what looked like two Arabs and a Somali. Some snarled reluctant answers to Ross's questioning. One, apparently, a Swede, understood no English until a bayonet-point was touching his throat, but then he was voluble enough and willing to identify the jailors. And not just the fat, balding man with the bloated red face and the Liverpool accent who described himself as fourth mate, but one of the Arabs, and an African, who must serve as an interpreter of sorts.

"Separate them from the others, Mr. Ross," Dawlish said. "We'll have work enough for them."

The captives could not be unchained all together. Too many coming up on deck at once, milling about in bewilderment and terror, could initiate another tragedy. This liberation must seem as incomprehensible and frightening to them as their first capture. The sounds from below – moaning, wailing, the occasional piercing scream – indicated that the slaves had realised that something was afoot. The thought of panic and of riot – and of the violence that might be needed to control it – was appalling.

Nothing more could be done until the reinforcements had come across from *Leonidas*. Dawlish walked aft, under the iron stanchions supporting the bridge, past the funnel and boiler-room ventilators, past the hatch-covering on the after-hold from which stench and sounds of misery drifted from the few inadequate gaps in it, on towards the small deckhouse that must contain the captain's quarters. His mind was churning over what would be needed – awnings rigged so that captives could be sheltered on deck from sun and rain while the holds were cleansed, wind-sails that must catch any breath of air and direct it below, food prepared in quantity, as much medical succour as might be possible, a modicum of decency for the inevitable burials, drinking water, scrubbed decks, some provision for sanitation.

Then too, selection of a prize crew. O'Rourke, the torpedo lieutenant, would be ideal to command it – decisive and confident, and with no prospect of his specialist skill being needed on *Leonidas* in the immediate future. For the *Lady Emmeline* must go to Bombay for adjudication – and for justice for those who had run this floating hell.

*Justice that would involve a noose if I had my way.*

And the slaves would have a future of a sort in a resettlement colony in India, their return impossible to the unidentifiable villages they had been swept from in the unexplored heart of Africa.

And prize money.

The thought was an unworthy one but once the initial disgust was past, every man on *Leonidas* would be thinking about it. Not just the meagre per capita payment for each slave but a share of the value of the captured vessel. Dawlish himself would gain most. The very idea seemed unclean and he knew that he would keep nothing of it. Florence could find a use for it at the Sailor's Rest.

The chartroom comprised the forward half of the deckhouse. It was neat, the workplace of a professional, rolled pilot-charts in pigeonholes, sextant and chronometer carefully stowed. A bound log – a new volume, opened for this voyage only, with nothing recorded earlier – lay open on the chart spread on the plotting table. The course from Mtwara was marked, noon and celestial sightings carefully noted. The *Lady Emmeline* had headed north-eastwards after leaving Mtwara, only swinging to the north when some four hundred miles from the African coast, staying well clear of usual shipping lanes. None of the three vessels she had sighted – their positions and headings logged – and to which she would most certainly have given a wide berth, could have guessed her cargo. For this was slaving on a new and more efficient basis, hundreds packed into a single ship that was independent of wind, that had no need to hug the coast, that need not fear detection by a Royal Navy patrol, that marked her track only by corpses that the sea itself would easily consume.

Dawlish searched for registration papers, anything of an official nature, and found none. The captain's quarters were directly behind the chartroom. Comfortably furnished, clean, the sheets of the well-made bed crisp and white when the sheltering curtain was drawn back. A swivel chair before an open roll-top desk that carried a framed photograph of a lady, thirty-five perhaps, stout, homely, with three smiling children and a baby. The smell of cigar-smoke. Tobacco ashes and butts in a tray next to a comfortable leather armchair beneath a shelf of books, all in English and little more than penny-dreadfuls. Under the bed was a bundle – four feet long, curved, wrapped in jute sacking. Ripped open, it revealed four elephant tusks. The captain was apparently doing some private trading in addition to his other duties.

Dawlish rifled through the desk drawers – no personal letters, no diary – but neither here, nor in any closet, trunk or locker did he find registration or personal identity papers. They must be on board somewhere, ready to reappear if the *Lady Emmeline* – registered in London, he knew – ever reassumed her true identity. And by then the slaves would have disappeared into the vastnesses of Arabia and Persia through markets in the Gulf.

Even in these quarters there were traces of the smell but when Dawlish stepped out on deck again it was like walking into a solid wall. Contempt that so much foulness should lie yards only from so much comfort welled in him. He walked back to Ross.

"Him." Dawlish pointed at the captain. "I want to see him. And I want a bayonet an inch from his back when I talk to him."

He turned and went aft again, stopping only at the counter. Anger had set his blood pounding, his pulse racing, and he knew he must tame it when he spoke to this man. Retribution must be left to others. What he needed now was information.

The captain's uniform might be smirched with ordure by his fall but he somehow kept his dignity as he came aft, ignoring the marine following him. He might be Dawlish's own age and he was dark-haired and clean-shaven but for a narrow moustache. He reached out his hand.

Dawlish ignored it. "There." He pointed to the deck, eight feet from himself. "Don't come any closer."

"As you wish, captain."

The accent was definitely British, but not pronounced, a hint perhaps of Northumberland. Thickset, heavy jowled. He had been well turned out – brass buttons gleaming, a tie worn on the collar of a clean white shirt. For all his air of truculence, his hands were trembling.

"What's your name?" Dawlish said.

The man paused, then said, "Smith will do. John Smith."

"You know that you may hang for this," Dawlish said. For sixty years, slaving had been recognised as piracy and the penalty, even if not often applied, was death. "You've got wretches enough on board this ship for you to hang a dozen times over."

No answer.

"You loaded this cargo at Mtwara," Dawlish said. "Where were you headed?"

"I've nothing to say."

"How many did you load? How many have you lost getting this far?"

"I've nothing to say." Smith's tongue was darting over his lips to wet them.

Dawlish felt his fury rising, his fist clenching, but he knew that he must not let his disgust gain control. It was enough for now that this man was frightened, was intelligent enough to know that his case was hopeless, that cooperation was his only chance for escaping the rope.

"I know that this ship's the *Lady Emmeline*." Dawlish loosened his fist. "I know that she was reported missing with all hands in the Timor Sea." *Lloyd's List* had revealed that much before *Leonidas* left Aden. "You're her captain – Charlton, Thomas Charlton – aren't you?"

A shake of the head. "Charlton's in Batavia or somewhere else in Java now. He'll be living like a king. He won't be calling himself Charlton any more. He was paid well enough and wanted no more of it."

"And you were his mate? First mate, perhaps?"

"No. No, never. I only met Charlton for a few hours. I never saw the *Emmeline* before I was approached."

"Approached where?"

Hesitation. Dawlish could see that the man was calculating how much to tell to improve his chance of leniency, how little not to incriminate himself still further.

"I asked you where, Smith."

"Singapore. A gentleman approached me in Singapore. A foreigner."

"European? Chinese? Indian?"

"European. Spoke English well but Danish or Dutch or German maybe. God's honest truth, but I couldn't guess better than that. You meet everything in Singapore."

Dawlish's heart missed a beat. *German.*

"He had a name?"

"Winter, he said."

"And he made you an offer?"

"I was down on my luck." Smith sought sympathy in Dawlish's eyes and found none. "I was between ships and I needed money. Not for me. Only to send to the wife and kids back home."

"You mean you'd lost your ticket." Dawlish had heard of captains who had been disqualified ending up as deckhands. "And you already had a reputation."

Smith's unwillingness to meet his eye was confirmation of something of the sort.

"So, what did this Mr. Winter want of you?"

"I could go Queen's Evidence, couldn't I, captain? You can see I'm being straight with you." Pleading in Smith's tone now.

"It might go easier with you if you tell me about this Winter."

"He wanted me to gather a crew – they'd be well paid and I was to bring them to Marang and..."

"Marang? Where's that?" The name meant nothing to Dawlish.

"South coast of Sumatra. A small place, just fishing people, nothing near it for miles, but a good anchorage. Winter had already chartered a schooner to bring us there."

43

"And the *Lady Emmeline* was waiting for you?"

"Charlton had already had the shelves built in the holds. They're clever with wood in Sumatra and he'd done a deal with the village headman for it. The schooner that brought us took Charlton and his crew away the next day. Heading for Java. That's the last I saw of him."

"And Winter had instructed you to take the ship to Mtwara? But you'd have needed to re-coal somewhere."

"Pondicherry. French officials never ask questions if the price is right. Winter had it all set up before we got there. The coal was already paid for. We just had to load it. Two days and we were gone."

"Had Winter said what was expected of you in Mtwara?"

"As God is my witness, sir, I never knew. I thought it would be produce. Cloves maybe, or copal. If I'd known the truth of it I'd never have taken a penny from Winter. God strike me dead, sir, if I'd known it was to be slaves."

No other cargo would have need for such shelving. This man was lying.

"When I did find out, sir, I was shocked. God's truth, sir." The words were tumbling out, the terrified eyes showing that he knew he was being disbelieved. "I'd have refused, I really would, sir, but there was no option. They'd have killed me, sir, no doubt of it, if I hadn't agreed."

"When your ship was packed with slaves and you were a few miles out from Mtwara, you never thought of steering for Zanzibar and looking for protection from the British consul? You set a course for the Gulf and you held to it."

No answer. Smith was looking away in speechless misery.

"Who did you deal with in Mtwara?"

"Arabs. Achmed This and Ibrahim That. It was hard to keep track of the names, they're all much the same. But they were the sultan's men. They'd have easily have cut my throat as –"

"Any European?" Dawlish cut him off. "English, Dutch, German?"

Smith was refusing to meet Dawlish's gaze. "I'm telling you a lot. But I'm not saying another thing until I know you'll put a word in for me, sir. I'll go Queen's Evidence, honest to God I will, sir, but I must be sure that –"

Dawlish stepped closer, put his mouth to Smith's ear, close enough for the marine behind not to hear.

"It's a long way to Bombay. Nobody will be surprised if you disappear overboard. Nobody is going to ask any questions." He sensed Smith trembling. He stepped back. "Now, Mr. Smith. You were going to tell me about your contact in Mtwara."

"Imker, sir, he said his name was Imker. That's all I know. He only came on board the once and then afterwards his people brought out the cargo."

"What was he like?"

"Thin. A tall man. Thin. Dark, sunburned. Talked good English but I could still see he was a foreigner. Like Winter. He knew Winter too, must have been thick as thieves to have set up all this."

"A foreigner, you said?"

"Dutch or German. He sounded like he might have been an officer. You get a feel for that."

"Was this to be the only voyage?"

Smith hesitated. "Imker said that there might be more. When I'd brought the *Emmeline* back to Mtwara, then…" His voice trailed off.

Dawlish felt his loathing boiling to a new pitch. This had not been intended as a single voyage but rather the inauguration of a new trade, faster than any before, difficult to intercept, shipping larger numbers, industrial in its efficiency, satanic in its cruelty. He felt his fist clenching again, knew that it was better to break off now, to question this man again later only when he was calmer.

He spoke to the marine. "Take this… this person back to the others. And my compliments to Mr. Ross. I want a word with him."

For Smith and his people must be set to work immediately, to unshackle the slaves, to cleanse the holds of their filth, to endure buffeting and perhaps worse from their erstwhile captives, to find by night the meagre rest they would be allowed in the very lowest levels. And so again, and again, and again until they reached Bombay. Even before parting company with *Leonidas*, many of Smith's mongrel crew would be glad to talk to save their own necks and help put a noose around his.

45

Now men from *Leonidas* were boarding. The long, filthy, soul-destroying work of mercy must commence.

*

Dawlish spoke again to Smith before the vessels parted two days later. The *Emmeline's* captain had been chastened by his labour in the holds. He was cringing and ingratiating when he was brought on deck, hosed down and taken to the bridge. A loose chain linked the manacles on his ankles.

"Is this the only ship?" Dawlish said.

"I can't say, sir. God's my witness, sir. I don't know." Fear rather than calculation in his eyes.

"This Mr. Winter you talk of. He said nothing?"

"I never asked him, sir," Smith said. "I didn't want to know, sir. And it was to be just the one trip for me. I've a wife and kids, sir. Just one trip so they'd be well settled, for them to –"

"Get him out of my sight," Dawlish said to the marine guard.

The *Lady Emmeline* carried four hundred and twenty-three slaves with her towards Bombay. Another four had died since the ship had been boarded and five who must have been dead for days before that had been buried with them. Dawlish had ordered them to be sewn into hammocks and weighted with shot, a dignity no less than what would be accorded to any of his crew – or to himself. They were to have dignity at this moment. The admonition in the Book of Common Prayer that the service of burial must not be used for any that die unbaptised deserved to be ignored. A dozen slaves, chosen because they seemed to have some authority among their fellows, watched in dumb incomprehension as Dawlish read the words, as the planks were raised, as the pathetic white bundles splashed and were gone.

Women – against all odds, twenty-seven of them had survived this far – were accommodated on deck beneath awnings but the male slaves were still lodged in the holds. They were docile and despite their bewilderment, despite the barrier of language, they seemed to understand that they had attained deliverance of a sort. They were brought on deck in batches for an hour at a time – a sequence that went on by night as well as by day – to be fed and hosed and then sent below again. It was still foul enough down there, though the shelving was cleaner by the day as Smith and his crew laboured under duress and slept there in chains, and as the wind-sails brought a marginal improvement in ventilation.

It was eight hundred miles to Bombay, six, seven days at the most. As O'Rourke and his twenty-man prize crew headed the *Lady Emmeline* there, Dawlish was satisfied that the passage would be completed without drama.

And *Leonidas's* bows swung southwards.

Towards Zanzibar.

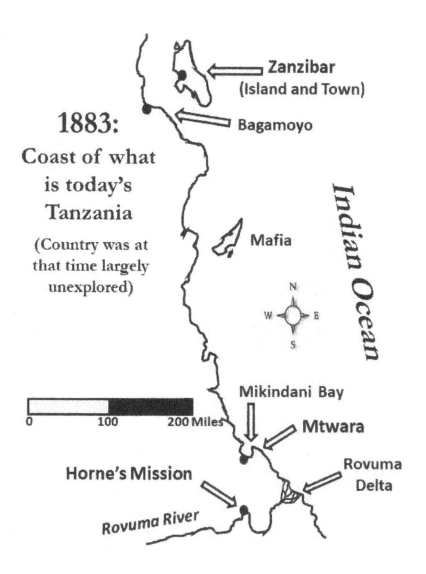

**1883:**

Coast of what is today's Tanzania

(Country was at that time largely unexplored)

Zanzibar (Island and Town)

Bagamoyo

Mafia

*Indian Ocean*

Mikindani Bay

Mtwara

Horne's Mission

Rovuma Delta

Rovuma River

0    100    200 Miles

# Chapter 4

Just how much Dawlish had loathed Zanzibar throughout the two years he had been stationed there flooded back as he saw the long line of low buildings rise up above the horizon. Stretched out behind a beach dark with sewage, and too often dotted with bodies cast aside as no longer of commercial value, a few European-style houses lay between more traditional Arab structures. The sultan's palace had its own extended frontage, grandiose of conception but squalid for its stained walls and rickety wooden balconies. And there was worse in the maze of narrow streets behind, Dawlish remembered, poverty, filth, disease, mutilated beggars squatting outside tiny mosques and, further on, what had been the shame of the slave market.

But there was wealth here too from sources other than human misery — trade in ivory, in copal, in the cloves that grew so easily here, and on the nearby island of Pemba, as they did nowhere else on earth. There were profits to be made here, large enough to draw merchants and factors from India, from Oman and the Persian Gulf, from Europe, from America. It was these outsiders who had shocked Dawlish worst of all, for it would have been too easy to become one with them. After six months here, he too had felt the temptation to step across the dying beggar, to take posed photographs in the slave market as curiosities for shocked relatives at home, to disparage the callousness of every other group, to assure oneself that each outrage was merely the custom of the country, to accept that this was how this world was. It was easy to convince oneself that change would of course come, next year, next decade, next century — economics would see to that — but change must not be rushed. And in the meantime, even if not here to trade, peace of mind lay only in deliberate blindness, in studied ignorance.

Yet something was missing now from the scene as he remembered it. Gone from amid the shipping moored offshore was the old wooden line-of-battle ship HMS *London*, one of the last in service. Dawlish had served on her as second officer, had cruised with her along the African coast, dropping off small boats to patrol and to capture slaver-dhows, had commanded several such small expeditions himself and had come close to death in one of them. The Royal Navy's anti-slavery activities in the Indian Ocean had been managed from this fully rigged relic with her twin rows of empty gun ports. Nelson himself would have found nothing strange about her except for the single thin funnel rising from the foredeck. Now she too, like the victors of Trafalgar, had passed into history, withdrawn for scrapping earlier in the year, her duties allocated to smaller, faster, more capable vessels.

Dawlish would shed no tears for *London* but it still gave satisfaction to order *Leonidas* to cast anchor where she had once swung. He had come far, very far, in seven years.

It was early afternoon, the humid warmth no less than it had been in the blazing midday, and it was uncomfortable to wear full uniform. The formalities of saluting had been completed, a small muzzle loader on the steam yacht that comprised the sultan's navy barking answers to *Leonidas's* deeper booms. Dawlish stepped down into his gig – slim, gleamingly white, a single one-inch gold-leaf stripe running beneath her gunwales, her crew turned out as smartly as he himself. Egdean, though the most senior man on the lower deck, had taken it on himself to act as coxswain.

"I believe you know where to take us." Dawlish settled himself in the sternsheets.

"Aye, sir. It's not to be forgotten."

For it was on *London* that Dawlish had first encountered Egdean and it was then that he had learned the man's worth.

The gig stroked across to the stone steps on the harbour wall. Dawlish stepped out and ascended. He brought nobody ashore with him.

"Captain Dawlish." The slightest hint of a Scots accent. A spare, bearded figure in white, Kirk looked older than he should have done – it had been only seven years, but he had aged twice that.

"Dr. Kirk." Dawlish shook his hand and was pleased that the consul had come to meet him. He had not known him well, had never had any especial link of friendship, but he had always sensed an integrity about the man that was simultaneously appealing and intimidating. And tough. Few Europeans had ever lasted as long in this pestilential location.

"A positive outcome, Captain Dawlish?"

50

"Satisfactory, Dr. Kirk. Most satisfactory."

Kirk had as little inclination as Dawlish himself to discuss the *Lady Emmeline* outside his office.

"You remember the way, captain? Only a few minutes."

Four Baluchis in white uniforms and red pillbox caps, with Snider rifles and bandoliers crossed on their chests, had stood at a distance. Now they fell in behind them as they walked. Two more went ahead, pushing aside anybody in their path. Not gently.

"Mathews' people. From Sultan Barghash's guard." Kirk had sensed Dawlish's curiosity. "He never wants me to be without an escort."

"And it's needed, Dr. Kirk?"

"I'm not popular in certain quarters. No more than His Highness himself. But Mathews has the situation in hand. He's lived up to every expectation."

Dawlish was not surprised. He had first encountered Lloyd Mathews in the Ashanti Campaign, almost a decade before. "One T if you please, not two" he had said on first introduction. Some five years younger than himself, Mathews had proved fearless on the contested track to Kumasi. Dawlish had met him again as a junior lieutenant on the *London* at Zanzibar, aggressive and relentless in the pursuit of slavers, relishing the degree of independence the duty demanded. He had jumped at the opportunity for secondment to the sultan's service.

"I did well to propose him," Topcliffe had told Dawlish. "Mathews would never have accommodated to fleet service. Too rigid for him, too formal. But he was the ideal man to recruit and train a small army for the sultan. Over twelve hundred by now – Baluchis, Somalis, rescued slaves, a few Arabs. A secondment initially but now he's resigned from the navy and the sultan has appointed him as Zanzibari brigadier-general."

"Is Mathews here at present, Dr. Kirk?" Dawlish said.

"No. He's up the coast near Malindi with a small column. There's bad blood between a certain sheikh there and the sultan. The sheikh will be rather more cooperative after Mathews' visit."

The streets – alleyways rather – were as Dawlish remembered them. The jostling without any apparent purpose, the plodding donkeys, the flies buzzing loudly around exposed meat on stalls. Petty trading, everybody seemingly selling and nobody seemingly buying. Arab women with covered faces. Indians gaudy in printed calico. Africans – they might have been slaves here since childhood – mingled cheerfully without any outward resentment of their status. They, or their parents, or their grandparents, had been torn from some forest village, had been strong enough to survive the march to the coast, lucky enough to avoid shipment to Oman and be brought instead into domestic service here. Tribal languages forgotten, knowing now only the coast's Swahili and nominally Muslim, they were the living examples that so many Europeans quoted to show that slavery, as practised here, was not necessarily a bad thing. It was the possibility of loss of ownership of such human chattels – and of the less lucky ones who toiled on Zanzibar's and Pemba's clove plantations – that so worried the sultan's relatives.

Kirk was as little addicted to small talk as Dawlish himself, and he said little before they reached the consulate. More Baluchi guards there, and a union flag limp on a pole above. His office there was high-ceilinged, thin wire-mesh stretched across the large, open windows. A punkah flapped slowly back and forth, connected by a cord through a hole in the wall to some unseen servant squatting on the verandah outside. Tea offered and accepted. A steward brought it and left. Now there was nobody else present.

"Now tell me about the ship, captain," Kirk said.

He listened intently, as proud of the interception of the *Lady Emmeline* as Dawlish was himself.

"I didn't quite understand why the vessel was in Mtwara," Kirk said. "It was fortuitous that my contact was there on some petty business for a shipping company. For a small fee he always keeps his ears open and he keeps me informed of what he finds. He'd heard rumours about this steamer but he found them hard to credit, not immediately. She was in port there for only two days and he learned that slaves were to be loaded by night."

"Over four hundred," Dawlish said, "though God knows how many would have been left to be landed in Oman. There were packed like herrings in a barrel."

"My man paid a fisherman to take him close enough to see what was happening. They were warned to keep clear but he saw the name clearly enough. *Lady Emmeline.*"

"It was good that he could read English."

"As well as you or me, captain. An Englishman called Wainwright, Acton Wainwright. Down on his luck, poor fellow. You'll meet him soon."

Dawlish's mention of Imker, Smith's contact, interested Kirk.

"There are reports about somebody of that name," he said.

"In Mtwara?"

"He arrived about year or so ago," Kirk said. "Ostensibly employed to smarten up the sultan's guard. But more interested in ivory, I suspect. He's apparently been working closely with a slaver, a damn ambitious one called Achmed Ibn Hamed."

"Ambitious?"

"He's got a private army. It makes sense, Achmed and Imker. One to supply – Achmed is operating on an unprecedented scale – and one to transport in a way nobody could have expected. Potentially a vastly profitable undertaking. And now you've nipped that transportation in the bud."

"Nobody in Mtwara will know that yet," Dawlish said. "No announcement will be made for now of the *Lady Emmeline's* capture." The documents that O'Rourke had carried with her to Bombay requested – no, demanded – that. Should there be any argument, then a telegram to Topcliffe would decide the matter.

"Then they'll be expecting to make a second shipment," Kirk said. "I've no doubt that Achmed is accumulating his stock in trade as never before."

"This Imker. Is he English?"

"Apparently not. Even Wainwright knows him only by repute but he's sure that Imker's not British. Perhaps Swedish or Dutch. Danish maybe."

"Or German?" Dawlish tried to sound casual.

"Possibly. Mtwara attracts scoundrels of every complexion. As long as the sultan gets his share of the profits, anybody's welcome."

And suddenly Dawlish was back mentally in Topcliffe's club for the last, crucial, meeting with him before *Leonidas* had sailed. When legal fictions had been set aside, brute facts admitted.

"No need to mention it to Kirk," Topcliffe had said. "There are few enough outside the cabinet and the Foreign Office who know about it. But it's possible, indeed plausible, that there's German interest in the area."

For it made sense that some in Germany might have colonial ambitions. The empire proclaimed a scant twelve years before lacked the aura of grandeur that overseas possessions brought.

"The chancellor's against the idea." Topcliffe always relished complexities. "The emperor is all but senile and he's content to let Chancellor Bismarck have a free hand. Bismarck's no enthusiast for colonies. And Friedrich, the Crown Prince, has little appetite for adventures abroad either. But I'm afraid that it's his son who's behind it."

"Isn't he too young to have any say?" Queen Victoria's eldest grandson was only in his early twenties.

Topcliffe had shaken his head. "Young Wilhelm knows that his father is ill. We know that he knows. It's a long, slow malady – he's seen British specialists as well as German, and we've spoken to them in confidence. Crown Prince Friedrich won't make old bones. He may even be dead before his own father."

"So young Wilhelm will be Kaiser sooner than expected?"

"Exactly, Dawlish. He's vain already, will be worse when he's on the throne and he won't be happy with an empire confined to Europe alone. There's a clique gathering around him that already feels the same. Not just courtiers or soldiers either, but Bremen and Hamburg merchants, and ironmasters in the Ruhr, and dye-masters and textile interests, all of them convinced that they need overseas markets that would be closed to all trade but German. They're feeding young Willy's self-importance and he's promising them that he'll get his grandfather's approval for any colonial *fait accompli* they can engineer."

"Mtwara?" It was obvious now that the Reverend Joshua Horne was just a pretext.

"I doubt the sultan would consent to a protectorate," Topcliffe had said, "but the hinterland is vast. It's ripe for the picking."

"But it could be ours just as easily, sir."

"You're underestimating Gladstone's distaste for more foreign adventures, Dawlish. He's frightened enough by having been forced into taking Egypt. As long as no other European power is lodged in East Africa he'll be content, and his supporters no less so. As long as we can offer protection to gentlemen like the Reverend Horne and his ilk."

"And show that we can intervene there as and when we need to?"

"You're learning, Dawlish, you're learning. *Raison d'etat*. Just a minor show of force to protect Horne should be enough. Sufficient for the Sultan of Mtwara to know that we value his continued independence as long as he behaves himself and understands what might descend on him if he doesn't. We'd need to give a bloody nose to the slavers whom he must disavow publicly but on whom he relies for his revenues – the people who've been discommoding Mr. Horne. Some little action, but decisive. Really little more than showing the flag. But memorably so. And enough to remind the Germans not to meddle."

"So, I'm to provide the minor show of force, sir?"

"Precisely, Dawlish. But appropriately. I'm relying on your discretion."

Always that word 'discretion'. Directives that were never explicit, blame that always flowed downwards, never up. A reminder that successful action would be endorsed, failure repudiated. And a career in ashes.

"This business with the *Lady Emmeline*," Kirk was saying, "it was something I never expected."

Dawlish's reverie had passed and he was back in the consul's office.

"I thought that slaving was nearing its natural end." Kirk said. "God knows I've spent long enough fighting it. But this! I never thought much of Mtwara's Sultan Saif, but this *Emmeline* abomination is worse than I ever could have feared."

"And damn clever too."

"Britain's been remiss – criminally remiss, Captain Dawlish, I can use no other term – for ignoring that place too long. My arguments for action there have fallen on deaf ears. If it were my decision alone I'd back Zanzibar to take Mtwara. No need for a British occupation. It would be enough if Sultan Barghash were to control it with Mathew's forces. And with just some discreet backing from ourselves."

"I'm going to ignore Mtwara for the time being," Dawlish said. "I intend to pay Mr. Horne and his mission a visit before anything else. The Prime Minister is personally concerned about it."

And could not afford to see it destroyed, Dawlish thought. Not when Horne is a saint to so many, not when a cruiser and a gunvessel have been sent to succour him. One fatal raid on the mission would be the death of my career. Horne is my priority at present.

"These missionaries," Kirk said, "they're well-meaning but they're naïve, all of them. I learned that the hard way when I was with Livingstone twenty years ago. It's not just that they throw away their own lives. They don't count the cost for others either. Like Livingstone himself, like Horne, like those Romans also on the Rovuma."

"Romans?"

"Catholics. The very thought of them downstream from his mission must be sticking in Horne's gullet. Some sort of monks, German, Benedictines, they call themselves. As fanatical in their way as Horne himself, I imagine."

And again that word. *German.*

The gunvessel, *Ibis*, should be here in another day or two and without her it would be difficult to move up the Rovuma. She could not be here soon enough.

*

The warship that steamed into Zanzibar the following morning was not the *Ibis*, but longer, sleeker, more elegant than any utilitarian gunvessel, a clipper-bowed, barque-rigged corvette, two ochre funnels rising above a gleaming white hull. Watching from *Leonidas* with Edgerton and Foxley, Dawlish was impressed by the precision of her anchoring, by the measured, clock-like timing of her individual salute-discharges, by the polished brasswork glinting as the sun caught it.

56

But what was least expected was the ensign. White, quartered by a black cross, a crowned eagle at the centre, a white-bordered iron-cross superimposed on the red and white and black stripes on upper rectangle next to the staff. It had a striking beauty that conveyed strength, confidence and pride. Seldom seen as yet on the world's oceans, the small navy of the newly created German Empire was already known for smartness and professionalism that the services of many long-established powers might rightly envy. It was a far cry from the puny Prussian gunboats Dawlish had seen off Heligoland almost twenty years before. They had been mere hangers-on then, liabilities, to the powerful Austro-Hungarian squadron that had confronted the Danes.

"What's her name, Mr. Foxley?"

The letters on the bow were indistinguishable at this range. Dawlish was unwilling to be seen focussing a telescope on her, though he knew he must be under scrutiny himself from the bridge of the other ship.

"H, i, l, d.... *Hildegarde,* sir."

A boat was being swung out, a mooring boom also, preparations in progress to lower a steam pinnace. All done smartly. A well-run ship.

It could be no accident that she was here and yet Kirk did not seem to have known anything about an expected German arrival, nor had any coded telegram arrived from Topcliffe to warn of it.

Purdon, had come to the bridge also.

"They look like four-inchers, sir." *Hildegarde's* weaponry was her only feature that interested the gunnery officer. "Krupps, I'll warrant. But I can see only one mounted on this side and there's probably only the same on the other. Just two of 'em. Yet she looks as if she's got positions for eight."

"They're certainly not expecting any trouble anywhere then," Edgerton said.

Dawlish said nothing, felt perplexed. Sending a partially disarmed ship here made little sense if Germany had designs on this coast.

The boat – a gig as graceful as Dawlish's own – was already stroking towards the steps in the harbour wall, the rowers in white uniforms no less immaculate than that of the officer sitting in the sternsheets. He rose as the craft swept past *Leonidas,* his hand arcing up in salute. Dawlish returned it. *Hildegarde's* captain was losing no time in presenting his emperor's compliments at the sultan's palace.

Dawlish needed to know more. Fast.

"Commander Edgerton – I want an invitation sent across immediately. Dinner this evening, say seven o'clock. The German captain and his senior officers. I've no doubt that *Leonidas* will be more spick and span than ever in her entire life. And the meal – better have a cow bought and slaughtered ashore this morning so we've something decent. None of that damn brown soup either."

"Understood, sir."

"And not a hair out of place on any of our people."

Eight hours available for holystoning already-spotless decks, washing down paintwork, polishing brass and boots and rifle stocks, whitening webbing, ironing uniforms. However impressively run, a parvenu from an upstart navy must know her place, must never forget the Royal Navy's almost three centuries of seniority.

\*

But it was Dawlish and three of his offices who were to be the guests that night because the *Hildegarde's* invitation arrived just as Sub-Lieutenant Leigh was leaving to carry across that from *Leonidas*.

*Fregattenkapitän Reinhold Kaunitz requests the pleasure of etc. etc.*

Courtesy demanded that it could not be refused and yet Dawlish felt uncomfortable – slightly ashamed indeed – that his counterpart had been ahead of him. By sunset, as his gig pulled away towards the German ship, he was already prepared to dislike her captain.

Yet when he met him it was impossible to do so.

Fregattenkapitän Reinholt Kaunitz was perhaps Dawlish's own age, tall, slim, fair-haired, and clean-shaven. The reception on board the *Hildegarde* was managed with perfect precision, and the vessel itself was as pristine as had been expected, but there was a sense of genuine welcome when Kaunitz introduced himself and his officers in pedantically correct English. Among the superbly tailored dress uniforms the dark clothing of seven civilians stood out incongruously.

Whatever function Professor Doktor Friedmann and Herr Doktor Ehrenberg and the five others fulfilled on board, it was a respected one. Kaunitz was deferential when introducing them. Dawlish's curiosity – and apprehension – grew. This could be no normal showing-the-flag voyage.

The dinner was to be in the ward-room but while the other officers – and the civilians – assembled there, the captain invited Dawlish first to his personal quarters. They were as sparsely furnished as Dawlish's own, comfortable but not luxurious. Wine was poured, white.

"Elbtal, Captain Dawlish."

"Elbtal!" Dawlish raised his glass. It must be a toast.

Kaunitz smiled. "Wine from the Elbe valley, captain, in Saxony." No hint of condescension. "From vineyards south of Dresden. A delightful city. I recommend a visit."

"You a native of there, fregattenkapitän?"

"No, captain. From Prussia, from near Königsberg."

"A Hanseatic city," Dawlish was glad to have remembered that much, though he knew little more. Valuable though to help the conversation along. "A city with a great tradition of sea-faring, I believe."

"And you Captain Dawlish? You have perhaps a long naval tradition in your family?" An impression of willingness to establish a personal link, not merely an attempt to make small talk until it was time to go to the wardroom.

"My uncle was in the navy," Even after a quarter-century, Dawlish still missed him. "A good man, a very good man, but he died young. I was proud to follow him."

"I don't doubt that your duty has taken you around the world, Captain Dawlish? It's said that the Royal Navy can be found wherever there is water enough to float a ship."

"Wet grass is enough," Dawlish said.

A pause, then Kaunitz saw the joke and began to laugh. He listened with undisguised fascination when Dawlish mentioned ships and voyages, but no action other than his experience as a boy in China. He said nothing about his previous involvement in anti-slaving duties, nor about any more recent activity. And it was diplomatic to make no allusion to the fact that he had once been in a town under siege by Prussian forces or to mention those gunboats he had seen in futile action in the North Sea.

"Our navy is a young one, younger than yours. The extent of its duties is much more limited." Kaunitz sounded almost wistful. It was easy to imagine him adding mentally *'For now''.*

"But this voyage has taken you far from home, fregattenkapitän. Training for young officers perhaps?" Dawlish had not noticed any disproportionate number of them but he could think of no other reason for a partly-disarmed ship being so far from home.

And again the impression of a straight reply, spontaneous, honest.

"Oh no, Captain Dawlish. A scientific expedition. Studies of the ocean depths and of the flora and fauna of islands on our route. Our Crown Prince Friedrich proposed the idea and ensured support. He was inspired perhaps by your own navy's *Challenger* expedition."

As well he might be. In a four-year cruise HMS *Challenger* and her team of experts in half-a-dozen disciplines had created a new science of oceanography.

"Professor Friedmann of the Friedrich-Wilhelms-Universität – he's a zoologist, you met him earlier – undertook organisation of the scientific aspects," Kaunitz said. "It was my honour to be entrusted with command of the vessel dedicated. You can talk to the good Friedman at dinner – he speaks excellent English. He'll be proud to show you the laboratories and the photographic workshop and the stores of preserved specimens."

Kaunitz's enthusiasm was unfeigned, boyish, attractive. The *Hildegarde* had left Wilhelmshaven three months before. She had completed seven weeks of sounding and of trawling for specimens south of Socotra and was now heading to a position south-east of Seychelles to undertake similar activities. After that to re-coal at Madras and then yet more investigations off the Maldives, in the Celebes and later in locations strung across the Pacific. In three years *Hildegarde* would circumnavigate the world and return home with hundreds of thousands of specimens. And no mention of activities off the East African coast which might be construed as having colonial implications.

"Do you intend to stay long at Zanzibar?" Dawlish said.

"Long enough only to take on fresh food supplies, but Doktor Ehrenberg is keen to botanise ashore, even if only for a few days. And …" Kaunitz's hesitation conveyed a modesty that was appealing, "… I am interested in botany myself. It will be my pleasure to accompany him."

Kirk was a botanist of some repute, Dawlish remembered, something of a zoologist too. And the Scot was even more skilled as a diplomat. It might be worth introducing him to the German captain and scientist. If the *Hildegarde's* mission was anything other than what it seemed, then Kirk could be relied upon to find it out during an afternoon's botanising in Zanzibar's interior.

It was time to go to the wardroom. Whatever initial stiffness might have been between the British and German officers was already relaxing with the aid of alcohol. Now to the dinner, then the toasts. To Queen-Empress Victoria, to Kaiser Wilhelm the First, to the Royal Navy, to the Imperial German Navy. And to Nelson's immortal memory – pleasingly proposed by Kaunitz. Then to the brotherhood of the sea, to the furtherance of science, to eternal friendship and – with much laughter and laboured explanations of unfamiliar language – to wives and sweethearts, that they might never meet. Conviviality, forced at first, but growing comfortable, intoxication just short of drunkenness, a mutual sense that, regardless of nationality, the others were men who could be relied on in extremis.

All the while Dawlish, abstemious, held his hand repeatedly over his glass to deter refilling He endured Professor Friedland's monotone droning about the phylogeny of crustaceans – it had been a mistake to ask him about his speciality – and probed Kaunitz as unobtrusively as he could. But the *Hildegarde's* expedition still seemed as innocent as it had been depicted. No guard dropped by Kaunitz, perhaps because he had none to drop, no careless reference to Mtwara, nothing about slaving or ivory, no allusion to colonial ambitions, no mention of Roman Catholic missionaries.

It should all have felt reassuring but as Dawlish was rowed back to *Leonidas* in the early hours, as he overheard his tipsy officers reassure each other than these Germans were fine fellows, damn-near as good as Englishmen, he remembered a similar dinner on a Japanese warship.

And that had been the prelude to Hell.

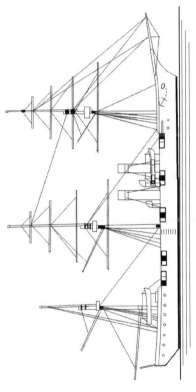

# SMS *Hildegarde*

Builder: Kiel Dockyard
Launched: November 1878
Completed: April 1880
Displacement: 2300 tons
Length: 260 feet overall
Beam: 41 feet
Draught: 18 feet
Armour: None

Machinery: Compound Engine, Single Screw
                    2200 Horsepower
Speed: 13 Knot (Max.)
          10 Knots (Cruising)
Armament: 2 X 4"Krupp Breechloaders
                  (Mountings for 10 but vessel; partially
                    disarmed for scientific expedition)
Complement: 260 (Scientific Party additional)

## Chapter 5

Dawlish was pleased that the *Ibis* reached Zanzibar the day after the *Hildegarde* had departed and not before. It was better that the presence of the gunvessel, in addition to *Leonidas*, was not known. The German naval vessel might indeed have headed for the Seychelles, as Fregattenkapitän Kaunitz had indicated she would, but Dawlish had retained a suspicion – he was half ashamed of it – that he might find her at Mtwara. He hoped he would not. He had liked Kaunitz and did not want to find him out in a lie.

The botanising excursion to the centre of the island had proved a success. Kirk had welcomed the suggestion – he even knew of Doktor Ehrenberg by reputation – and had arranged horses from the sultan's own stables. The consul and the savant had got on well together, Kaunitz assisting them like a humble acolyte as they examined roots, scrutinised stems and clipped leaf specimens. Dawlish was less lucky, finding himself helping a myopic entomology professor from the university of Hohenheim to catch beetles scurrying from under overturned stones and drop them into glass jars. Lacking a language in common, the experience was wearing.

Kirk had enjoyed Doktor Ehrenberg's company. "That man's an inspiration," he told Dawlish afterwards. "We've arranged to correspond and I'll be forwarding specimens to his university."

"Will he be returning there soon?"

"He'll be leaving the expedition after it reaches Singapore. He says he'll have enough gathered by then to keep him busy for the rest of his life. He only regrets he won't have more items from Africa, so he'll be grateful for anything I can send."

"But I understood that the expedition would be making several more stops along the African coast?" Dawlish knew that Kaunitz had mentioned nothing of the sort.

"Oh no," Kirk said. "Doktor Ehrenberg was so taken with Zanzibar's flora that he suggested just that to Fregattenkapitän Kaunitz. But Kaunitz said that there could be no deviation from his orders. Very systematic, very unyielding, these Germans. There's a strict schedule for when the *Hildegarde* must reach the Seychelles, when she must reach the Maldives, and so on. Kaunitz joked that his career would be in ruins if he was more than two days late for the date set for his arrival back in Wilhelmshaven the year after next."

"Impressive, damn impressive," Dawlish said. "I hope we'll never see the Royal Navy run on those lines." He left unspoken the suspicion that Kaunitz's career depended on something other than a punctual return, that the *Hildegarde's* presence here was not so innocent.

The dinner that Dawlish gave on *Leonidas* for the German officers and scientists had gone as well as that on the *Hildegarde*. No less cordial were the boat races organised the following day and the tug-of-war held on the beach. It seemed somehow appropriate that *Leonidas's* crews would win most of the pulling and sailing races and the *Hildegarde's* crew the straining contest ashore, British mastery afloat, German strength on land. Dawlish noted that both his upper and lower decks showed none of the animosity they would have held for French counterparts. He sensed a genuine warmth in the cheers he ordered from the crew lining *Leonidas's* side as the immaculate German corvette slipped from the harbour.

Heading for the Seychelles.

*

Dawlish was always pleased by the sight of a well-run ship, by the sense of trimness and smartness that came through dozens of small indications that fused, even from a distance, into a single impression.

HMS *Ibis* did not disappoint as she entered harbour under sail and anchored flawlessly. She was typical of the Navy's work-horses, the small gunvessels that operated on remote foreign stations, often alone for months at a time. The massive ironclads of the Channel and Mediterranean Fleets, with their flocks of scouting cruisers, guaranteed Britain's supremacy but their service, year in, year out, was a steady, monotonous routine of peacetime exercises. It was the humbler craft like *Ibis* that bore the burden of the small, often vicious, actions that maintenance of empire demanded. Larger then gunboats, slow, as dependent on their sails as on their engines when far from coaling stations, heavily armed for their size, they were unarmoured and not designed to fight other vessels. Their task was to deliver force wherever needed, to bombard shore targets and land bluejackets and marines to suppress unrest, restore order or exact retribution.

Commander Daniel Jarvis, *Ibis's* captain, came across. The necessary courtesies were exchanged and Dawlish invited him to his quarters afterwards. He was older than Dawlish – closer to Edgerton's age – and it was difficult to know if his forbidding aspect was habitual or whether it was due to resentment of subordination to a younger officer. Thickset, swarthy, with heavy eyebrows and a permanently downturned mouth, there was a sense of brutality about him despite all his begrudging courtesy. It was easy to imagine him having been the gun-room bully, the sub-lieutenant who terrorised young mid-shipmen, later the bluff young tyrant who made life a misery for those below him, now the embittered middle-aged man who would never see high command. But *Ibis's* fast passage from Singapore and her brief patrol up the East African coast before returning to meet *Leonidas* in Zanzibar – it had resulted in capture of two dhows and thirty-seven slaves – had demonstrated competence. Topcliffe would not have nominated Jarvis otherwise. He could be useful – very useful – but he must be handled carefully.

Coffee was brought, then Dawlish outlined as much as he intended to share at this time.

Jarvis was not surprised when he heard of the *Lady Emmeline's* conversion in Sumatra. "Nothing in the East Indies surprises me anymore. The Dutch don't have a serious grip there. The place is too damn big for them."

But there was a glint in his eyes that might be greed – or perhaps envy – when he heard details of the *Lady Emmeline's* capture. "Prize money, I'll be bound. You're a lucky man, sir."

Dawlish let it pass, but he did not like it. He mentioned what Kirk had found out through his informant at Mtwara. "It's consistent with what the wretched Captain Smith of the *Emmeline* told me. Some European seems to be managing the business, maybe for himself, maybe for the sultan. Somebody called Imker."

66

"Imker?" Jarvis was visibly surprised.

"Maybe a Dane or German or Dutchman."

"I knew an Imker. Two years ago. In Borneo. The Dutch part."

"How did you know him?"

"He was a Dutch officer, a commander. He was disgraced after what happened there."

"A bad business?"

"Bloody bad," Bitterness in Jarvis's tone. "There's a lot of pirate activity off Borneo. The Dutch normally sort it out themselves but this time it was a British ship that had been taken off the south coast. A small barque, the *Johanna*, bound from Singapore to New South Wales. Most of the crew were killed but a small boat got away and made it to Singkawang, God knows how. Three men only, more dead than alive."

"And *Ibis* was on station?"

"Off Sarawak. We'd been involved in pirate suppression there. The Dutch got word to us and suggested that we might want to join them in rooting out the nest to which the *Johanna* had been taken. A place called Soengaiamang, on one of those big river estuaries."

"What did the Dutch assign?"

"Just the one gunvessel. But a powerful one, the *Carel Reyniersz.*"

"Imker was in command?"

"He was," Jarvis said. "The Dutch are always short of vessels so they make up for it in other ways. Willem Imker had a name for using local groups against each other. There was talk that he'd no hesitation about employing head-hunters, and I can believe it."

Dawlish had already guessed what was coming. "It got out of hand?"

"Badly. I know I'm not a sensitive man, but what happened went too far. We bombarded the village – a big one – where the pirates were cornered. A dozen shots to put the fear of God in them, and then I landed men to burn the boats on the beach and to come off again, nothing more. Imker was to do the same, but he kept firing – the barrels must have been red hot. Then he let his savages loose. He'd got men enough of his own to control them, but he didn't even try. They burned the place to the ground and killed God knows how many, did yet worse

67

also. I tried to reason with him but he laughed in my face." Jarvis paused, then said, "Imker likes killing. He had a reputation for that sort of thing but it was worse than I could have imagined."

"You said he was disgraced. Was that afterwards?"

"Imker's luck ran out. There was a missionary in the village, an old Dutchman who'd been there for years and who'd baptised half the locals. He escaped into the forest and got the story back to the provincial governor. It transpired that the village had nothing to do with the pirates – they'd merely put in there. You can imagine the rest. Fear of scandal back in Europe if somebody wasn't held accountable. And that somebody was Imker. He was cashiered, dismissed with ignominy."

"And you, Commander Jarvis?"

"Damn lucky not to have been court-martialled. Private censure, nothing official. I should have been more sure of the facts before committing myself, I was told. I should have protested, should have been able to restrain Imker. The sort of thing that's easily said by those who weren't there. And the sort of thing that's never forgotten, that ruins a man's prospects."

Better not to pry further, not to rub salt in the wound. No need for Dawlish to confirm to Jarvis what he already knew, that the Navy would always find him useful, but would never advance him.

"It's more than likely that it's the same Imker." Dawlish was reminded of an ex-Confederate colonel in Paraguay, brutal, courageous and deadly, reliable until the next payment. Imker sounded little different, another of those rootless European or American mercenaries who turned up in the service of petty tyrants.

"If it's the same Imker then the loss of the *Lady Emmeline* won't stop him." Jarvis said. "He'll find another way."

Dawlish shook his head. "Not if Mtwara's blockaded."

For that was the first step in his plan. It was time now to fix the details. And those details must make no allowance for private account settling. Commander Daniel Jarvis must be kept on a tight rein.

# HMS *Ibis*

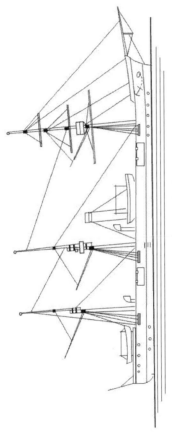

Builder: Laird, Birkenhead
Launched: March 1877
Completed: August 1878
Displacement: 780 tons
Length: 158 feet overall
Beam: 29 feet
Draught: 13 feet
Armour: None

Machinery: Compound Engine, Single Screw
720 Horsepower
Speed: 11 Knot (Max.)
7 Knots (Cruising)
Armament: 1 X 7" Rifled muzzleloader*
2 X 6" Rifled muzzleloader*
.45" Gatling in Foretop
Complement: 105
* Behind hinged bulwark

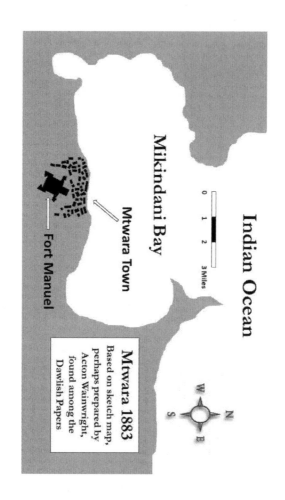

Indian Ocean

Mikindani Bay

0 1 2 3 Miles

Mtwara Town

Fort Manuel

**Mtwara 1883**
Based on sketch map,
perhaps prepared by
Acton Wainwright,
found among the
Dawlish Papers

N W E S

# Chapter 6

"That's Mtwara."

Settled with a telescope in *Leonidas's* foretop as she steamed slowly across the mouth of Mikindani Bay, a safe two miles offshore, Dawlish followed Wainwright's pointing finger. He adjusted the focus slightly. Low buildings and thatched huts and a half-dozen minarets sharpened in his disc of vision. A white beach with boats drawn up on it, ragged palms behind, eleven dhows at anchor, several more along a stone quay. A single steamer swung on a mooring at the centre of the semi-circular bay. She looked more like a Crimea-era gunboat that Dawlish had served on in China as a boy than a merchant tramp.

"That ship," Dawlish was surprised by the sight. "Did you see her before?"

"No," Wainwright said. "She must have arrived after I left."

Kirk's informant, an Englishman, had arrived in Zanzibar two days before on a dhow that had taken three days to crawl up the coast from Mtwara. The steamer could have arrived there any time in the last five days.

"And no word before you left of new slave shipments?"

"Only that Achmed Ibn Hamed's column is expected back sometime soon. 'Soon' can mean anything here – a week, a month, two or three. But there'll be no shortage of slaves when he returns."

Wainwright had spoken of it before. The slaver had headed west four months previously with some ninety armed men, a few of them Arabs but mostly Somalis or Baluchis, and two hundred porters. In that time they might well have crossed the Congo's watershed and when they returned they would bring ivory as well as captives.

Dawlish wanted *Leonidas* to be seen from Mtwara, just as he wanted *Ibis* to remain unseen over the horizon to the east. It was better that the presence of a second ship not be suspected.

He swept his glass further to his left and the great bulk of Mtwara's Fort Manuel filled the lens, its discoloured walls still massive, cannon muzzles jutting between the pointed crenellations along their tops, the angles of the bastions as sharp as when Portuguese engineers had laid them out three centuries before. Wainwright had made a rough plan of it for Dawlish. It looked like a crouching toad, its head a jutting citadel, its stubby limbs the protruding bastions from which flanking fire could be directed towards any point along the walls. The Dutch had tried, without success, to take it. But a Sultan of Zanzibar had captured it – by a ruse – a century later. In the aftermath a half-brother who had failed to murder him had himself taken possession and proclaimed himself Sultan of Mtwara. Since then Mtwara had been a separate, independent sultanate, no more than a minor irritant to Zanzibar, too small to interest any European power.

"Saif Ibn Rahman, the sultan, occupies the fort," Wainwright said. "It's the closest he has to a palace, but I can assure you that it's damn uncomfortable and unimpressive inside those walls. Worse still for his women. They're never let outside it. At least fifty if rumour is to be relied upon."

"You've been inside yourself, Mr. Wainwright?"

"Twice. Once to get a permit to travel to the interior. More recently to get payment for a cargo of silks that Saif had ordered for his harem but showed no inclination to pay for after delivery."

"You got the money?"

"I got it. A small commission to Saif's half-brother Ibrahim worked wonders." Despite his short stature and emaciated frame, and the yellow complexion and receding chin, Acton Wainwright gave the impression of a steel core within.

"You'll find him invaluable," Kirk had said. "Not just as an interpreter but for what he understands about the coast and hinterland. He came out with a scientific expedition four years ago – he's an entomologist, specialises in beetles. The other members died of fever and he wouldn't have survived himself if a slaver column hadn't found him when he'd been abandoned by his porters."

"They saved him?"

"Strange people, these Arabs," Kirk said. "They'll kill and kidnap and enslave Africans without remorse yet they'll sometimes treat a European in distress with endless kindness. Wainwright could have gone home but he's stuck it out here ever since, always writing letters to possible backers in Britain and hoping to gather the funds for another expedition. He speaks fluent Arabic and Swahili and he scrapes a living by interpreting and assisting shipping firms. And for a small payment he's glad to do a little for me now and then."

Now Wainwright was doing a little for Dawlish also, for five pounds per week as long as his services were needed, services Dawlish had authority and funds from Topcliffe to engage. For Wainwright had been up the Rovuma before. His knowledge of the shallow, winding, fever-sodden river that had killed his fellow expedition members could be priceless.

Dawlish returned to the bridge, leaving the seaman who had helped Wainwright up the shrouds to get him back down again. Foxley had the watch but the other officers had gathered on the bridge also, eager to see where the *Lady Emmeline* had sailed from. Among them Dawlish could sense persisting anger and disgust at what they had found on board her. He felt as much himself. And something deeper also, more troubling, something which he could not discuss with anybody else on *Leonidas*, for the captain must never be seen as anything but calmly confident. It was the consciousness that had first come to him when, as a midshipman, he had boarded a slaver off Brazil and it had never left him since.

It was an awareness of evil, of a force almost otherworldly in its malevolence, a recognition of a depth of degradation of the human spirit that his mind shrank from. The foul holds and packed bodies had not just happened. They had been integral to a calculated plan for gain – logical within its own set of values, or lack of them – that had been conceived in minds alien to all goodness. It worried him that men could descend into this abyss. He admitted reluctantly that he had himself slipped at times some way down that slope – not far, but there must always be a start – for it was too easy to cloak callousness with the excuses of duty and necessity. He had already come to dislike this mission and his abhorrence of what the *Emmeline* embodied had made it all the worse.

As always, action was the antidote to depression.

"A few blasts on the steam whistle would be in order, Mr. Foxley."

*Leonidas* was in full view of the town and of the fort now and her six long shrieks must have drawn the attention of everyone awake there, a challenge no less than a warning. This boldly advertised presence of a British cruiser served notice that, however legal slavery might remain within the sultan's domains, shipment of human cargo would not be tolerated.

From this moment Mtwara was under blockade as regards slaving. No matter how many wretches Achmed Ibn Hamed might return with from the interior, it would be impossible to export them. *Leonidas* might move further offshore, over the horizon indeed, would on occasion return briefly to Zanzibar for fresh supplies, but it must be known that she was close, could always reappear. In the coming period she would make her presence known when least expected, steaming again across the mouth of Mikindani Bay, dropping boats to swoop on any dhow leaving port, harassing even those carrying inoffensive cargos. Edgerton could take care of this duty – the routine that Dawlish would have found tedious would be welcomed by the capable but unambitious commander.

Dawlish himself would soon transfer to *Ibis*.

And then the real work would begin.

*

*Leonidas* closed with *Ibis* ten miles off the Rovuma Delta, some thirty miles south-east of Mtwara. The two vessels lay a cable apart on a mirror-smooth sea as *Leonidas's* whaler carried Dawlish across to the gunvessel. Wainwright was seated with him in the sternsheets, flanked by Tadley, the surgeon, and Ross, the marine lieutenant. Five marines sat with the seamen manning the oars, all men whom, like their Scots corporal Shand, had performed well in Korea. A second whaler was following, laden with medical and other supplies for Horne's mission, supplies allegedly provided by some anonymous benefactor and, officially at least, not funded by government. The crates and bundles stacked between the thwarts gave scarcely enough room for the crew of six trustworthy seamen. Dawlish glanced astern and pride welled in him, as it always did, when he regarded *Leonidas's* elegant lines. Edgerton was now in temporary command of her and the thought gave Dawlish no qualms.

"Those guns, captain," Wainwright gestured towards the gunvessel ahead that he was viewing as intently as he might a zoological specimen. "Those guns, are they as powerful as those on the *Leonidas*?"

"They're relics," Dawlish said. "Muzzle-loaders, a seven-inch and two six-inch. But they're powerful – the seven-inch, throws a 150-pound shell and the others 68s." Jarvis had told how cruelly effective they had been against that unfortunate village in Borneo. They would be no less effective here also if circumstances demanded.

The whaler nudged against *Ibis's* side and Dawlish boarded, was welcomed by Jarvis. The ships parted, *Leonidas* swinging north again to loiter off Mtwara, *Ibis* to nudge towards the mouth of the Rovuma. An increasingly dark stain of brown silt marked the sea's blue as the gunvessel crept closer at half-revolutions. Leadsmen were already positioned in the bows and finding bottom – still twelve fathoms but with the depth decreasing. *Leonidas's* two whalers trailed on tow cables, the men on board slumped in uncomfortable rest, sennet-hats pulled down over their faces against the merciless midday sun.

The green fringe on the horizon ahead resolved itself into dark mangrove with gaps indicating individual creeks. There was no mistaking the main channel. A mile or more wide, the sluggish brown river flowed between mudbanks and patches of sand-beach with solid walls of vegetation behind, the tidal range marked by the bareness of the lower branches. While still offshore, the air had still had a salty freshness but now it was dead and humid. Dawlish knew it would be worse further upstream. A memory stirred of another mangrove swamp, a vastly larger one on the other side of Africa, and Dawlish prayed inwardly that what lay before him now would be nothing to what he – and Egdean – had survived there.

*Ibis* crept slowly up the centre of the channel, along what was, in theory at least, an international boundary. The Sultan of Mtwara's territories lay to the north, and Portugal's' colony of Mozambique stretched southwards from the other bank. In neither case was sovereignty much more than nominal. The channel was still wide but there were exposed banks a mile ahead – sand rather than mud – and what looked like a long low island dotted with scrub. There was no sign of human presence on either shore.

"Eight fathoms." Jarvis repeated the leadsman's call and looked expectantly towards Dawlish.

"Far enough." *Ibis* drew much less but sandbars could be unpredictable in a broad estuary subject to seasonal floods. "Let's find how well the ground holds."

The anchor splashed down, the engine stilled, the vessel drifted with the current, the cable tautened and the anchor held. *Ibis's* steam launch was being lifted off its chocks and swung outboard, her fire already lit and pressure building. The gunvessel's whaler had already been dropped alongside. Ten men under a young lieutenant called Maddox boarded it, all armed, like those in *Leonidas's* boats, with Snider rifles, fifty rounds of ammunition, a cutlass and a pack with spare clothing and personal necessities. Dawlish had agonised over how to clad the river-party and had settled on light duck shirts and trousers – standard shipboard uniform for the tropics. The seamen, accustomed to going barefoot aboard ship, were uncomfortable in boots but the marines wore them without hesitation. Each man carried a single rolled blanket to ward off night chills.

Or worse.

More terrible than any chill would be the uncontrollable teeth-chattering agony of malaria with its rapidly changing extremes of fever and of cold. And malaria would inevitably attack many – Dawlish himself too perhaps. The steaming atmosphere that lay dead on the river, the hint of miasma from the banks, were redolent of the scourge's name – bad air. How air was transformed into a killer deadlier than any bullet was a mystery. All that was known was that quinine, which the crews swallowed so reluctantly, could hold it at bay.

A few words between Dawlish and Jarvis, confirmation of what had already been agreed. *Ibis* would drop back to the open sea and remain at anchor off the estuary. Jarvis's irritation that the expedition upriver had not been entrusted to him was unspoken but Dawlish detected it as he shook his hand. It was understandable. The thrust upstream had much in common with the good work Jarvis had done off Sarawak before Imker's madness had engulfed him also. His chances for redeeming and distinguishing himself were decreasing with every year. Being first on the scene with relief for an admired missionary, a virtual saint, would have earned him prominence, perhaps promotion. For relief was all that Jarvis and the rest believed the expedition to be about. Nobody suspected the real reason.

Germany.

*

*Ibis's* steam launch advanced up the centre of the main channel, a seaman in the bows prodding with a long pole to find bottom. The three whalers trailed astern in a single towed line. Smaller channels lay to either side after the first mile of progress, snaking between exposed sandbanks, dividing, uniting again in an unpredictable pattern that must shift after every flood. Another two miles of slow, cautious south-westerly progress saw the mangrove dwindle away and the banks rise slightly. Beyond them lay dry, dusty open ground scattered with low scrub.

Dawlish was in the launch and it worried him that, though the craft had not yet grounded, the depth beneath its keel was decreasing steadily. He turned to Wainwright.

"How much beyond here did you get?" He knew that the expedition that had killed the entomologist's companions had gone badly from the start.

"A dozen miles, if that. We'd sent ahead to hire Horne's steam launch. It had managed to get downriver from the mission without problem – it was damn nearly worn out for lack of proper care – but by the time we were ascending the level had dropped to about the same as this. And a few miles further on the launch grounded and we couldn't shift it. We must have been close to where those German monks are now."

"They weren't there then?"

"They came later. I've never met them."

"And then?"

"We'd been towing a boat, shallower draught than the launch. We put some of the supplies into it and managed to get to the mission, poling, getting out and dragging when we had to. Askey, our geologist, was already down with fever by then and he died two days after we reached Horne's place."

"And you pressed on afterwards?"

"We did, and it killed my other companion. Me too, almost."

It was a bad precedent and Dawlish sensed the Wainwright did not want to say more. He let him continue undisturbed with the observations he had been jotting in a notebook.

Dawlish surveyed the banks, passing his field glasses to Tadley as he spotted some new feature. The surgeon had never been inland in the tropics before and he was enthralled by hippopotami wallowing in a cut-off channel and, at intervals, crocodiles lying basking on the banks. Rustling foliage close to the water's edge and occasional glimpses of darting brown within the dusty green betrayed troops of monkeys.

Animal life there might be, and in abundance, but there was still no sign of human habitation. Dawlish wondered if it was centuries of slaving that had made the country so empty so close to the coast, for he had been told that the first settlement to be encountered would be the German mission, still another ten miles or so ahead.

Progress slowed through the afternoon. A canvas awning shielded the launch's cockpit from direct sunlight – even with that, Dawlish's clothing was saturated with sweat – but it must be worse for the men in the whalers. The novelty of their surroundings had palled already and most had drifted into cramped lethargy, conscious that though they had been saved the labour of rowing in this steam-bath today, it might be unavoidable on the morrow.

The sun would set in an hour and continuing in darkness could only result in grounding. An island close to midstream, a long sand bank that tapered at both ends and would be gone with the next flood, offered a site for bivouacking. The water close to the edge provided depth enough to anchor the launch. One of the whalers took a party across to the northern bank to cut firewood. It was too green to blaze but its smouldering gave enough heat to boil water for tea to accompany the meal of biscuits and canned beef. The men were mustered before they ate and the tots of quinine wine were issued, swallowing enforced by calling of name.

The soft darkness enveloped them as they passed an hour before sleep, some playing cards in the cooking fires' meagre glow, some talking, others, more pious, joining Lieutenant Ross in a small knot that prayed together. The insects were active now, mosquitoes inflicting bites that would not be felt until the itching began, their whines close to dozing faces shocking tired men into wakefulness. From the banks came a continuous cacophony of frogs and crickets, broken at intervals by the distant wailing screams of jackals or by the roar of some larger beast.

Dawlish moved between the groups around the fires, a word of approval or encouragement here and there, answers to questions hesitantly asked about the country around. Even here, where he would sleep surrounded by many whom he knew by name, he felt as alone, as isolated, as when he was on board *Leonidas* herself. He smoked a cigar around a fire with Tadley, Wainwright and Maddox. Ross joined them when his prayers were done but he refused a cigar, just as he would have refused an offer of spirits.

And yet for all the camaraderie of the moment, Dawlish still detected caution in their conversation, deference that was not servile. He was with them but not of them, and could never be again. He wondered if it would have been otherwise had he been more gregarious by nature – he knew that many had always judged him as reserved – but he comforted himself that advancement must always be at the cost of loneliness. And it was thirst for advancement that had brought him here.

It was eight o'clock, wisps of cloud drifting across the moon's face and the stars a million dots of light against the dark velvet above. There was no prospect of rain and he was thankful for that. He rose, wished the others good night, and made a final round of the sentries.

Then, because he did not want to be seen availing of the small comfort of the launch's cockpit, while his men lay on the sand with holes scooped out for their hip-bones, he wrapped himself in his blanket, laid his head against a pack, tried to keep his face covered against the mosquitoes, and slept.

Chapter 7

The German mission was two rows of buildings – ten or twelve, some of them substantial – with a small church and several acres of neat vegetable patches along the river bank. No African village close by, no curious women looking up from cooking chores, no naked children running excitedly along the bank, only the impression of a tiny, orderly and self-sufficient settlement bounded by a low ridge a half-mile inland.

The launch was sighted as it advanced up a broad reach in late afternoon with the whalers in tow. Two men – Europeans, white shirts and trousers, straw hats – could be seen waiting on a wooden jetty. One lifted his arm in greeting as the launch drew alongside and the other caught the mooring rope cast by a seaman and secured it to a bollard. Dawlish stepped on to the lowest rungs of a vertical ladder and, as he climbed, noted that the structure was solidly built, its piles and beams rough-hewn but securely fastened. Two pulling boats were moored on the far side.

The men he met at the top had wooden crosses – three or four inches long – hanging around their necks. Their sleeves had been rolled up to show arms as deeply tanned as their faces. The younger was perhaps his own age, slightly shorter but powerfully built. His cheeks were scarred, two long-healed slashes on one side, three on the other. His grip was firm when he extended his hand and he bowed slightly from the waist as he shook Dawlish's.

"Albrecht von Hohenfels. Abbot of the monastery of Saint Adalbert." His English was hardly accented and he spoke with as much assurance as if the collection of huts behind him was some vast and venerable foundation.

"Captain Nicholas Dawlish, of Her Britannic Majesty's Ship *Leonidas*. I trust that I find you well, sir."

The second man was introduced as a Father Wolfgang. "Our prior," the abbot said, "and also our lexicographer." He was taking in Dawlish's own perspiration-sodden uniform. "Visitors are always welcome, Captain Daw... Dawl – forgive me, yes, thank you – Captain Dawlish.

But I take it that you've not come to see our abbey, that you're on your way to see our brethren upriver."

"We're headed for the Horne Mission." Dawlish doubted if the author of *With Cross and Bible among the Heathen* would welcome inclusion in the word brethren.

"My community will be pleased if you spend the night here," the abbot said. "Plain lodging, I fear, and plain food too. But you're welcome to what you need."

As they watched the men disembark, several other Europeans – presumably monks also, because of their wooden crosses – joined them. None spoke and Dawlish realised that they must be bound by a vow of silence when speech was not strictly essential. A Brother Heinrich was directed by the abbot to see to accommodation for the men.

"Perhaps you'd like to walk with me, captain," Albrecht said. "You may wish to see what we've created here."

What Dawlish saw impressed him. The perfectly rectangular wattle and daub huts with thatched roofing lay at regular intervals along either side of a beaten-earth roadway. At one end was the church – built apparently of mud-brick – and at the other the refectory, a hall with tables and benches. Four of the huts appeared to be sleeping quarters but the remainder were open-front workshops, including a smithy. Several barnlike structures lay behind, close to the nine or ten acres of cleared ground marked out into vegetable patches.

"Who does the work, abbot?" Dawlish said.

"We do. Sixteen of us. We used to be seventeen but fever took a brother last year."

"I don't see any Africans."

"We didn't come to ask others to work for us. What we need, we make or grow or do ourselves. Time and patience are our allies. When local people come it's for help only, for medicine, for treatment."

The most impressive building proved to the hospital. It was well built – thick sun-baked bricks rather than mud and wattle – and there were at least five separate rooms leading off a central corridor within. A glimpse through one open door revealed two unoccupied wooden beds covered with immaculately white cotton sheets and protected by draped

81

mosquito nets A canvas ceiling blocked off the underside of the thatch. The doors were well made, the wood-framed windows openings no less – their right-angles exact – and woven screens took the place of glass. The floor was packed earth, perfectly level. Well ventilated as it was, there was the slightest whiff, not unpleasing, of some disinfectant.

"Brother Ruprecht's pride," Albrecht said. "We're blessed with his presence among us."

They walked on among the crops, their path bordered on one side by neat drills of what must be kassava and on the other by a small field of maize.

The abbot stopped. "I apologise, captain – I must talk practicalities and I trust you won't be offended. You must be gone from here tomorrow. We live here on sufferance and your presence will compromise it."

"Sufferance?" Dawlish said. "The slavers?"

"They tolerate us, partly because we treat some of their people on occasion. We turn nobody away. And partly too because we don't try to convert anybody."

"Why are you here then?" It seemed impossible that anybody would establish a religious settlement here for any other purpose.

"Conversion will come, captain. But in time. When we're trusted, when we're accepted. The local people come for medical treatment, sometimes a long way. When they do, they see that our farm is worked in ways they might imitate with satisfaction. In time they'll also want to hear us. Willingly, sincerely, without coercion. Our work is no different to Mr. Horne's. But we advance more slowly."

"I heard in Zanzibar that you are Benedictine monks…"

"… and you're surprised not to find us in long habits." Albrecht said. "You won't be disappointed, captain, you'll see them. We wear them only for formal prayers, early morning, evening. We're a Benedictine offshoot – part of the Community of Saint Gebhard. We're all men who heard the call after having had other lives, previous careers. You've met our lexicographer – he was a professor at the Ludwig Maximilian University. Our doctor's a surgeon. Our cook used to be a lawyer and our carpenter a master cabinet-maker. We all work daily on this farm. It's managed by a market-gardener."

"And you yourself, abbot?" Dawlish was trying to avoid looking at what must be duelling scars on his cheeks.

"A soldier." The answer invited no further probe. "We'll sing Vespers in half an hour, captain. You're welcome to join us. But first we must get your people fed and settled." He paused. "I understand that you'll need to post your guards. I've no doubt you'll do so unobtrusively."

There was a dignity about the request – and a sense too of a shared brotherhood of arms – that made it easy to warm towards this man. It seemed natural to converse as equals, as men charged with responsibility and happy in it, as they walked back together.

It was not what Dawlish had expected.

*

Dawlish stood at the back of the austere but well-constructed church – the wooden roof trusses were almost works of art – and listened to the sixteen monks chanting Vespers. Now robed and cowled, shadowy in the light of flickering torches, as if an apparition from a lost medieval world, it was hard to recognise them as the practical business-like men he had first encountered three hours before. This monasticism dropped alongside an African river was at once moving, impressive and bizarre.

The rise and fall of the Latin were pleasing and as he listened Dawlish suddenly remembered his much-loved old nurse, Mrs. Gore. She must be turning in her grave at this moment and dreading his damnation. Her idea of Sunday afternoon entertainment for a motherless boy had been readings from *Foxes' Martyrs*, the more gruesome the better. Now he was in the bosom of the Roman enemy she had so much loathed and yet he felt no strangeness. The chanting brought a feeling of tranquillity, freedom for the first time since he had stepped on board the *Lady Emmeline* from the oppressive awareness of evil. He saw that several of his people had come also. He knew only one, an Irish seaman, to be Catholic.

It pleased him to think that a new era of tolerance had grown up in his own lifetime. There were Catholic officers in the Navy now, something almost unheard of in his youth. O'Rourke of the *Leonidas* was one, liked and admired in the wardroom and on the lower deck alike. Jews too were gaining acceptance. He had been seated with one at a dinner once – a practising one, he learned, not baptised a Christian, as had been Benjamin Disraeli, the late Prime Minister. The impression was no less of a worthy man than an agreeable companion. There might be setbacks but tolerance, acceptance of difference, generosity of spirit could only conquer as time advanced. The twentieth century was only seventeen years away.

It would surely be a golden one.

\*

The early sun was burning away the last wisps of the night's mist on the river and steam was being raised in the *Ibis's* launch.

"Tell him that we'd welcome closer ties with him and his people."

The abbot was on the jetty with Dawlish, watching baskets of fruit and vegetables being loaded into the whalers, gifts not just for the naval party but for the Reverend Horne. "It pains us that whenever they pass downriver or up they do so on the other side." He paused. "We understand that there's no doctor at that mission now. Tell Mr. Horne that Brother Ruprecht is at his service, if ever needed."

Tadley, *Leonidas's* surgeon, had been impressed when he had been shown around the hospital by the German surgeon. "Remarkable fellow," he had told Dawlish afterwards. "But I'm damned if I can understand how he could end up here. He could make a fortune back home."

"One other item, Captain Dawlish." Albrecht dropped his voice. "A sensitive matter."

Dawlish had sensed that he had been weighed since arrival. Whatever had been behind the scrutiny, he had passed muster. Confidences could be exchanged. But cautiously.

"We're not the only Germans you may encounter here, captain. You can take my word, as an officer and as an ordained priest, that we have no dealings with a certain gentleman you may hear of."

"A gentleman called Imker?"

"No. A Doktor Lutz. We know of him, but he has never come here. He renders to Caesar – or rather to the Kaiser – and we render to God."

Lutz. The name was new to Dawlish. "Do you know what he's trying to achieve?"

"We talk no politics here, captain." Albrecht held up his hand. "If we did then our three Alsatian brothers might be at their German brethren's throats. We've left all that behind."

And yet there was something that the abbot had not left behind. He was eyeing the marines' Sniders and Dawlish saw something like hunger in his gaze.

"Corporal Shand!" Dawlish called him over. "Let me see your rifle."

He took it, checked that the breech was empty, then handed it to Albrecht. He accepted it in silence, his hands gliding lovingly over the polished furniture, pulling back the breech-block, flipping up the back sight, lining up the barrel, feeling for balance.

"Speed of fire?" The abbot's voice was a whisper.

"Nothing acceptable to me under eight per minute. But Shand's been known to manage eleven on the range, bull's eyes and inners at three hundred yards."

A sigh. A silence longer than a minute after Albrecht handed the rifle back. At last he said "The vows of poverty and chastity and obedience have been no burden. But this… it's hard to miss it."

"A soldier, you said, abbot?"

"Second Bavarian Guards Infantry." Said with pride. "Lieutenant at Kissingen in '66. Fighting against the Prussians then. And a captain and brevet-major by their side in '70 against the French. Bloody stuff, though I came off lightly. Wörth and Bazeilles and Sedan and the campaign along the Loire."

"You tired of it?" Dawlish knew cases of officers, good men, courageous, who had recoiled from the reality of war, most often in

India, and had sought solace in civilian life. His own experiences in Paraguay, still relived in nightmares, had almost done the same for him.

"I loved it, captain," Albrecht said. "I enjoyed it too much. I still would. That was why I had to turn from it."

It was time to go.

The relief that Dawlish had felt the previous evening was suddenly gone. The concerns that Topcliffe had expressed about German penetration had seemed so exaggerated when the reality seemed to be no more than this peaceful religious institution. But the abbot was a man of the world, had no illusions about its brute realities. If he dissociated himself from this Doktor Lutz then it was for good reason.

*Rendering to the Kaiser…*

Nothing was to be gained in pressing the abbot for more than he was willing to say. He would not yield easily, if indeed ever.

As the launch began its laborious plod upriver Dawlish looked back to see only a solitary figure left on the landing stage. He rose to his feet in the tiny cockpit. He snapped to attention and raised his hand in salute.

And Abbot Albrecht von Hohenfels returned it, holding it immobile until he was lost from sight at the first bend.

## Chapter 8

The twenty-five miles to Horne's mission at Kitaya took two days. They felt like ten.

Dawlish was determined, at the very least, to get the whaler carrying the medical supplies there but by the end of the first day even this seemed over-ambitious. The steam-launch had grounded several times – was poled free at three points, and towed free twice by seamen straining on the whalers' oars – but the increasing frequency of shallow sandbars indicated that the problem could only get worse. It was difficult to predict what might lie beyond the next bend of the meandering river, sometimes a long, broad, calm reach but at other times several smaller, faster channels that brought the challenge of deciding which to chance. Often too, a stretch of a hundred yards or so of narrow choppy water must hide obstacles beneath but gave no indication of their depth. The steam launch's advantage – its towing of the whalers saved the occupants from exhaustion – was eroding as the men were called upon to free it, each effort more strenuous than before and bringing with it the danger of damaging the vulnerable propeller. The climate was beginning to tell upon them now, the damp heat sapping energy, the sweat-soaked clothing chaffing, the endless discomfort of mosquitoes in the night.

The launch was left behind on the morning of the second day, anchored in midstream in a placid reach with two seamen to guard it. The whalers stroked on upriver. Dawlish himself took his turn at the oars and the other officers, though not ordered to do so, followed his example. Holding to the steady rhythm of men who were mostly younger was harder than he had expected. Middle age was upon him, he realised, and the vigour he had always enjoyed, though still strong, had started its unavoidable decline. He would fight it to the last, he told himself, and the resolve drove him to join several of the men in the water in the next shallows when sand scraped beneath the keel and the whaler had to be dragged for fifty yards. Awareness that crocodiles were near, the thrill of fear when they were so often seen slithering off the banks and disappearing beneath the brown stream, made entering water even to knee-level a test of courage, a challenge against showing fear.

And so on through a long day's laborious progress that was rewarded in late afternoon by swift progress along a long calm section. One last bend and then, a quarter-mile ahead, sight of a collection of grass-thatched huts on a high bank that sloped towards the river. Only a large wooden cross atop a hillock behind told it to be something other than a normal African village.

"That's the mission?" Dawlish felt vaguely disappointed. He had expected something more impressive, something akin to the German settlement, and his tone must have conveyed it

"Kitaya's a miserable place," Wainwright said. "You'll see."

The whalers had been spotted and a figure was running up, shouting, from the foreshore to the huts. His cries drew others and they, calling and gesticulating, drew more still to follow them. A bell began to toll, a plaintive summons to yet more. Soon several dozen people, Africans and half-naked, but with three or four in white clothing among them, were hurrying to the water's edge. Dawlish could see a small ramshackle jetty there. Just beyond it a decrepit steam launch was drawn far up on the bank and half-hidden in long grass around it.

The crowd was still growing as the whalers drew in, the men clad with little more than loin cloths but many of the women wearing shapeless, ragged European-style dresses. They were chattering and pointing and some older children were entering the water and splashing towards the arrivals. Pushing through the throng were what only could be Horne and two of his assistants. He must be the tall gaunt figure in a black coat, for the Africans were stepping back, almost shrinking, to clear a path for him.

The whalers grounded and several Africans rushed into the water to help drag them further. Dawlish moved to the bow and jumped down on to dry sand. Horne was standing still, twenty yards away on the slope above, his face solemn, his two helpers at a respectful distance behind him and gesturing to the crowd for silence.

Dawlish had an instant impression of calculated theatricality in which his own role had already been decided without him. Horne must have known that such a moment would come, must have rehearsed it in his mind. This was a contrived scene that would be imagined by illustrators in missionary magazines and in framed engravings that would grace the walls of chapel halls and pious households. It annoyed Dawlish that he was already cast to be this Livingstone's Stanley and he was damned if he was going to play along.

"Lieutenant Ross! Be so good to get your men ashore. Keep those people back if they come too close. Gently, if you please."

It was unnecessary, but he wanted to impose his own pace. Then he turned back towards Horne, who had made no movement towards him.

He walked slowly up the slope, his own face as impassive as the missionary's. He knew his age — two years younger than himself — but Horne had the look of a much older man, one worn down by disease and privation, hair prematurely white, a luxuriant beard but no moustache, complexion yellow, yet still vital because of willpower alone. He was hatless but Dawlish raised his own broad-brimmed hat — like

Stanley, but there was no avoiding it. Horne had extended his hand. Dawlish took it.

"Captain Nicholas Dawlish, of Her Majesty's Ship *Leonidas*." Nothing like Stanley, no presumption. "I trust you're well, sir."

"As well as the Lord vouchsafes," Horne said. "You and your men are welcome."

"Mr. Gladstone knows of your work here and values it highly. It's at his request that we've come, to assure him of your safety." The words were Topcliffe's, not his own, and Dawlish had been told to use them verbatim. "They'll filter back in Horne's letters," the old Lucifer had said. "Grist to the People's William's mill."

"God be praised," Horne said. "Our needs are pressing and the moment is opportune. The Lord indeed tempers the wind to the shorn lamb."

"And these gentlemen are?"

The two missionaries were still standing back. Horne beckoned them forward.

"Mr. Dalton, my brother in Christ and my strong right arm since we first came here together."

The small man in grimy white looked as weathered and as resilient as Horne himself. He was smiling, the only one here who was, and for that Dawlish found himself liking him.

"And Mr. Joyce, our reader and our blacksmith." A large, swarthy man on whom his flesh now hung loosely and whose eyes were yellow and whose sun-scorched face was livid with mosquito bites.

Dawlish sensed subservience in the Devon tones when Joyce took his hand and was pleased to meet him. The humility seemed genuine and moving, the more so since his health was all too obviously ruined.

"Our sister, Mrs. Joyce, is indisposed," Horne said, "but she will be pleased to meet you later. And our brothers Miller and Buckwell are labouring in the Lord's vineyard at outstations some distance from here. I trust that you may meet them also."

As they spoke the crowd of Africans was still growing, this meeting an entertainment and a mystery, the formal exchanges between the Englishmen opaque but fascinating. It was hard to gauge whether the arrival was as welcome to them as it was to Horne, for glances that might have been either fearful or relieved were stealing towards the weapons carried by Ross's men.

"I believe that you know Mr. Wainwright already." Dawlish had noted polite coldness in the nod the entomologist had exchanged with Horne.

"Mr. Wainwright will not be turned away as long as he keeps his commitment to Mr. Darwin's ravings to himself." Horne did not venture to shake his hand.

"And may I introduce my officers?"

Horne was especially pleased to meet Tadley. "We have sore need," he said. "Your medical supplies are as manna to us, doctor." He looked around to see if the blacksmith was close and, seeing that he was, dropped his voice. "Sister Joyce's case is urgent. It would be a singular mercy if she could be seen immediately."

"Your German counterpart downstream asked me to convey his regards," Dawlish said. "Abbot Albrecht said that…"

Horne cut him off. "The Whore of Babylon is ever on the watch, captain! I'll thank you to make no mention of the foul leaven of Rome!"

Dalton had pressed closer. "Have you brought kerosene, captain?" His voice was conciliatory, as if to make up for Horne's outburst.

"Doctor Kirk was insistent that we should bring you ten gallons," Dawlish said. It was a troublesome charge, its smell unpleasant and pervasive even though the tins seemed well sealed.

"Light is precious to us," Dalton said. "We've been reduced to allowing ourselves a single lamp only, and that for only two hours each night. It makes reading our bibles difficult. And my work even more so."

"Your work, Mr. Dalton?"

"Translating Luke's gospel." The slightest hint of pride. "I've reached the thirteenth chapter."

"Into Swahili?"

"Into the tribal language. I had to start by making a dictionary first."

"Can these people read and write?"

"A few, in English. But they all will in time."

If he had come with Horne then he had been here for six years. Thirteen chapters. It must be brutally demanding work but Dalton spoke of it lightly.

It was dusk now, the tropics' brief minutes of twilight that would soon be full darkness. Accommodation would be provided in the church for the men, for Dawlish and Wainwright and the officers in Horne's and Dalton's bungalows. Both had been fabricated in Britain, wooden structures that had been broken down and transported here by almost superhuman effort. They had been reassembled – drawings of them, surrounded by happy converts, had appeared in numerous missionary magazines – but by now the climate had exposed their inadequacies and they were dilapidated. A British slum-landlord might have been ashamed by the glassless windows with ill-fitting slatted shutters, jammed frames locking doors open and crude wooden furniture. Insects scurried underfoot and dust cascaded from the rafters as a room was entered.

Offloading of supplies must wait and marine sentries must protect the whalers through the night. Won for Jesus though they might be, Africans who had almost nothing might find the temptation to pilfer irresistible. This was the first batch of supplies only – more would be ferried upstream later – and Dawlish apologised to Horne for the delay in bringing them ashore. That would happen in the morning.

The missionary could barely contain his indignation. "Are you not aware that tomorrow is the Sabbath, captain? There is no labour here on the Lord's Day! Monday will be soon enough. We want no bad example here for our benighted brethren."

"Only the most essential items then," Dawlish said. "Medical supplies perhaps?"

"Even the Lord healed on the Sabbath. Medical supplies then. Just the medicines. Nothing more." Horne paused, as if regretting his harshness. "I understand that naval captains read divine service to their crews when no chaplain is carried. Perhaps you might join with me tomorrow in conducting the service?"

Dawlish had a quarter-century's experience of shipboard services, first listening, later leading them himself. "A pleasure, Mr. Horne. I'd be honoured."

91

"And nothing that smacks of Rome, if you please, captain. No ritual! A reading only. The words of the Good Book alone. Nothing more."

"Most assuredly not," Dawlish was glad that the darkness could hide his amusement.

Theology was the least of his concerns.

*

Tadley came to see Dawlish before he slept.

"It's Mrs. Joyce."

"Bad?"

"Worse than that," Tadley said. "Her life's not worth a fortnight's purchase unless she gets proper care. And I can't give it here."

"Fever?"

"Worse. She's *enceinte* and there's a serious complication. Very serious. She's had half-a-dozen miscarriages before, each worse than the last, I gather. This time she'll die if she's not helped."

"Can you help her here?"

"It would be butchery. It needs proper facilities, cleanliness, a full set of instruments. I've seen what this place has and it's not enough. And I've little experience in that area. I delivered a few babies when I was a student, but since then…" Tadley held up his hands. "I know my limits."

"So, she'll die?"

Dawlish felt cold. Fear and pity mixed. Something very similar had all but taken Florence from him, had taken also any chance of future children. He had never loved her more than at that instant of almost losing her, nor had that love diminished since. He hadn't seen this Mrs. Joyce yet but the insect-inflamed face of her humble blacksmith husband was fresh in his memory. A worthy, selfless, naïve sense of dedication had brought these simple people to this nightmare. They deserved better.

"The only chance is to get her to that German surgeon," Tadley said. "That Brother Ruprecht has vast experience. He could do it. I'd trust my own wife to him in similar circumstances."

"We'll need to speak to Mr. Horne then," Dawlish said. The proposal would not be welcome but he must try. "In the meantime, get

92

one of the boats ready but say nothing to anybody. Not yet." Better to wait until after the service in the morning.

And, for all his fatigue, he slept badly. He was not relishing the discussion he must have with Horne.

*

The sun was still low, the shadows long, when they gathered in the church, a large wooden building inexpertly assembled and now falling apart. A decrepit harmonium, lugged across from shelter in Horne's house, stood at one side of the platform at the front, a crude lectern too at which Horne, sombre in faded black, positioned himself. Dawlish and his party stood at the front of the congregation with Dalton and some sixty or seventy Africans crowded behind, men on one side, women and children on the other. A sense of expectation, no sound but shuffling of feet on the earthen floor within, and hens clucking and a goat bleating somewhere outside. Horne was leafing through an enormous bible on the lectern and glaring up at intervals through his steel-rimmed spectacles, clearly impatient to begin.

Then, at last, louder shuffling, murmuring from behind. Dawlish looked back to see a path opening through the crowd to make way for three figures. Tadley was at one side, Joyce at the other and in the middle, supported by them, a tiny woman, her pinched features all but hidden by a black bonnet. A threadbare grey dress was stretched across her enormous belly. Horne made no move as she was helped two steps up on to the platform and into the crude chair – the only one in the church – at the harmonium. An African in a frayed shirt began to pump the bellows behind it.

Sweat was running down the woman's face and great dark blotches of it stained her clothing. She must be in extreme discomfort, perhaps even pain. She turned to look at Horne. To Dawlish it seemed that her eyes mixed dread with a desperate hope for approval, like some faithful dog who feared offending its master. Horne's nod was curt and she launched into the first notes of a hymn. Even before the congregation's voices – led by Horne himself – took up the words it was clear that her

93

playing could never have been better than inept, and the discordant instrument made it even worse. Dawlish felt himself moved by the woman's fierce sincerity. She was suffering and she must know that she was on the brink of death.

The hymn was unknown to Dawlish, though one of the seamen knew it and was joining in loudly. The voices were at full strength now, more musical, more pleasing, than might ever be expected and the surprise was that the words – English words – could be distinguished.

*"Who will go and work today? Fields are white, the harvest waiting. Who will bear the sheaves away?"*

Dawlish wondered if one in ten, one in twenty, of the Africans understood what they sang, for all that their pleasure in it seemed so unfeigned. Joyce was standing by his wife's chair, tears running down his face as he sang, and Dawlish looked away. Horne, dry-eyed, was beating time on the lectern but he was nodding towards somebody to Dawlish's left, as if prompting readiness.

The words died away and a young African in a loose white shirt and trousers mounted the platform.

"Brother Christopher will read from Jeremiah," Horne announced.

Dalton nudged Dawlish and whispered "Our catechist. Our first true convert."

Christopher had been well schooled for his enunciation was clear, his English pronunciation perfect.

*"I will gather the remnant of my flock out of all countries whither I have driven them, and will bring them again to their folds; and they shall be fruitful and increase."*

Horne was nodding slowly, grim satisfaction on his face. Dawlish glanced back and saw the congregation listening with reverence to words they could not comprehend. He wondered if for them the reading seemed like some magical incantation, some glimpse of mystic power from the world beyond.

The reading ended. Another hymn, no less familiar to the throng, no less well sung.

*"Bear the news to every land. Climb the steeps and cross the waves. 'Onward!' 'tis our Lord's command."*

Dalton was singing with them, the seaman also, and Mrs. Joyce was pounding the harmonium keys with desperate intensity.

As the notes faded Horne was at the lectern again, grasping it firmly, clearing his throat, glaring down with an expression that somehow merged sorrow and contempt.

He preached in what must be the local language for fifteen, twenty, thirty minutes, his voice strong, threatening, starting low and rising almost to a shout. The crowd was responding, individual voices calling what must be assent and by Dawlish's side Dalton was nodding furiously. On the platform the Joyces, husband and wife, were nodding too, but it was clear that they understood little of the words and that, in their terrible years here, mastery of the language had been beyond them. The woman was swaying on her chair, steadied by her husband's hand on her shoulder.

And, through all this, time is slipping away, Dawlish thought, precious time when the whaler should be stroking downriver, minutes that might save this woman's life.

Horne reached his climax — it seemed like a warning that a bad-tempered Old Testament prophet could not have delivered with more surly passion — and again there were cries of what must be concurrence from the congregation. Horne stepped back, mopping his brow and gesturing to Dawlish to come forward

He had wondered what he should read and at last could think of only one text. His religious belief was lukewarm, his doubts strong, but those words had always inspired and challenged him, even though he had so often failed to live by them.

He spoke to Dalton. "Come with me. Translate."

They ascended the platform.

The bible — folio-sized, leather bound — was still open at Jeremiah but he flicked forward, almost to the back, searched and found Corinthians. He located the verses he wanted and began to read.

*"Though I speak with the tongues of men and of angels, and have not charity, I am become as sounding brass, or a tinkling cymbal."*

He paused and Dalton translated, too fluently, too easily, to be exact but probably well enough to convey the thought. For the first time

Dawlish could see the faces of all present. There was bewilderment there, fascination and respect too, but he wondered how much there was of understanding. He read on, stopping at the end of each verse to allow Dalton to interpret. He was moved himself now and he was afraid to glance across towards the Joyces lest emotion master him. The scene, and his own participation in it, were bizarre, incongruous, even foolish, and yet there was a dignity, a nobility, about it that could not be denied.

Then the last verse.

*"And now abideth faith, hope, charity, these three; but the greatest of these is charity."*

He looked across at Mrs. Joyce as Dalton translated and he made the slightest inclination of his head. He saw that she was frightened, in pain too perhaps, and already exhausted, but she nodded to him. He saw gratitude on her face and he looked quickly away.

A last hymn, this time in the local language. Dalton could not keep the pride from his voice when he whispered to Dawlish.

"My translation. *Souls in death and darkness lying, where no light has broken through.* Our converts love it."

They did, for they were beginning to clap and sway as they sang. When it finished Horne dismissed them with what must be a stern reminder not to labour on this Sabbath day.

"A word with you, Mr. Horne, and with Mr. Joyce". Dawlish drew them aside as the congregation dispersed and beckoned Tadley to join them.

They listened in silence as Tadley explained, Joyce with half-comprehending but rising fear, Horne with ill-disguised impatience, until the German mission was mentioned.

Then Horne exploded.

"You propose handing our sister over to the attentions of some lascivious Romish monk? How do you dare, Captain Dawlish?"

"She'll die unless she gets the attention she can only get there." Dawlish saw Joyce beginning to weep and looking helplessly to Horne.

"And your Royal Navy surgeon is powerless to help? Is this the…"

"No!" Tadley cut Horne off. "Anything I could do would almost certainly kill her. It would be little short of murder."

"Mr. Joyce!" Dawlish turned to the husband. "It's your decision, nobody else's." The man did not turn towards him, seemed incapable of breaking his gaze from Horne's fierce frown.

"I know Staff Surgeon Tadley well," Dawlish said to Joyce. "I've seen him tend the worst wounds, have seen him draw men back from the threshold of death. Listen to him! He can accompany your wife to the German mission, bring you with him too and …"

"Peace, man!" Horne shouted and held up his hand. "Mr. Joyce will not entrust his wife to the care of some Roman charlatan, nor would she wish it herself. His trust and hers will be in the Lord, here in our own vineyard." His voice was calm but infinitely cold. He turned to Joyce. "You will assure the gentleman of that, will you not, Brother Joyce?"

The man was in agony, tears on his cheeks, his lower lip quivering, his whole frame shaking. He looked to Dawlish, his eyes pleading.

"Tell them, Brother Joyce!"

Dawlish tried to hold Joyce's gaze. The blacksmith shook his head slowly, then looked back to Horne.

"Here." He began to sob. "It will be better here."

"Well, captain?" Horne could not hide the triumph in his voice. It was clear that he would not yield.

Dawlish had been prepared for this, but it was still bitter. He and Tadley had discussed the alternative. An undesirable one. He caught the surgeon's eye, nodded slightly. *Go Ahead.*

"I could attempt it on our ship, on the *Leonidas*, if I had to," Tadley said. "The facilities needed are there. I'd risk it, but there'd be still much danger. It would be better still at Zanzibar. There must be some qualified *accoucheur* there for the foreigners' wives."

"Could she be got safely downriver?" Horne was biting.

The question raised another fear – an unworthy, shaming concern that Dawlish tried to ignore. It would be bad enough if she were to die here, but she would be revered as another martyr of the mission field. But if she were to die in a whaler or on either *Ibis* or *Leonidas*, she would be a heroine condemned by his own bad judgement. Gladstone would not forgive. And another voice of temptation, meaner still. Topcliffe had other officers aplenty to do his work, men as hungry, as ambitious, as competent as Dawlish himself.

"We'd need to get her to the *Ibis* first," Tadley must have dreaded this moment even more than Dawlish. "There wouldn't be much room in a whaler if… if it was suddenly necessary to intervene. But if we got her to the steam launch… then it would be easier. And it would be faster to get downstream than up. But until Mrs. Joyce is lifted on board *Ibis* then…" His voice trailed off, the unspoken words telling all.

"But she'll die if we don't take the chance?" Dawlish said.

"She'll die if we don't take the chance." Tadley did not hesitate.

"Mr. Joyce?" Dawlish spoke directly to him. His quarterdeck voice, intolerant of delay.

The husband was standing in mute misery. At last he nodded.

"But no contact with the German Romans as you pass downriver." Horne said. "On that condition only!"

Dawlish ignored him. "I trust you can depart within the hour, Surgeon Tadley? Good! And Mr. Joyce, you'll break the news to your wife, put her mind at rest? Yes? Excellent! She'll be relieved that you'll accompany her. I'll send men to carry her and her things to the jetty."

An hour later, he watched a frightened and bewildered Mrs. Joyce being lowered into the whaler in which Tadley and four seamen would carry her and her husband downstream. He hoped that it would not be too late.

But there could have been no other choice. Not if he was ever to look himself in the mirror again. Nor to face Florence.


Chapter 9


It was important to mend fences with Horne – Dawlish knew that his own career lay at the mercy of this man, that a negative report in the missionary press could not be ignored in Downing Street.

He stood watching with Horne until the whaler disappeared around a bend, then asked him to show him the mission. He sensed that the missionary also wished for something of a truce, even if he made no outward sign of concession.

But for the imported bungalows and church, the settlement looked little different to any African village – mud-walled thatched huts, beaten earth around them clear of vegetation, small vegetable gardens in between, an impression of order and cleanliness that had reigned long before the missionaries' arrival. But it felt somehow unlike any such village as Dawlish had ever seen. The women fanning cooking fires outside the huts were not chatting with each other and they looked away as Dawlish and Horne approached. The few children who had been playing – most stark naked and carrying smaller siblings on their backs – scurried away also. The men were nowhere in evidence and nobody was working in the gardens. The sense of bustle, of happy gossip, of slow but purposeful activity that Dawlish had always found appealing in Africa, was missing.

They walked in silence. Dawlish was unsure how to initiate a conversation with this man. He suspected that Horne felt the same. Only once did the minister speak, talking sternly to a woman who was stringing fish on a twig for smoking over a smouldering fire. She said nothing but stood up, fetched a gourd and poured water from it over the embers. She mumbled a few words that must be of apology, but her eyes were blank.

Horne turned away. "Unforgivable on the Sabbath," he said. "Preparation of today's food is acceptable but that work she was doing could have waited until tomorrow."

"Where are the men?" Dawlish welcomed the break in the silence.

"I'd like to say that they were resting in their huts, but I'm no fool, captain. Many of them will have gone straight from our service to devilish rites at their heathen shrines beyond the village." Horne spoke with a degree of relish, of satisfaction in confronting an immense evil and not being cowed by it. "Satan is never idle. Many who profess belief in Jesus, many who have stood with us in our worship today, are the Evil One's most willing instruments."

An open space lay behind the church with six low mounds in a single line marked by black crosses. None carried a name.

"Matthew Bannister. Our earliest martyr." Horne spoke with something like pride as he gestured to the first grave. "He was a mechanic in a Lancashire mill when he heard the call. His health was always frail but his faith was unconquerable."

Then Thomas Phillips, the mission's only doctor, four years in the field before fever had taken him. Jacob Grigg, a grocer who had sold the family business when his father died and had come to labour here.

Horne's voice had the slightest quaver at the fourth.

"My dear wife Rachel. Our infant daughter lies here in her arms. Both wear their crowns of glory now."

There was a gap between this mound and the two last.

"My own resting place, close to my precious darlings." It seemed to give Horne mournful comfort as he pointed to it. "A temporary rest only, Captain Dawlish, until the final trumpet calls for reuniting at our last resurrection."

The fifth grave was another woman, Miss Ellen Jessop, a catechist who had been a housemaid. The last was of Edward Frensham, previously a draper's assistant, dead at twenty-eight after a scant eight months here.

There would have been another here soon, Mrs. Joyce's, if we had not arrived, Dawlish thought. And there might yet be a grave, an even more humble one, if Tadley did not get her to adequate help in time, a mound above the flood mark on a riverbank downstream or the plunge of a weighted bundle from the *Ibis*.

"Could they not have left when their health began to fail?" Dawlish found himself half-impressed, half-angered by the ignorant conviction that had brought these innocents to their deaths here.

"Some who came did leave," Horne said. "Shepherds who deserted their flock in the face of sickness. It is for the Lord to judge them, not men." But it was clear that he did so himself.

Dawlish felt his dislike for this man growing. Horne was an inspired writer, had seemed like an inspired preacher, was able to impose an alien, iron discipline and joyless virtue on a personal fief by force of character alone and yet... He had something in common with another whom Dawlish had once known who, in self-conscious humility, had called himself The Poor Man, *El Pobre*. He too had been driven by a vision of

100

paradise that discounted the sacrifices demanded of others to achieve it. The outcome had been a hecatomb.

*Though I speak with the tongues of men and of angels, and have not charity…*

"I gather that you won't be leaving, Mr. Horne?"

"No, Captain Dawlish. My place is here."

Horne's tone was level, civil and cold. And beneath it recognition. *I understand you, and you understand me, and there is no common ground of sympathy between us. There never can be, never will be.*

"You've been harassed by slavers," Dawlish said.

"A murderous attack, four months ago. We were never threatened directly here before – their routes lie slightly to the north – but some wretches who had escaped from one of their columns made their way here. It was a miracle that they found us. They knew no local language, knew nothing of the area. The Lord guided them here."

"You gave them sanctuary?"

"They were tracked here," Horne said. "By three Arabs and a half-dozen of their hirelings. Most of our people here fled into the bush when they saw them coming. But some, a few, brethren who had accepted the Lord Jesus, remained. It was…" His voice caught and he turned away, embarrassed by his emotion. "Isiah, my first convert, struck down. Simon, a boy who had embraced the word so joyously…" He paused, overcome now. "They cut his throat before us. And our brother Joyce, who has the courage of a lion, him they tied to a tree and flogged senseless even as his wife watched. And when these jackals left they took the fugitives and five of our converts with them."

A silence. It seemed all the more terrible to Dawlish that Horne and his flock had been unarmed, powerless. And some of those snatched from here might have ended up on the *Lady Emmeline.*

"Have they come back since?" Dawlish said

"No. But they can at any time," Horne said. "Our brother Buckwell at our outstation at Nanguruwe is under constant threat. Their columns pass regularly through there." He looked straight at Dawlish, his only emotion now cold fury. "Britain has turned her face from us, captain. Here is a land crucified by greed, a land hungry for the word of Christ, a land where the bearers of his message are persecuted unto death. And

101

until this land is purged of slavers Britain can never stand high in the sight of the Almighty. Never until it has picked up this gauntlet."

It was easy to imagine Horne's words printed in a pamphlet, easy to imagine them read out to tears and indignation in chapels and meeting halls. Easy to understand Gladstone's need to respond, despite his distaste for foreign adventures. Easy too that the nature of that response should be left to an officer whose success could be endorsed, whose failure could be repudiated.

They walked on past the huts towards the tilled patches of yams on the edge of the scrub beyond. An easy slope brought them to the top of a low ridge. Below it lay a small lake. Perhaps a mile wide, it stretched for about three to the north west. Several canoes lay stationary on it. A net was being cast from one.

"It's called Chidya," Horne said. "There's better fishing in it than in the river. The Lord vouchsafes us yields there as generous as those of Galilee. And there," he pointed towards the further end. A brown cluster of huts and signs of cultivation was just discernible. "That's our outpost at Sali. Mr. Miller supervises there. And Nanguruwe, where Mr. Buckwell labours alone, is ten miles beyond."

"A useful base for further activity inland?"

"So we had hoped, captain. Our efforts thrived for a while, gave great hope. But now..." Horne suddenly sounded defensive. It was clear that his influence extended little more than a dozen miles from the river, his foothold even less. His writings, so admiringly and so uncritically received in Britain, had held the promise of so much more. He seemed embarrassed by what he had to admit. "All that Mr. Buckwell has achieved at Nanguruwe, is brought to naught. The chief, Kikuwa, accepted baptism three years ago, put away his plural wives, seemed steadfast in his faith. Dozens followed. But since then the slavers have grown bolder, more importunate in their demands for porters. Kikuwa has lapsed, mocks all he once professed and persecutes our flock. He's the Arabs' creature now and in thrall to one of them above all others, the one whose men came here to kidnap and to murder."

"Achmed Ibn Hamed?" The slaver Kirk had mentioned in Zanzibar.

102

"Him," Horne said. "He's better armed than any like him before, and he thrusts further into the interior each year. He needs way-stations where his columns can rest, where they can get food and engage labour."

"So Nanguruwe is now such a station?"

"The nearest to the coast, but there are a dozen or more like it further inland. Achmed needs porters, not slaves, from this region, if he's to loot the unexploited territory far to the west. He's clever. He pays for what he gets and so makes confederates of Kikuwa and the other chiefs. They sell their souls for less than Esau's mess of pottage."

"For trade goods?"

"Printed cotton. Brass wire. Cast iron pans. Tin mugs and bowls and tawdry women's trinkets. Trash that Europe can probably find no market for elsewhere. It floods in through Mtwara."

"German trade goods?" An opportunity to slip in the word casually.

"German, British, even American. What does it matter, captain? But this country has German imports of another sort to plague it. You've seen them yourself. Papists, vassals of Rome."

"I saw decent men, Mr. Horne, as sincere as yourself."

Horne stepped back, fury on his face.

"A nest of vipers, nothing more than a mask for Popish ambition, captain! The Arab slaver may yet earn forgiveness for the blindness of his heathen faith but there can be none for the machinations of the Vatican."

"You haven't been to that mission, Mr. Horne. I can assure you that you'd be welcomed there without any danger to your faith."

An angry shake of the head. "No! We'll have no truck with them, nor want any." He smiled for the first time. "Local people tell us that this Romish venture has not prospered, that there has not been a single convert, not a single baptism, even though they tempt the heathen with medical care. The Lord's displeasure is manifest."

Dawlish did not respond. Horne's mission was even more vulnerable than he had been prepared for. And the outstation at Nanguruwe, through which the slavers' columns passed, must be more exposed still. Until he had seen that outpost it would be impossible to know just how Horne's activities might be protected.

*

Nanguruwe would be reachable in a day's march – not an easy one in this heat, but a start in the cool of dawn and an easy three miles up the Chidya lake in canoes, would mean substantial progress before the sun's full heat began to bite. Mr. Dalton, the gospel-translator, would act as guide and Wainwright would be essential as he was fluent in Swahili. Lieutenant Ross, Corporal Shand and four marines would provide the armed escort. The expedition would be a short one – two days at most – but the standard landing-party equipment of packs, water bottles, ammunition and weapons would be carried.

The sun was rising as the three canoes stroked through the tendrils of mist drifting over the lake. It was still cool, and there was a scent of freshness, and birds singing on the shores and, once, a troop of monkeys calling. Three early fishermen were casting nets, hauling them back, searching in the meshes, then casting again. Voices carried far across the calm water – and Dawlish suddenly felt something like joy, a delight in the calm beauty of the brief hour of the passage.

At Sali, the outpost at the lake's far end, they were greeted by Mr. Miller, a harried-looking young man whose manner indicated that he might soon be a shepherd who would desert his flock. It would be hard to blame him – his hut and his small wattle and daub chapel must be little inducement to stay. He stammered thanks for the small packet of tea that Dawlish gave him and seemed even more grateful for a few minutes of conversation with fellow Englishmen before they left.

They followed what were paths rather than tracks, scarcely wide enough for two people to pass, but they were well-trodden enough to confirm frequent usage. The ground was for the greater part open, low scrub, some thorn, grass often waist high, the occasional thicket of trees and undergrowth, all parched at this time of year.

The sun rose higher, and the heat with it, and the pace, which Dawlish had deliberately kept slow, became more onerous, the packs heavier. Yet for all that his pleasure in the surroundings remained undiminished – the unexpected beauty, the distant cry of some predator,

104

a baboon sitting defiantly on the path and only stalking reluctantly away at the last moment, the chatter of crickets, the birds now largely silent but splendid in brief flashes of colour. Once they encountered a flock of goats, two boys tending them, and in mid-morning they passed through a village – a half-dozen huts – where Dalton was welcomed with genuine pleasure and where courtesies were exchanged through him with the headman. A break was taken there, tea brewed. Naked children stood watching, silent at first, but laughing as Dalton joked with them in their dialect.

It would be easy to like this country, these people, Dawlish thought, and yet death was always close, not just the threat of slavers but the yet more insidious one of disease. Few Europeans lasted long here – Dalton and Horne and Wainwright and Kirk were exceptions. If the Germans, or anyone else, wanted this land, then they would have to pay a high price for it.

The march resumed, the distance longer for the paths' ramblings than any crow might fly, a break of five minutes in each hour, a longer one at midday, rest snatched in shade, other life also quietened by the heat, only the cicadas' clicking chatter unstilled. Lookouts had been posted and most of the others drifted into light dozes. Only Wainwright was active, poking under bushes and lifting stones, falling in delight on some insect and dropping it into a sample bottle. Dawlish noticed him pushing on into long grass, his head and shoulders dropping from view, then lifting again.

Just as it was time to move again, as men were lurching to their feet and drawing on packs, a cry rang out.

"Captain Dawlish!" Wainwright's voice, urgent but lacking fright. "Over here. Look here!"

Dawlish hurried through the waist-high grass, Ross and the others following.

"They're human." Wainwright was pointing down at scattered bones, ribs, a pelvis, further off a femur. He beat the grass aside to reveal a skull – the jaw had been torn away but lay close by. A further jumble, more ribs, vertebrae, what might have been a humerus before it was broken. There was no sign of digging, none either of remaining flesh. The fragments had been here for weeks, maybe months.

There was no mistaking what they saw. A human body that had lain here on the surface and had been dismembered by animals.

"It might have been a lion," Dalton said. "More likely a leopard. They're common around here and they're –" He stopped, pointed. Something brown lay half-concealed among the untrodden grass to one side.

Wainwright lifted it. Three feet of rusty iron chain, the links light, still loose, at one end a ring, four inches or so in diameter, not fully closed. "It's a shackle," he said. "They slip the hand through, then hammer it to fit."

The bones of the wrist it had enclosed must have been carried away though a few of the smaller ones remaining might have been from fingers.

"A slave?" Even as he asked it, Dawlish realised that the question was superfluous.

"He must have escaped from a column somewhere near Nanguruwe," Dalton's voice was weary with resignation. "Like those poor wretches who reached the mission."

Dawlish felt again the pity and anger that had surged through him on the *Lady Emmeline*. His awareness of the strength of evil was back, the joy of the previous hours set at nought. He turned to Dalton.

"We'll bury them," he said. "I trust you can say a few words."

Whoever the fugitive had been, he – or she – deserved that much.

And then they must hurry on, for the sun was well past its zenith.

*

They reached the Nanguruwe mission outpost in late afternoon, a handful of huts and a tiny makeshift chapel set among cultivated patches. The women who had been toiling there were already trudging home, babies slung on their backs. The main village lay a mile further east, Dalton said. It was better to wait until the morning to go there. They should meet Mr. Buckwell first.

106

There was no smile of welcome from the sinewy, sun-darkened, tough-looking missionary. Dawlish wondered if he ever smiled. Cromwell's Ironsides must have looked like this.

"You're doing no good by bringing these people here." Buckwell spoke directly to Dalton as if nobody else had been present. He had already ignored Dawlish's outstretched hand.

"Let's step over here." Dalton took Buckwell's arm and drew him away from the group, clearly unwilling to have a confrontation in earshot of the marines. Dawlish followed.

"Captain Dawlish has been sent to –".

Buckwell cut off. "Captain Whatever-his-name-is can go back to wherever he came from. He'll no doubt be leaving immediately anyway. He'll be leaving us to the Lord's protection after we've heard some empty words of solicitude."

"You're a British subject, Mr. Buckwell." Dawlish kept his voice measured despite his rising anger. "You're resident – you're toiling selflessly, and I admire you for it – in an area where the Sultan of Mtwara has no control, an area outside any national sovereignty, and Her Majesty's government is –"

"Her Majesty's government is somewhat late in its concern," Buckwell spoke with cold venom. "Where was it when Achmed Ibn Hamed – you've heard of him, I trust – took possession of this place, when my work of years was undone? Where was Her Majesty's government when Mr. Lutz, Doktor Lutz he called himself, came here with his so-called treaty and…"?

"Lutz?" Dawlish interrupted.

"L-U-T-Z," Buckwell said. "That's how he spelled his name on the document he induced Chief Kikuwa to sign."

Dawlish let it go. Better to probe later, when Buckwell's ire had cooled. He glanced towards Dalton. *Help me.*

"We can't refuse hospitality, Brother Buckwell." Dalton's tone was soothing, conciliatory. "These gentlemen have come in good faith. They've brought welcome supplies and they've succoured Sister Joyce in her hour of travail. Captain Dawlish has arranged for her to be brought to Zanzibar. He has proved himself a friend already."

Buckwell made as if to speak, then paused, and reached for Dawlish's hand.

"You're welcome, Sir, you and your men." He seemed embarrassed now by his earlier outburst. "The only accommodation I can offer is in the chapel."

He must be stretched to the limits of his endurance, Dawlish thought. He must know the danger. Nothing but blind determination is keeping him here.

"The chapel will be more than welcome," Dawlish said. "I'd be honoured if you'll share our rations with us."

It was time to tell Ross to post sentries. Nanguruwe must be regarded as an enemy's camp.

*

Buckwell's testimony, told around a flickering fire, indicated that the crowded holds of the *Lady Emmeline* had been perhaps not the worst of the crimes inflicted on the victims of Achmed Ibn Hamed's ventures. The afternoon's finding of the scattered bones and rusty chain did not surprise Buckwell. Hundreds more could be found between here and Mtwara, he said, thousands between here and the lands further west that had previously been free of raids.

"But they leave you in peace?" Dawlish asked

"They tolerate me," Buckwell sounded weary. "For now, at least. But only the bravest of my converts dare come near me anymore. It was warning enough when two were taken away for sale at Mtwara. I can't blame the remainder. Nor will Jesus."

"I understand that Achmed may even now be leading a raid," Dawlish said. In expectation of the *Lady Emmeline's* return, though he did not say it.

"He passed through towards the west two months ago," Buckwell said. "He'll be back in another six or eight weeks."

Dawlish heard a small voice within him urging a way ahead. When Achmed returns we must be here in force to meet him. As Topcliffe

108

wants. Some little action, but decisive. Memorably so. And enough to remind the Germans not to meddle. Germans who come with treaties.

"This man Lutz you mentioned, Mr. Buckwell. You spoke of a chief signing a treaty. Have you seen it?"

"Briefly. Not the whole thing. Only the signature and the red wax seal – it looked like a bird, an eagle or vulture perhaps. Chief Kikuwa was especially taken by that."

"What does it say?"

A shrug. "Who knows? Nothing good, I've no doubt."

"You met this Lutz yourself?"

"No. I believe that he's some sort of explorer, Danish or German. He travels with a dozen porters and as many armed men, I gather. But he has signed these so-called treaties, trading concessions, I understand, with several places north of here."

Where the writs of the Sultans of Zanzibar and Mtwara peter out, Dawlish thought. Ripe for the picking.

"Does Achmed know of these treaties?"

"I've heard that he laughed when he learned of them," Buckwell said. "I doubt if he's concerned about the type of trade Lutz has in mind. The usual type of cheap trash that Europeans dump in Africa."

"Can I see Chief Kikuwa?"

"Tomorrow," Buckwell said.

Just then a marine, Rigby, appeared at the edge of the firelit circle. He waited there, reluctant to come closer. Dawlish rose and went to him.

"Mr. Ross's compliments, Sir," Rigby kept his voice down. "He asked if you could come. Mr. Wainwright also."

Dawlish gestured to Wainwright to follow. The marine led them through a moonlit vegetable patch. At its far side Lieutenant Ross was facing two turbaned men in white robes, bandoliers across their chests, rifles – Chassepots – in hand. Two marines stood behind Ross with fixed bayonets but there was no air of threat or aggression, only of an impasse caused by absence of a common language. Dawlish was impressed that Ross had called for Wainwright to translate, not either of the missionaries. He had recognised that they must be kept neutral.

"Translate for me," Dawlish said to Wainwright. "And add all the embellishments I can't think of."

He stepped forward, bowed gravely, hand on heart. The two Arabs did likewise.

Then the formalities. The exchange of meaningless courtesies, the pleasure in hearing of each other's health, of that of their fathers – God be praised. The careful, endlessly circuitous, enquiries. For each word of Dawlish's, Wainwright's translation – in Arabic, for Dawlish recognised individual words, and not in Swahili – seemed to require a dozen. Voices never raised. Assurances that the British visitors were here only to honour their countryman Mr. Buckwell – Her Majesty herself would value one hair on his head above a dozen rubies – and to pay their respects to Chief Kikuwa. Regrets that there would be no opportunity to meet the revered Achmed Ibn Hamed.

They parted – with yet more fulsome courtesies – each side with the measure of the other.

"Barbarians," Dawlish said when they had disappeared back into the night.

Evil incarnate.


Chapter 10


Nanguruwe, next morning, deepened Dawlish's perception of evil.

It would have been easy for a strong, heathy man to break from the wattle and thorn-hedged slave pens, but those who would occupy them – the surviving women and the few children, no less than the men – would be to too broken in body and spirit ever to imagine doing so. Each large enough to contain two hundred or more people, the pens were empty at present, their foulness undiminished by absence of captives. The handful of Arabs lounging by them – all, like those met the previous evening, armed with modern Chassepot rifles – watched sullenly as Dawlish's small column marched past. They made no attempt to impede its progress as it headed towards the large jumble of huts that constituted the village. It was clean and orderly and what surprised Dawlish was the air of easy contentment he sensed about him. There was nothing of the oppression of spirit – he could think of no better words – that had been apparent at Horne's mission. The Africans working in the fields seemed under no duress, nor did the women cooking outside huts or carrying produce to some unseen market, nor the men, few of them young, nor the naked children, show any degree of fear. By local standards this was a prosperous, contented community and Achmed Ibn Hamed's power lay lightly on it.

And then Dawlish realised – the recognition was chilling – that it was because of the slaver, not despite him, that this place was prosperous, was contented. It was a willing participant in the trade of humans, a purveyor of food and comfort to the predatory columns, a supplier of young men as porters and perhaps also as armed auxiliaries, its location on the route of misery between the coast and the deep interior an asset to be exploited. The villagers here, and in similar places to the west, might once have been the prey of slavers themselves. Now they too were persecutors.

Dawlish had refused Dalton's and Buckwell's offers to accompany him to Chief Kikuwa's compound. It must be known that they, as missionaries, could rely on British protection – and that had been conveyed unambiguously the previous evening – but it was essential that they not be seen as agents of government. Wainwright would serve as interpreter and he possessed a worldly pragmatism that the missionaries lacked.

A small and curious crowd of Africans had hastened from the huts and fields and was following the column by the time it reached the chief's compound. It was enclosed by a low stockade, scarcely higher than a fence, and within could be seen a single large hut at the centre and twelve or so smaller ones around the perimeter. Somebody must have run ahead because, by the time the entrance was reached, three men in cotton wrappers were waiting there. Some two dozen women and children crowded behind, chattering and pointing. There was no sign of weapons – the only armed men seen in the village this morning were Arabs.

Ross might have had only five marines with him, but he had ensured a degree of smartness that could not but impress. Uniforms dusty from the previous day's march had been brushed clean, buckles and boots polished, webbing washed and freshly pipeclayed. The rifles' furniture had been oiled and fixed bayonets gleamed in the sun. Dawlish himself was as well turned out – a marine had seen to his uniform – and he regretted only that there was no flag to carry as a standard. Notice was being served that, however much others might aspire to control this territory, however that control might be settled in the future, Her Majesty's arm was long enough to reach here.

The column halted and Wainwright, as agreed, went forward.

It was impossible to gauge how the exchange proceeded after the initial courtesies. The oldest of the men in wrappers – shrunken, withered and white-grizzled – was alone talking, the others nodding vigorously at intervals. The initial impression was of suspicion, with much pointing at Dawlish, who was standing in silence with a deliberately impassive face. Slowly, Wainwright's explanations and answers seemed to gain ground and at last there were bursts of laughter in which he joined. Dawlish was tall enough to see over the heads of the crowd and beyond he saw a large rotund man in a garish robe emerging from one of the smaller huts. Two men were hurrying with him and a third came running towards the back of the crowd, pushed through and spoke to the oldest of the men in wrappers.

Wainwright's negotiation continued, almost jovial now on both sides. The old man was smiling, looking approvingly towards Dawlish, and then he was coming forward, his hand outstretched.

"Karibu," he said.

*Welcome* – it was a good start, but close to the limits of Dawlish's Swahili. "Nafurahi kukuona," he said. *I am glad to meet you*. And there his command of the language failed. He was answered by an incomprehensible flood that Wainwright translated.

"Chief Kikuwa is happy to welcome us." He dropped his voice. "Be careful what you say. Two of these fellows tell me they've been to the coast. They may have picked up some English."

The crowd was opening to allow a pathway. Dawlish turned to Ross and nodded. No words needed. *Follow me. Don't relax your guard. Be vigilant.* Then he strode forward.

112

The central hut was clearly a meeting place rather than a residence, for there was no door, and the sides were largely open, and its thatched roof was high. On a small platform at the far end a robed figure was seated on a huge Rococo armchair, all tarnished gilt and frayed and faded scarlet velvet. It might have seemed at home in the decayed palace of some impoverished European princeling. The grossly fat man on it, who was peering at Dawlish though thick-lensed spectacles, was the same who had scurried here from a hut only minutes before. What had seemed a robe were swathings of brightly coloured cotton. A flat beadwork collar, larger than a dinner plate, encircled his neck.

Now another long exchange of empty courtesies. Kikuwa was apparently forbidden by tradition to speak directly to outsiders but as his spokesman relayed Wainwright's words in a whisper, the eyes behind the thick lenses never left Dawlish. If the unexpected arrivals concerned him – and they must – Kikuwa gave no outward sign of it. Fifteen minutes passed and still the exchanges had nothing of substance, only ritual compliments and circumlocutions in which Wainwright seemed as skilled as the withered old man who spoke for the chief.

Dawlish was losing patience and at last he could contain himself no longer. "Does he pay tribute to the Sultan of Mtwara?"

"It'll take time," Wainwright said. "I can't ask directly."

When the answer did at last come it was announced by the chief's first display of animation, by his audible, and angry, contemptuous words. Wainwright did not wait for the spokesman to relay them.

"He's paramount here himself, he says. The sultan counts for nothing. He's got more powerful friends now, stronger supporters than any sultan."

"Achmed Ibn Hamed?"

"Him, yes. And now the mzungu too, the European, who will bring riches. And the mzungu's master is more powerful, more rich, more generous than any sultan."

"Who's the mzungu?" But Dawlish already knew the answer.

"Lutz."

"And who's Lutz's master. Ask! Press him!"

More exchanges, but now a smile of smug contentment had settled on Kikuwa's features. He beckoned to a young man, who dropped to his knees before him. He whispered an instruction and the youth left. He was back minutes later and had in his hand a gilt frame no larger than a book. He mounted the dais and stood by the chief, holding a coloured lithograph aloft. There, frowning slightly from behind the glass, was the aged Kaiser Wilhelm, generously whiskered, bald-pated, tunic tightly buttoned, medals overlapping in a single line across his left chest, victor over Denmark, Austria-Hungary and France, first emperor of a united Germany.

Dawlish hoped that his surprise did not show. "Tell the chief that His Majesty Wilhelm is also honoured in Britain. That his son is married to our queen's daughter." He paused. "And tell him that I wonder how the good old emperor, generous and powerful as he may be, has come to extend his protection here."

Kikuwa responded directly to Wainwright's long, rambling translation of Dawlish's question and his tone sounded proudly triumphant. As his words were translated, Kikuwa beckoned again to the young man and sent him off once more.

"Lutz has been here before. Twice in the last two years," Wainwright said. "He brought what sounds like a treaty, and gifts, and the promise of more, and the chief signed."

"I want to see it," Dawlish said. There was a formality about these contacts that he did not like. He had thought of this Lutz as a trader, an opportunist, an adventurer, perhaps a dealer in ivory. But this garishly coloured portrait, as bizarrely out of place in this thatched hut as the Rococo chair, hinted at something much more ambitious. And official. The embodiment of Topcliffe's concerns.

When it finally came – it was extracted from a long tin tube in which it had been kept rolled – Kikuwa seemed even prouder of the treaty than he been of the portrait.

The sheet of thick, heavy paper was as large as a newspaper. Dawlish asked for it to be brought closer and saw symbolic eagles flanking an ornate title at the top. The heavy Gothic lettering was just decipherable as *Die Bremen und Oldenburg Ostafrikanische Handelsgesellschaft*. Below it the text was grouped in three vertical columns, the first in German, again in Gothic script, the second in Arabic, the third in English. Kikuwa's X was scrawled at the bottom and, next to it, what was clearly the signature of Doktor Eitel-Heinrich Lutz – identified in small letters below it as authorised-representative of the Bremen and Oldenburg East African Trading Company. Blotches of red wax, linked by a black, white and gold ribbon, and each bearing the seal-impression of an eagle, confirmed the date of signature, the nineteenth day of April, 1883.

Dawlish scanned as quickly as he could, his eyes dancing over the dozen numbered articles, picking up individual phrases – *sole right of trading, minerals exploration, exclusion of third parties, concession of authority, mandated licence* – that might mean anything or nothing. Yet at this first glance there seemed to be nowhere any allusion to the government of Germany, no reference to Kaiser Wilhelm, no endorsement by some imperial ministry, nothing but mention of a regional trading company. The English seemed awkward, convoluted, but so too did legal language in Britain also. It would need a competent lawyer to determine what this document was worth and, even then, the German and Arabic texts might bear little relation to the English wording.

Kikuwa was gesturing to his man to take it back. Dawlish had seen the document for all of ninety seconds but he realised that it was not the text that mattered, only that an untold number of such documents might already have been signed across the region. Lutz had been busy, had got here first, had prepared the ground. Britain might not want this territory, but she wanted nobody else to have it either. Topcliffe had spoken of Bremen and Hamburg merchants, of ironmasters, dye-masters and textile interests, all hungry for markets. And here was evidence that they were already here, had a foothold, had a presence, however nominal and tenuous, that could grow into something much more formal. A private entity this trade association might be, but it could only be here if it had powerful, if clandestine, backing.

Sheltered by the Sultan of Mtwara's tenuous sovereignty along the coast, the hinterland was set to become the domain of a trading empire. Britain had established herself in India by similar methods. The young German Empire was learning fast.

115

"Has Lutz been back since?" Dawlish said.

He hadn't, not personally, it appeared, but Kikuwa was pleased that a small caravan promised by Lutz had arrived from Bagamoyo with gifts three weeks before. Four men were despatched to bring samples. They returned with cheap tin trays adorned with images of Alpine villages, with hand mirrors, scissors, alarm clocks and cast-iron cooking pots of several sizes. The cheapest of trade goods, largesse for the chief to distribute at will to his villagers.

Had other chiefs received the same? No direct answer but it appeared that some of no account, worthless leaders of insignificant villages in Kikuwa's estimation, might also have benefitted.

Low-quality items that would have found few buyers at a sixpenny-stall on an English marketplace were purchasing a network of goodwill. And were posing no threat to the trade in slaves or ivory. Not for now.

Another twenty minutes, but nothing more of real substance before leaving. Dawlish had Wainwright emphasise, as he had done to the Arabs the night before, that Buckwell's person was sacrosanct, as was that of his converts and adherents. He had little confidence in Kikuwa's bland assurances. It was time to leave, to brush off the chief's request for gifts – which descended into shameless wheedling – and to exchange the last meaningless courtesies.

"An Arab column, a very small one, is due from the west. It may even get here tonight. It sent word ahead," Wainwright said as they headed back to Buckwell's residence. "That old chap, the vizier or chancellor or whatever he might be, told me as we left."

"With slaves?"

"Not many. But a lot of ivory. They'll need food and a few days' rest. Kikuwa will be doing well out of it. One of Achmed's lieutenants is with it and he'll pay well."

They passed the slave pens again. Empty for now.

*

It was midday and there was nothing more to be done here.

116

Dawlish had no desire to confront the approaching slavers, nor any slavers for that matter, not until he had more men available. A forced march should get his party back to Sali before darkness and a quick passage across the lake by canoe would have them at Horne's mission in late evening. His apprehension had grown, his concern at the breadth of this man Lutz's ambition.

They ate with Buckwell before they left. He had had one of his few chickens killed that morning. It was barely enough to flavour the stew made with it but the missionary was savouring each mouthful, as if a pleasure he could but seldom afford. Dawlish was touched. He had a small tin of boiled sweets in his pack and he was glad that he could press them on Buckwell before leaving. He would probably taste none of them himself, would divide them among his shrunken congregation.

Dawlish drew him aside before he left.

"I'd try to convince you to leave if I thought I could, Mr. Buckwell."

"It's where I'm needed."

"Believe me that I admire you for being here. But your presence is a provocation, you know that. Not just a danger for yourself, but for your converts also. I've seen Kikuwa. He can't be trusted."

"You've come all this way to tell me that, captain? You think that I don't see that?"

"It's not just your life, Mr. Buckwell."

"Do you really want to help? Then when you get back to whoever sent you, then you can tell them that my presence here reminds Britain of its duty. Tell them that Britain has abandoned this land to the heathen and to worse, that the vengeance of heaven will someday fall upon our nation if it does not come to stand between the benighted multitudes here and their oppressors."

The words were pouring in a flood now, the pent-up anger of hundreds of solitary nights spent brooding on that same incarnate evil that Dawlish himself had sensed.

"You are appalled by Kikuwa, captain? Let me tell you that he is the least of sinners in this land, fallen away from the light though he may be. The corruption that has enveloped him, has enveloped this whole village."

117

"I can't protect you here," Dawlish said. "If you return to Mr. Horne's mission then there'll be a degree of security. I'll see to that. But here... Here I can do nothing for you, not yet. Or for the innocents who've placed their trust in you."

"You'll never understand, captain, though I pray to God that you will." Buckwell reached out his hand. "Goodbye, sir."

He turned away and walked back to his hut. He did not look over his shoulder.

\*

The march in the afternoon's heat was hard, but they reached the head of the Chidya lake before sundown, were gliding across its clear moonlit surface as darkness fell, were back at Horne's mission by eight o'clock.

And, all the way, the sense of evil, and of his weakness in the face of it, lay even heavier on Dawlish than it had before.

## Chapter 11

Dawlish was clear now in his mind what must be done and to effect it he needed to return to his two ships. He must assume that Mrs. Joyce would have survived the journey down the river to the *Ibis* and that the gunvessel would carry her to Zanzibar. Allowing for passage time, it could be up to a week before *Ibis* could be back in the Rovuma delta. There would be time enough for he himself to reach her there if he were to set off downriver in three days' time. Until he could get back, Maddox and his *Ibis* bluejackets, and Ross with his *Leonidas* marines, must remain here. He had already instructed Ross to pick defensive positions, small entrenchments – rifle pits – that would guard the landward approaches to the mission.

Horne had been emphatic before in his demands for protection but now, when the realities involved were dawning on him, he did not like them.

"Our work here is a labour of peace," he said when Dawlish showed him Ross's sketched plan. "We wish no shedding of blood."

"Should I take my men away with me then? If you so wish then…"

"No, captain, no. It shouldn't come to that." Horne was suddenly conciliatory. "I've no doubt that your men would act only in extremis, only if there were as an incursion like we had before. And even then, that any violence would only be a last resort."

But he was less accommodating when Dawlish suggested bringing back Miller and Buckwell from their outposts.

"They are as confident as myself in the Lord's protection."

Dawlish felt his own temper rising and he turned and left Horne before he lost it. He spent the afternoon inspecting the defences that Ross had laid out on the edges of the village, with one look-out post situated on the ridge above the lake. The matter of who should command in his own absence was easily settled – Ross's commission, predated that of Maddox by two months. He avoided Horne in the evening, unwilling to risk a confrontation. He made his rounds – sentries had been posted – and slept early.

Ross woke him in the early hours.

"There's somebody here from Nanguruwe. He's babbling about Buckwell. We can't understand him, but it seems bad."

"Fetch Dalton."

Dawlish pulled on his boots and followed Ross outside. In the glow of an oil lamp he saw a half-naked African crouched on the stoop, a marine behind him. The man's upper body was streaked with red, as if he had been dragged through thorns. His face was bruised and swollen but it was from terror rather than from pain that his eyes were bulging. He was shaking uncontrollably.

"Throw a blanket over him and give him some water."

Dalton appeared, rubbing sleep from his eyes. He started when he saw the man.

"Isaac!" Horror in his voice. "Oh, what have they done to you, Isaac?" He turned to Dawlish. "He's one of Buckwell's. A catechist."

The man dropped, grasped Dalton around the knees and burst out weeping. Dalton cradled him to himself and began to speak softly in what must be the local dialect. The sobbing stilled. Horne appeared, tried to push forward. Dawlish gestured for him to stand back, be silent. Better to leave it to Dalton.

119

Isaac was talking now, his words coming in a rush, then interrupted by new weeping, then briefly calm again, and all the time Dalton was gently pressing his questions. At last he turned to Dawlish.

"Buckwell may be dead," he said. "Slavers arrived at Nanguruwe just before sundown. A small column, some of Achmed's people, ivory as well as slaves. One of their porters had to be taught a lesson. They tied him to a tree and started to flog him."

"And Buckwell intervened?" It seemed inevitable.

"He tried to take the whip from one of them," Dalton said. "Madness, I know, but Buckwell's afraid of nothing." He paused, reluctant to say the words. "So they tied him to another tree and..."

"Is he dead?"

Isaac must have understood some English for he lifted his head and said. "No, sir. Thank God, sir." He lapsed again into his own language, his words a flood. Then more sobbing.

"Buckwell was still alive when Isaac managed to get away. But only just," Dalton translated. "Two of the other converts tried to help. One was shot, the other killed with a sword. The porter was flogged to death. Isaac watched, was afraid to go closer. He's ashamed he couldn't do anything but come here for help."

It had taken him seven or eight hours of panting exhaustion to get here along the moonlit tracks, his body lacerated by scrub as he rushed, his feet bleeding. He had nothing to be ashamed of.

Silence now. The full implications setting in, shock, dread and, most of all, bewilderment.

Dawlish felt a surge of anger as every eye turned to him.

Buckwell had known what he was doing. Create a martyr. Force intervention. No half-measures, no warnings of inviolability of hairs of heads, only full-fledged confrontation that would end the slavers' dominance. His own life a low cost to pay.

And my own hand forced before I can bring my full power to bear. No choice.

"Mr. Ross," Dawlish said. "The same party as yesterday. Light, arms, ammunition and water only. Ready to march in fifteen minutes."

*

The canoes grounded at the head of the lake as the sky was brightening. Miller, badly frightened, greeted them and seemed relieved that Horne had consented to him returning to the main mission. Maddox and the remaining bluejackets would be the only protection there until Dawlish returned.

The pace was fast, faster and more punishing than two days before, hardest most of all for Dalton. Older than the others, he had not hesitated to act as guide. He had refused the offer of a revolver but he carried a small pack of medical supplies.

Dawlish felt something bordering on hatred for Buckwell welling inside himself. He had chosen martyrdom not just for himself but perhaps for dozens of others.

*And the first victims may be my men and myself.*

Faced with such loss, such an outrage, no British government – and most especially Gladstone's – could resist demands for annexation. Dawlish sensed the same anger among the marines, a resentment that would never be voiced, that would not mar their discipline or deadliness when the trial would come, but bitter acceptance nonetheless that they too had no choice.

He had thought of negotiation – an entry as open when he had come before to Nanguruwe, but now under a white flag of truce. A meeting with whoever commanded this column of slavers. His handful of men standing around him with fixed bayonets. The slaver's mercenaries – Isaac had thought that there must be at least two dozen of them – standing in a circle around them. A demand for Buckwell's release. If he still lived, then that release must be immediate. And if there was a refusal? Outnumbered, the marines' bayonets and rifles would avail little.

*They must expect us. They've heard how few we were when we came before, and they must be confident in their own numbers if they were to dare us by flogging Buckwell.*

That confidence was their weakness. With surprise as an ally then seven disciplined and battle-hardened men must be a match for marauders accustomed to easy terrorising of the defenceless.

121

No negotiation.

His decision was made. A fast raid from an unexpected direction, sowing shock and confusion to cover Buckwell's rescue, and then a fast withdrawal. The plan resolved itself in his mind and he shared it with Ross and Dalton during a five-minute water break. He sensed their fear even as he suppressed his own. They must know that the tactic was desperate and that Buckwell, if alive, would need to be carried when retreating.

No option. The words he hated.

They made a wide detour around the small village they had passed through previously and, though the heat was rising, they pressed on.

"We shouldn't follow this track any further," Dalton said. A smaller track lay across it at a tiny crossroads. It was just after ten o'clock. "We're about three miles from Nanguruwe."

"Better to loop north or loop south?" Dawlish said. The scrub was thinning both ways. He intended to approach the village from the east. Attack would be least expected from that direction.

"Around along the south," Dalton said. "There's a small village a few miles to the north. It's better to avoid it."

The pathway led over increasingly open ground, exposed red earth with small patches of thorn. The going was slower, sheltering in shadows and looking for undulations and gullies that might offer cover as they moved forward. To the north, two miles perhaps, a haze of woodsmoke rose over what must be Nanguruwe. Sighting a large herd of goats, and two boys with them, necessitated a diversion that almost brought them into a scattering of huts and vegetable patches, an outpost of the village proper. It was almost noon and the heat must have driven the residents into their huts, for no alarm was raised. Fast, crouching movement carried the party to cover in the nearest scrub.

They were tired now – and only willpower must be keeping Dalton going, for he looked close to collapse – but there could be no let up. Dawlish was conscious that this might be a fool's errand, that Buckwell might already be dead, that he was advancing towards defeat and worse. The might of *Leonidas* and *Ibis*, their crews, their guns, availed him nothing at this moment and he cursed Buckwell's arrogant fanaticism.

122

But to the men around him he let nothing show except calm confidence and he felt the solitude of command weighing heavier than it ever had aboard his own ship.

Another hour. Nanguruwe's woodsmoke was drifting above the shimmering ground to the west. The sun was at its zenith and its furnace heat would still be keeping slavers and villagers alike dozing under shade. Yet a break was essential before further action, fifteen minutes at the most, time for a few mouthfuls of water and brief rest in the shelter of a bush before rising again on aching joints and screaming muscles. Dawlish grudged each minute. With them the advantage of surprise might be ebbing. For he had determined to bank all on one unexpected, fast and violent thrust in which murderous efficiency with bayonet and rifle would multiply his numbers.

They moved forward, in an open line, covering each other as they flitted from one meagre concealment to the next, Dalton staying close to Dawlish. For an unarmed man on the edge of heat-stroke it must be a torment.

The village's edge was visible now, a straggling line of huts. Dawlish halted the advancing line to crouch in a slight dip – the last cover, for the five hundred yards of intervening ground was cleared of scrub and chequered with vegetable patches. Even in this heat a few women were bent in toil there. No sign of pacing guards, no hint that the slavers suspected danger from this direction.

A last, brief conference, Ross joining Dawlish and Dalton.

"That's the chief's compound." The missionary's finger pointed towards a thatched roof to the left, higher than those around it. "You can't see the slave pens from here," he gestured to the right, "but they're behind those huts. You see there?"

Two trees rose beyond the roofs, shading a space between the two largest pens, Dalton said. It must be to one of those trees that Buckwell had been tied.

Time now to move. Dawlish was the first to rise from the dip, revolver in hand. Twenty yards to his right Ross was following suit – he carried a Snider with a fixed bayonet like the two marines who followed at ten-yard intervals. To the left Corporal Shand was also moving forward, two more marines trailing him. Dawlish glanced back. Dalton's sunburnt face was ashen now with fear, but he was following manfully.

They moved at a fast crouch. A woman who had been stooped among the crops to the right rose, seemed transfixed by the sight, stood up, watching, but raised no alarm.

Two hundred yards covered and then a flurry of movement as several goats startled from their grazing in long grass. The boy herding them, resting somnolent in the shade of a bush, rose unsteadily, fright on his face at the sight of the advancing men, and he scurried silently away after his charges. Dawlish's heart was thumping, his whole being focussed only on reaching the huts ahead, no concern for any future but the coming minutes.

On across the parched ground, the vegetable patches more thickly grouped, small pathways of beaten earth between them making progress faster. Two women were surprised where they were hoeing, cowering from the oncomers, one with a baby tied on her back uttering a low cry but nothing louder. They dashed away to one side, shocked into silence by the sunlight glinting on the bayonets.

Closer now, another hundred yards, then two. Somebody was moving between the huts, a woman carrying something on her head, unobservant, unsuspecting as she passed from sight.

The last hundred yards.

Ross and his two marines, Shand with his pair, were heading towards the gaps between the huts to left and right. Dalton was panting loudly but was still following Dawlish closely. The trees were rising over the huts directly ahead.

And then a shriek.

Away to the right a woman had emerged from the huts, had spotted them, was crying out even as she turned and dashed back as she had come. Unseen now, her shrieks continued.

Ross and his men were plunging into the mud-walled alleyway before them and disappearing from sight. Other voices were rising now to their right, shouting, men's, an edge of panic to them. Shand's group had also gained the huts, were passing from view, but no sound of alarm from that direction. Dawlish headed now for the narrow passageway directly before him and could still hear Dalton stumbling behind.

Sudden, shockingly, the sound of a single shot to the right – a rifle, not a musket, no way of telling if it was a marine's Snider or an Arab's Chassepot. Then louder shouting and another shot. Alarm had been raised.

Pistol cocked, Dawlish moved carefully between the huts. A small open space lay ahead, further huts beyond, and the ground was strewn with millet spilled by some woman desperately seeking cover. He paused before crossing – a glance behind told him that, however terrified, Dalton was keeping pace. A look forward revealed open doorways, from any of which a threat might emerge. Sobbing sounded closely, the unmistakable sound of children's uncontrollable terror and of women's trembling voices trying to still it.

"Buckwell must be there." Dalton's voice was rasping, his chest heaving for breath and he was pointing towards the trees looming over the huts ahead.

No sound of action from the left – Shand must not have encountered opposition and must now be close to the edge of the slave-pens – but there was more firing now from the right, still single shots.

Across the open space at a run, down the next alley, a man's head – African, not Arab – emerging from a doorway and then quickly withdrawn. Dawlish raced past, was confronted by a mud wall, darted to the right – the way was clear – and paused at the corner of the next lane. It too was clear, though he could hear women's voices and a crying child on the other side of the wall. Now he could see the wattle and thorn fencing of one of the pens. As he advanced cautiously down the alley a crash came from the right, unmistakable as Ross and his marines firing in volley. Sudden silence, the shouting suddenly cut off, and then seconds later another volley, and then another. Not silence now, but something more dreadful, intermittent half-smothered cries of pain and terror. No further fire, but the promise, the threat of it, hanging in the air. Ross had secured the right flank for now.

"All clear here, sir!" Shand's head was protruding beyond a hut to the left and he was calling softly.

Dawlish gestured – *Go forward, occupy the pen.*

Followed by his two marines, Shand flitted across towards the fencing, could find no immediate entrance, ran along it, found a weak spot in the wattle and battered a gap. Yells of fear from within – there must be slaves lodged there.

"We can see him, sir! It's Mr. Buckwell – he's there!" Shand shouted as he reached the far end of the pen. It was shaded by the two trees in the space between it and the other pen. "It's clear, Sir! We have you covered!"

More shooting from the right – individual shots, irregular, then a volley – as Dawlish pounded from the alley and towards the trees, Dalton close behind. The trunks were thick – four feet or more in diameter – but there was no sign of Buckwell. Then a flash of white just beyond, a robed figure behind the nearer tree. A shot from the left – Shand had risen above the fence and was firing from the shoulder.

"Watch out. sir!" he yelled "There's a bugger with Mr. Buckwell! He's got a sword! I missed him!"

"Keep him there!"

Shand fired twice again, his rounds knocking bark from the trunk as Dawlish raced forward, enough to keep the Arab cowering in shelter. The distance was yards only, yet crossing them took aeons.

Left around the tree, or right?

The choice instinctive – right, leaving his pistol hand free. The urge was strong to throw himself against the trunk, to work his way slowly around it but reason told him that surprise was on his side. Shand fired again, and then another shot, one of the marines joining him, and splinters flew off the leftward tree.

Boots sliding on the dry earth, Dawlish skidded around the trunk. He was remotely conscious of something kicking weakly above him but it was the white-clad figure crouched on the ground and turning towards him that had his full attention. He fired instinctively, saw blood erupt on the man's upper body, heard him cry out. The Arab was twisting in agony, screaming as he tried to reach out a curved sword in submission, hilt first. A moan from the right and above caused Dawlish to glance up – bare feet and calves, striped with blood, barely twitching. The Arab on

126

the ground was babbling now – it might have been a plea for mercy – but loathing was boiling in Dawlish and his heart was unmoved. He cocked the pistol again, aimed towards the wretch's face, saw terror in his eyes, heard the last despairing plea, then fired.

"Oh, dear God!" A voice behind him – Dalton, appalled by the bloody heap on the ground, by the scarlet spattering Dawlish's uniform, then more horrified still when he saw what was hanging above.

Buckwell had been stripped naked and hoisted by a rope passed over a branch above and knotted on his wrists. Savage weals, many bleeding, had crisscrossed his body, arms and legs. Blood had dripped down into a congealing puddle on the earth below. Flies buzzed around him and his face was bruised, his eyes barely visible through black swelling. Yet he was alive – just alive perhaps – for he was moaning softly. Dawlish felt all his resentment against this man pass from him.

"Poor fellow! Poor fellow!" Dalton was weeping, bewildered, incapable of action.

Shand had burst through the fence with one of his men. "It's clear this side, sir."

"Get him down," Dawlish said. "Gently." He turned to Dalton. "Help me hold him. Don't let him fall."

They held his knees as Shand gave the marine with him a leg up on his closed hands. Buckwell cried out as the knots burrowed deeper into his wrists as the rope that suspended him was sawn through with a bayonet. He screamed more terribly as he came free and as they laid him unhandily on the ground.

The shooting and the tumult to the right had died. Ross had either subdued or driven away all opposition. Shock had won the day – for now.

Dalton was kneeling by Buckwell, had lifted his head and put a water bottle to his lips. "He's alive, he's alive," he mumbled through his tears. "Thanks be to Jesus that we could save him".

Buckwell had escaped the extremity of martyrdom he had sought. He still lived.

And now, broken and lacerated, he would be a burden.

## Chapter 12

Buckwell would need a litter, something like a hammock that could be hung from a pole. There would be no shortage of men to carry it since thirty or forty terrified wretches were chained to posts beneath open-sided palm-thatch shelters in the nearer pen. If they were strong enough to have survived the journey from the Congo basin, laden with ivory, then the wounded missionary might be no great burden.

"Don't move him until I come back," Dawlish told Dalton. He turned to Shand. "Get back in the pen – watch for any attack from over there, from the chief's compound. I'm going to see Mr. Ross. I'll be back directly."

He hurried along the side of the other pen, towards where the sounds had come of Ross's brief battle. There were slaves chained in this enclosure also, cowed, bewildered, frightened. A silence reigned over the village, one of dread rather than of peace, one hinting of terrified people not daring to venture from the shelter of their huts' mud walls. A little further on he encountered the first body – an Arab in a soiled white jibbah lying on his side, a Chassepot still in his hand, flies already buzzing around the great wound in his neck that only a bayonet thrust could have inflicted. Dawlish recognised him as one of the men he had engaged in such circuitous enquiries and with such meaningless courtesies on the night before last. He rounded a corner, cautiously, pistol at the ready – he had fed in fresh rounds. An open space beyond between a scattering of huts. More bodies here – one an Arab but three others that were unmistakable from their features as Somalis, mercenaries, bandoliers crossing their chests, rifles, curved swords in scabbards, all cast down like rag dolls by one of the marines' volleys.

"Captain Dawlish, sir!" Ross was emerging from an alleyway ahead. "It's secure for now. The scoundrels have fled."

Dawlish followed him to where the two other marines were keeping watch over the open ground at the village edge. They passed solitary bodies – Arabs and Somalis – in the passages between the huts. All were still. Bayonets had completed whatever the marines' volleys gunshots might have left unfinished. Another seven bodies littered the open ground, smashed down as they ran from the village.

"We caught them napping, sir," Ross said. "They ran. They're gone for now, but they'll be back. Let me show you what we found."

He led Dawlish to a substantial hut with a wide doorway. Stacked inside, like firewood, were elephant tusks, four, maybe five dozen at the least. A fortune already, a king's ransom by the time they would reach European markets. For Achmed Ibn Hamed, recovering it would justify any expenditure of mercenary lives.

"How many got away? Dawlish said.

"Fifteen, twenty maybe. Hard to say. But most of them armed."

Once the initial shock had faded they must surely come back. An hour, two at the most? Essential to be gone by then for they would have numbers enough to outflank, to attack from different directions.

"Keep watch," Dawlish said. "If anybody leaves their hut then drive them back inside. I want it quiet here."

He returned to Dalton and Buckwell. A few Africans had approached timidly, Christian converts apparently, terrified and devastated by what had happened to the missionary. Dalton had sent two of them to Buckwell's house for clothing and for anything that could be fashioned into a hammock. With his meagre medical provisions, he had begun to clean the weals and open wounds, the half-conscious Buckwell gasping with pain as the antiseptic stung. A call to Corporal Shand, at the far end of the pen, confirmed that all was quiet on that side also. Dawlish beckoned for him to come back, to bring his two marines with him also. The slaves chained in the open shelter shrank back as they passed. A man with a gun, any man, was an enemy.

"Find tools, hammers, chisels, whatever's to hand," Dawlish told Shand. "Anything that can break a chain. Then free a half-dozen of the strongest looking and bring them here."

The converts returned – clean clothing for Buckwell, a patched cotton bedsheet, two substantial blankets. They had found a rope too, and an axe, for they had understood the need for a litter. Dalton set them to freeing a substantial pole from the pen's fencing, thick enough to support a man's weight.

129

"Raise him up," Dalton said to Dawlish. "I must clean his back."

Buckwell failed to suppress a groan as he was propped into a sitting position. His lacerated skin was streaked with red clay and it had entered the open weals. The wounds were already contaminated. Dalton cleaned them as best he could and wrapped strips of torn sheet around Buckwell's torso – blood was seeping through even before he finished. With Dawlish's help he managed to get a shirt on Buckwell – an agony – and they wrapped his lower body with the remnants of the sheet. As they worked they could hear sounds of hammering – an anvil and blacksmith's tools had been found in a nearby hut. The captives needed for labour were the only ones who could be liberated. The remainder must remain in their chains until the slavers returned and Dawlish could only hope that vengeance would not be wreaked on them.

The litter was taking shape, a ten-foot pole, springy, a hammock formed of blankets and held together with rope suspended from it. Dalton was still busy with the wounded man, cleaning his face now, dosing him with laudanum.

Shand had freed the six captives he needed – all emaciated, whip-scarred, terrified, confused by any instruction but the simplest gestures, their language, from somewhere far to the west, incomprehensible to any here. They had been set now to dragging wattles from the pen fencing, to carrying them to the hut where the ivory was stored, to piling it on the tusks. Dawlish did not know if they would burn, but he was determined that when the slavers returned they would find them damaged beyond commercial value.

"Pick up all the rifles you can find," He told Shand. "Ammunition too. Wedge it between the tusks. And find where these scoundrels have their quarters. We'll burn them too when we leave."

Dalton approached, asked Dawlish to speak privately.

"Buckwell's bad." His voice was hushed, weary. "There's nothing broken, but he's lost so much blood and the wounds…" His voice trailed off.

"Gangrene? It's too early to be certain."

"It'll come. Almost certainly. And if not that, then lockjaw. I've seen it happen again and again, faster than you can imagine. Even if he survives as far as the river he'll die anyway. He needs attention that we can't give him. Not since our Dr. Phillips died." Dalton dropped his head, covered his face with his hands, embarrassed by his tears. "It's hard, Captain Dawlish. It's always been hard. But this... Buckwell's been the best of us, a rock, a hero. It's as if God has deserted us." He sobbed, a soul in despair.

And Dawlish heard a small, unworthy voice within himself, pragmatic, worldly, shameful.

Buckwell will have the martyrdom he craves and I will have failed to prevent it. The forced march, Ross's battle, the rescue. For nothing. No forgiveness for failure, not from Topcliffe, still less from Gladstone. My career in ruins even if I survive this nightmare.

Yet even as his mind spurned the squalid selfishness of the thought, he remembered the doctor at the German mission. Tadley – competent himself, no easy judge – had been impressed by him. Horne might regard him as a Roman charlatan but there was nobody else to turn to.

It was more than twenty miles by water between Horne's mission and the German abbey downstream, but the river curved over that distance and the chords linking the extremities must be considerably shorter. The relative locations were forming a diagram in Dawlish's brain. This village of Nanguruwe must be all but equidistant from Horne and from the Germans. There must be a path – and indeed one that the slavers would be unlikely to follow, for they would most likely guess that the rescue party would head back directly towards Sali, at the head of the Chidya lake. It must be possible to reach the Germans by nightfall, for it was still scarcely an hour past noon.

Buckwell's only hope.

It was good that he had lapsed into a drugged slumber. He might die of indignation were he to know that he was to be carried to sanctuary with the Whore of Babylon.

*

Chief Kikuwa approached them before they left, trembling, blinking through his round spectacles, clad in a cloth wrapper he must have been sleeping in and lacking the dignity of his beaded collar. Only the old man who had been his spokesman previously was with him, clutching the tin tube that held Lutz's treaty. They were at once pathetic, and yet dignified, and that they had come while the rest of the villagers were still cowering in their huts spoke of courage.

"He knows we're leaving," Dalton translated. "He's begging you to know that he had nothing to do with Buckwell's treatment. None of his people either. He'd have stopped it if he could, but he can't stand against the Arabs."

"Tell him that we can stand against them and we will," Dawlish said. "We're leaving now, but we'll be back." *In force*, he added mentally. "He can tell the slavers when they return that I'll shoot two of them for any of Kikuwa's people whom they kill. And three for any one of those slaves." He gestured towards the pens. It was galling to have to leave them in chains.

Kikuwa was holding up the tin tube.

"He asking if this too can protect him," Dalton said. "Whether Lutz can bring soldiers."

The parchment inside the tin was little better than an amulet.

"Just tell the chief that I'll be coming back." Dawlish said.

They left the village with the seven large huts which had accommodated slavers burning behind them. Exploding rifle ammunition was crackling in the blazing ivory store. The party was dangerously large now. It took two of the liberated salves to carry the litter and their fellows must relieve them in turns if a fast pace was to be maintained. They were endlessly biddable, all will and hope beaten from them since they had been snatched from their homes, bewilderment and fear and despair manifest in their cringing acquiescence. Four of Buckwell's converts had begged to come also, could not be refused, for they knew what would befall them when the slavers returned. Swinging in his hammock, Buckwell was tossing and moaning in his half-coma but it was Dalton now who worried Dawlish most. Will power had carried him this far, but now his untrained, unexercised, middle-aged body was close to its limit. He too should have had a litter but there was nothing for it but for two of the converts to half-carry him between them, his arms around their shoulders.

Nineteen men in total. Only seven armed.

The numbers haunted Dawlish as they headed up the path that led directly towards Horne's settlement. He was fearful that they might encounter somebody from the small village ahead – it was essential to turn away towards the German mission before reaching it. The parched bush was increasingly thick now, the track narrower and the afternoon sun at its most fierce. The pace was fast, the marines acting as rear-guard and relentless in prodding already exhausted stragglers onwards. Smoke still stained the sky behind them, but thinner now, as the fires burned out in Nanguruwe. The slavers driven from it must be regrouping outside, must be returning soon, must be learning of this pathetic column's flight and deciding whether to hunt it down. Everything would depend on the resolution of the most senior of the surviving slavers, whether he would risk confrontation with an enemy that had proved itself murderously effective despite its paucity of numbers.

No startled goatherds, no detection, and at last the small crossways. Here they must turn left, along an even narrower track. One of the African converts led the way. He had confessed shamefacedly, as if to some secret vice, that curiosity had once led him on this pathway to the German mission. Fearful of Buckwell's anger, he had not tarried there and had never mentioned it until now. There were no villages on the way, he said, but there had been several streams.

The watercourses were almost dry at this season, but steep-sided, demanding endless care to get Buckwell's litter across. It was dropped once, drawing agonised cries from him. He was feverish now, raving weakly as he drifted in and out of consciousness. Dalton was in a little better state, his feet trailing between the converts struggling to support him.

It was hard to get moving again after the first halt. It had been in a dry streambed, precious minutes snatched in the shade, freed slaves and converts alike thirstily scooping up muddy water from the few remaining pools and enviously watching the marines drink from their bottles the few mouthfuls that Dawlish allowed them.

There was no indication of pursuit, yet even so the hours that followed were an agony, exhausted men, sun-tormented, gasping, sweat-soaked, muscles screaming, each locked in his own stupefied misery. Yet somehow they continued placing one foot before the other, and again, and again, deaf to the mockery of the shrill afternoon insect chorus.

For Dawlish there was anger as well as fear that an Arab force might still be on the column's heels. The anger was stronger now, no longer directed towards the pathetic bundle of suffering in the litter. It was rather the same loathing he had felt on the *Lady Emmeline,* a hatred of the vast evil that had enchained the captives he had been forced to leave behind in the pens at Nanguruwe. One thought alone sustained him, awareness that he had the makings of a naval brigade on his two ships. He had been granted discretion and he knew how he must use it. Achmed Ibn Hamed and his locusts must suffer some fraction of what they themselves inflicted.

But only if he himself survived.

\*

Darkness fell as they stumbled along the last mile that brought them to the ridge above the abbey. There was barely enough moonlight to make out the neat rectangles of buildings and cultivation below. The sound of chanting carried through the still air – the monks were at Vespers. Dawlish left Ross and the marines at the crest to cover the track they had followed, then pushed down the slope with the rest of the party, led by Buckwell's litter and the converts dragging Dalton. They halted at what Dawlish knew to be the hospital – nobody there – and he hurried on alone towards the dim light illuminating the church.

The voices never faltered as he strode between the cowled figures on either side of the tiny nave. As he was about to call out, one head was raised and recognition was instant. Abbot Albrecht threw back his hood and raised his hand. The chanting died.

"I take it that this is not a social visit, captain?"

Dawlish explained as quickly and as simply as he could.

Albrecht turned to his monks, spoke rapidly in German, his tone authoritative, singling out individuals for specific instructions. The church emptied. Dawlish had a strong impression of a man welcoming crisis, radiating joy in challenge and decision and action. Together they hurried towards the hospital – torches were bobbing there as brothers reached it.

"I've heard of Mr. Buckwell," Albrecht said. "A good man. Brave, but foolhardy too. So often the two go together. I hope that with God's help Brother Ruprecht can save him."

"Your doctor has experience of wounds?" Dawlish said.

"As much, and probably more, than you or me, captain. He served as a surgeon major in the Bavarian Army. He saw wounds enough for a lifetime at Wörth and Sedan."

Preparations were already in hand when Buckwell was carried into the now-candlelit hospital. Ruprecht – long, intense looking, closely cropped iron-grey hair – was waiting in a crisp white overall, probably freshly donned. He introduced himself curtly to Dawlish, bowing slightly, then supervised Buckwell's lifting on to an examination table. Two shelves on the wall behind were lined with bottles and jars. Another monk, also in an overall, was laying out a set of surgeon's implements in pre-determined order on a white cloth.

Lying naked on the table, unconscious but for the odd moan, the makeshift dressings stripped carefully away, Buckwell's body showed itself all but flayed. The slaver's whip had spared nothing and Dawlish suddenly found himself praying inwardly that this man should not live, that his sufferings must not be prolonged. Ruprecht's face showed no emotion as he examined each cut closely, silent except when directing his helper to move the body slightly to reveal yet another weal. When at last he turned away from the table and spoke, in German, Dawlish saw anger as well as compassion in his eyes even if his features remained impassive.

"Ruprecht says that our brother has suffered the wounds of Christ," the abbot translated. "It is an honour to be asked to help him. But it will take a long time. Days, weeks. But now Ruprecht wants us to leave. He has a long task ahead tonight."

135

Dalton had already been laid on a pallet in another room, a net surrounding him. His clothes had been removed, a cotton robe replacing them and he was sleeping soundly. It was clear that he needed only rest.

It was dark when Dawlish emerged with the abbot. He felt his words inadequate when he thanked him.

Albrecht held up his hand. "No need for thanks, captain. I'm confident that our friends upstream would have done as much for us were the situation reversed, no matter what our slight doctrinal differences."

"You doctor indicated that Mr. Buckwell can't be moved, not immediately," Dawlish said. "You know that keeping him will endanger you?"

"Slavers have been here before. They were grateful when we gave treatment. One was as badly hurt as our friend is now and yet we saved him. If they come searching here I won't lie if I tell them that Mr. Buckwell is one of our brothers who is ill. We can deal with them again if we have to, but," he hesitated, "there must be no armed men here, captain, no liberated slaves."

"That's understandable." Dawlish felt a pang of embarrassment. A captain – a commodore of a small flotilla in fact – and yet no vessel at his immediate disposal to transport his people. "Did you see any of my craft pass downriver two days ago?"

"Your steam boat with a smaller craft in tow astern." Albrecht said. "We exchanged greetings – your surgeon hailed us. He said that the case was urgent and that he could not land."

So Tadley and his charges had reached the moored launch and had passed downriver with it. He must have reached the *Ibis* by now and she might even now be carrying Mrs. Joyce to Zanzibar.

"It pains me to trespass further on your goodwill," Dawlish said. "You have two boats. Other than Mr. Buckwell, could they carry my people upriver?"

"It can be done," Albrecht said.

Ross and his marines would be needed at Horne's mission. The abbot might be willing to risk the slaver's hostility but his stern counterpart upriver would not.

"I understand that you'll need to post your guards tonight, that your professional obligation demands no less," Albrecht said. "But mount them on the ridge above, beyond our boundaries. I know you won't take offence if I ask you to pass the night up there with them yourself. I speak as an old soldier."

There was a dignity about the request – and a sense too of a shared brotherhood of arms – that made it impossible to refuse.

They shook hands and Dawlish started back towards the ridge through the soft, warm darkness.

## Chapter 13

The night spent bivouacked on the ridge was uncomfortable. Dawlish, his body aching and crying for rest, had himself woken at each change of sentries to reassure himself that there was no indication of pursuit. Nothing, only the loud chatter of a tropical night, insects and frogs in perpetual chorus. At first light, the sound of the monk's chanting of Lauds washed up from their settlement, the beginning of another day lived to a rhythm established a millennium and a half before.

One of the monastery's two boats was large enough to carry Dawlish's whole party, less Buckwell and Dalton, back to Horne's mission. They would be close packed but number enough to drag the craft easily over shallows. Four monks would come too and they seemed to accept patiently that getting the boat back downriver afterwards would be slow and laborious. None spoke English, but Dawlish, fluent in French, was pleased that two of them, Alsatians, also spoke it.

Buckwell, his wounds cleaned, salved and lightly dressed, had survived the night in drugged sleep, still unaware of where he was. The surgeon, Ruprecht, was cautiously optimistic. It would take two to three weeks, maybe more, before Buckwell could be moved.

Dalton was on his feet again, even if aching and painfully slow. He drew Dawlish aside as preparations for loading were in hand.

"A favour, captain. Tell Mr. Horne that I must remain here longer." Embarrassment in his voice, guilt that he was stretching the truth. "Tell him that I'm not fit yet to travel and that Buckwell needs me to be near and …"

Dawlish tried to make light of it. "You're not deserting to Rome, are you, Mr. Dalton?"

"It's Brother Wolfgang, and his dictionary. It complements mine." Dalton's despair of the previous day was gone, enthusiasm sparking again. "And he's far advanced with his translation of Matthew. If we can share our knowledge…"

"I fear that the sun may have befuddled you, Mr. Dalton." Dawlish was smiling. "You seem to me to be a patient who needs a long period of recuperation before he can travel again. And you'll be a comfort to Mr. Buckwell amid this host of idolaters if the abbot will allow it."

"Brother Wolfgang has raised it with him. He's agreeable."

It was time to board, to pack the bewildered liberated slaves between the thwarts, Buckwell's four converts too, although they were reluctant to leave him. The marines followed, would join the monks on the oars. Dawlish stood in the sternsheets as the boat pushed out into the sluggish current and drew away.

And, as before, he saluted the one figure, Abbot Albrecht, remaining on the jetty. The salute was returned.

There was more than one form of brotherhood.

*

It took a day and a half to reach Horne's mission – the night spent on a sandbar was made miserable by mosquitoes – but there were hands enough to drag the boat through the shallows. That the settlement had not been attacked was a relief but Horne's welcome was cold. Dawlish suspected that he would have sent the four monks away again without a meal had he himself not made a point of demanding one for them. They received only surly thanks and seemed happy to start back in mid-afternoon, content to spend another night on the river.

"You're sure that there was no alternative to leaving our brothers Buckwell and Dalton there?"

The fact that they were lodged at the abbey seemed to concern Horne more than the near-martyrdom of one and the exhaustion of the other. For the rescue itself his gratitude were meagre. Had Britain provided adequate protection earlier, there would have been no occasion for it.

Dawlish felt sick of the man, was glad to be leaving – for now. He told him no more of his plans than that Ross and the marines would remain behind, Maddox and bluejackets also. Horne had accepted that the outpost at Sali, at the far end of the lake, must be abandoned for now – indeed already was, for the broken-spirited Mr. Miller had no intention of returning there – and that the handful of converts there must be withdrawn to this main settlement on the river. This must now be defended like an armed camp. Further well-sited rifle pits had been dug and now – against Horne's protests – Dawlish ordered the arid bush beyond the vegetable patches to be torched. Flames roared, crackled, burned themselves out, and then another area, and another and another were similarly devastated. Any force approaching the settlement would have to cross three hundred yards of open blackened earth that would offer no cover against the lash of well-aimed rifle fire. There was only one weakness. The armed party had come upriver with fifty rounds of ammunition per man and almost a quarter of the total had been expended at Nanguruwe. However resolute, defence against a determined assault could not be sustained. Everything would depend on whether the enraged slavers and ivory traders had the necessary determination. Dawlish doubted it, but he knew that the thought would nag him until he returned.

*

He slept well, would indeed have been grateful to sleep as long again, but he wished to be gone soon after dawn. He was leaving the whalers behind – as last means of escape if disaster did befall the settlement – and was heading downstream in a dug-out canoe, similar to those used on the lake. Wainwright was coming with him – reluctantly, since he was convinced that he had found a new species of beetle, and was confident of finding more – and so too were two of Horne's villagers as paddlers.

139

A few last words with Ross and Maddox, handshakes, confidence expressed on one side, assurances on the other. But Horne did not appear.

Dawlish looked back at the first bend. No lone figure on the shore, no petty tyrant of his own New Jerusalem, stood watching as the canoe stroked out of sight.

*

Dawlish resisted the urge to land at the German mission. It was reached soon after midday for the canoe's shallow draught had allowed it to speed across shallows that had demanded dragging of the whalers against the current. It was better not to land, but he hailed briefly, was assured by Dalton calling from the jetty that Buckwell was responding to treatment. There had been no sign of vengeful slavers.

The night's rest, again on a midstream sandbank, was disturbed by trumpeting of unseen hippopotami. There was no need to tarry in the morning. The water level was falling, exposing ever more shoals, and Dawlish was not surprised that the *Ibis's* returning steam launch had not pressed on this far upriver. He was resigned to another comfortless night when, rounding a bend in mid-afternoon, the trim craft could be seen anchored in a broad, calm stretch, sun glinting off her brass funnel. The canoe had been spotted and a seaman was waving in greeting.

Dawlish and Wainwright were helped on board. The mission's two paddlers were thanked and given a bag of hard tack and a can of bully beef each before they began their passage home against the stream.

"Mrs. Joyce?" Darwish asked. "The lady from the mission, did she…" He hesitated to enunciate his fear of what might have befallen her.

"She looked at death's door when she reached us, sir," the launch's coxswain said. "But the lady's a tough one and she made little of it – patient as an angel she was, sir – and we got her an' her husband safe to the old *Ibis*. Rigged a sling, they did, to get her on board and she was heading for Zanzibar – full steam ahead, sir, maximum revolutions –

before she'd even been taken below. Then we turned back here to wait for you, sir."

"Has *Ibis* returned?" Dawlish expected that she would have sent a boat to check on the launch if she had arrived.

"Nothing from her yet, sir." The coxswain paused, reluctant to ask a superior directly why he had arrived virtually alone. "All's well up the river, sir? The lads doing fine?"

"A spot of bother," Dawlish said, "but the lads did well. Very well."

No need to say more. All that mattered immediately was to drop down to the delta to await *Ibis's* return from Zanzibar.

They reached the first mangrove by nightfall, anchored in a quiet stretch, and Dawlish enjoyed the comfort of uninterrupted sleep on a cockpit bench. Soon after dawn the launch was chugging seawards over calm mist-wreathed water. The haze burned away with the climbing sun, the river widened, separate channels branching off to either side. And at last the long blue streak of the sea's horizon broken by the profile of a white hull brilliant in the sunshine.

*Ibis* had returned.

*

Jarvis of the *Ibis* listened hungrily to what Dawlish told him of the raid on Nanguruwe. His countenance did little to disguise his disappointment – resentment rather – that the responsibility for it had not been his. But the first concern now was to get reinforcements up to the mission, another ten bluejackets, more ammunition and a half-dozen Hales rockets with a launching frame. The nine-pound projectiles would dominate the scorched area beyond Ross's defences. The whaler carrying them was away three hours before sunset.

Mrs. Joyce had been delivered safely to Zanzibar and Kirk, a medical doctor before he had become an explorer or a consul, had personally arranged for the attention she needed. The prognosis was good. Dawlish felt shame that the news relieved him – the Horne mission needed no other martyr for whom he might be held accountable.

"Any news from Mtwara?"

The *Leonidas* was still maintaining her vigil outside but, faithful to Dawlish's command that the two ships not be seen together, Jarvis had made no contact with her.

"No word. Dr. Kirk said he'd lost his eyes and ears in Mtwara when you took Mr. Wainwright away with you. But we might get something, now that Wainwright's on board. We've got prisoners, but we couldn't talk to them, no interpreter. I trust that Wainwright can."

A dhow had been sighted close inshore, just south of Mtwara, as *Ibis* had ploughed back to this rendezvous.

"I thought we deserved some sport," Jarvis said, "so I dropped a cutter. The blackguards ran but we took her anyway. One of her crew was shot – no damn loss – and the other five were glad enough to yield, and nineteen slaves with them."

"And the dhow?" Dawlish asked.

"We burned it." Said with relish.

A stupid decision, Dawlish thought. There might yet have been a use for it. There was nothing subtle about Jarvis's mind.

The interrogation was as long and as frustrating as Dawlish remembered from when he had hunted slavers off this coast himself. The prisoners were brought on deck individually and Wainwright's patient questioning determined that three of them were no more than deckhands – two of mixed Arab-African parentage and the third himself a slave of long-standing, who seemed quite contented with his lot. But even from them valuable information was forthcoming.

"They had to sneak out from Mtwara under cover of darkness," Wainwright said. "All traders are forbidden to leave the port."

"Forbidden? By whom?"

"They don't know. I've phrased the question a dozen different ways but I think that they genuinely don't know."

"Fear of *Leonidas*? They must know she's there."

"They're clear that whoever is responsible is in Mtwara itself. 'Sultan's men' is all they can say."

"Where were they headed?"

"Southwards, down the coast. There's always a market for slaves there, wherever Portuguese control is weakest. Maybe even where it isn't."

The two other prisoners were by their looks pure Arabs, and more truculently uncooperative. They proved – after endless evasions – to be related to the man who had been shot.

"They say he was their uncle and that he was the captain. It might or might not be true." It had taken Wainwright's questioning the best part of a half-hour to tease out that much. "It doesn't really matter. What does is that they had a financial interest in the business."

"So why did they have to leave Mtwara surreptitiously?"

"It's going to take time, captain. Bear with me."

"If we leave it to my bosun he'll have them talking in five minutes." Jarvis had grown increasingly frustrated by the slow progress.

"Leave it to your bosun and they'll tell us whatever they think we want to hear, true or not," Wainwright said.

Unwilling to disagree openly with his deputy, Darwish said, "Carry on, Mr. Wainwright."

First one prisoner, then the other, then the first again, a quarter-hour's questioning each the time, repeated through to midnight on the open deck in the light of a hurricane lamp. And some inkling of truth was emerging.

"There's to be no private trading until further notice. A decree by the sultan," Wainwright said at last. "All slaves arriving in Mtwara to be kept there for now. Two hundred or so in the pens there at present but it appears that a lot more are expected."

"Achmed Ibn Hamed?"

"I asked about him. His column is due back soon. Whenever he returns from a raid he brings at least four hundred slaves, often a lot more."

"So, they're waiting for a full cargo," Dawlish said.

It was obvious now. Nothing was yet known in Mtwara of the capture of the *Lady Emmeline* and she was expected to return soon from the Gulf to pack her holds with another cargo of misery. Not just

Achmed's captives but any stock-in-trade of smaller slavers also – whether or not they liked it.

And like it neither of the prisoners did. The relentless routine was slowly wearing them down as they were questioned separately. Their resentment was manifest as Wainwright probed further. Small-scale dealers, they were alarmed by threat of compulsory purchase of their stock at Mtwara, at a lower price than they could expect in Portuguese territory. And it made it worse that the buyer in Mtwara was a *Nasara*.

"Christian." Dawlish recognised the word. *Nasara – Nazarene*. The name Europeans were often known by along this coast.

"Not much of a Christian, I suspect," Wainwright said, "but a name we've heard before. Imker."

"Imker." Jarvis spoke the single word with infinite loathing.

"The prisoners hate him," Wainwright said. "He's hand in glove with the sultan, they say, and with Achmed too, and between them they've cornered the market in ivory as well as slaves."

The prisoner now under questioning, the older of the two, had caught the sense of the English conversation and was nodding vigorously. He interrupted with a stream of Swahili.

"Imker is like Satan himself," Wainwright translated. "He hanged three traders from his yardarm when they were caught trying to slip slaves out of Mtwara. This gentleman thanks God that his dhow was captured by us, and not by Imker's ship."

"What ship?"

"A steamer that arrived a month ago. Imker is so proud of her that he lives on board. A ship with guns. Very big guns."

And already Dawlish knew what he must mean.

A craft glimpsed once only inside the Mtwara anchorage, something very like a Crimea-era gunboat on which he had served in China as a boy.

The sultan of the sovereign state of Mtwara had acquired a one-ship navy but it was difficult to imagine it as a threat. With her few antiquated smoothbores, like so many decrepit gunboats like her that could be picked up cheaply from the petty navies of half-bankrupt Latin American republics, she could be no match for *Leonidas* or *Ibis*.

144

The challenge was on land, not on water. The solution lay in Zanzibar. And that was where *Ibis* was now heading.

## Chapter 14

The slowly swishing punkah above made no impact on the hot, dead afternoon air. Through the wire-meshed windows Dawlish could see *Ibis* lying among the dhows and steamers in the Zanzibar anchorage. He was alone with Kirk in the consul's office, alone as befitted two men who were planning an acquisition. No distrust between them, but no full disclosure of knowledge or of motives either, two men cautiously feeling their way towards an understanding to their mutual benefit. A word lay recognised but unspoken between them.

Annexation.

Zanzibar's acquisition of Mtwara would be relished by Topcliffe and approved, after the event, by those whom he served. But there would be no official endorsement ahead of the action.

And no support in the event of failure.

For there was only one solution if the series of treaties being signed between petty chiefs and a German trading consortium was not to grow into something more official. Britain did not want Mtwara's hinterland, nor the East African coast, but Germany was not to have it either. Better to act now to counter the threat Lutz represented while it still had no official backing. Zanzibari control of the lands north of the Rovuma would allow exclusion of Lutz and all like him. Kirk's unofficial role as adviser to Sultan Barghash could see to that.

Dawlish echoed Kirk's words from their earlier meeting.

"You said that if it were your decision alone then Zanzibar should take Mtwara." He sensed that Kirk was already guessing what was to come. "That if Sultan Barghash had it, he could control it with Mathews' force."

Kirk nodded. The former naval lieutenant turned Zanzibari brigadier-general was due back from Malindi within the week. Word had already come back of success there – merciless success that left no doubt

145

about the cost of disloyalty. A sheikh who had challenged the sovereignty of Sultan Barghash had died with several dozen of his followers.

"Mathew's people could control Mtwara," Kirk said. "But they could never take it. Not that damn great fort. I don't doubt that Britain would welcome Barghash having the place if it was presented as a *fait accompli* but Gladstone's not going to send troops to take it." He paused, looked directly into Dawlish's eyes. "And Britain hasn't sent a cruiser and gunvessel to take it either, has it, captain?"

"Certainly not." Dawlish smiled. "I didn't come here for that. I'm here only to succour a British missionary. Nothing more."

"Most certainly nothing more, captain."

"And that missionary and his followers are at this moment under threat from a barbarous slaver," Dawlish said. "Only a small and inadequately armed detachment from my crews stands between those people and annihilation. A detachment that I'll be reinforcing as soon as possible, a process that may well bring us into conflict with that slaver, a process that will be most certainly to his detriment. And if we do then…"

"There will be a vacuum." Kirk's lips were also forming into a smile. "A vacuum all the way from the outskirts of Mtwara to Lake Nyasa. One that Mathews and his people could most effectively fill."

"And cut off all trade from the interior to Mtwara."

That sultanate's prosperity depended on a constant flow of slaves and ivory from that interior. It lacked the soil and climatic conditions for the clove plantations on which Zanzibar's wealth was built.

"There would be no hurry thereafter," Kirk said. "Mtwara would be Zanzibar's in time. At least three of the sultan's half-brothers there would be glad to see him off. They'd be happy to swear allegiance to Zanzibar if they were to be recognised as vassals. That fellow Ibrahim, with whom Wainwright has had some rather shady dealings, isn't the least of them. One could well imagine certain gentlemen in London welcoming such an outcome."

As long as that outcome came to pass without embarrassment. For the price of embarrassment would be repudiation, the ignominious end of two careers.

"So, I understand that you will be returning to Mr. Horne's mission, captain," Kirk's voice was devoid of any hint of conspiracy. "With a powerful force, I take it?"

Dawlish's voice was no less neutral. "A powerful force, Dr. Kirk. A small naval brigade. Probably a short punitive action to follow and a quick withdrawal afterwards. I've no doubt that Mr. Horne will be thankful for the temporary security it will guarantee him."

"Most pragmatic, Captain Dawlish."

"And I suspect that Mr. Horne would be even more grateful if Brigadier General Mathews were to follow in our tracks," Dawlish said. "He might establish a permanent presence, perhaps a settlement for liberated slaves at Nanguruwe. A fallow field awaiting Mr. Horne's cultivation. Muslim or not, Sultan Barghash would no doubt be recommended fervently to the Almighty in Mr. Horne's prayers."

"God moves in mysterious ways," Kirk said. "I'll see His Highness, the sultan, this evening. I think we understand each other, captain."

"Assuredly, Dr. Kirk," Dawlish said. "Most assuredly we do".

*

It was essential to act quickly, to get a sufficiently powerful force ashore before news of the engagement at Nanguruwe could reach Achmed's column approaching from the west. *Ibis* could contribute fewer than a dozen, for her crew had already been depleted by the detachment of the men now at Horne's mission. The greater number must be supplied by *Leonidas*, drawn from the marines and bluejackets who had been so relentlessly exercised with bayonet and cutlass on the voyage out. The cruiser was still maintaining her tedious patrol outside Mtwara and a cutter was despatched, under sail, to locate her, carrying orders for rendezvous twenty miles east of the Rovuma Delta.

While Jarvis saw to supplies – including fresh fruit and vegetables for *Leonidas* as well as *Ibis* – Dawlish concentrated on planning. Tradition would yield his force the courtesy title of naval brigade, but the name belied the numbers, just over a hundred and twenty men. It was discipline, training and confidence that would make it powerful, that and

147

the seven-pounder field gun the cruiser carried and a six-barrelled Gatling from her main-top. Both were mounted on wheeled carriages that could be broken down into their components for transport across obstacles.

*Leonidas* would be left with two-thirds of her crew and still remain the most powerful warship off this coast. The challenge would lie onshore, not in the brigade's fighting ability, but in supply of food and ammunition and medicines and the myriad of other items needed to keep it in the field. All must be transported up a shallow river, with its shoals and sandbars, even before the first loads could be carried ashore at Horne's mission. Food would be a concern from the start — the settlement was already surviving at bare subsistence level — and husbanding of supplies must be draconian.

Hanging over all was the threat of fever, the malaria that Dawlish knew so well, its burning sweats alternating with icy cold. Worse still was the menace of the blackwater fever that almost invariably ended in death. Quinine discipline must be relentless, no matter how much the men might dislike it, and Dawlish was glad that he would have Tadley back with him again.

*Leonidas's* surgeon had brought Mrs. Joyce safely to Zanzibar. A resident English doctor who ministered to the foreign community, and who was more acquainted with feminine complaints, had made an essential intervention. He was hopeful that her imminent confinement would pass off safely and in the meantime she was lodged with an elderly missionary couple who had been caring for years for worn-out and abandoned slaves. Dawlish visited her, was touched by her stoicism and by the gratitude of herself and of her husband. All but destitute, they had been advanced limited funds by Kirk. Mr. Joyce had accepted temporary employment in his old trade of blacksmithing at a small ship-repair yard, similar to others in half the world's harbours, all seemingly run by tireless and enterprising Scotsmen. Joyce — and even his wife, despite her still precarious state — seemed different people here, less cowed, more confident than they had been at the mission. If Mrs. Joyce survived the coming weeks it would be easy to imagine them settled here, proselytising zeal forgotten, prospering in congenial labour.

A shepherd who deserted his flock, Horne might judge him, but Joyce was showing no sign of remorse.

*

That there was a telegraphic link to London was a temptation to seek endorsement. Dawlish recognised however that any reply from Topcliffe, even if it might have Downing Street's approval, would be couched in terms so ambiguous as to allow later repudiation. Should what he now planned fail then he would have misinterpreted the approval, would have exceeded his authority. Only success, should it come, would be viewed with favour and any credit would be eagerly claimed by others far distant from the steaming Rovuma.

It was unfortunate that Mathews had not arrived before *Ibis* departed, that there had been no opportunity to discuss practicalities of supply and transport or to review the quality of his mercenaries.

"They're reliable enough as long as they're paid," Kirk said, "but it's the opportunity for loot that drives them most."

For all that he was ostensibly here only as British consul, Kirk's role was to influence – the more diplomatic word for control, Dawlish recognised – Sultan Barghash's most important affairs. That the ruler had so quickly approved the proposal to cut off Mtwara from the interior had come as no surprise. Not only were Mathews and five-hundred of his men to be committed, but a small British cargo steamer, a tramp shallow-draughted enough to penetrate the Rovuma Delta, had been chartered to transport them there. A tiny steam tug, in use until now by a chandler as a harbour transport, had been purchased to tow boats up the river and to remain there to provide longer-term support. Sultan Barghash was clearly committed to recovering what a distant predecessor had allowed a half-brother to usurp and set up as an independent fief. Zanzibari and British interests coincided fully.

Though Mathews did not reach Zanzibar before *Ibis* departed there was another arrival, no less welcome. An unarmed despatch vessel, signalling herself as HMS *Vole*, steamed into the harbour with a bone in her teeth as *Ibis's* anchor was being raised. She dropped a gig and minutes

149

later Lieutenant O'Rourke was clambering up to the gunvessel's deck. His face was flushed with delight as he approached Dawlish and saluted smartly.

"Reporting for duty, sir! And the whole prize crew with me."

"The *Lady Emmeline?*"

"Secure at the Bombay dockyard, and her captain and crew in less comfortable accommodation." Satisfaction in O'Rourke's tone. "I saw to that personally. The slaves, poor devils, are at a settlement. Five more of 'em died before we reached port."

"What about the prize court?"

"From what I saw, there won't be a decision about the *Emmeline* for years – the lawyers will make a meal of it. I reasoned that I'd be better employed with you, and the lads with me, than kicking my heels there."

"So, somebody put the *Vole* at your disposal?" Dawlish could sense the young officer's enthusiasm and had already guessed what had happened.

"Better not to ask, sir. Let's just say that I ran into an old shipmate who's now commanding her. It just happened that he was to carry despatches from Bombay to Mauritius and there was space enough on board. And let's say that concern about a bearing running hot obliged him to make a detour to Zanzibar. And let's say..."

"Enough!" Dawlish held up a hand. Formalities had been massively breached and it was better that he himself could plead ignorance. But O'Rourke had done well. "You mentioned the prize crew?"

"All twenty, Sir. All glad to get back to the old *Leonidas*."

Many of them men who had been blooded in a brutal battle on an island off Korea. Invaluable.

A half-hour sufficed to get them transferred. *Vole,* headed now for Mauritius, left the anchorage just ahead of *Ibis*. As the sun faded in crimson glory over the dark mass of Africa, Zanzibar lay thirty miles astern of the gunvessel.

The birth of Dawlish's naval brigade was imminent.

*

*Ibis* ploughed south-south-eastwards under steam. A steady breeze blowing from almost dead ahead offered some relief from the morning heat. By midday the large island of Mafia lay off the starboard beam and the bows swung further to the south on a course parallel to the unseen mainland. The meeting point with *Leonidas*, twenty miles off the Rovuma Delta, should be reached by the following dawn – a cutter, carrying instructions, had been sent from Zanzibar two days before to find her. Preparations for landing continued through the day, inspection of equipment, stacking of stores along the bulwarks for fast transfer to boats, selection of crew from *Ibis* to go ashore. The gunvessel had already yielded her lieutenant, Maddox, at present upriver at Horne's mission. The only officer who could now be spared to command her twenty-strong contingent was a fresh-faced sub-lieutenant called Johnson. Dawlish sensed the *Ibis* men's resentment of O'Rourke's erstwhile prize crew. Service in *Leonidas*, and victory in a hard-fought ship-to-ship action in the Yellow Sea, was already a temptation to arrogance. Invidious comparisons were no doubt being made with *Ibis's* bombardment of an innocent East Indian village. It didn't concern Dawlish unduly. Rivalry between ships' companies was traditional and it evaporated during emergencies.

Of more concern was the sullen resentment he sensed again from Jarvis, stronger now than when he had previously been denied the chance to lead the expedition up the Rovuma. It was resentment that was not blatant enough to justify confrontation, only surly agreement and grudging compliance that fell just short of insolence. It was better to ignore it, better to allow Jarvis to immerse himself in the work in hand.

By late afternoon the wind was rising. Dark storm clouds advanced from the south-east like a rolling rampart, thick columns of rain spread intermittently across its front, lightning flashing in the murk. There was time enough to secure gear, take down yards, turn ventilators sternwards, rig lifelines and send unwanted hands below before the full force struck, but when it did it was more violent than might have been expected in this season. The wind grew stronger still, was a full gale as darkness fell and *Ibis* altered course slightly to take the full fury directly on her bow. Revolutions were reduced to hold her all but stationary against the blast.

By midnight the sea had risen further – long slopes down which the gunvessel slid into deep troughs, climbing up steep gradients ahead, topping foaming crests and commencing the slide again. And again. And again. The decks were awash, water surging with each pitch and roll and seeking entrance to the decks below. Yet, for all the movement, stokers were somehow keeping their feet in the boiler-room and feeding the grates, and the engine's beating pistons were driving the single screw as regularly as on a mirror-calm sea.

"Is this serious?" Wainwright was pale, was perhaps fighting down the urge to retch, was clearly fighting fear.

"Serious? No." Dawlish said. "It can be expected."

The spray on his face was welcome, the gale's anger exhilarating. He had survived worse in an open boat during anti-slaving duty further up the coast seven years before. "This ship and this crew will have met the like a dozen times or more."

These were conditions that *Ibis* and dozens of other sturdy gunvessels were designed to cope with as routine. The vessel was Jarvis's to command and he was doing so with skill, standing rain-lashed in oilskins on his bridge, something like joy visible on his face, the first time that Dawlish had seen it. It was a manifestation of pride that was moving, of determination to withstand the rage of nature itself, of a resolve that was no more unexpected in Jarvis than in thousands of other officers.

The best assistance Dawlish could offer was to demonstrate his confidence by going below and taking to his bunk in what had been Maddox's cabin. Water was sloshing in the passageways and even here it was ankle deep. He wedged himself to accommodate to the vessel's pitch but sleep did not come easily. He knew that this same storm would be hitting *Leonidas* off Mtwara and Edgerton, now in temporary command, and as competent a seaman as Jarvis, would be taking her further out to sea. The blockade the cruiser had maintained would be interrupted briefly but that hardly mattered. The storm itself would prevent any vessel leaving the anchorage in Mikindani Bay and any dhow unlucky enough to find herself creeping inshore along the coast would face almost certain destruction. What did matter was that the thrust up the Rovuma would be delayed – these conditions might persist for another day or more – and all the time Horne's mission would lie under threat of retribution.

In the end, sleep did come, but a slumber never deep enough to cancel awareness of the storm's continuing fury.

*

It lasted through the night and continued through most of the following day, abating only as evening drew on. The wind died in the night but as dawn broke the sea was still rough. *Ibis* had come through all but unscathed and normal watches had been maintained. Jarvis and his crew had performed admirably. With daylight it was time to alter course and to head again towards the point of rendezvous.

*Leonidas* was loitering in an empty sea when *Ibis* found her in late afternoon. The sky was still overcast, flurries of rain still drifting slowly from the south-east. Dawlish crossed to the cruiser in Jarvis's gig – he arrived soaked, as a rising wave caught him on the lowest rung of the Jacob's ladder – but the experience convinced him that it was still too hazardous to transfer men and supplies to *Ibis*. As before, the gunvessel was to bring them as far up the Rovuma Delta as possible before dropping boats for the ascent upriver. Transfer would have to wait until the following morning when the sea state was more favourable.

Edgerton had little to report. His blockade of Mtwara had not been challenged and the only incident of note was when he had sent a boat close inshore to inspect a dhow. It had proved to be carrying copal only and so had been allowed to proceed. No other shipping had entered or left the port. The instructions that Dawlish had sent from Zanzibar had been executed meticulously. Names had been selected for three companies of bluejackets – a hundred and twenty men in total – and organisation of equipment supplies had been far advanced before the storm halted these efforts.

Now to finalise command allocations. O'Rourke's return – Dawlish had brought him across with him – guaranteed competent and aggressive leadership for a company drawn entirely from *Leonidas* personnel. A second, which would include all marines remaining on both vessels, with the numbers made up by seamen from the cruiser, would come under Ross when it reached Horne's settlement. The third company supplied by *Leonidas* would be assigned to Sub-Lieutenant Leigh, whom Dawlish regarded all the more favourably since he had begun badly before Korea but who had responded well to advice since and had proved himself reliable. The fourth group, all men from *Ibis*, would be assigned to Johnson for now. Once they reached the mission they would join their shipmates there to form a company commanded by Maddox.

The night passed, effort unceasing to ready the stores for transfer. Weapons were checked, kit inspected, paperwork completed.

And time was slipping by, four days lost at the least.

Up the Rovuma, Ross and a handful of marines and bluejackets were all that stood between Horne's mission and annihilation by a vengeful slaver whose wrath knew no bounds.

However much he pushed the thought away, it still troubled Dawlish. Because of those four lost days, this entire mission might well end in disaster.

## Chapter 15

The transfer of men, stores and equipment proceeded quickly on a calm sea after dawn broke. By midmorning *Leonidas* was steaming back to her station of Mtwara, leaving her contribution to the brigade packed on the *Ibis's* deck. Six of the cruiser's pulling boats, and her steam pinnace, all laden with supplies, bobbed on tows in the gunvessel's wake as she headed directly towards the delta. A green streak was soon visible on the horizon and the sea's blue grew brown with silt.

Half-revolutions, then quarter, as the *Ibis* crept up the Rovuma's main channel, leadsman calling monotonously from the bow, mangrove thickening on either bank as she progressed, mud and sandbanks exposed by an ebbing tide, steaming heat growing as the sun neared its zenith. Another hour and the point would be reached at which the gunvessel had anchored previously and where the men could be loaded into the boats. *Ibis's* steam launch should be waiting there, ready to assist in towing. By nightfall much of what was now being referred to as the

Dawlish Brigade – not his term, but one that seemed to have emerged spontaneously from the men themselves – should be camped on a sandbank upriver, the first and easiest stage of the ascent complete.

"Deck there!" A call from a lookout on the fore-top. "Something ahead! It could be a buoy!"

Surprise on the bridge, where Dawlish was standing with Jarvis.

"Is it the launch?" Jarvis bellowed up to the look-out.

"No, Sir! Smaller! Like a buoy!"

Dawlish felt a chill of fear.

*It shouldn't be here. Nothing like that should be here!*

He turned to Jarvis. "Hold her stationary. I'm going aloft!" He reached for a telescope, moved forward along the packed deck between the waiting men stepping back to let him pass – he could sense their unease also. He mounted the bulwark, swung himself on to the shrouds and climbed.

He could spot it without the telescope – a single bright yellow dot in the middle of the two-hundred yard wide channel – but as he adjusted the lens to his eye it sharpened into what looked indeed to be a small cylindrical buoy. It must be moored, for the current had canted it over and a tiny ripple of foam surged around it. It had not been there when he had passed down this stretch so recently and it looked newly placed, for it showed no streak of rust. Behind it lay a wall of mangrove, for the channel was curving around just upstream of it, blocking view of the stretch beyond.

Down quickly to the bridge again. Jarvis was no less surprised and alarmed by what he heard.

"Better to man the one-fifty," Dawlish said. The seven-inch muzzle-loader on the foredeck was mounted on the centreline, could not fire directly ahead and the gunvessel must manoeuvre if it were to be brought to bear. But against what? Against a harmless tethered buoy?

There must be more to it than that.

Jarvis snapped orders and the gun crew moved to ready the weapon and drop the hinged bulwarks to either side of it. The men crowding the deck and equipped for landing were pushed back. *Ibis's* slowly churning screw was holding her immobile against the current.

Silence on deck and on the bridge. Dawlish felt every eye turned to him, Jarvis's most of all, felt the expectation for decision, knew that he had little – nothing – to base it on. This was the enormity of command, the burden of responsibility his alone. An aeon passed in seconds. Then the die was cast.

"Proceed upriver. Slowly."

More of the channel beyond the buoy became visible as *Ibis* crept closer to the bend. There had been a long, straight stretch beyond here, Dawlish remembered, with wide side-channels branching off it into the delta's fan.

Nearer to the buoy now. There was nothing unusual about it – the type seen mooring small craft in harbours across the world – and it had recently received a new coat of paint. Nothing unusual except that it had not been here before, had no apparent reason for being here at all.

Into the long sweeping bend to port, the buoy off the starboard bow as the gunvessel crawled forward. Now the anticipated long broad stretch was revealing itself, calm brown water, three-hundred yards wide, thick mangrove to either side, a solitary fish eagle, its black and white plumage starkly demarcated, wheeling slowly overhead.

And then, suddenly, a sharp report from somewhere ahead that sent a thousand alarmed birds streaming skywards. It was a sound that Dawlish recognised immediately, knew all too well, and it chilled him with the realisation of what must even now be reaching the apex of its long, low trajectory.

The shell fell fifty yards upstream of the buoy, throwing up a skidding plume across the surface before it sank. *Ibis* ploughed past the dispersing foam and now the full length of the stretch ahead revealed itself. There lay, a mile or so distant, a vessel still wreathed in the smoke of her gun's discharge.

"Fall back!" Dawlish called, his knuckles white as he grasped the rail ahead, fear coursing through him. "Don't turn! Drift back!"

Jarvis had already brushed past the quartermaster, was dragging back the telegraph handle to call for the engine's stilling. With a half-dozen boats trailing on tow astern, any attempt to turn could result in chaos.

The report had been unmistakable, a crack rather than a boom, the bark of a Krupp breech-loader, almost certainly a six-inch. Armed with such weapons, an Ottoman gunboat under Dawlish's command had once wreaked destruction on Russian vessels, unarmoured like *Ibis*, smashing hundred and twenty-pound explosive shells into their vitals and blasting them apart.

*Ibis* was drifting back, past the buoy that was now clearly an aiming mark. As the curve again blocked off the reach ahead from view Dawlish had a glimpse, broadside on, of a short hull, a single funnel, a long bowsprit and three raked masts, little different from the gunboat on which he had endured his blooding in China twenty-four years previously. It was the craft that he had seen moored in Mtwara's anchorage when he had surveyed it from *Leonidas's* foretop. In the aftermath of the storm that would have kept her trapped in Mtwara, while *Leonidas* was off station and meeting *Ibis* twenty miles offshore, she must have slipped out and hugged the coast to the delta and passed upriver.

The moment could not be worse. *Ibis's* deck was packed with blue-jackets and marines ready for landing. A single shell landing among them would cause carnage.

Dawlish turned to Jarvis. "I want as many men as possible in the boats! Just as they are. Rifles and ammunition only!"

The nearer bank was to port and a force landed there would be hidden from any craft coming downriver until it had rounded the bend. He looked down, saw O'Rourke's upturned face.

"Get our people along the bank, over there! Out of the boats if there's footing! Hold fire until *Ibis* opens on that ship. Then pick off all you can, anybody on the bridge first of all."

As the *Ibis* drifted with the current the boats astern were being hauled in. Under O'Rourke's and Leigh's direction, haversacks and blankets and other equipment were being dropped on deck and men were being herded aft. That the haste was well ordered was confirmed by all happening in a near-silence, broken only by brief commands and the shuffling of feet. The disembarkation was in good hands.

"Hold her steady now, Commander Jarvis." Dawlish said. The *Ibis* had drifted two hundred yards downstream from the buoy. "Be prepared to drop a kedge off the stern, then move across the current to starboard. We'll drop the bow anchor, then hold her fore and aft."

"We'll be a sitting duck and …" Jarvis stopped himself. "Very well, captain."

"And guns to bear to port. Bursting shell. Range on the bend."

Understanding dawned on Jarvis's face as he called the commands. Moored fore and aft, lying broadside across the current just downstream of the bend, there would be one opportunity, one only, to cancel the superior range and accuracy advantage of the Krupp – was there only one? – carried by that gunboat upstream. Like *Ibis's* own weapons it could not fire directly ahead. Should that gunboat come downriver, she would emerge around the bend at point-blank range for *Ibis's* antiquated muzzleloaders firing on the port broadside.

The first boats were already away and pulling towards the shore. The others were filling. The hinged bulwark sections in line with the centrally-pivoted one-fifty and the sixty-eight inch on the port broadside were thudding down and the guns themselves were being slewed over by their crews.

The kedge dropped from the stern. Jarvis telegraphed for quarter revolutions and directed the quartermaster to nudge the vessel diagonally across the current. The mooring party was ready at the bows and as the cable running aft to the kedge tightened and strummed Jarvis called for the bow anchor to be released. Now its cable also was being drawn in taut, deckhands straining at the capstan – *Ibis* carried no steam winch. The seven-inch and the six-inch crews were grouped at their stations around the weapons with rammers and sponges and loading tongs, and each gun captain had raised his arm to confirm readiness to fire.

Dawlish's gaze was fixed on the bend, chilled by the realisation that should that gunboat appear, and should either or both of *Ibis's* muzzleloaders miss, then there could be little hope. He remembered the Krupps his Turkish crew had managed five years before and knew that *Ibis's* guns could never match such fire. Once that gunboat – now that enemy vessel – could swing across the current, and bring her Krupp to bear, *Ibis* would be overwhelmed.

Minutes passed, five, ten. And still no sign of the gunboat.

Dead silence on *Ibis*, every eye locked on the buoy at the channel bend. She was firmly anchored now athwart the current, the mooring lines fore and aft rising and falling, shaking off drops, as she rocked gently. The loudest noise was of the slow surge of water around her. Well over half of the landing party had gained a strip of hard mud exposed in front of the mangrove by the falling tide. O'Rourke was positioning them in small groups behind whatever cover could be found and the boats were returning to take off the remainder from *Ibis*.

"It's Imker, isn't it?" Jarvis was affecting the same calm as Dawlish but his hand was white-knuckled as he grasped the bridge rail. "It can't be anybody else."

"If it's him then he'll be too damn clever to come down to meet us." Dawlish himself would not have done so either. "He's got the range advantage and he's got a Krupp – I've no doubt of it, I'd recognise the sound to my dying day. If he stays where he is then he can block passage indefinitely."

"But what does he want?"

"There's only one way to find out. We'll have to talk to him."

\*

Sub-Lieutenant Leigh was supervising the transfer of the last of the landing party.

"Take the gig," Dawlish told him. "Take four of your best men. Rifles, nothing else. You remember seeing a creek on the southern bank about a mile downstream?"

"Yes, sir. Narrow, wasn't it?"

It might have been forty yards wide, curving off between thick walls of mangrove, one of the myriad cross-connecting waterways that linked the delta's larger channels.

"I want you to push up it," Dawlish said. "Find where it leads. See if it connects somehow with this channel further upstream. You may need to follow several other creeks off it. Get out and drag if you have to. You'll need a compass. Keep a log – estimated distances, turns, intersections. Don't get lost. It's too easy to do so in a swamp."

"Very well, sir. And then?"

"Get back here. I'll need a sketch map." Dawlish sensed Leigh's trepidation – his fear of failure perhaps greater than of danger. "If you encounter anybody, even just fishermen in canoes, just fall back. No confrontation, you understand?"

Dawlish left Leigh to it, then dropped down himself to the whaler waiting alongside. He looked up to see Jarvis glowering down from the bridge wing, his face still flushed with anger. He knew Imker, Jarvis had said, knew him better than any man. He had argued with Dawlish to the point of insubordination that it should be he himself who should parlay with the Dutchman. He had all but spat out the name, could not disguise his loathing, and it was for that reason that Dawlish did not want the two men to meet. Better that Imker should have no idea of the *Ibis* commander's identity. Jarvis had yielded with bad grace and Dawlish had to choke down his own rising impatience with the man. Officers and crew alike should never see superiors at odds, most of all not at a moment like this.

A seaman, holding vertical a boat hook to which one of Jarvis's white bed sheets had been attached, was standing in the whaler's bows as it stroked upstream. Dawlish, in the sternsheets, could sense the rowers' fear – their backs would be exposed to any threat – and he forced a show of impassivity. His mouth was dry, heart thumping, as the yellow buoy ahead drew closer. Along the bank to port the men already landed were half-hidden in the mangrove. O'Rourke emerged briefly and waved what seemed like reassurance.

The whaler held the centre of the channel as it swung into the bend. The curve seemed endless, nothing visible ahead but the green line of mangrove on the far bank and the buoy straining on its cable. And beyond it, unseen, that deadly Krupp.

"Wave that flag!" Dawlish called.

The seaman began to sweep the boat hook back and forth, the white sheet streaming from it. It was unmistakable as a flag of truce but, from what Jarvis had told about Imker, it might well be worthless.

160

Now the curve was easing and then, just short of the buoy, the long straight reach came into view. And there lay the gunboat, as securely moored fore and aft as the *Ibis,* and too far off to determine detail. If she was to open fire, it would be now.

The fear in the whaler was palpable. An inner voice screamed to Dawlish that this was madness, that every stroke lessened the chance of safe retreat, that at this moment a shell was certainly in the Krupp's closed breech, that the gun captain was holding aim, was waiting for Imker's word.

Only silence, broken by the oars' dip, the laboured, frightened, breathing of a rower, the distant screech of an unseen monkey troop. The buoy dropped astern and the whaler nudged on against the sluggish current, a hundred yards forward, two hundred, soon a quarter mile, the gunboat ahead looming larger. Dawlish could see that a section of the starboard bulwark had been dropped – hinged like *Ibis's* – and through it he could see what must be the Krupp, its crew in position around it. No second weapon was visible. A flash of reflected sunlight from the bridge abaft it identified a figure there studying the approaching whaler through a telescope.

Imker.

Dawlish resisted the urge to stand up, to wave his hat, to give some signal other than the flapping sheet, to establish some contact with a man with whom he shared a profession. Any action, any movement, seemed preferable to sitting here immobile as the whaler crawled forward.

On up the river. A narrower channel split away from it towards the north, one of the dozens of waterways that formed the delta's fan. Closer now, close enough to recognise this gunboat for what she was, a wooden-hulled, spindly-funnelled, barque-rigged relic, dangerous only because of the single large weapon she carried. Dawlish had seen craft like her shattered by Chinese cannon fire when he was a boy – she might indeed have been some surplus Royal Navy craft sold off in the early sixties and passed from one minor navy to another in the years since. One had restored her potency by the purchase of the Krupp. Imker, once terror of the Borneo coast in a modern Dutch warship, had fallen far.

161

Three cables distant and still no response. There was no hope of covering fire – O'Rourke's landed men had been left far behind. Somewhere over to port Leigh might already be probing through the winding mangrove channels but there could be no support from his small group either. Nothing for it but to press forward.

Then, suddenly, a single shot, the sharp report of a rifle, a spurt of water fifty yards ahead of the whaler's bow.

"Hold water!" Dawlish yelled.

The shot was clearly a warning, for a good marksman could have hit the whaler. It would be suicide not to heed it. The dragging blades killed all forward motion.

"Easy all!" The strokes now slow enough to hold stationary against the flow. The seaman standing in the bows was trembling but he was still sweeping the flag in long, steady arcs.

Long minutes passed. No second shot, though two figures in the gunboat's maintop might well have rifles. And then at last figures dropping into a small boat secured against the vessel's side. As it pulled away, a white flag, as large and as makeshift as the whaler's, was being waved.

Imker was on his way.

*

Dawlish had expected a florid, moon-faced, blustering Dutchman but there was a cold remoteness instead about the slim, hawk-featured, saturnine officer in a white uniform with brass buttons and rings on his sleeves who exchanged salutes with exact formality. His English was almost devoid of accent.

"Admiral Johannes Imker of the Navy of His Highness Sultan Saif Ibn Rahman of Mtwara." Said without any awareness of the absurdity of the title, said indeed with a hint of pride.

"Captain Nicholas Dawlish, of Her Britannic Majesty's Navy." It was difficult to keep wholly dignified when trying to stand ramrod straight in a slightly rocking boat.

Dawlish was taking in the manning of Imker's craft – three Europeans and what might be two Somalis, none in uniform, tough-looking but with no great air of disciplined professionalism. Six yards separated the two boats, held as if anchored in midstream by slowly stroking oars.

"You've got business here, captain?" Imker said. "You'd better state it, and then be gone. You're intruding in territorial waters."

Dawlish ignored the question. "I suggest, sir, that we might adjourn either to your ship or to mine, if we're to talk."

"I don't see much to talk about." Something of a smirk on Imker's features. "I'm quite content to speak to you here, though I imagine you've little to say that interests me. When you're finished you'll be welcome to find the Indian Ocean a few miles downstream."

"There may be a misunderstanding." Dawlish kept his voice calm, was uncomfortable that he must haggle like this in front of this own crew. "This waterway –"

Imker cut him off. "This waterway, sir, is under the shared jurisdiction of the Sultan of Mtwara and the King of Portugal. At this moment you are directly on the median line that runs down it. And you see over there, the northern bank? That belongs to Mtwara."

Something of the same grim certainty in Imker's voice as in Horne's, something of the same unwillingness to count cost or to see the world on any terms but his own.

"And you see that southern bank – yes? – that's Mozambique, Portuguese territory. Unless you can show me written authorisation from the Portuguese governor you have no right to navigate this channel."

"I've no such authorisation and I need none. I'm here to bring succour to a Christian mission under threat. People who've put their own lives at risk to help others."

Even as he spoke Dawlish realised that no words of his would sway this man. Slave shipment by steamship was almost certainly his idea. He likes killing, Jarvis had said. It had cost him an honourable career. A pariah in his native land, he was prepared to serve anybody who would offer compensation of a sort, even if only a ludicrous single-ship navy and a preposterous rank.

"You've been up this river before, haven't you, sir?" Imker said. "On the same pretext, wasn't it? And you and your people attacked legitimate traders entitled to the protection of His Highness of Mtwara and murdered several of them and destroyed their property."

"You're talking about slavers and…" Dawlish stopped himself. He felt his temper rising – recollection of the *Lady Emmeline's* holds was suddenly powerful – but knew that it would avail him nothing. "There's no profit to either of us if you force this issue." He tried to sound conciliatory as well as determined. "You know that I've no intention of turning back and –"

"And I've no intention of letting you past, sir. Bring your vessel around that bend again and I'll blast it to matchwood." A tone of absolute determination, no hint of doubt in the cold eyes. "I can assure you that the Sultan of Mtwara will approve the action and that he'll have international legal justification for it also."

"International support? That's ludicrous, sir." Dawlish wondered if this man was mad. Jarvis would certainly have said so. There was nothing more to gained by talking to him. "I believe we understand each other well enough," Dawlish said. "I'll wish you good day and trust that I'll have safe passage as far as that buoy downstream."

"I'll give you that much."

No salute as they turned away.

The challenge still stood.

Stupid, ridiculous, insane, futile. The words churned in Dawlish's brain as the whaler dropped downstream.

And another, worse still.

Unavoidable.


Chapter 16


The Krupp barked again and its shell tore a strip of spray upstream of the buoy as Dawlish's whaler passed unharmed around the bend. Imker's message was clear.

*Come on if you dare. I'm ready for you.*

And there could be only one response to such a challenge.

Not meet it head on.

A hundred yards downstream O'Rourke emerged from the mangrove on to the strip of mud. He shouted confirmation that there was drier ground behind him.

"The tide's turning", Dawlish called. "Can you remain there when it's high?"

"We can stick it out, sir. There's ground above the tidal mark." That was easy to gauge with mangrove – the glossy leaves sprouted just above high-water level. "And we've cut across the bend. We can see that gunboat."

"Keep your people under cover. Do nothing unless that vessel comes down. You're going to remain there for the time being."

"We'll need water, sir."

"You'll get it. I'll take ten of your men back with me. Your best, strongest. They'll return to you soon with water. And more."

When Dawlish boarded *Ibis* he was met by Jarvis.

"It's him, isn't it, sir?"

"It's Imker," Dawlish said. "And he's determined not to budge."

"That's like him. If he's got an idea in his head then –"

Dawlish cut him off. "Has Leigh left?"

"A half-hour ago."

"Let's assume he's successful. We'll plan on that."

"And if he isn't, sir?"

"Then we're as well placed as we can be for the time being."

And Dawlish's brain shrank from considering what the 'time being' might entail.

*

*Ibis's* painting float was a square wooden platform with four barrels lashed beneath it, large enough for two men to stand on when working on the hull's flanks. With more planks hurriedly secured to it there was just enough room for the Gatling that had been taken down from the foretop and mounted on its wheeled carriage for land service. A whaler, hastily loaded with ammunition and a cask of fresh water, headed back upstream with O'Rourke's men. It had the painting float and Gatling on tow astern. It would take brutal labour to drag the weapon through the mangrove. When under cover however, upstream of the bend, it would menace the straight channel below Imker's moored gunboat even though the vessel herself would be out of effective range.

Leigh returned in mid-afternoon, mud-smeared like his crew, but elated.

"There's a passage." His words spilled in a torrent of delight in the achievement. "That creek we entered – it narrowed quickly and it forked after a few hundred yards. We were damn lucky, we chose the correct branch though it got narrower still and shallower. I was going to turn around when we saw that it seemed to connect with a larger channel. We had to get out and drag the gig, hard going, but there was deeper water beyond and –"

"So, you found another creek? Did it branch off the main channel?" All that Dawlish wanted to know.

"It did, sir! Nearly mile upstream of that gunboat. We got that far. We could just see her."

"She didn't see you?"

"No, sir. Sure of it. We just got back as fast as we could."

"Could we get anything larger than the gig across where you had to drag?"

A pause, then Leigh said, "Maybe a whaler. Certainly not a cutter."

That would have to suffice.

Leigh had done well. And he would have an opportunity to do better still that night. There would be a half-moon and just enough light for what Dawlish intended.

*

Jarvis was enthusiastic, perhaps too much so, for Dawlish feared that settlement of a vendetta might impair judgement in the heat of the moment. But Jarvis's *Ibis* was as well prepared for any eventuality as she could be, her guns ranged on the buoy, sledgehammers ready to knock away locking pins from shackles on the mooring cables, precious

166

anthracite ungrudgingly fed into her boiler to keep the safety valve just short of lifting, should she need to run herself. Dawlish had allowed Jarvis the authority for any such decision.

Six of the marines who had landed with O'Rourke were brought back on board, all specified by name by Dawlish. Another six were bluejackets, all from *Leonidas*, no less tried, no less trusted. With himself and Leigh, fourteen in total. Rifles, forty rounds per man and cutlasses. No bayonets – a menace in a small boat in darkness. Revolvers for Dawlish and Leigh. And most important of all, six nine-pound Hale rockets and a firing frame for them secured in the whaler's bows. Time to snatch two hours' rest, essential for the men, no less than for Dawlish himself, and for a hurried meal on being awoken.

The laden whaler stroked downstream two hours before midnight. The sky was clear, the moonlight reflecting silver on the water's surface, enough to make it easy to identify the creek entering the channel from the south. Into it then, Leigh in the bows, scanning ahead, Dawlish at the tiller, holding the craft in the centre of the quickly narrowing waterway. The silence was oppressive – no chatter of monkeys or cries of distant jackals, not even the buzz of mosquitoes, for there were few where the water was tidal, nothing but the ghastly plops that might mean some snake or crocodile slipping unseen into the muddy water.

Soon the fork that Leigh had discovered earlier. The bows nudged over into the creek to starboard. It grew narrow quickly, its banks a yard or less beyond the oar blades' tips, until at last the growth on either side met overhead and the creek became a tunnel. At last, rowing impossible, the craft could only be propelled forward by poling with the oars. Twice it grounded and was pushed free but the third time there was no option but to begin dragging. Dawlish moved to the bows, steeled himself against the fear of what might be lurking near, and heaved himself over the side. The tepid water reached his thighs but the mud underfoot was firm.

"Right lads! Let's have you out!"

Leigh joined him as the men dropped over, six to a side.

"It'll be harder than with the gig, sir. I think we got much further than this before we had to drag. It's difficult to judge in the dark."

Unburdened of its occupants, the whaler floated free and the only problem in moving it forward for the next five hundred yards was the unevenness of the creekbed underfoot. Sudden drops in depth and exposed roots brought men – Dawlish himself twice – plunging into the water and emerging spluttering. But eventually the craft herself grounded, and now the real labour began. The straining men hauled her forward, keel scraping on the hard mud, sometimes stumbling, sometimes falling, all with wet and filthy clothing plastered to them. The creek was only a trickle now, even though it was high tide, and the mangrove closed in so closely that the battle was now as much against the restraining branches to either side as against the mud and exposed roots. Muscles screaming, rasping for breath, progress, however slow, was maintained.

At last Dawlish ordered a ten-minute break, let the men half-slump over the whaler's gunwales, have water passed around to give each a mouthful. While they rested he went forward with Leigh to investigate the creek ahead. Fifty yards beyond, the trickle died, the mangrove too, revealing a bare low ridge of white sand perhaps fifty yards across. Beyond it, another wall of mangrove.

"There, sir," Leigh pointed towards it, "that gap, you see it? There's another small creek there. The channel I told you of isn't more than two cables length further on."

What followed was the worst toil of all, the sand grinding beneath the keel as the whaler must be pushed rather than dragged over it. Reaching the crest of the low ridge felt like a triumph and the descent down the slight incline beyond it was a blessing. Dawlish knew that Imker's gunboat must be all but directly to the right now, unseen a mile or more beyond the thick mangrove. No sound of alarm, no shooting, no attempt to run downstream to surprise the *Ibis*, no answering fire from O'Rourke's hidden Gatling. Yet silence was no reason for complacency. Imker, seasoned commander that he was, must have his own plan, must have his own ship in a state of readiness as high as Jarvis's.

The mangrove was all but closed at the head of the next creek and it took a quarter-hour to hack the branches to either side and to smash the whaler through. But the trickle underfoot was widening, and deepening, even though the tide was on the ebb. Another hundred yards and the whaler had shaken free of the mud, was floating, was easy now to drive forward. Water rose to knees, to thighs, then suddenly to waists. It was possible to heave men back into the boat, for them to pull others after them, to rest panting before grasping the oars and poling forward. The mangrove drew back – two distinct banks again, rather than a tunnel, and wide enough apart for the oars to be shipped and for the whaler to glide smoothly forward.

And at last the broad creek ahead that Leigh had spoken of, the creek that flowed off the Rovuma's main channel.

Upstream of Imker's gunboat.

*

"She's got steam up." Dawlish passed the night glass to Leigh.

There were no lights, no sign of movement, on the dark hull silhouetted against the moonlit waters downstream. The faintest glow above the thin funnel indicated a stoked boiler.

"She's still moored, sir. Fore and aft," Leigh was studying her. "There might just be somebody in the maintop. I thought I saw ... yes! There it is again! There's definitely somebody posted there."

And that would be the greatest danger in the minutes ahead. The whaler must be all but invisible as it lay shrouded in the shadows of the thick growth on the south bank, but a single gleam of moonlight on a wet oar blade could be enough to alert a vigilant lookout.

Last checks before getting under way. The men not rowing were facing forward at a crouch, a round in each Snider breech. The trough of the rocket frame lashed at the bow was raised slightly above the horizontal, a single missile cradled in it, ready for firing. Leigh and a marine would serve it. Dawlish, at the tiller, could sense the men's apprehension, the realisation that action was imminent, death a possibility. Several must be praying silently, some confronting the dread – he felt it himself also – that his own courage might fail at the moment of crisis. An internal voice, wheedling, coaxing, reminded him that it was still possible to hold back, that the rockets could be launched from here. On a high trajectory they might just reach Imker's vessel. One hit would create havoc, a second would be devastating… Easy afterwards for *Ibis* to come up to finish the work…

He smothered the temptation. Hitting even a large target a mile distant with a Hale rocket would be a matter of pure luck and the blazing trail of the first launching would rouse even the most inattentive of lookouts. There was only one way to employ the rockets tonight.

Point blank.

The tide's ebb was still weak, but enough to carry the whaler slowly with it. Only an occasional oar stroke, only the slightest movements of the tiller, were enough to hold it in the shadows as it drifted downstream. Two-hundred yards, three… and still no alarm on the gunboat.

Now a terrifying section where the mangrove had receded from the muddy shore, where for a full minute – an eternity – there were no shadows, where the whaler glided in the moon's full illumination, where the urge to order hard pulling was almost irresistible. Yet still luck held. Shadows of high mangrove with branches trailing in the quickening flow embraced the craft again as it slipped onwards.

The channel here was scarcely narrower than where *Ibis* was moored – some two hundred yards – and the final approach to the gunboat must be across open moonlit water. But not yet, not as the stealthy advance continued in the shadows until at last the gunboat loomed large, three hundred yards distant along the diagonal from the bank.

Time now.

"Give way together!"

The whaler surged forward as the oars bit and, as the speed built, Dawlish swung the tiller over. Into the open water now, stroking as fast as in a regatta. The range was closing, all but point blank

A sudden cry from the gunboat. An instant later a muzzle flash and the bark of a rifle from her maintop. Shouting, another shot, the thump of bare feet running on deck.

The whaler was lined up with the centre of the black flank a hundred yards ahead as Dawlish shouted, "Rocket!"

170

Leigh jerked the firing cord. Fizzing before the first sparks spat from the missile's rear, then a great whoosh of flame as it blasted up the trough. Impact with the gunboat's side was almost instantaneous. A blinding flash, an explosion deafening at such close quarters, smoke billowing, debris thrown high overhead before hailing down in a myriad of splashes.

A rower was crying out in the whaler, a high inhuman scream of agony torn from him by a splinter smashed into his back, and already he was being pulled aside for another to take his place. The marine in the bows with Leigh was laying the next rocket in the trough.

Dawlish threw the tiller over to bring the whaler curving over to starboard in a wide circle, oars beating in steady rhythm. The first rocket had been launched too close, could indeed have inflicted even worse unintended injury on the whaler's crew, and he wanted greater separation before launching again. The smoke was clearing from the gunboat's wooden side to reveal a jagged hole some three feet across. Faint red flames flickered within. Panicked shouting above, one voice louder, calmer, then the others – Imker perhaps – calling for order, then the unmistakable report of a pistol, a scream, another shot, another scream, and then the hubbub subsiding. Figures rising above the gunwales fore and aft, then the crack of rifles and rounds screaming past the whaler.

"Ready, sir!" Leigh's hand raised in confirmation.

The turn was almost a full circle now, the gunboat's foremast in line with the whaler's axis, the range longer than before.

"Rocket!"

Now again the short flaming flight, the explosion on the dark flank that was hidden instantly in rolling smoke, the shower of debris. Dawlish had his riflemen on their feet as the whaler curved into another circle, bracing themselves against the thwarts and firing at any visible movement. Amid the din the wounded rower was moaning softly – "It's a wicked splinter, sir", one of the seamen had told Dawlish. "We'll kill him if we try to take it out."

But Dawlish was worried now. Despite the second hit, the initial panic on the gunboat seemed to be subsiding, less shouting, more men at the gunwales firing back. The flames glanced briefly through the first

171

rent in the side had either died out or had been extinguished. The second rocket had done less damage, blasting a gap in the gunwale forward. Even an old wooden vessel like this could survive at least a dozen of such hits, probably many more, and Imker must know that. But the gunboat's vulnerability was human, not material, and on that Dawlish still banked. Whatever mongrel crew the renegade Dutchman had assembled, their training and discipline could only be inadequate. Their rifle fire, ineffective so far, confirmed that. If somehow Imker had quelled their initial panic, then it must be provoked again. And that would be best accomplished by attack on the far side.

Dawlish nudged the whaler out of its turn to run parallel to the gunboat's side towards her bows. His own men were now maintaining a steady fire – probably as ineffective as that of Imker's people, but well aimed enough to keep many of them cowering behind the bulwarks. As the whaler drew level with the bowsprit he pushed the tiller over to curve just under it, then straightened out to run downstream. As it emerged from the blind spot before the bows, rifle fire was renewed from the gunboat – brief jets of flame from the foretop told of at least one man keeping his nerve there.

Now the tiller was thrown over again to run downstream before arcing back for the next attack. Dawlish's feeling of vulnerability was intense now, all reason urging him to crouch low, but the eyes of the rowers were on him and he owed it to them to preserve the same outward calm with which generations of officers had exposed themselves to fire on open decks.

He glanced back towards the gunboat and through a lowered section of the starboard bulwark saw the outline of the Krupp pointing downstream. It was unmanned – inadequate as a defence against Imker's current attacker – and if a rocket could be landed there then success would be absolute. But for that he needed range – the launching frame was too securely lashed in position to allow fast raising of elevation. He must be further downstream, a cable's length or more, if the rocket was to rise high enough on its trajectory to drop on deck.

A sudden cry brought him whirling around in time to see one of the seamen pitching backwards and disappearing down between the thwarts.

Dawlish recognised him – Grove, a reliable man. A marine bent and tried to raise him, then yelled "He's gone." Shock in his voice. "Just like that. Just gone!"

The rowers were pulling furiously – looking astern, as they must, without even the solace of a weapon in their hands, they could see what menaced them. Dawlish glanced back again and saw that a shower of sparks was shooting from a strengthening red glow above the funnel.

Imker intended getting under way.

And *Ibis* lay unseen, athwart the channel, just beyond the downstream bend, with her one-fifty pounder ranged point blank on that yellow buoy. And, before that, O'Rourke's Gatling. The gunboat was being driven towards destruction like a pheasant urged on by beaters.

The whaler sped forward, a hundred yards, two hundred, then time to sweep around, for the bows to swing again towards the gunboat.

"Ready, Mr. Leigh!"

"Ready, sir!"

"Two in immediate succession! But on my word!" The order must not be given until the whaler's axis was lined up on the Krupp.

Into a sweeping curve now, the whaler arcing towards the gunboat. At that moment Dawlish saw a splash beneath her bowsprit and he realised that the anchor cable had been cut and was falling into the water. Beam on to the current as she was, Imker's craft began to drift around, foreshortening as she turned, swinging on the anchoring cable astern. No hope now of destroying the Krupp, but still a chance – a rapidly diminishing one – of hitting the hull.

Dawlish shifted the tiller ever so gently, judged that the whaler was lined up on the gunboat's vomiting funnel.

"Rockets!"

The first was still in the air as the second sped up the trough, and Dawlish saw with sickening certainty that neither would strike. Imker's vessel had already swung too far and the fiery trails shaved past where the foremast might have been an instant before, plunging uselessly into the water beyond.

"Reload! Wait for my word!"

Foam churning beneath the gunboat's stern now and she was starting to gather way – the stern mooring must have been cast free also. A bow wave was building up and she was bearing straight towards the whaler. Dawlish threw the rudder over to head for the south bank's shadows.

"Cease firing!" he shouted. "Double bank the oars!"

Speed increased slightly as men scrambled on to the thwarts next to the rowers to pull with them. The gunboat had drawn almost level, but the rifle fire from her had all but died and Imker was intent only on escaping downriver and ignoring her tormentor. She passed the whaler at fifty yards separation, screw beating, heavy smoke vomiting from the funnel and enwreathing her masts and yards. In another minute she would be in range of O'Rourke's Gatling, and that range would be closing by the second, and the hail of heavy rounds could scour the bridge and upperworks. Her Krupp, unable to bear directly ahead, was useless for now, and only speed and luck and resolution could save her when she would round the bend and meet the fury of the *Ibis's* one-fifty pounder.

A last chance now to speed her to destruction.

"Ready, Mr. Leigh! On my command! Immediate succession!"

Two rounds left, and the gunboat already two hundred yards downstream, foreshortening quickly, a difficult target, but not impossible.

Again the tiller thrown over, again a broad sweep, now to port, again the whaler's bow sweeping over to seek its quarry. Seconds more to line up on the retreating gunboat.

"Fire!"

The rockets – the last remaining – climbed into their low parabolas, fiery tails reflected in the waters beneath. Even as they flew, Dawlish realised that he had miscalculated. The first dropped in a running splash twenty yards or more to starboard of the gunboat and the second fell directly astern.

No matter, Dawlish consoled himself, Imker was running, and that was all he had set out to achieve. The Gatling would be opening in another minute.

And then – his heart almost stopped, his spirit screamed within him in protest against Fate – he saw the gunboat nudging towards the south bank before sweeping over to port. She was beam on to the current now, forging towards the northern shore. She must be heading for the mouth of the narrow channel that he had seen branching off there when he had been rowed upriver to meet Imker. It had seemed then too slender to give passage to a large vessel.

Dawlish raged inwardly against himself. He should have seen it, should have realised that an officer as experienced as Imker would never have allowed himself to be trapped without chance of escape. He would have charted the delta's channels long before now, would have determined which were passable and which not, had perhaps buoyed this one, and probably others too, so that he could weave through them with confidence.

As he was now doing. And without fear of being followed.

O'Rourke's Gatling opened, a stutter of a half-dozen shots, a protest rather than an attack, as the gunboat's silhouette merged with the north bank's black wall of mangrove. Only the receding plume of smoke that rose above it indicated that she had ever blocked this waterway.

Imker might have escaped to fight another day, but the Rovuma's main channel was open again.

Time to resume the advance up it.


Chapter 17


It was midday before *Ibis* could move the last three miles upriver to the previous point of anchoring, three miles bought with two lives. Chloroform had eased the removal of the splinter from the seaman's back but neither that, nor all of Tadley's skill, could save him. While O'Rourke's landed men and their equipment were ferried back to *Ibis*, Dawlish sent her steam pinnace ahead to find the launch that had been sent back to wait after he had last descended the river.

The safe return of both craft did little to lift the gloom that hung over the gunvessel. Dawlish sensed the awareness of crew and officers alike that he had failed, detected it in the caution with which they approached him, felt it in Jarvis's ill-concealed resentment.

The steam launch that had been left behind had taken shelter in a creek when Imker's vessel had probed upriver three days previously.

"She weren't all around the bend before we saw she weren't the old *Ibis*, sir," the coxswain said. "We moved pretty sharpish into cover, we did, but she was turning back, didn't want to risk grounding, I'd warrant. She never saw us."

"Anything from upriver?" The nagging concern that Dawlish kept to himself, the possibility that Horne's mission might have been overwhelmed by now.

"Nothing, sir."

The pinnace and launch took the pulling boats in tow and followed *Ibis* up the channel. The mangrove thinned, drier ground and scrub lying just beyond it along the stretch where she had moored before. The men were exhausted, had been standing-to or with Dawlish all night, and he knew that he himself was near collapse. The advance upriver would be as gruelling as before and more haste could mean less speed. Better to allow a night's rest and prepare for a dawn departure.

But first must come the burial. Dawlish and Jarvis conducted it jointly, a duty all-too familiar, the words of the service known by heart. The dead men's closest shipmates carried the canvas-wrapped bodies. There was no plunge overboard with weights at the feet, graves instead dug high above the flood line and stones laid on top of the pathetic bundles to protect them from scavengers. During the slow filling with red earth, the terrible silence was broken only the scrape of spades and faint, distant, animal calls.

Dawlish felt desolation, a sense of futility, yet knew that he must not let it engulf him, most of all must not let it show. He had brought these two simple men here to their deaths — even their graves could not be marked less they provoke desecration by slavers — and he could not evade admission that yet more might follow. He could not shrink from that responsibility, would not want to. He had put his hand to the plough.

Like Joshua Horne, like Albrecht von Hohenfels.

176

The two low mounds were being patted firm now. Time to return to preparations for the morrow.

\*

There would be no rest for Jarvis and his men after Dawlish's force moved upriver. The possibility of Imker's gunboat returning could not be discounted. Since disappearing down the northern side channel she might have either stayed somewhere within it, or slipped back to Mtwara, evading detection by *Leonidas* under cover of darkness – Imker had managed it once before to get her here. If he could slip out of Mtwara again and again, avoid *Leonidas*, then Imker might either come up the Rovuma's main channel or else approach by that which he had escaped through. Blocking the main channel would demand *Ibis* dropping downstream and mooring fore and aft, as she had done before, so that her main armament would dominate the waters upstream. But the side channel was still a concern.

Jarvis volunteered the solution. "We could mount one of our sixty-eight pounders on the opposite bank. A single bursting-shell would tear that old gunboat apart."

A gig carried Dawlish and Jarvis back downstream to inspect the possible site. The thick mangrove on the southern bank would give ideal cover. The mud was reasonably firm but would still require construction of a base solid enough to carry the sixty-eight's four-ton weight. Building a platform for O'Rourke's light Gatling had demanded massive effort. This would cost immeasurably more – palm trunks cut down on higher ground and dragged here to make a mat, the gun itself lowered from the *Ibis*, ferried to shore and hauled here along a cleared path on an improvised sled, by blocks and tackles and screaming human muscles. It would be brutal, back-breaking work, yet a type not unknown in a navy that had hauled heavy guns across half of India during the Mutiny.

"Five days at best, a week at the outside," Jarvis said. "And then there'll be an unpleasant surprise for Willem Imker if he shows his face."

It sounded as if he relished the prospect.

177

Departure just after dawn. The moored *Ibis* was left astern, half-hidden by the last wisps of the night's mist above the river.

Smoke drifted from the brass funnels of the pinnace and launch as they strained against the current at walking pace, the strings of loaded boats on tow astern. And here, above the tidal reach, Dawlish noted that the water level was lower, the exposed shoals more frequent, than when he had first come here. The dry season was biting.

By midday the deeper-keeled pinnace was touching bottom and the craft she towed – three heavy cutters and as many whalers – must now move forward under oars, carrying with them almost three-quarters of the landing force. O'Rourke, in command, would not be tardy in driving them on. Dawlish, taking Wainwright with him, pressed ahead with the launch. It towed three whalers with Leigh's company of *Leonidas* bluejackets – some thirty men. With luck her shallower draught might allow the launch to reach the German mission before the fallen water level would defeat her. She scraped twice on shoals and was dragged across, but it became unavoidable soon thereafter that she too must be left behind with two men. An hour under oars brought the whalers to a sandbar high enough to allow uncomfortable bivouacking for the night.

And it was all the worse because it rained heavily for an hour just after midnight.

So much for the dry season.

Misery.

*

The dawn brought little comfort, just saturated clothes steaming as the temperature rose, and a hurried meal of hard biscuit washed down by water. Three hours' rowing, then shallows that demanded men dropping into the water to lighten the boats as they were poled forward. And all too soon, nothing for it but to drag the craft across the increasingly frequent sandbars. Dawlish was fretting inwardly about the slow

178

progress – he had expected to reach Horne's mission at least two days before this – and each delay increased the threat of failure.

But what was to come was worse than he ever feared.

By mid-morning a succession of sandbars had been passed and the boats, again under oar, rounded the bend leading to the long stretch on which the German mission stood. Dawlish found the prospect of meeting the abbot again pleasing – he liked the man, admired him – even if only an hour might be spared to rest there. The wooden jetty projecting from the shore was visible now and he waited for white-clad figures to appear in welcome there.

None came.

Closer now, Dawlish urging his crew to stroke faster, unease rising. A smell now, weak, depressed by the night's rain, but one that he flinched from recognising. Birds wheeling slowly above. No boats moored at the jetty, no sight of the thatched roofs that should be visible by now, no sign of life

"Mr. Leigh!" Dawlish called back to the whaler astern. "Land your men two hundred yards short of that jetty!"

"Aye, sir!"

"Get two men up there," Dawlish pointed to the overlooking ridge where his group had previously camped. "Sharp lookouts, under cover. Who can best semaphore?"

"Canavan."

"Put him up there. And a man to stay with you who's not to take an eye off him. If there's anybody beyond that ridge I want to know it. Move forward into the mission with the rest of your people."

"Very well, sir. And you?"

"I'll land at the jetty. I'll move in from it and meet you in the centre."

He knew what he would find even before the blackened remains of the buildings came into sight. The thatch had burned away, the wattle and daub walls were scorched and many had collapsed. No movement other than a few dusty vultures flapping clumsily in the ashes in search of carrion. No smouldering wisps, only the impression of hell unleashed long days before.

The mission's two boats lay water-logged by the jetty, bottoms smashed. A body was floating in one of them, face down, half of the head missing, the white shirt ripped from its back by some bird to reveal a rotting pit of decay beneath.

Up on to the jetty itself, Dawlish leading from it at a run, revolver in hand, his bluejackets fixing bayonets to their Sniders as they followed. Anger – fury – was rising in him and he steeled himself for what he must now find. Near the end of the jetty was another body, hacked, worried by scavengers so that the rib cage was exposed, the flesh on the thighs eaten away to reveal the bones beneath. Past a roofless hut and beneath the charred beams fallen within was another body, half-burned, the stench unbearable.

Leigh met him at what had been the refectory.

"We haven't found a soul alive, sir." His face was pale. "Two bodies back there." He gestured over his shoulder to where his men were moving from one ruin to the next. "And three more in there. They didn't have a chance. Whoever did it are long gone Cowardly animals!"

"There's no doubt who did it." Dawlish felt rage almost overpowering him and he forced calm on himself. "I want to see the bodies in there."

He recognised none of them – their own mothers could not have done so – though the remaining shreds of white clothing told that they were monks. Three more were found soon afterwards in the gutted church – these men had died very hard, lashed to benches and left to the flames rather than butchered outright. Another body at the open-fronted smithy – the brother who had worked there had been an Alsatian, the abbot had said.

The search continued. It was not just that the buildings had been torched and the occupants slaughtered, but that the vengeance visited on this community had been so absolute, so merciless, in its contempt for all it had stood for. The crops in the fields beyond were partially burned, the barns also, the fences broken, goats killed and left to rot. A few chickens wandered about still, escapees from the blaze that had destroyed the poultry shed. Tools, cooking utensils, ransacked chests, bottles and jars, even the white habits worn for services, littered the spaces between the huts. Books had evoked especial wrath, covers ripped off, pages torn out and trampled underfoot.

And all the while Dawlish dreaded finding what he still sought.

"There are two more in here, sir." A seaman at a doorway. A trace of vomit on the front of his shirt. "It's bad, sir, very bad," he said as Dawlish pushed past him.

It had clearly been a study or an office, the remains of two desks just visible below the tangle of fallen rafters. On the wall to the left a blackboard, the two columns of words chalked on it just discernible beneath the dusting of ash. Shelving on the opposite wall, a section all but unharmed and with books – large ledgers – still stacked there. At the far end a large cupboard, only partially burned, a smaller at an angle in front of it. Dawlish realised where this place must be, whom he would find here.

"They're behind there." The seaman gestured toward the cupboards. "It's hard to get to them, sir."

Dawlish feared that the smell here would induce him too to vomit as he clambered across the debris.

Only the remaining scraps of half-burned clothing – the white of Father Wolfgang's rent shirt, the black of Dalton's trousers – identified the two translators. They must have retreated here, had dragged the cupboards to create a barrier to hide behind, had been speared and hacked when discovered, had died together. The words on the blackboard, painful steps towards a first dictionary, must be their epitaph and the Gospels of Matthew and Luke must wait for other interpreters.

I brought this upon them, upon them all, when I brought Buckwell here. And yet I had no option…

Dawlish had hung back from going directly to the hospital, knowing too well what would be there. Now he could delay no longer. He found Wainwright and Leigh outside it, both silent, looking up and shaking their heads as he approached. This had been the most solidly built of all the structures and it had partially withstood the fire. The charred rafters were still largely intact though the half-consumed canvas ceiling hung in strips below them. He passed in silence down the central corridor – the doors to either side had been shattered, the rooms ransacked. In the last he found whom he sought. A cot and cupboard and chairs had been piled in the doorway to create a barricade that still stood. The bodies lay beyond, struck down by attackers who must have gained entrance through the window on the far wall. Another cupboard lay tumbled before it, a last desperate measure to block it.

Dawlish went back outside and Wainwright and Leigh followed him, without a word, to the window. He climbed through. None of the bodies had been burned – they had escaped that, if little else. Buckwell, stern Ironside, had risen from the cot that had been used to block the doorway and, still in a cotton nightshirt, was slumped in a corner on top of the body of the surgeon, Brother Ruprecht, in a what must have been an effort to shield him. They lay behind a bench and a low cabinet dragged there as a last barrier. In front of it lay Abbot Albrecht von Hohenfels, late of the Second Bavarian Guards. He had died as he would have wished, defending his brethren, facing enemies whom he might have forgiven at the very last.

The massacre had occurred something of a week before – the decomposition alone told that story – and it must have been in daylight, for all the victims were in working clothing. It would not have needed many men, perhaps little more than a few of the traders incensed by the destruction of their ivory at Nanguruwe. The force left with Ross at Horne's mission would have been sufficient to withstand any such attack there but it could be a different matter if Achmed Ibn Hamed's large slaving column, expected imminently from the west, had assaulted there. It was imperative to get to that mission as quickly as possible. But first, one duty.

Dawlish ordered a pit dug beside the church's ruin. There were hands enough for it, the labour less disagreeable than the gathering up of the bodies. Sixteen were recovered, the number of which the community had consisted, but they included the two English missionaries. Two German brothers were therefore unaccounted for, even after a search beyond the farm boundaries.

The burial was hurried, though the remains had been laid down with respect and covered with the few trampled habits that could be found. Their small wooden crosses had remained around the necks of several of the dead and these were laid on top of the bodies before the earth was shovelled back. Had O'Rourke been here, Dawlish would have asked him to lead the brief prayers, but in the Catholic officer's absence he himself recited the Anglican words. He doubted that von Hohenfels would have resented them, nor the dedicated Nonconformists Buckwell and Dalton either.

Leigh came over, stood by his side as he came to the end.

"Canavan's signalling, sir. They've seen something."

Just below the ridge crest the tiny figure was moving its arms in short jerks, the movement cut off abruptly between each letter.

"Column. One mile…" Leigh was reading the signals himself.

Dawlish pulled out his field glasses, brought Canavan into focus, was not fast enough himself to read the rapid movements, could see the signaller's companion prone on the slope beyond him and peering over the crest.

"Twenty. Armed." Leigh said.

"Get everybody up there!" Dawlish could see no danger of flank attack. Any hostile thrust must come directly across the ridge. The approaching force must still be unaware of his presence here, could be taken under fire as it toiled up the opposite slope. Savage delight surged through him. This could be a massacre. His massacre, his retribution.

He sensed something of the same among the men as they pounded up the track, a shared outrage that only action could assuage. Lungs bursting, chest heaving, he halted them fifty yards below the crest, split the party, ready to move forward in line when called. Then he went ahead at a crouch with Leigh.

Canavan met them.

"They're a rum bunch, sir," he said. "Like soldiers, they are."

Dawlish dropped just short of the crest and crawled to join the other seaman in cover behind a low bush.

The slope ahead was gradual, open but for scatterings of thorn, the track that wound up it all but indistinguishable from the parched grass and red earth to either side. But on it, a thousand yards distant, an extended column was moving fast, two by two, clearly disciplined, the advance steady, resolute, a quick lope rather than a march, dust kicked up by its regular tread. This was no gang of slavers.

The idea flared in Dawlish's mind that these men must be Mathew's Zanzibari force but it died as quickly – Mathews had not passed up the Rovuma and could not easily have reached here overland. He wriggled forward, raised his glasses, focussed.

Nineteen men in all, nine ranks, three or four yards between them, a single figure leading. They wore a semblance of a uniform, a tunic and soft round cap that might have been brown even before being caked with dust. Canvas bandoliers crossed their chests, shoulder straps indicated backpacks behind, water bottles and sheathed bayonets hung from their belts. Their legs were bare below the knee and they appeared to be either barefoot or wearing sandals. They were carrying what were clearly rifles, not muskets.

And they were not Arabs, not Somalis, not Baluchis, but clearly Africans, sinewy men with black faces and curly hair, not tall but with an air of strength, and above all, of endurance. These men could maintain this pace all day.

All Africans, except for the single figure at the head of the column.

Dawlish realised exactly who he must be.

Doktor Eitel-Heinrich Lutz.

*

He was of a kind with Horne and Imker, even with Albrecht von Hohenfels, Dawlish saw, men driven by some vision that brought them to the edge of madness – for even the abbot must have known that his venture had been all but suicidal. This vast anarchic country, sparsely populated by docile people, and plundered by barbarians – a beautiful country at that – had obsessed each of them with the dream of possessing and controlling it, whether by belief or by naked power. They saw no impossibilities, were blind to constraints, counted no cost too high either for themselves or for others.

And Lutz was the most impressive – and frightening – of them all.

184

After the handshake, the brief exchange of names, there was a long silence. Lutz stood staring down at the devastated settlement. Seen from the ridge, and despite the burning, the layout's almost mathematical precision, the regular crop patches and the scale of the larger buildings, could only impress.

At last he asked, "Did anybody survive?"

"Nobody," Dawlish said. "We buried fourteen, and two Englishmen with them."

"Englishmen?" Lutz made it seem like an accusation.

Dawlish ignored what might have been provocation. "I can show you the grave," he said.

"You will show me everything, captain." A statement, not a request, not a demand, more like a command that assumed compliance without argument. And Dawlish let that too pass.

Lutz might be anything between thirty and fifty – the tropics did that to a man. He was taller than Dawlish, but thin to emaciation. His face was an unhealthy yellow, the closely clipped moustache and hair showing beneath his sun helmet steel grey, the eyes red-rimmed and inflamed behind round thick-lensed, blue-tinted spectacles. His uniform – it was hard not to regard it as such, though it bore no badges – was little different to his men's, the jacket and breeches of brown serge, puttees wound around his calves, short boots, good for marching. A huge holster hung from his belt. Sickly as he looked, he radiated a fierce energy, as if willpower alone would sustain him over endless marches.

They passed down the track, Lutz's troops – they well merited the name – following him, with Dawlish, Leigh and the bluejackets behind.

"Have you been here before, Dr. Lutz?" Dawlish knew he had not, but wanted to break the silence.

"No. My business did not take me here."

"How did you learn of what happened?"

"I had matters to attend to in a village here, in Nanguruwe. They told me about you, captain, and about the trouble you had caused there. How you brought this catastrophe on these people here. On these German people."

185

The cold fury in Lutz's voice seemed to have little sympathy in it for the slaughtered missionaries. He seemed affronted, insulted, not outraged.

"So, you met the men who did this, Dr. Lutz? The slavers?" Dawlish said.

"They'd fled from Nanguruwe before I came. They were afraid of you and they were afraid of me. They knew that we would come for them, either together or alone. They had murdered Germans. They knew that there would be no mercy."

He spoke as if he had an entire army at his command and not merely a half-platoon of African mercenaries. His English had a clipped precision, with only the slightest trace of a German accent.

They were among the burnt-out buildings now. Terrible as it had been while still littered with bodies, it seemed even worse now, more desolate, deserted even by the vultures. Dawlish felt painfully the memory of von Hohenfels showing him around here with such restrained pride. More than a vision, an ideal rather, had been destroyed. He identified each building, told which bodies had been found where. Lutz listened in silence.

At last the grave.

"They died with courage," Dawlish said. "Sixteen men who died in brotherhood."

"Fourteen," Lutz said. "Fourteen subjects of the German Reich who lie in what will be forever German soil."

Not only fury in his voice now.

Exaltation.

Chapter 18

Dawlish and Lutz stood in the shade of the church's ruin, out of earshot of others. Each cautious of what they said, each probing for information only reluctantly imparted, each uncertain of the other's motives. Dawlish admitted that a larger force was following him upriver but said nothing about the encounter with Imker's gunboat. In time Lutz would know about that, but better not now. Even less should he know that Mathews was due to arrive soon with some five hundred Zanzibari troops to occupy the area inland of Mtwara and to cut it off from the interior. Lutz acknowledged that his troops – his *askaris,* as he referred to them – had been trained by a retired German sergeant-major, dead now of fever. Dawlish envied them their Mauser rifles, superior to his own men's ageing Sniders.

Lutz had come from the north west. Another nine communities had signed commercial treaties there, he told Dawlish, all based on the same terms as concluded at Nanguruwe. That brought the total to twenty-three, he said with pride, a firm foundation for German trade. He had arrived at Nanguruwe the previous evening. Chief Kikuwa and his people had told of the party of slavers and ivory traders setting out for the German mission, had heard their savage boasts when they returned, had feared that their rage might now be turned on their village.

"But they'd left before you arrived in Nanguruwe, had they not?" Dawlish asked.

"To the west," Lutz said. "To meet the caravan expected soon with slaves and ivory."

"Achmed Ibn Hamed?"

"Him. He'll have a powerfully armed group with him."

"Was there news about the British mission? Mr. Horne's?"

Lutz shrugged. "I never asked. He's not my concern. But you, Captain Dawlish, kicked over a hornet's nest on Mr. Horne's behalf in a village where you had no business. Achmed uses Nanguruwe as a staging post. That's of no concern to me as long as he did not intrude on the trading rights that the treaty gives Germany. But you interfered, captain, and because of that fourteen German subjects died."

"A treaty with Germany?" Dawlish knew that sarcasm would gain him nothing, but Lutz's arrogant tone had provoked him. "I understood that you represented a private trading company, Dr. Lutz. That you've been negotiating with petty African chiefs, and turning a blind eye to the slave trade, so you could peddle tin trays and mirrors and scissors and cooking pots."

187

Lutz ignored the accusation. "The question is what you are going to do now, captain. German blood has been spilled and I'll avenge it. But English blood was spilled too. Will that remain unavenged?"

How much to share with this man?

Dawlish had intended that the force he had brought this far would bolster the defences of Horne's mission. Only with that wholly secure could he risk using any of his force to strike at Achmed. And that too would be folly until the larger group that was still crawling upriver under O'Rourke's command had arrived. That force would be unlikely to get this far for another two days…

"And what do you intend to do, Dr. Lutz?"

"I'll uphold German honour." He said it quietly, with no hint of arrogance now, a simple declaration of intent. "Chief Kikuwa signed a treaty. I owe it to him to defend his village. And I'll destroy Achmed and his people when they arrive."

Dawlish felt a flush of pity. This man was as suicidal as Horne, as Buckwell, as von Hohenfels. "You've got eighteen men, doctor. That's not enough. I've seen Nanguruwe. It would take two or three times as many to defend it. You haven't got the men needed."

"But you will have, captain," Lutz said. "You'll have the men."

Dawlish was silent. Topcliffe's words echoed in his mind.

*A man who's prepared to take decisions on the spot. Decisions appropriate to the circumstances.*

There was an opportunity now to place Lutz and his masters under an obligation – there was so much talk of honour that any such obligation must be respected. No need either to mention that Mathews would follow with Zanzibari troops, that they would claim this area in their sultan's name and afterwards exclude Lutz and his treaties and his tin trays and his lithographs of his emperor. But for now Lutz was useful, knowledgeable in the ways of this country and its tribes, with trained mercenaries at his disposal who could be a useful augmentation.

And Lutz is thinking much the same, Dawlish thought, weighing me up, wondering how he can make use of me, how he can exploit my concern for Horne, how far he can trust me.

At last Dawlish said "Are you proposing an alliance, Dr. Lutz? A temporary one? For mutual benefit?"

"To uphold German honour, Captain Dawlish. To uphold British honour also."

Dawlish reached out his hand, and Lutz shook it, and each knew that there would be more to it than that. And that a plan must be hammered out in the coming hours.

Slowly, carefully, with mutual but unstated distrust.

*

Horne's mission was Dawlish's immediate concern. Following the arc that the river traced between here and there had taken two days previously, and the water level had been higher then. Cutting overland across that arc would allow reaching the mission in a day of hard marching. He took Leigh and Wainwright aside.

"I'm leaving two men here with a message for O'Rourke. He'll be here in two days, with luck. Select men who won't panic."

Leigh paused, then said "Hatton. Davis too."

"I'll leave them a boat to use if they have to." Drifting with the current, two men could just about manage a whaler if they must flee. "And I want six men in each of the other boats to go upriver. Determined fellows. They'll have to pole and drag in places, but nothing's to stop them."

"The rest of us, sir?" Leigh said.

"We're marching." Dawlish turned to Wainwright. "You're up to it I trust?"

"I'll manage."

"Full marching order, sir?" Leigh asked.

"No. Light as possible. No blanket. Just haversack, water bottle, one night's rations, forty rounds and a quinine dose to each man before we leave. Everything else to go in the whalers. Departure at dawn."

A few questions and then Leigh left to initiate preparations.

Still depressed, Dawlish felt solace in commitment to action. Small as the force might be, but it would be heavily armed and surprise and

189

discipline would be on its side should it run into slavers. There was no map, just his mental picture of this devastated mission, Horne's settlement and Nanguruwe village as the points of a triangle. With a pocket compass the general direction could be maintained along bush tracks like those encountered before. Any villagers met could be questioned by Wainwright, perhaps conscripted as guides.

As he walked down to the jetty to check the loading, he passed the hut where the translators Dalton and Wolfgang had died. A thought struck him and he went in. The wreckage had been dragged aside to recover the bodies and it was easy now to reach the wooden shelving. The seven thick ledgers still stood on what was left of it and, despite the ash heaped on them, they looked unharmed. He took one, dusted it off and flicked it open.

Each page was split into two columns and the handwriting was in what he guessed was Gothic script. It hard to understand initially but after leafing through several pages, and finding chapter headings, he realised that the left column must be the Matthew's Gospel in German. The other column was impossible to understand, the words probably phonetic renderings of the local language. He checked another book – the same – and another and another, lines crossed out, words modified, annotations in the margins. The last volume, quarter-full, seemed to be an uncompleted dictionary. A life's work.

He called a seaman, had him bring a blanket, a square of canvas and some rope. He bound up the books carefully himself and had them brought down to a whaler. In some uncertain future he, rather than Lutz, would have them returned to the monastic order to which Wolfgang had belonged.

A bequest a man could be proud of.

And Dalton had left another like it at Horne's mission.

\*

Dawlish's force bivouacked among the ruins that night. There was no air of cheerful relaxation around the cooking fires – the seamen's mood was subdued and the full enormity of what they had witnessed was sinking in. Lutz's men, exhausted by their forced march, camped further away. He was determined to return to Nanguruwe on the morrow. The fifty porters who normally accompanied his column had remained there.

Dawlish strove not to let the depression that had settled on him be seen. He remembered how the sense of evil that had lain heavily on him had been lightened when he had listened to the men, now dead, chanting vespers here. Now that sense was back. His mood hardly brightened when Lutz accepted his invitation to share food. There were long silences, no convivial exchange of experiences, none of the easy conversations that Dawlish had enjoyed with Fregattenkapitän Kaunitz of the *Hildegarde*. It struck him again, as it had so often since he had taken command of *Leonidas*, that something within him was crying out for relaxed companionship such as was impossible with subordinates onboard ship. It was no less difficult with naval contemporaries who, once midshipmen together, now saw each other as middle-ranking officers who had become rivals for preferment. And it would get no easier in the years ahead.

"Will you be sending a despatch back to Zanzibar, captain?" Lutz broke the silence.

"Yes. When I know about the situation at Mr. Horne's mission."

A boat would drop downstream to the *Ibis* and a sailing cutter would carry the missive to Kirk. Two-hundred mile journeys in open boats had been normal undertakings for the anti-slavery patrols off this coast. Dawlish himself had made several in earlier years. A good opportunity for an ambitious young officer on the *Ibis* to show his mettle.

"Will you extend the courtesy of bringing a report to the German consul there also?" It sounded more like a demand than a request

"Write it before you leave, doctor. Seal it. One of the boats arriving here in two days or so will take it downriver."

"Thank you, captain." Lutz stood up to go. "I will meet you in Nanguruwe. You, and the men you say are coming."

The first step of the plan.

\*

A start at sunrise allowed steady progress in the morning's brief cool, both columns, Dawlish's and Lutz's setting out at the same time on diverging tracks.

The pace must needs be slower than Dawlish would have liked – exercise on ship, however intense, had not fully prepared the bluejackets for marching in such conditions. After the first hour there were some signs of human presence, small winding tracks, goat droppings, once the faint smell of woodsmoke from some unseen village away to the left. The ground was mainly open. Detours around thicker brush cost time, but always the compass readings kept the advance roughly as intended. By ten o'clock Dawlish estimated that half the distance had been covered and that Nanguruwe must now lie five or six miles almost directly to the right. At this rate it should be possible to reach Sali, the mission outpost at the end of the Chidya lake, by mid-afternoon.

A noise ahead. Dawlish held up his hand, stilled the tread of boots behind. It was clear now, the distant bleating of goats just audible above the insect chatter. He turned to Wainwright.

"There must be a herder there. Could you understand him?"

"Possibly. I don't know the language here, but he might know a few words of Swahili. I might get something from him."

Dawlish beckoned Leigh to join them.

"I want you to go ahead. Take a man with you. Mr. Wainwright will be with you also. If you can find somebody, then bring him back. Don't hurt him." He looked to Wainwright. "Reassure him as much as you can. I don't want anybody too frightened to talk."

The wait seemed interminable and the youth they brought back – they had crept up on him resting in shade – was mute with terror for the first five minutes. Sweat ran from his face and his eyes were locked on the bayonets until Dawlish made a show of turning them away.

"Have we anything we can give him?" Wainwright said. "A gift. Something he'd value?"

Dawlish fished in his pocket and took out a small penknife. "Will this do?"

The sight of the tiny blade scared the herder even further when Wainwright opened and closed it several times. He at last flicked it shut and, speaking softly, put it into the lad's trembling hand and closed his fingers around it. Smiling, he gestured that it was his to keep.

The questioning went slowly, with frequent incomprehension on both sides, much searching for words, much head-nodding and shaking. The boy was relaxing, was as pleased as Wainwright when some small step in understanding was gained, was at last chattering so fast that he must be slowed, be made repeat himself. And then a sudden stop, the words halting again, fear once more in his voice and on his features. The word 'Sali' was repeated several times.

Wainwright turned to Dawlish. "He seems to know about what happened to the Germans," he said. "Somebody from his village went there for medical treatment and found it burned. And Sali seems to have been attacked too. No – he doesn't know what happened there. Now the villagers are frightened that they'll suffer the same if the slavers come again."

The terror in this innocent's eyes, the trembling as he spoke, his rational dread for his family and village, moved Dawlish's spirit. It suddenly set his depression at nought and made him grateful to be here.

Evil existed, scourged this land.

To have the opportunity and the means to confront it was a privilege, a gift.

Which he now had, and was glad.

\*

The boy proved a willing guide, remaining with them for over an hour and setting them on a track that brought them to Sali by three o'clock.

The smell of burnt thatch quickened their pace when they were still a mile away, but they arrived to find no bodies among the wrecked huts. There were no canoes drawn up on the lake's foreshore. It was clear that the occupants had been evacuated to the Horne mission before the slavers had struck.

Ross was in the first of the canoes to come down the lake – his alert lookouts at the far end had observed the arrival of Dawlish's party. His immediate report was heartening. The slavers who had burned Sali had probed half-heartedly towards Horne's mission, probably suspecting an armed presence there. They had got no closer than the edge of the open belt of burned ground in front of the marines' and bluejackets' rifle pits.

"Shand got one of them," Ross said. "A single shot, three-hundred yards, downhill, a nearly impossible one. They turned tail then and we haven't seen them since."

Horne was waiting at the water's edge as the canoe grounded at his mission. Mr. Miller was there too, looking less terrified than when Dawlish had last seen him. But it was the two other Europeans on either side of Horne, one speaking animatedly to him in what sounded like fractured English, whose appearance surprised and elated Dawlish. Emaciated, clad in ill-fitting clothing that must have been donated, he recognised them as the German brothers who had been missing from the bodies found at the ravaged abbey. They had somehow made it here.

Maddox of the *Ibis* had drawn up his men in line and they presented arms in salute as Dawlish stepped ashore. Horne advanced, grasped Dawlish's hand, his eyes brimming.

"You must know it all, captain. Of our brothers Buckwell and Dalton." His voice was breaking. "That they have their crowns of glory now. And other good men, martyred too." He gestured to the Germans, who seemed no less moved. "Thanks be to God's mercy that he cast his mantle over these two friends."

One of the brothers broke in, his words a confused mix of English and German. Dawlish recognised him – he had glimpsed him once before, contentedly planing wood in the abbey's carpentry workshop. The name came back – Brother Albert, identified by von Hohenfels as an Alsatian.

"I speak French," Dawlish said. "Tell me about it in French."

"They came without warning." Albert's voice was trembling. "There was no mercy. I saw Abbot Albrecht and ..." He could not continue.

Horne reached over, put his arm around his shoulder.

When Albert could speak again he said "Brother Friedrich and I, we hid in a ditch. They didn't find us but we saw all. There was nothing we could do. Nothing." He paused, tears welling, clearly oppressed, as he always would be henceforth, by his inability to have helped. "We stayed until darkness fell. There was nobody alive. But we knew of this place and we hoped for its shelter. And this good man gave it." He began to weep.

"God guided them," Horne's voice was again steady. And solemn. "They were half dead when they reached here. The Lord vouchsafed miraculous deliverance, just as he preserved us all from persecution in your absence, Captain Dawlish."

It was not the time to point out that Ross's and Maddox's men might have assisted the Lord in that. Before all else, Dawlish must confer with these two officers and to enlighten them about next steps. They would have another part to play now.

No longer defence.

*

Horne seemed like a changed man when Dawlish spoke to him in his bungalow. The same grim resolve was there as before but his eyes filled and he had to turn away when Dawlish answered his questions about Buckwell and Dalton.

"They died as well and as bravely as any man might hope for." Dawlish had held no detail back. "We buried them in dignity and…" He paused. "… and with men with whom they would have been glad to lie together with in death."

A long silence in the darkness lit by the weak flame of a lamp fed by the kerosene that Dalton had valued so highly. It would have brought him into the fourteenth chapter of Luke. That gospel might now remain untranslated for years, perhaps forever.

"They're misguided." Horne said. "Misguided, but there's no malice in those two men, those two foreign brothers in Christ. None either in those who died. The sin was mine that I did not see it, that I refused to see it, before this visitation, that I turned my face from Christian fellowship."

"None of them would have held it against you. Their abbot least of all." The memory of von Hohenfels caressing the rifle, the embodiment of all he had renounced, was strong. "When the time came you had charity in your heart, Mr. Horne."

"They pray separately from us and they don't preach their Popish doctrines here." Something of the old Horne in his tone, determined to show that his tolerance of error extended only so far. "But they offer their labour willingly – Brother Albert has been tirelessly repairing our dwellings – and their toil is accepted gladly. Their friendship too. Good men."

He was glad to hear of Mrs. Joyce's hopeful prospects, disappointed but not surprised that her husband was unlikely to return. "They laboured long enough in the vineyard," he said. "The Lord will not ask more of them."

Then time for business, to tell Horne as much as he needed to know about what was planned.

And afterwards, sleep.

## Chapter 19

Eight days had passed. Nanguruwe was secure, its food supplies, its provision of porters, all now denied to Achmed Ibn Hamed and any like him. The force that O'Rourke had led upriver arrived there three days after Dawlish had occupied it with the men he had brought on ahead, supplemented by Ross's marines. Only a few bluejackets remained at Horne's mission, its security now assured by the larger presence at Nanguruwe. The slave pens were empty, for the wretches who had been left behind when Dawlish had retreated with the rescued Buckwell had been taken westwards by the slavers when they had fled. Nanguruwe was an armed camp now, a base from which patrols could be sent to locate Achmed's column expected from the west sometime in the near future.

Those patrols would have been impossible without Lutz. The German's askaris were tireless, patient, wise in the ways of survival in arid bush terrain, immune to the heat that exhausted the British force and to the insects that tormented it. Their tracking abilities, their genius for finding cover where there seemed none, their cheerful tolerance of every discomfort, made them invaluable. Dawlish knew that he needed Lutz, realised now that he had over-estimated what his own landed force could achieve in this terrain and climate. Seizing, and if necessary defending, a position like Nanguruwe was easy. Locating a mobile column that could so easily lose itself in the vastness of Africa was more difficult, even one slowed by a horde of bewildered slaves, shackled or staggering under ivory tusks. Reluctantly, Dawlish recognised that he needed Lutz. And he resented it.

Upwards of half the bluejackets were occupied in maintaining the supply line from the *Ibis*. The Rovuma's falling level meant that the German mission was now the furthest point the larger boats could reach. Egdean was in charge there, supervising landing of supplies – tinned beef, ammunition and medical supplies, especially quinine – and forwarding them on to Nanguruwe, carried by porters provided by Chief Kikuwa. The chief's loyalties had shifted, however temporarily, from Achmed to Lutz and to Dawlish, and he was clearly calculating which would be the more valuable to him. Only whalers could progress beyond the German mission to reach Horne's settlement with the bulkier supplies sent for it from Britain. A regular shuttle upriver and down was in operation now, and the first boat to drop downstream to *Ibis* had carried Lutz's despatch as well as Dawlish's. By now these documents must be half-way and more to Zanzibar in a sailing cutter.

*

The heat had cooled a little as Dawlish sat in mid-afternoon in what had been Buckwell's hut. He was writing up his journal, embittered by recollection of the argument with Lutz just after arriving here. All approaches to Kikuwa for more porters, Lutz had insisted, must go through him. The treaty that the chief had signed with Die Bremen und Oldenburg Ostafrikanische Handelsgesellschaft established that right, he claimed. A compromise was reached – Lutz himself would now accompany Wainwright, Dawlish's deputy in such matters, when the chief must next be approached. A rational internal voice told Dawlish that the concession cost nothing. Once Mathews reached here with the Zanzibari troops, Lutz's treaty would be worthless.

Concern about Mathew's whereabouts nagged Dawlish. Over a week had passed since occupying Nanguruwe and there should have

197

been word by now of the brigadier general and the five hundred mercenaries he commanded. A small steamer had been chartered to get them to the Rovuma but reports carried upriver from *Ibis* indicated no sighting of her yet. Anything could have delayed Mathews – an overheated bearing, a burst boiler, stormy weather. Until he arrived, the entire burden of finding and destroying Achmed would fall on Dawlish – and on Lutz.

Tadley entered.

"Another one," he said. "Woke up in the night, fever, raving soon afterwards."

"One of Ross's people?"

"No, sir. From *Ibis*. Only got here two days ago."

Five men were now shaking in alternating hot and cold sweats, half-delirious in the two huts that Tadley had converted into a hospital. The first three had been of Ross's marines, had been ashore longest. Now newcomers were succumbing too, despite all the daily tots of quinine wine. Most, probably all so far, would recover, but it would be weeks rather than days before they could be fit for anything but the lightest duties. The dysentery that had struck a half-dozen others, humiliating and enervating as it might be, could clear up in days but the fever was more devastating.

"The longer we're here, the more there will be."

Dawlish had seen it himself a decade before in Ashanti, the expedition's effectiveness eroded as the sick list lengthened. Strong and healthy though he had been when he arrived there, he too had fallen victim and had suffered intermittent, unpredictable, bouts ever since. The threat still hung over him.

"If we only knew what caused it we could do something but…" Tadley shrugged, held up his hands in something like despair. "If you can authorise doubling of the quinine wine ration, sir, that might help."

"Do it," Dawlish said. Egdean had forwarded six cases, twenty-four bottles in each, the previous day.

The surgeon left and behind him there remained the concern that had Dawlish had felt from the beginning, that disease might prove a deadlier enemy than any slaver.

198

Leigh arrived soon after, blinking as he entered the hut and passed from bright sunlight into cool shadow.

"We've sighted the patrol, sir. They should be here in a quarter hour. I've sent men to meet them."

"Very well. My compliments to Mr. Wainwright and ask him to join us immediately."

The patrol had been gone five days, Ross with five of the best marines, Lutz accompanying them with as many askaris. They had headed west to reconnoitre known tracks and to return immediately, and unobtrusively, should anything significant be sighted.

Dawlish and Wainwright waited for them by the small redoubt hastily cast up at the western side of the village. Spurts of red dust rose above the half-shuffling, half-marching feet of the small column coming down the track. Women hoeing in the fields to either side glanced up briefly without curiosity, then stooped again to their work.

Ross and Lutz were heading the column and, tired as they must be, Dawlish sensed purpose in their quickening steps. Directly behind them, two askaris were carrying something slung on a pole between them. As they neared, he saw that it was a crude litter, similar to that in which Buckwell had been carried to illusory safety.

Ross was beaming when they met. "We've got one of them, sir. He was sick. He still is, but we thought you'd like to meet him."

Lutz moved to the litter, pulled aside a cloth that had covered the face of the Arab swaying beneath the pole, his brow drenched with sweat. He mumbled what might have been an appeal for pity. Dawlish felt none.

"He was with Achmed," Lutz said. "He had a fever and he was left behind in a village called Mahuta. About fifty miles west of here. It profits from working with Achmed, just like Nanguruwe."

"Achmed's caravan?" Dawlish said. "It passed through? When?"

"Five or six days ago, it's hard to be certain," Lutz said, "but it didn't pass through. It turned back. It was heading this way but the slavers who fled from here, the swine who murdered the German brothers, had reached Mahuta. Achmed is no fool. He retreated westwards when he

199

heard that we were here, he went back the way he'd come. He's no longer coming this way."

"We followed for half a day," Ross's elation was gone. "It's bad, sir. It's very bad. We could see that they must be moving fast, flogging the poor devils on to get to Mtwara before we reach them. There are bodies every mile or so. Not just men but —"

Lutz cut him off. "Whatever other route he takes to Mtwara will be longer. Achmed will abandon the women and children if he has to, but he'll save the ivory at all costs."

"How many men?" Dawlish's brain was churning. It was going to be a race, and his men would be exhausted if they caught up. Most of his force lacked endurance in this heat. He did himself. And there must be a fight at the end of it. He needed to know the odds.

"How many, captain?" Lutz echoed the question. "Many, this prisoner says. But his answers lack precision. No numbers."

"He's been delirious most of the time, sir," Ross said.

"Treat him well for two hours, captain." A hint of relish in Lutz's voice. "Have him tended to, let him sleep, reassure him, put him at ease. And then I'll waken him. Leave him to me. He'll talk once my men have had ten minutes with him. I assure you that he'll be glad to tell us all we need."

"This is stupidity." Wainwright was looking angrily towards Lutz.

Dawlish ignored him, turned himself to Lutz.

"We'll leave him to Mr. Wainwright's care," he said. The entomologist's patient questioning had been effective before, on the *Ibis*, with the evasive prisoners from the captured dhow. Let him try it again.

"This is an outrage, captain!" Lutz's voice rose to a near scream. "He's my prisoner and..."

"You'll see to him, won't you, Mr. Wainwright?" Dawlish ignored the outburst. And to Ross he said, "Get the prisoner into one of the huts and have Surgeon Tadley see to him." He turned back to Wainwright. "I trust you'll have something to tell me in an hour. Not longer"

"A disgrace, captain!" Lutz was trembling with rage. "An outrage. An insult to..."

200

Dawlish moved closer to him, kept his voice low. "Shut up, Doktor Lutz. You're making a bloody fool of yourself."

He did not wait for the response and strode away.

Three hours of daylight remained, too little to allow anything but a hurried and ill-prepared departure. Better to wait until dawn, with the men well rested, with a clear plan and adequate supplies.

*

Surprise would be critical and surprise would demand speed, a pace fast enough to get ahead of Achmed's column, wherever it now was. How far could it progress in a day? Ten miles, twelve at most, however brutal the encouragement meted out to captives already exhausted to the point of death? Intercepting it, marching on a converging course, would demand a faster pace still, fifteen miles a day, more if possible. The patrol just returned had achieved as much, but Dawlish knew that less than half of the men he had here could manage that. But where to intercept?

While Wainwright questioned the prisoner in another hut, Dawlish called in his officers, O'Rourke and Ross, Leigh and Maddox. Men were to be selected, all reliable, tested in combat if possible, all healthy so far, endurance already proven, and more promised, by their fitness. Light marching order, rifles only, forty rounds, a single blanket, rations to be carried by porters. Chief Kikuwa would have to provide those porters. O'Rourke would act as Dawlish's second in command. A small force must be left to hold Nanguruwe, the sick also and those unlikely to sustain a rapid pace, and men also held back at the landing point at the German mission.

Together they worked through the list of names. It came in the end to forty-three. Half the men selected – marines and bluejackets – were assigned to Ross, the remainder, all bluejackets, to Leigh. Maddox and all others would remain at Nanguruwe. The seven-pounder that had been transported here at such effort would have to stay behind.

Lutz's askaris were likely to be invaluable, and he himself would be essential, for they would take orders from nobody else. Achmed's column must be moving through an area where Lutz had concluded petty treaties and that alone should be an incentive for him to cooperate. But first his ruffled feathers must be smoothed, hasty words regretted, an apology given, a hand extended, and only then negotiate an acceptable arrangement for the coming days with mutual cold calculation and cautious trust.

As his officers hastened to set preparations afoot, Dawlish left to seek out the German. It would not be an easy meeting.

*

"There will be no unified command. You understand that, captain?"

Lutz had already asked the question three times in three different ways. Each time the answer had been the same.

"Cooperation only, doctor," Dawlish said. "A working alliance. I'll supply your people, I'll hear your advice, give it due weight, reject or accept it as I decide fit. And when I propose action I'll request your cooperation and if not –"

"And no authority over my askaris," Lutz cut him off. He had said it several times already. "They remain under my direct command."

"I accept that, doctor. I repeat, your counsel will be invaluable. I look forward to our cooperation."

Triumph gleamed in the eyes behind the blue spectacles. Dream as he might of a vast trading empire, Lutz also clearly enjoyed petty and vindictive victories. He might have repeated his terms yet another time if Wainwright had not joined them.

"The prisoner's name is Omar Ibn Said," Wainwright said. "He's just one of Achmed's lieutenants, a very minor one, according to himself. The slavers who fled from here met Achmed's caravan at a village called Mahuta. This fellow was already ailing with fever but he heard enough from Achmed about the likely new route before he collapsed. Achmed had no option but to leave him behind at Mahuta. That's where we found him. He's terrified that we'll let Doktor Lutz' askaris loose on him. He knows about the murders at the German Mission and expects no mercy from us because of it."

"So, he talked?"

"I took the liberty of using your name, Captain Dawlish. That you'd authorise his release once the worst of his fever is past – Tadley thinks it's common malaria, by the way. So yes, this Omar talked, even if finding the truth of it was like getting blood from a stone."

"How large is the caravan?" The critical question.

"About eighty armed men, Arabs and Somalis. It started with four hundred slaves from somewhere far to the west, maybe even in the Congo Basin. They were down to three hundred by the time it reached Mahuta. It's carrying ivory too, Omar thought about three hundred tusks."

But it was the armed men that mattered, ruthless and effective mercenaries who had trekked half-way across Africa to devastate enough villages to yield so many captives, so much ivory. If they were armed like the slavers encountered in the first attack on Nanguruwe then they would be equipped with Chassepots, more effective than the Sniders carried by the bluejackets and marines, equals of the askaris' splendid Mausers.

Eighty enemy, more than the force that must find them. Only surprise and discipline could even the odds. But even if an ambush could prove successful, a yet greater problem would remain. Three hundred captives – cowed, emaciated, bewildered, and yet more terrified still by the attack that would erupt around them – would have to be got back here.

"Where could Achmed be now?" Dawlish asked.

Wainwright flicked open a leather-bound notebook, briefly exposing closely written text and meticulous drawings of beetles. The page he held to view carried a list of single words. He pointed to them. "They're names of villages the prisoner thinks the caravan will pass through to avoid us. But he wasn't clear enough about where they are. He wasn't too coherent."

Lutz was staring at the list. "Chinugutu," he said, "I've been there. And Masasi – a big village, slave pens there and a cooperative chief, porters for Achmed, good for resting a few days. I signed a trade treaty there. And what's this? Chingwar? Never heard of it. Could it be Chinguru?"

"It could be," Wainwright said. "I wrote down what I though he said, but he's damn near delirious again."

"Almost certainly Chinguru," Lutz said. "Another treaty village but it's off the usual slaver's route – it's easier to come through Nanguruwe. And Nangaka? Probably Nanganga, a small place. But Mtama's big, and I've a treaty there."

"Could you sketch the relative locations, doctor?" Dawlish said.

Lutz could do better, could produce the map that he had been painstakingly constructing and updating ever since he had come to Africa. He left for his hut, was back almost immediately with a long tin cylinder from which he produced a rolled sheet, some three feet by two. He smoothed it out on the table and Dawlish and the others held down the corners.

Stained, creased and blotted though the map was – it had clearly been worked on in leaking huts – and with huge voids still to be filled, it must be the result of months of meticulous observation. Coloured inks had been used and the various features had been identified in Gothic script so perfect that it might have been type set, some crossed out neatly and replaced by a correction of name and location. The river lay in the bottom right, crawling sinuously north-eastwards towards its delta and the sea. Mtwara and Mikindani Bay roughly north-westwards of the delta and close to the top of the map. Without surveying equipment, acting on compass readings and observation alone, with no way of estimating distance other than by experience and from reports, Lutz's achievement was impressive.

"Here's Nanguruwe," Lutz stabbed his finger at a point almost directly south of Mtwara. A winding dashed line indicating the track between them. He traced westwards. "Here is Nanyamba –"

"About twenty-five miles from here," Ross said. "We bivouacked near there the night before last. We'd come from Mahuta, where we found this wretched Omar fellow and –"

"You can see Mahuta here, captain," Lutz was irritated by Ross's interruption.

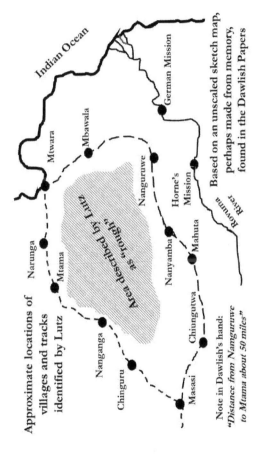

Indian Ocean

German Mission

Mbawala

Mtwara

Nanguruwe

Horne's Mission

Rovuma River

Narunga

Mtama

Area described by Lutz as "rough"

Nanyamba

Mahuta

Chiungutwa

Nanganga

Chinguru

Masasi

Approximate locations of villages and tracks identified by Lutz

Note in Dawlish's hand: *"Distance from Nanguruwe to Mtama about 50 miles"*

Based on an unscaled sketch map, perhaps made from memory, found in the Dawlish Papers

205

"And Chiunguta a long way to the west," Lutz continued, "and beyond it again, Masasi, where Achmed was retreating to with his caravan. There's a reasonable track all the way from Masasi to here and it's the route the caravans normally take when they're heading west or coming back."

North of the track linking Masasi and Nanguruwe the centre of the map was all but blank. Elongated west to east, the area was bounded to the north by a dashed line denoting a track, with annotations marking what must be villages, strung out like beads on a necklace. Some were identified in black ink, others in red. Dawlish asked why.

"Treaties were signed at those marked in red," Lutz's tone of pride was justified. Virtually alone, he had explored and mapped a huge area.

"What's here?" Dawlish swept his hand across the void.

"That rough terrain I referred to," Lutz said. "Hilly, broken by ravines, a few small lakes, unsettled. But look to its east and north – that track there, you see it? Running from Masasi in a great curve towards Mtwara. There's Chinguru – what Mr. Wainwright thought was called Chingwar – not ten miles from Masasi, and beyond it Nanganga – you misheard it as Nangaka, sir – and on to Mtama. On to Narunya from there – you see it? Just north east of Mtama. And from there, straight east to Mtwara itself."

"A track suited to a caravan?" Dawlish asked.

"Little used. But on occasion, yes. It's a more difficult route than coming through Nanguruwe, rougher going."

"So Achmed would have to retreat to Masasi before he could follow it? He'd have to retreat west before he could turn north-eastward?"

"About fifty miles back to Masasi, captain. And then from Masasi to Mtama, another fifty at the least. It's hard to think in terms of distance. The tracks wind so much, get washed out by rains, loop around hills."

Dawlish's mind was racing. Mtama could not be further than fifty miles north-westwards of here across the space Lutz had classified as rough. A column of bluejackets, marines and askaris must surely be able to cross it in – what? Three days, four at the most, however hard the going. But Achmed's ivory laden caravan and its surviving slaves would have over a hundred miles to cover since turning back at Mahuta.

Achmed had a head-start, yes, five days, but it was inconceivable that his caravan could sustain more than ten or twelve miles a day, day after day, however many wretches might be flogged to death to speed them. It might be a near-run thing, Dawlish realised, but it must be possible to get his force to Mtama before the caravan.

"Have you crossed this area, doctor?" Dawlish pointed again towards the blank.

"Once, captain, when I first came south."

"And it's passable?"

"Not easy. It's barren and I encountered no village, not even tracks. But, yes, passable."

"In four days at the outside, doctor?"

"In four days at most."

"And you know this village of Mtama?"

"Like I know this village of Nanguruwe. Its chief has signed a treaty with me."

The chief there had signed to get a lithograph of Kaiser Wilhelm and for tin trays and cheap alarm clocks, Dawlish thought, not one that obliged him to facilitate an ambush on a slaver warlord. But let that pass. First get there.

"An ambush at Mtama must be possible," Dawlish said. "Would you be willing to bring your askaris to join in?"

"German blood had been spilled, captain," Lutz said. "Even without you I'd be marching."

Now to confront the most daunting problem of all.

"You said the route from here to Mtama was passable, doctor," Dawlish said. "Will it be passable for three hundred slaves if we can liberate them?"

"You want to bring them back here, captain?" Lutz was looking at him in genuine surprise. "Why?"

Dawlish failed to disguise his disgust. "You're not proposing we abandon them?"

"Why not?" Lutz said. "I'm joining you for one reason only, Captain Dawlish. I want German blood avenged. What becomes of those slaves afterwards is none of my business."

"I'm not asking for it to be. But it'll be mine." Dawlish felt a surge of pride as he said it. "I asked if the way from Mtama might be passable for them."

He could imagine them – weak, stumbling, terrified, unaware that this new path of misery would be to deliverance of a sort. And hungry. It had all seemed so straightforward before – intercept Achmed's caravan here at Nanguruwe and hold the liberated slaves until Mathews would arrive with his troops to declare a Zanzibari protectorate, then withdraw the *Leonidas* and *Ibis* personnel. But now there was still no word of Mathews.

"Those slaves survived this far from the Congo. Another sixty miles won't kill most of them." Lutz shrugged. "They'll be your concern, captain, not mine."

Let it pass, an internal voice told Dawlish. Argument with this man will get you nowhere.

"My people will be ready to depart at dawn, doctor," Dawlish said. "I trust yours will be ready also?"

"At dawn, captain."

"We're not carrying rations for longer than six days, and I suggest the same for your people either, doctor," he said. "Any more and we'll be slowed too much. Can we get enough food at Mtama to get us back here?"

"Enough for you," Lutz said. "Maybe not enough for those slaves you care so much for. But that's not my affair." He turned to go. "I wish you a good evening, captain. I'll see you at dawn."

He left, the others too, to commence preparations. Dawlish gestured to Maddox and Wainwright to stay back.

"Select another dozen men, Mr. Maddox. Solid, reliable. As fit as possible, even if we didn't choose them before. But capable of getting half-way to Mtama and of supervising porters." He turned to Wainwright. "See Chief Kikuwa, but not for an hour after we've left – I don't want a confrontation with our German friend about that. Negotiate for porters – at least fifty, more, a lot more, if possible. And food – yams, whatever else you can find, enough to feed three hundred mouths. Tell Kikuwa he'll be paid, but I don't want him threatened until there's no other option."

"And then, sir?" Maddox said.

"The column will leave a trail – cairns, rags tied on trees. I want that food moving up behind us. There'll be a place for a cache marked clearly – it'll be about half-way. Dump the supplies there, leave a guard, then get the porters back here and repeat the process. We'll need every mouthful at the cache when we get back from Mtama."

And even as he spoke Dawlish knew he was assuming that an ambush of Achmed and his armed slavers would be successful.

It was a very large assumption.

## Chapter 20

Already by noon on the first day it was clear that water would be a problem. Marching north-westwards on a compass bearing, with no assurance that this heading would take it to the Masasi to Narunya track, either to the east or to the west of Mtama, the column had soon entered the terrain Lutz had described as difficult. He had not exaggerated. The fertile area around Nanguruwe, with its well-tilled vegetable patches, dropped behind and the ground ahead was more broken, littered for the most past by low thorn bush, dry and arid in this season, with no breath of wind to rattle the shrivelled leaves on the few parched trees. The last winding pathways beaten by goatherds and their flocks petered out, forcing sinuous skirting of the densest thickets. Progress was good in the first cool hours after departure but by the time of the first break – Dawlish would allow five minutes in the hour – men were already glancing longingly at the water bottles from which they would be permitted to swig a mouthful only at every second halt.

Two small groups advanced ahead of the main column, to right and left of it, a half-dozen of Ross's most seasoned men in one, an equal number of askaris in the other, led by Lutz's sergeant, Hassan. Men returned from them at intervals to warn of the need to march around obstacles ahead. Dawlish and Lutz were at the head of the column, both loaded and armed like their men, a frigid politeness between them in their few interactions. Ross's and Leigh's small contingents, separated by Lutz's askaris, marched behind in single file. O'Rourke ranged up and down the column, urging or cajoling when necessary, sometimes praising with a joke, radiating a sense of cheerful determination that the askaris responded to no less positively than the seamen and marines. At every two hundred yards he tied a strip from a roll of four-by-two rifle-cleaning rag to a branch. Wainwright's negotiations with Chief Kikuwa should already be underway and the first column of food-laden porters should be following this marked path within twenty-four hours.

The sun climbed, the dead blanket of heat grew ever heavier, the insects shrilled ever louder and there was no other sign of life than occasional birds circling slowly overhead. The red earth underfoot had been broken by fissures as it dried. Throat-searing dust billowed up from the marching feet. It was hard, almost impossible, to estimate the direct, crow's-flight, distance covered but by noon, when Dawlish ordered a two-hour break – to drink, to sleep in discomfort in whatever scant shadow could be found – he doubted if it was much over eight miles. Most worrying of all was that there had been no sign of water, not a single rivulet, not even a single stagnant pond.

He mentioned this to Lutz.

"There is water," Lutz did not seem unduly worried. "I saw it in several places here before, green vegetation thick around it."

"We must find some by nightfall." Dawlish's voice rattled in a dry throat.

"Some of my askaris can all but smell it. I'll send four ahead. If we fire a single shot every half-hour they'll answer if they've found it."

Joints aching, the respite insufficient, the column's march resumed, quickening as more open country lay before them, mottled with sparse scrub and broken by a succession of low ridges and shallow dry gullies. The heat had hardly lessened since midday and water breaks were now three hours apart, rather than two previously. Rifles and other equipment grew heavier and clothing chafed, but the askaris' shuffling gait, never slowing, set a pace which pride alone drove the naval personnel to maintain.

A single shot from the column at five-thirty was answered by another from the askari scouts somewhere ahead and to the left, some two miles distant, judging by the sound. A second shot from the column acknowledged it, was answered again by the unseen scouts. The direction of advance was shifted a compass point leftwards. A long gentle slope lay ahead and as he reached the crest Dawlish saw a small streak of green, dark amid the brown landscape, several trees protruding above the dense foliage below.

Water. And a camping place.

Just over an hour of daylight left to reach it.

\*

It was little more than a pond, a long hollow, without a spring or a stream flowing from it, filled only by rain, its edges retreated far back in this dry season. But it was water, however stagnant, and there was no shortage of dry kindling for boiling it, enough for meal-porridge made with it to be made edible, if not palatable. Enough too for the British to brew their inevitable tea, for a can of preserved beef to be divided between each four men. The mosquitoes came with the darkness and all but the sentries, who would be rotated through the night, pulled their blankets close around their faces and dropped into comfortless sleep.

It had not been too bad a start, Dawlish reflected when, rounds completed, he finally lay down on the hard, red ground, a hollow scooped for his hip. The final distance covered might have been as much as fifteen miles. The warm darkness enveloped him and for all the loud chorus of croaking frogs he drifted into slumber.

The march resumed with first light. As the column continued north-westwards, dense scrub alternated with more open areas, and much of the ground was broken as before. Progress was steady – seven or eight miles by the time of the noontide break, twice that or more achieved by evening, when they bivouacked by another small lake, this one fed by a muddy stream. Animal prints were baked into the dry mud at the edges, but the presence of so many men ensured that no beast approached in the night, call plaintively as they might.

211

After the men had been settled and the sentries posted, it seemed churlish to Dawlish not to invite Lutz to eat with his own officers and himself, frugal as the meal might be. The mood was tense as they sat around a fire, attempts to maintain a conversation on neutral topics – the ground they had passed over, the unseen wildlife – petering out despite all O'Rourke's attempts at humour. Lutz's few interventions were dismissive, even contemptuous, of the reactions of men inexperienced in this country. One by one, the officers excused themselves to make their rounds, leaving Dawlish and Lutz alone together in uncomfortable silence.

"Are you a medical doctor, sir?" Dawlish asked at last, conscious that he knew so little of this man or of his agenda and that he must know more.

"No, captain!" Lutz came close to a laugh, one with a hint of condescension. "A doctor of philosophy, earned at Göttingen."

"Is that a university?" Dawlish felt humiliated by his ignorance.

"A university indeed, captain, a university." Lutz might have been speaking to a child. "You are unaware perhaps that it was founded by your King George the Second, also King of Hanover? But then so many Englishmen seem unaware of their own history. A pity, captain, a very great pity."

The temptation to stand up and walk away was strong, but Dawlish needed this man, might rely on him for his life, and for his men's. Better not to show offence, better to milk him of information while he was in boastful mood.

"Of philosophy, you said, doctor. Natural philosophy perhaps, zoology or such?" The most likely explanation for first bringing him to Africa.

"My dissertation was on Schopenhauer, captain." Lutz seemed pleased that Dawlish showed no recognition of the name. "On his thinking on the world as will." He could see that Dawlish was mystified and he rubbed in the salt. "*Die Welt als Wille und Vorstellung*, captain. A concept you are clearly not familiar with."

The words were deliberately wounding, but Dawlish let them pass. "And that – that will – brought you to Africa, doctor?"

212

"I might have been a professor myself, but after I spent time in London with distant relatives – I can see that you've been wondering about my fluency in English – I saw how British power and prestige were fed by your colonies. I wondered why Germany too should not have its place in the sun."

"And that place is East Africa, Doktor Lutz?"

"It could be anywhere where your countrymen and the French haven't already staked claims. But yes, what I heard of East Africa interested me. So, an expedition. Poorly funded, myself and two friends of student days. A steamer to Zanzibar, a landing on the coast, twenty porters – we could afford no more – and a march of three hundred miles. One of my companions dead of fever before we reached the coast again. But enough to see the promise of this land. For agriculture, for mining too perhaps, for settlement by German families. And no shortage of African labour."

It sounded no different to Britain's presence at the Cape and in Natal and yet there was a note of exaltation in Lutz's voice that hinted at a vision of something more.

"And you're now an agent of Bremen trading houses, doctor?"

"Of Oldenburg as well as Bremen companies. Signing commercial treaties that may in time lead to mutually beneficial business. Purely mercantile concerns, captain."

"And for that you need your askaris?"

"It's a dangerous place, captain – you know that. A man without official backing would be a fool to travel here without armed escort. As those well-intentioned but naïve German subjects whom I intend to avenge learned at their cost." Lutz stood up. "Good night, captain." He faded into the darkness.

What he had last said had been the most offensive of all, Dawlish thought. There had been nothing naïve about Abbot Albrecht von Hohenfels, and it seemed unlikely that he would ever have wanted to be avenged.

And certainly not by Lutz.

*

213

Another dawn departure, another long morning of steady but exhausting progress, something almost trancelike by now in the action of putting a foot forward, and then another and then another yet again. All sense of time vanished in the rising heat and dust, ability to maintain alertness a struggle.

Two of Ross's men returned to the column just before midday. They were hurrying a shambling figure between them. As they approached, Dawlish saw that it was an almost naked African, his body skeletal, his hair a matted clump, his face a mask of terror as he glanced from one flanking marine to the other as if fearful of a blow.

"Mr. Ross's compliments, sir. He said you'd like to see this poor chap." Pity in the marine's voice.

The man was cringing, his head bent, his whole body trembling. A rusty iron ring encircled one ankle, a foot and a half of chain trailing behind. The flesh above and below was heavily scabbed as if repeated rubbing raw had bloodied and dried and bloodied the flesh again in endless succession.

"Where did you find him?" Dawlish, appalled, kept his tone steady.

"He blundered into us, sir, accidental like. Then he turned and ran. We found him hiding in a gully."

"We must be near the slaver's column, sir." O'Rourke was by Dawlish's side. "The poor fellow must have escaped."

The man had sunk to his knees now, was throwing his sticklike arms around Dawlish's calves, touching his head on his boots. The action was simultaneously pitiful and repellent. Dawlish stepped back, leaving the wretch sprawling in the dust. He had an instant feeling of shame that he had reacted so.

*Am I not a man and a brother?*

Lutz had joined them. "I can talk to him, captain!" He reached down, caught the man by his hair and dragged him back on his knees.

"I won't have that, doctor." Dawlish repressed the urge to strike him. "Stand back."

A look of venom, but Lutz stood back. "You've haven't got the language to get anything out of him, captain. You don't know what they're like. There's only one thing they understand."

Wainwright would have managed it better, more effectively, more humanely, but Wainwright was not here.

Dawlish spoke to O'Rourke. "Take this unfortunate into the shade of that tree over there. Sit him down. Give him water and something to eat. It's time for the noonday break. We have time." He turned to Lutz. "We'll try him again in a half-hour. There'll be no brutality, you understand?"

No answer. Lutz stamped away.

It would have taken hours, perhaps days, before the captive's terror could wholly fade, but in the half-hour allowed O'Rourke calmed him enough to accept a few distrusted mouthfuls of water and crushed biscuit sweetened with sugar.

Lutz – no fool – had recognised that nothing but slow systematic questioning would be permitted. He squatted with Dawlish in front of the captive, whom O'Rourke now-part cradled in his arms, and he began in what was recognisably Swahili.

No reaction. Not from fear alone, but from bewilderment, the terrified eyes flitting from one face to the other.

More questions, still no response. At last Lutz said, "He doesn't understand a word."

"Any of the tribal languages?"

"I've only a smattering in three. But I'll try."

Incomprehension no less profound than before.

"He must be from far west of here. Maybe six or eight hundred miles." Lutz pointed to the man's hair. "That didn't grow in months," he said. "That took years. He must have escaped from some column long before now. He's probably been afraid to go near any of the villages." He stood up. "I'll talk to Sergeant Hassan. Some of his men have been to the west themselves with slavers before I took them on. They might be able to help."

215

They did not – indeed the very sight of dark-skinned men with bandoliers and weapons frightened the prisoner into whimpering terror. That in itself told a lot.

"If you leave him with me I might get something from him, sir," O'Rourke said. The prisoner was clinging to him now, comforted by his enclosing arm. Only the few spoonfuls of pap he had accepted from the Irish officer had done anything to establish a modicum of communication.

"An hour," Dawlish said. "We can't afford more." The track that Achmed's caravan was following could not be more than twenty miles ahead now. Information was vital.

From a distance, Dawlish watched O'Rourke gesturing to the African, offering more food, nodding vigorously when the man gestured back, holding fingers up as if counting, pointing to the iron ring and chain. He was clearly frustrated by the slow progress but working patiently to build trust and comprehension by signs alone.

At last O'Rourke looked towards Dawlish, his silent message clear – *Approach, but slowly.*

The man's hand was held in O'Rourke's now, gently, as a child's or dying man's might be held. Dawlish squatted before them and reached out his own. The African's hand drew back but seemed to relax as Dawlish touched it. A long silence before O'Rourke spoke very softly.

"Doktor Lutz is right. This poor fellow's been here for a long time. I don't think he knows how long or where he came from. Just a long way away. God knows how he escaped or how he survived ever since."

"Was he alone?"

"No. Two or three dozen, I gather – though I could be wrong. There must have been enough to overpower some guards."

"Any left?"

"Eight or ten, I think, but again I can't be sure."

And so, the questioning continued, Dawlish himself joining in now, desperately attempting signs and gestures that might convey meaning, detecting increasing trust when he waved the approaching Lutz away. The African – his name appeared to be Nguza – trembled and sobbed when Dawlish called for a seaman to break the iron ring. It was so

216

corroded that doing so took little effort. Dawlish held it dangling from its chain for Nguza to see, screwed his face deliberately into an expression of disgust, and threw it away into the undergrowth. More water then for the prisoner, more food – he was accepting and wolfing it without hesitation now – and there was a sense that he was somehow reassured, wanted to tell more, was trusting more, was himself frustrated by the difficulty of communication.

Another quarter hour – the halted column enjoyed its unexpected extra rest in shade – and progress with Nguza was infinitely slow. But at last progress.

There was apparently a settlement of a sort ahead.

Nguza would guide them there.

*

They found it before sundown, no huts, just a pathetic collection of shelters made from branches and leaf-thatch that showed signs of being hastily abandoned. Those who had made it, who had survived here for however long, had had no tools, no resources of any kind. The fire smouldering in the centre must have been harvested from the embers of some lighting-ignited blaze in the bush and the blackened bodies of two small animals – cane rats perhaps – were skewered above it. No sign of pottery, but several gourds, no metal, no cloth of any kind. These people had survived here as primitive man might have eked out an existence millennia before, captives of terror and of ignorance of their whereabouts, fearing to venture far from this haven.

And a safe enough haven it was too, Dawlish recognised, for it lay in a small bowl-shaped depression fringed with thick brush, almost invisible unless directly encountered, easy to miss if passed by a hundred yards on either side. A pool at the centre, green and stagnant and shrunken back from caked-mud edges, could only be rain-fed.

It was ideal, Dawlish thought, not just for the night's camp, but as the depot where food must be cached for when he led his force back with – he hoped – as many liberated slaves as possible. And then on to Nanguruwe. With them, he hoped, would come Nguza's vanished companions. O'Rourke was attempting to convince the African, who now appeared to trust him implicitly, that he must search for them tomorrow and bring them back here.

A sense of foreboding hung over the evening's conference. The track being aimed for must now be within a day's march and the morrow might well bring action. Achmed's caravan might not have yet reached there, in which case an ambush would be essential, but the worst case was that it had already passed through, and was now closer to Mtwara. If so, following it would almost certainly lose the advantage of surprise.

Information was essential, and lacking. Dawlish knew that reconnaissance far in advance of his own column must be essential. The ideal men for it were available – Ross's marines and Lutz's askaris, who had done so well in recent days.

And he himself must lead it.

*

Yet again departure in the cool dawn when the eastern sky was still only faintly brightening. A cold and formal handshake with Lutz, a few last words with O'Rourke – command of the column would devolve on him should the worst happen – and confirmation that two seamen were being sent back to guide the porters with whom Wainwright must be bringing food from Nanguruwe. Then out through the thick brush, heading north-northwest, reaching more open ground an hour after the sun had risen. The scrub grew thinner and was at last dwindled to only scattered clumps. Progress was fast, as Dawlish, and Ross, with two marines, and Sergeant Hassan with two askaris, pressed onwards in the growing heat. Like his men, Dawlish was carrying only a rifle, bayonet, water and ammunition, his revolver left behind as unwelcome weight.

At close to nine o'clock came the first sign of settlement, a small herd of goats moving through the open a half-mile distant to the right, a single human figure among them. More cautious now, darting in silence from one patch of ragged thorn-bush to another. Insects shrilling, birds circling patiently overhead and the noontime heat driving all other life into shade or underground. A mile to the left, a brown cluster of huts, mud-walled, grass thatched, a streak of green before them indicating cultivation. Dawlish felt his heart thump harder at the sight, his mouth drier, and knew that this must be too small to be one of the villages – Nanganga or Mtama – that Lutz had identified as lying on the track. But one or other of them must be close.

The mile that Dawlish did not realise would be the last proved to be the most difficult of all, almost wholly open and dotted with only occasional thorn that gave minimum cover. And the track, when they came upon it, was hardly distinguishable as such, a broad strip of dust that was not scuffed by recent footprints. A patch of fresh goat droppings showed that a herder must have driven his flock though here shortly before, his own footprints hidden by the tiny hoof-marks. No discarded bodies, no human waste, no detritus, no hint of suffering and misery trudging along here for days, even weeks, past. There were scattered bones at one point, but they had whitened long since, and might have been either animal or human.

The race had been won. Achmed Ibn Hamed's caravan had not yet reached this point and was still on its way.

Now for the reckoning.

*

Communicating with Sergeant Hassan was difficult, but not impossible. He had a few words of German and Dawlish had even fewer, picked up on that excursion that Kirk had organised for the *Hildegarde's* scientists at Zanzibar. A few minutes of questions and answers, frustrating for both parties, confirmed that Hassan had been on this track before, trekking with Lutz to negotiate treaties.

"Chinguru?" Dawlish pointed south-westwards. He had to repeat it several times, with minor variations in pronunciation, before Hassan said, "Ndiyo!" Yes.

"Nanganga?" The next village on the track through which Achmed's caravan must pass.

"Ja," Hassan said, "Ja, ja! Ndiyo, hakika, ndiyo!" Yes, with certainty. Dawlish turned, pointed north-eastwards. "Mtama?"

Hassan was sure of it.

Mtama was a big village, Lutz had said, and he had signed a treaty with its chief. Achmed's column would be expecting food, water and rest there. Dawlish's plan had been to occupy the place but now the memory of his raid on Nanguruwe returned. He had carried it off successfully, but surprise had been on his side. Had there been a larger slaver force there, then the fighting in the alleyways between the huts would have been desperate. And Achmed's column had up to eighty armed men, hardened Somalis and Baluchi mercenaries as well as Arabs.

Better, if possible, to catch them on the open track where they would have little chance of taking cover.

A stealthy advance a mile north-eastwards parallel to the track, away from the village seen earlier, found a small ravine patchily fringed with scrub. On for another half-mile – the thorn bush was less scattered here, the cover better – and then a larger hollow, on the northern side of the track, another ideal hiding place. Provided a goat-herd did not blunder directly into either, the hollow and the ravine would provide ideal staging posts for an ambush, one to halt the head of Achmed's unseen but oncoming column, the other to block the rear.

Dawlish made his decision. He would fight here.

It was almost eleven now. It was essential to get word back to the main column – the bluejackets and marines, and Lutz's askaris – and to guide them to their positions. Dawlish pondered his options. Achmed would almost certainly place the majority of his armed followers at the head of his column, and leave a smaller force at its tail to deter escape by the slaves. Better then to concentrate the greater part of the ambushing force in the hollow. Ross's contingent of marines and bluejackets could be relied on for steady fire and iron discipline as regards concealment. Better too to group the askaris with them. Cooperating or not, Dawlish was reluctant to allow Lutz's force to operate wholly independently. He himself was going to remain in this position to command the combined force – and to ensure compliance from the German. O'Rourke, with Leigh's group, must hide itself at ravine further back so as to deal with the rear of the slaver column. Theirs might be the most difficult task of all, to remain in bated-breath concealment as the column plodded past, waiting for the sound of attack on its head before launching their own assault on its tail.

The decision whether to remain here himself, or to go back to guide the main force to their positions was a hard one. He decided finally to stay and to send back Ross with a scribbled instruction for O'Rourke and a more courteously worded request to Lutz. An askari would accompany Ross as guide – these men's tracking and concealment skills were priceless.

After Ross had left there was nothing to do but wait below the hollow's lip, to watch the track for movement and to fret silently over the fact that there was no water here, that the positions selected, ideal though they might be for ambush, would be made untenable once water bottles had been emptied. No matter how strict the drinking discipline could be – a sip every two hours would be the maximum allowable – these positions could not be held for longer then twenty-four hours. And if Achmed's column did not arrive in that time...

Dawlish banished from his mind – for now – that possibility of failure. Most important was that the remainder of his force get here undetected and take cover. Better ambush positions could not be desired.

Success was within his grasp.

## Chapter 21

The wait seemed endless, the noonday's heat a parching oven as Dawlish's small group - Hassan, two marines and an askari – kept watch from the hollow. Once, in the distance, a herder and a line of goats moved slowly across open ground before losing themselves again in the scrub. There was no other sign of life. Dawlish had deliberately not brought his field-glasses – a single reflected flash of sunlight could be disastrous – and his eyes ached in the glare as he searched for any sight of his oncoming force.

"There's something there, sir." Addison, one of the marines. He was pointing to the slightest smudge rising above the line of scrub to the south-west. "It might be smoke but..."

"It's dust," Dawlish said.

The recognition sickened him. There was no mistaking the growing streak for what it was, hundreds of plodding feet throwing up red dust. It was at most two miles distant and the head of the slaver column would be here in an hour at best, at worst sooner. His own people could not reach here in time. His ideal ambush position was worth nothing now.

"There, sir. There's some of 'em coming," Addison's whisper told that he was as horrified as Dawlish. "And yes, there's more."

They were close, five hundred yards distant at most, six figures coming into view as they rounded a bend in the track, three ahead, three behind. Even at this distance they gave an impression of wariness, pausing briefly to scan the ground to either side, moving forward again with caution, clearly scouting ahead for the column that followed a mile behind. It would be impossible to leave the shelter of the hollow without being seen by them.

Dawlish gestured to the others to stay crouched down and he edged along the lip towards the thickest clump of scrub there. Through it he could make out part of the track at least, even if the oncomers were temporarily blocked from view.

Two, three minutes passed, and then he could see them again through the tangled bush-stems. Their once-white robes were brown with dust and had been gathered up for easier movement. Their rifles looked like Chassepots. Bandoliers crossed their chests and short swords hung from their leather belts. The faces beneath their head cloths looked Somalian. It would be easy to take them down – a single volley, followed by the bayonet, would see to that – but there could be no gain in it, not with the larger party following close behind.

Dawlish slid back down, gripping his rifle hard to stop his hands trembling, saw the questioning faces of the others. He raised a finger to his lips. It was essential now to remain still, to listen for the oncoming tread, to hope that no call of nature might draw a scout from the track in this direction.

The sound of voices, no hint of alarm in them, once a laugh. They must be level with the hollow, must not have suspected its location behind its fringe of bush. Slowly the voices weakened but Dawlish waited until they must be well past before he raised himself to peer through the cover of the bush again. He could see their backs a hundred yards distant, wholly unaware of his group's presence. He craned forward to get a better view to the south-west. The rising cloud was closer now and, even as he watched, more brown-dusted figures were emerging at the curve there, two dozen or so, armed like those who had gone before, and with no less an impression of wariness. A gap of fifty yards, and then a similarly sized group following, not marching in any obvious order, but still giving an impression of some discipline and purpose. They were almost level with the ravine where O'Rourke's force should have been sheltering had it reached here in time.

Dawlish watched with mounting dismay as more of the column came into view, individuals still indistinguishable, a solid mass crawling painfully forward like a dying caterpillar. Still they came on, a line already two hundred yards long, and still more emerging into sight. The head of the column was close to Dawlish's hiding place by now, plodding forward with only the occasional, weary-sounding, remark between the guards, not only Somalis, as before, but also Arabs and many black Africans, most in variations of robes but a few in semi-European dress. They too were oblivious of his presence and clearly forcing a pace that must be killing in this heat. Their faces were tired, their eyes dead, men marching in a trance of heat and sweat and fatigue.

At this moment some fifty men – seamen and marines and askaris – should be rising above the hollow's lip, pushing forward through the screening brush, dropping to one knee and pouring a volley into them, and then another and another, before driving with their bayonets towards the stunned survivors. A minute's work would have killed the majority and, a half-mile behind, O'Rourke's contingent, alerted by the firing, should be launching itself from the ravine to butcher the rear-guard.

*What might have been, would not now be.*

The vanguard had passed. The caravan's most precious commodity followed. The Africans who carried the loads were clearly not slaves – they looked neither cowed nor poorly fed, but rather strong, fit, men who must be porters supplied by villages such as Nanguruwe. They were working in pairs, one before, one after, poles carried between them and resting on pads on their shoulders. The long, curved, items wrapped in coarse cloth and slung beneath the poles could only be elephant tusks, two or three together. A few guards kept pace alongside but needed no brutality in their urging. These porters had crossed half of Africa, east to west, and now their homes, and their rewards, were within reach. Dawlish counted – ninety-seven loads in all, at least two hundred tusks, probably much more. A year from now their ivory might be billiard balls, or carved cameo brooches on ladies' dresses, in Europe or America. More porters followed, the loads on their heads probably food or other supplies. Behind them rode a single figure on a donkey, his robes clean, jewels sparkling on the curved dagger on his belt, a look that seemed almost benign on his white-bearded and wrinkled face.

At another time and place Achmed Ibn Hamed would have been taken for a kindly grandfather. An Arab servant was leading the animal and another was keeping pace alongside, holding a fringed parasol above his master's head. A cluster of guards marched behind. Two thirds of Achmed's armed followers must be assigned to the vanguard for protection of his person and his ivory. There was clear method in it – should the caravan come under attack, this portion could make a fighting escape, leaving all else abandoned.

And now came Hell.

It had been pitiful, and angering, to see slaves packed in the filthy holds of dhows, worse still in the industrialised squalor of the *Lady Emmeline*, but Dawlish saw now that their plight had been nothing compared with the agony of the march that would have brought them to the coast. The men came first, skeletal, emaciated figures, some wholly naked, a few with loin-cloths, many streaked with their own ordure, barely able to totter forward, their eyes bulging in terror as they cringed back from the whip-armed guards ranging back and forth along their ranks. Most were unbound – it would be hard to imagine them capable of making any break for freedom – but a few had shackles around their ankles, joined by chains, the flesh above and below the iron rings chafed red-raw. Worst still, for it seemed more liked a punishment than any necessary deterrent to escape, were the dozen or so pairs who were

224

linked by forked branches secured around their necks. As they drew level, Dawlish saw one leader of a pair collapse forward, dragging his companion with him. He lay moaning weakly, then crying out in agony as the second man tried to rise, wrenching the fork around his neck as he did. The stream of slaves passed around them, eyes cast away, too terrified to help, and trudged on. A guard moved towards the pair, dragged them to their feet and slashed his whip at them as they stumbled forward again.

There seemed no end of them – some three hundred before Dawlish, repelled, gave up the attempt to estimate numbers. They staggered forward in silence, shamed by their own stench and filth, by the absoluteness of their subjugation. The only sounds rising above the shrilling of the noonday insects were the clink of chains and the intermittent shouts of the guards.

At last, and worst of all, came the women, fewer than a hundred – though there must have been almost as many of them as of men to start with. Their heads were bowed, their shrunken breasts flapping, despair incarnate in their dead and uncomprehending eyes, hope abandoned long before with the bodies of their children.

Dawlish, sickened to the point of nausea, could not tear his eyes away. His own fear of detection was as nothing compared with the anger, the vengeful hatred, that was boiling up within him, made worse by the acceptance that his delay in getting his force here had let the opportunity for retribution and liberation to slip through his fingers. A decision to have pushed forward with his full force, rather than to reconnoitre ahead, would have been enough.

At last the rear-guard, two dozen Arabs and Somalis, as well armed as those who had gone before and with whips in their hands to drive the last of the women onwards.

Then the caravan was past, shuffling, stumbling, plodding north-eastwards towards Mtama and leaving dust rolling in its wake. Dawlish waited for five minutes after the rearmost guards had disappeared around the distant bend before he beckoned to his men to rise. The fear in which they had crouched was plain on their faces, yet it was perhaps the significance of smell that had reached them that worried them most. It implied more than any sight.

"Was it bad, sir?" It took a lot for a man like Addison to question an officer directly.

"Bad," Dawlish said. "Very bad. But we'll make it better."

Somehow

*

No time for regret. All focus must now be on salvaging the situation. It was almost two o'clock – some four hours of daylight remained. Provided the remainder of his force arrived in the next hour, Dawlish knew that he would still have a chance of catching the caravan. His people would be tired, but their fatigue would be as nothing when compared to that of Achmed's column. They must be capable of moving faster and of overhauling it. He decided to wait here rather than go back to meet them – Ross knew exactly where to bring them.

They arrived less than an hour later, moving stealthily forward in Indian file, two hundred yards separating them, the twin columns of brown-clad askaris and of Ross's force heading towards Dawlish's position. They advanced in ones and twos, waiting in cover, flitting forwards, fading into the shadows, then darting on again. Lutz himself was the first to arrive, and there was confirmation that a half-mile to the right, guided by the askari who had accompanied Ross, O'Rourke's and Leigh's group was pressing forward towards the ravine. Dawlish sent Addison with a message to O'Rourke to leave his men resting in cover there and then come to join him.

The conference in the hollow was short. The churned-up dust of the track had already told Lutz and Ross and O'Rourke that the caravan had passed. Disappointment was written on their faces.

"What now, captain?" The usual arrogance was missing from Lutz's tone. He seemed beaten, the others also, and they were all tired, as their men must also be.

Dawlish had been ready for this, the sense of deflation, of failure despite best efforts, for he had felt it himself. But as he had waited here he had decided what must be done. There could be no subtlety about the tactics, only reliance on shock and brute force. And he himself must manifest an absolute certainty, however little he must feel it himself.

"Your askaris can move faster than my people, doctor." A statement of fact. "Quietly too. And they understand the terrain."

Lutz nodded.

"They set a cracking pace. It's damn difficult keeping up with them." Grudging respect in O'Rourke's voice.

"Achmed's caravan isn't much more than an hour ahead at the rate it's crawling," Dawlish said. "We could overhaul it in two if we can keep up that same cracking pace. We'll still have an hour of daylight to settle the business."

"We'll do it, sir" O'Rourke spoke as if to forestall Lutz. Ross was nodding.

"A Prussian sergeant-major trained my askaris." Lutz snapped.

Pride was at stake on both sides – no bad thing.

"This is the caravan." Dawlish traced its features in the dust with a twig – the vanguard, the ivory, Achmed and his escort, the slaves, the rear-guard, the approximate numbers.

"I want your fellows to get ahead of the caravan, doctor. In silence. Absolute silence," Dawlish said. "I trust you can get them there?".

"Do not doubt it, captain." Lutz spoke as if the question had been an insult.

"You'll need to move parallel to the track – on the southern side, quietly, under as much cover as possible, but fast, damn fast. You'll block the track when you get there – at least a half mile ahead of the vanguard. Take it under fire from cover – from under cover, mind you – as it nears."

"We'll be outnumbered," Lutz said. "We can't hold for long."

"You won't need to, doctor," Dawlish said.

And he detailed the rest of the plan.

No subtlety, a gambler's throw indeed, and just three hours of daylight left.

*

227

The brush was mercifully thick on both sides of the track, dense clumps with only the shortest of intervals of open ground between them. Lutz and his askaris were pressing ahead, unseen, parallel to the track's southern side, while Dawlish, with Ross and twenty-five men, was moving fast, never less than a hundred yards from it on the north, but still close enough to see it in places. A half mile behind, O'Rourke and Leigh were following with eighteen bluejackets.

Dawlish sensed that the men's fatigue had faded with the prospect of imminent action, as indeed his own had done. The pace was better than he could have hoped. Rough, scarcely literate, prone to drunkenness and brawling ashore, many of his men might be, but what they had encountered of the slave trade in recent weeks, afloat and ashore, had aroused their fury as well as their contempt. The officers felt no less strongly. That anger, coldly directed, would partly compensate for lack of numbers.

Glanced briefly through gaps in the scrub, the track was still empty, the caravan still somewhere ahead. A half hour passed, then forty minutes. The shadows were lengthening – the sun slipping fast now towards the horizon. Still onwards, each footfall, each crunch of gravel or dried herbage seeming to the marchers like pistol shots loud enough to carry for miles. Then, through a gap, half-hidden in the fog of red dust, the rear of the column was glimpsed at last, its guards intent only on driving the lagging women forward. No sign of alarm, no awareness of armed men overtaking the column – and the askaris must be even further ahead than Dawlish's group. He resisted the urge to order advance at the double. Everything depended now on remaining concealed as the distance to the head of the column lessened. O'Rourke and Leigh were following behind – the rear-guard would be their concern.

Five cautious minutes more – the briefest sightings showed Dawlish that the ivory-porters were now two hundred yards to the right. Another five minutes would carry his group level with the caravan's head. The scrub ahead was thinning, concealment would be more difficult and…

A volley crashed out ahead, almost a score of rifles – Mausers – blasting as one. Silence that lasted seconds before panicked shouting that was then drowned in another volley, and then the firing settled into an irregular staccato.

Lutz's askaris had edged ahead of the vanguard and were attacking.

Time to join the battle.

## Chapter 22

They drove forward in two groups, half with Dawlish on the left, the remainder with Ross to the right, pounding through the gaps between the thickets towards the rifle fire and noise of confusion ahead. They emerged suddenly on open ground, the track some fifty yards before them. Panicked by the askaris' firing, figures were breaking from the caravan. Ivory porters had dropped their loads and were dashing for cover, some directly towards the bluejackets emerging from the scrub, pausing in shock as they saw them, then turning back to add to the chaos they had left. Achmed's escort was directly before them, had made no attempt to move forward to support the vanguard, and their master must be sheltering behind them. They too had seen the attackers, were frozen in shock that could last only instants longer.

"Kneel! Rapid fire!" Dawlish and Ross shouting in unison.

The drill had been practised a hundred times and more on ship and shore, the seamen and marines – and Dawlish himself – dropping to one knee, raising their Sniders, sighting, firing, pulling the breech block open and flipping the weapon over to drop out the spent case, reaching into ammunition pouches, feeding in another round, sighting and firing again. And again, and again, five rounds in succession.

Lashed by the leaden hail, jerking and falling as the terrible half-inch slugs ripped through flesh and shattered bone, half of the guards went down without firing a shot in return. The remainder were breaking and running back towards the brush beyond, one dragging a donkey with him, the rider crouched on its back and barely keeping hold. Guards and porters breaking from the column were now mixed in a confused mob with no thought for anything but flight. Shackled slaves were stumbling after them, even the wretches linked by forked yokes, and from even further back along the caravan came the sound of yet more pandemonium.

"Cease firing!"

The threat here was neutralised for now but there was still shooting forward, and to the left, where Lutz's askaris had the vanguard under fire. The sharper bark of the Mausers was interspersed with the deeper reports of Chassepots – the hardened Somali mercenaries there must still be holding their own. Onwards now at the double, bayonets extended, pushing on through more fugitive porters dispersing before them. Further firing was erupting behind – O'Rourke and Leigh had fallen on the rear of the caravan, must be wreaking similar havoc there.

A half-dozen men – dust-covered robes, bandoliers, rifles, something like resolution on their faces – were running towards Dawlish's force, their nerve breaking as they saw them coming, turning to dash back as a marine's shot took one down. Another tripped, fell, was trying to rise when a bluejacket's bayonet smashed into his chest. The remainder fled back the way they had come, another falling as a marine's shot – an impressive one, delivered while standing – tore into his back.

But these were the only fugitives – so far – from the slaver vanguard. As Dawlish's group thrust forward past the confusion of porters, past the heaps of discarded ivory, a long streak of rolling gunsmoke told that the greater part of the mercenaries had taken whatever cover they could find on either side of the track. A hundred yards ahead, crouched behind any scrap of vegetation, or in the slightest hollows, they were firing slowly, deliberately – no panic here – towards the thicker brush ahead. Wreathing smoke was drifting there also, orange flashes stabbing through it, the askaris holding their position with all the tenacity of which that Prussian sergeant-major who had trained them would have been proud.

"Spread out! Down! Hold fire!" Dawlish realised that amid the screaming rounds and rolling smoke, and intent only on the enemy ahead, the slaver's vanguard was oblivious of his approach. That could not last.

"Select your targets!" Better to bring them under fire from prone positions here, better not to risk blundering into the askaris' rounds, even if those were less frequent now, for their ammunition must be all but expended.

Even as he spoke he saw fifteen or twenty of the mercenaries rising from cover on the left of the track. They were bunching – stupidly – as they rushed towards the askari position, some with rifles cast aside and swords in their hands, while over to their right their fellows were pouring an intense fire to cover them.

"There! Rapid fire!" Dawlish was rising to his feet to point towards backs of the racing attackers. He dropped to one knee, raised his Snider, drew bead on a dusty torso – it was hard to hold aim on the running figure – and fired an instant after reports rippled along his line. He saw that he had missed, others too, but three of the Arabs or Somalis were down, one struggling to his feet but flung down by another round as Snider-fire scourged them again.

Caught between two fires, the mercenaries were slowing, hesitating, diving into whatever cover they could find, while to the right of the track their comrades there, alerted at last to the menace from behind, were turning to face it.

"Yours, Mr. Ross!" Dawlish pointed towards them but shouted to his own dozen to maintain fire on the broken assault. The vanguard's fire was spasmodic now and the urge to drive in on them with the bayonet was almost too strong to resist.

And then, suddenly, they were breaking, running from cover towards the scrub patches on the far side of the track, some dragging wounded companions with them.

"Keep firing!"

It was no time for mercy, the open ground now a field of slaughter. A few were throwing down their weapons, raising their arms in despair, spinning and falling as the bluejackets' and marine's drum-fire blasted into them while the askaris – they were emerging from the brush – lashed them from the flank.

The resistance was dying, the survivors plunging into the formless mob of porters and slaves and guards fleeing into the bush. Dawlish and

Ross were moving forward now across the track, their men in line, five or six yards between them, bayoneting any wounded guard struggling to rise, brushing past cowering porters who were pleading on their knees for mercy. From far to the right, rifle fire was still sounding above the cacophony of fear rising from the slaves bunched where O'Rourke and Leigh were still pressing their attack.

The vanguard had disintegrated, was no longer a cohesive force but a scattering of terrified individuals, intent only on their own survival. Several had fallen to their knees, weapons cast aside, arms held high, terror on their faces as they begged for quarter. Dawlish found one directly before him – a Somali, abject despair in his eyes, his pleading a babble. He lifted his rifle to smash its butt against the man's temple, and as he did he felt something within him suddenly stay his hand. *I can't kill like this, I'm not like them.* He held the man's gaze, then jerked his head back, the message instantly comprehended – *Go back to the track, submit, live.* Screams to the right told of a guard writhing on the ground as a marine stabbed a second and a third time before pushing forward again with the line of his fellows.

"Mr. Ross! Here!"

The marine lieutenant joined him.

"Hold the line here with half your men, Ross. No further advance."

The shadows were long, the sky red in the west, darkness less than a half-hour away. Pursuit of fugitives – slaves and porters as well as guards – could soon be no more than blundering in thickening scrub.

"And I want prisoners. Truss them up with their head cloths, with anything you can. We'll need them."

Lutz approached, elation glinting in the eyes behind the thick spectacles. His askaris were clearly exhausted but were still advancing towards the brush. There was no mercy for any in their path.

"Well met, Captain Dawlish!" Lutz extended his hand as if he were Blücher meeting Wellington on the evening of Waterloo. "Success, captain, success and retribution!"

Brief discussion, and Lutz too saw the wisdom of not pushing on. His men were all but out of ammunition. Two had been killed, one badly wounded. Dawlish's own force had suffered none.

To the right, towards what had been the tail of the caravan, spasmodic gunfire still sounded. The slaves had been there and many must already have lost themselves in the scrub, their plight as bad now as it had been before this attempt at liberation. And Achmed was somewhere there also, and Dawlish wanted him.

He took a dozen men, *Leonidas* bluejackets all, and hurried back down the track, littered as it was with dropped loads of ivory. Then bodies, those of Achmed's escort who had been smashed down by the first volleys before the remainder had taken flight. Most lay still but a few, moaning, were crawling towards some imagined deliverance. Further on, slaves were clustered in small groups, too terrified, too bewildered, too shocked even to fly, whimpering and shrinking back as the armed men approached. And beyond them, south of the track, Dawlish saw O'Rourke's force, crouched in the cover of a small ridge, rising to fire towards a dense thicket, dropping back again to reload. There was still resistance there, gunsmoke wreathing from the scrub, intermittent flashes in the murk indicting that slaver guards – and not a few – were still holding out there.

Dawlish brought his men forward at a running crouch, took shelter below the ridge – it rose only three feet or less above the surrounding ground. There were less than ten men there, O'Rourke with them. He edged carefully towards Dawlish.

"Leigh's on the far side," he said. "We've got them hemmed in, but they're damned if they're coming out."

"How many?"

"Thirty or more. And their boss must be with them."

"Achmed?"

"Take a look, sir. Carefully now. There's one of the fellows who's a bloody good shot. He got poor Higden straight through the head."

Dawlish raised himself carefully, eyes just over the crest. Half-way towards the scrub, collapsed on the open ground, was the grey donkey, a little further on a slumped body, its robes dusty as well as blood-marked – not Achmed in his finery.

It was almost dark. A quick conclusion was essential.

"Can you get word around to Leigh?"

"Staunton's the man. He's like an eel. They won't see him."

"Get him."

Dawlish recognised him as an *Ibis*. He handed him a box of lucifer matches taken from his pouch.

"My compliments to Mr. Leigh. He's to get fires started on his side. Dry kindling in bunches thrown into the bushes. You understand?"

Staunton did, and he scurried off into the increasing gloom.

"Have your men ready for them, Mr. O'Rourke," Dawlish said. "They'll hang on as long as they can, but when they do come it'll be in a rush. Hold fire until then. But I want Achmed alive. He's easy to recognise. He's old, he's in clean robes."

The word was passed along the line. The firing died. An odd flash from the thicket's dark mass identified a defender shooting at some imagined movement. Behind, and to the right, was the sound of women wailing, of distraught voices calling to lost companions, of the clinking chains of shackled men seeking cover.

A long five minutes. The sudden tropic darkness fell, the first stars in the velvet dome above, only dim light from the thin crescent moon. The waiting was worse than the rage of battle, hands beginning to tremble, stomachs hollow, hearts pounding in recognition of what had just passed, what might be yet to come.

At first the faintest whiff of wood-smoke, then a yellow glow, barely glimpsed through the shielding tangle, and another, and another. Then the first shouts of alarm, a glow exploding into scarlet life, another following, flames suddenly rushing high as the tinder-dry thorn caught light, sparks cascading upwards in the rolling smoke. Figures were now silhouetted against the inferno behind, hesitating, all but paralysed by recognition of the stark choice confronting them.

"Stay down! Wait for my word!" Dawlish felt revulsion at what he had unleashed, knew he had no alternative.

A ripple of shots from the burning thicket, an ineffective diversion for the group that now burst from it on the left, black shapes outlined against the inferno behind, robes and head-cloths flapping, swords upraised. They shouted as they came on, their cries of despair or

234

desperate prayers lost in the cracking of the blazing thorn and the roar of the spreading fire.

"Up now! Fire at will!"

Dawlish's Snider was resting on the ridge-crest and he swung the weapon to hold a figure bounding directly towards him in its fore and rear sights. To his left and right other men were rising also, to kneel or stand, all selecting their targets, reflected flames dancing on their fixed bayonets. The Arab charging at him was screaming hatred, his sword drawn back across his opposite shoulder for one last, deadly swing. He was twenty yards distant when Dawlish squeezed his trigger, felt the kick into his shoulder, saw his victim spin and collapse. Other rifles were barking now, other figures falling, and yet the wave of fugitives from the flames still rolled forward, even as another group of them burst from the thicket to the right.

Time only for one shot more – the Snider was a clumsy weapon from which to eject. Dawlish took another man, scarcely ten yards from him, and other rifles were throwing yet more down, but there was no time to reload before the human torrent would crash over the low ridge.

"Bayonets!"

No other order needed – the men to Dawlish's left and right were already snapping into the stance that he had himself practised for a quarter-century, back bent and chest drawn in, weight behind the deadly spike directed at the height of any oncomer's chest.

Then the clash, a melee of thrusting and slashing in the flame-shot half-darkness, the first of the attacking slavers impaled as they crested the ridge, those following stumbling across them to be met with savage thrusts. Dawlish drove at an Arab blundering towards him with only a knife in hand, felt his blade rip through the soft flesh on the man's right side, dragged it free, saw him fall, was ready as another rushed towards him, sword upraised. He swung his rifle across and up, the bayonet-tip tearing diagonally across the attacker's chest. The sword dropped and, as the slaver clutched at his wound, Dawlish was throwing his rifle back, then driving it forward again into the man's throat.

He drew breath, glanced to left and right. The line was holding, the slumped bodies along the ridge-crest an obstacle that sapped the momentum of the slavers' charge. Some were hesitating now, edging back towards the flames behind them, a few were even casting down swords and rifles, falling to their knees and raising empty hands. But over to the right, where the flickering light was weakest, a knot of slavers was still advancing from the shadows, slowly at first, then gaining confidence as they came on, then breaking into a run, screaming as they did. Their concentrated mass – fifteen or twenty men – reached the ridge, its progress maintained even as its leaders died on the bayonets of O'Rourke's men there. Now they were across the obstacle, their numbers concentrated at a single point, but they were slowing, surprised by their own success, uncertain where to drive next as O'Rourke drew his bluejackets back to form a thin steel-tipped hedge.

That moment of indecision could not last.

"Hold here!" Dawlish yelled to the half-dozen men to the left, and to those on his right he called "Follow me"

Bayonets levelled, they rushed towards the line's breach, but as they did, the slaver mass was suddenly hurling itself towards the screen before them. Too intent on smashing through, they had no eyes for Dawlish's group rushing from the semi-darkness towards their flank.

O'Rourke's men were falling back – one, at least, was down – and the slavers' momentum was forcing yet further retreat. In the flame-illuminated hell bayonets were parrying and thrusting as swords swung and chopped. Now Dawlish and his six men drove from the shadows, one Arab caught by a bayonet in his side and falling even as his companions swung around to meet the new threat.

And then the last savage fracas that might have lasted seconds or minutes – no survivor would ever remember how long – before the attackers broke, their last fury expended, panic taking hold. At one moment they were still slashing, their wedge on the point of breaking through, and then, an instant later, they were turning and stumbling back as they had come, screaming as the pitiless bayonets behind impaled those who tripped. A new obstacle confronted them, Leigh's bluejackets skirting around from the opposite side of the blazing thicket and charging towards them from the right.

That ended it.

The survivors, many of them wounded, were on their knees, arms raised, abject terror on faces that had inflicted a thousand times worse suffering without conscience. Dawlish ordered the killing to stop, for the prisoners to be trussed with their own garments. He turned back towards the area of slaughter, dreading what he would find. The raging will to survive that had carried him through the storm was now ebbing fast, a depression flooding in him that he knew he must not let master him. Only now did he realise that his left forearm was bleeding – the shirtsleeve was torn and flapping, wet with blood. He had no recollection of how it had happened, found with tracing finger that it was a gash of some three or four inches, superficial, no muscle ripped, no artery severed. He jerked the sleeve free and with his right hand and his teeth managed to bind it around the wound.

A seaman was approaching – an *Ibis*, he did not know his name.

"It's Mr. O'Rourke, sir." His tone said it all.

The body was one of three. O'Rourke lay on top of a man he had died defending, and another was to their side. All had been hacked badly – only his besmirched uniform identified the officer – but they had died hard, a half-dozen slavers slumped around them.

Leigh came up, stood appalled.

"Any other dead?" No time yet to mourn.

"Wylie. His head was split." Leigh said. "And three wounded, one badly. Fairbairn, from *Leonidas*."

Dawlish remembered him – he had landed on Socheong.

"Will he make it?

"He won't last the hour. He's bleeding badly. He's lost consciousness."

And there was Higden too. Six dead, the price a high one.

Back then to pass among the squatting prisoners. Dawlish felt only contempt for them as they cringed and trembled as he moved between them. His mercy began and ended with granting them their lives. He stared into faces numb with dread, dragged back the occasional bent head to scrutinise the features, intent on locating one individual only.

It was two seamen from *Leonidas* who found him.

"He's here, sir! We've got him!" one called.

They were dragging Achmed between them, his feet trailing on the ground, the robe so recently pristine now streaked with dust and smuts, the jewelled dagger gone from his belt and probably now hidden in a seaman's shirt. If so, he was welcome to it.

They flung him on the ground before Dawlish. He tried to rise to his knees, his bruised old-man's features twisted in hatred and despair, but he fell forward. And grovelled.

"Tie him up with the others," Dawlish said and turned away.

The long, dreadful night had only started.

## Chapter 23

At least half the slaves had disappeared into the surrounding darkness but the remainder crouched by the sides of the track, faces blank, eyes dead, most silent, a few mumbling to themselves. Leigh was set to rounding them up. They cowered from his men as they raised them to their feet and urged them, not ungently, to an open patch where they could be easily overseen. Communication was impossible and signs must suffice, but every gesture, however well meant, was interpreted as a threat. Almost a hundred dazed and emaciated figures had been gathered already and more were being brought in. Their misery deepened Dawlish's bitterness, all the worse since there was little more to be done for them for now.

As his anger against Achmed and his slavers seethed within him a small internal voice told him again *I'm not like them*. Small, but persistent, impossible to ignore. Yet still there must be a reckoning.

Satisfied that Leigh had the matter in hand as best he could, Dawlish headed back towards what had been the head of the caravan. The fire had spread, flying sparks igniting other tinder-dry thickets to the south of the track, and the whole area was now bathed in flickering red light. Dawlish met Ross coming towards him.

"We've got the prisoners secured, sir. Forty-seven, no fight left in them. We won't be finding any more tonight." Ross gestured towards the line of burning brush. "If there's any beyond there they're still running."

"They can keep running," Dawlish said. "We've got enough,".

There was better news also. Ross's people had gathered a score of porters and had conscripted them to gather the loads of food and other supplies they had thrown down when they fled.

"Water?" Dawlish's greatest concern now.

"Only a few gourds, sir."

And maybe three hundred parched mouths, perhaps more, to satisfy Dawlish's own men, the slaves, whatever porters he would take with them. The captured slavers' needs would come last.

The recovered loads of food were piled in the middle of the track, three marines guarding them with fixed bayonets, the porters squatting near-by, compliant, relieved that they had not been tied up like the guards who had been herded into a low hollow.

A little further on, more dropped items were being gathered. Supervised by askaris, captured porters were dragging the fallen ivory into two long rows along the track and stripping away the sacking wrappings. A slaver, his head bare and his face bloody, was moving between the rows with Sergeant Hassan, babbling ingratiatingly in Swahili and apparently indicating which tusks might be the more valuable, which should be left in one row, which shifted across to the other. Three porters had been assigned to each row, rearranging the individual tusks according to length, longest to the right, shortest the left.

Lutz was standing between the rows, jotting with a pencil in a small notebook. He looked up as Dawlish neared. The elation that had radiated from him earlier seemed no less powerful now.

"All well in hand, captain," he said. "It'll take another hour to get it right, but the classification is well advanced. The shares will be fair."

"Shares?" The word was offensive. "Shares, Doktor Lutz?" Two hundred yards away liberated slaves, not yet safe, were trembling in misery. Bodies – friends and comrades – were awaiting burial.

"Fair by excellence as well as by number, captain." Lutz had not noticed Dawlish's disgust. "These items here," he gestured to the row at his feet "are of higher quality. And those, in that other row, somewhat inferior, but still valuable. It'll be easy to go down the lines, select from either row in turn alternately, my share, yours, the total equalised as regards quality as well as length. Nothing could be more fair."

"Ivory didn't bring us here, doctor," Dawlish said.

"No, but retribution did! Revenge for German blood! We'll have that when we hang them in the morning," Lutz's voice was rising, was on the edge of a scream. "And payment in ivory too, captain. You think it costs nothing to arm and pay a force like mine? Do you captain?"

"Nobody is going to hang." Killing in the heat of battle was one thing, in cold blood another.

"Shoot them then? You've got ammunition to waste, captain?" The tone shrill, contempt flashing in the eyes.

"Do you believe that Albrecht von Hohenfels would have asked that question?" Dawlish dropped his voice, moved closer to Lutz. "My men are guarding the prisoners. I'll have you shot, doctor, you or any of your people, if you come near them. I'll have work enough to get the slaves moving at first light. That's my concern now."

"And not mine, captain." Lutz spat the words. "I told you that from the start. Our cooperation is at an end!"

Dawlish stepped back. "I'll leave you to sorting your ivory then, Doktor Lutz, and I'll wish you good night."

He turned and walked back through the drifting smoke towards the prisoners. His idea of retribution was different to Lutz's.

*

A few slaves drifted back out of the darkness during the night, even a few porters also. Distribution of food, and of whatever little water there was, went some way to assuaging the slaves' terror of the white newcomers. Those shackled and fork-bound thrashed and whimpered when the first efforts were made to free them from their bonds. A few short sawing cuts with a bayonet easily released the forked branches tied close around the necks but the metal restraints were more difficult. Even though the necessary tools were found among the discarded loads, prising open the u-shaped metal rings that had been hammered close around ankles was of necessity painful and terrifying. And yet, as one

240

slave, and another, and yet another was released and helped to their feet with rough kindness, realisation was dawning that deliverance of a sort was at hand.

Dawlish felt moved as he watched the bonds being levered free. At last twenty-one rusty three-foot chains with now open rings at either end lay in the dust. There was a new use for them now, hammered closed around the ankles of Achmed and a score of his men. The old man raged when he saw Dawlish, his fury worsened as he heard the sound of his shackles clinking as he rose to rant.

"Have them stripped," Dawlish told Ross. "They can find their way home stark naked."

Albrecht von Hohenfels would not have wanted that either, but there was a limit to Dawlish's own compassion and forgiveness.

The flames died during the early hours, though the hot, dry air remained acrid with smoke. Thirst was a torment, one that might be a killer for many on the trek back. The objective must be that well-screened hollow where previously-escaped slaves had found refuge. Wainwright might have arrived there with food by now and the foul pool of water there could represent salvation. The newly-liberated slaves must be herded there – he could think of no other word. Recoil from the idea though he might, there would need to be a degree of compulsion to keep them moving.

Then, suddenly, he remembered the escaped slave who had brought him to that hollow. Nguza, that was his name. He had spoken no language that either Lutz or his sergeant could recognise and must have come from far west of here, perhaps from an area where many of these newly liberated slaves had been captured also. O'Rourke had gained his trust through kindness and, though that officer was gone, Nguza's memory of him – and the striking free of shackles – must still be fresh.

Dawlish sought out Ross, who was now supervising collection of discarded weapons. The French-made Chassepots would have been valuable booty – beautiful rifles, Dawlish recognised, as he examined one – but the extra weight would be an intolerable burden on what already promised to be a nightmare march. They would have to be destroyed. He had already decided another use for their ammunition.

241

"I want two of your best men to head back to the camp at dawn," he told Ross. "Reliable, fit, able to move fast." It was asking a lot after the events of the last twenty-four hours and the lack of sleep.

Ross paused, then said "Gibson. And Foster. They'll do it."

"That slave we found, Nguza, they're to bring him back. There might be some chance of him being able to talk to the slaves we'll have with us, to still their fears, to keep them moving." There were dozens, perhaps hundreds, of tribal languages, Dawlish knew, but there might just be something in common. "And if Mr. Wainwright has reached there then he's to bring his porters forward with as much water as they can carry."

Now another duty.

All burials were bad, but this was the worst of all, a hurried affair, macabre in the dim red light and drifting smoke, with the six bodies laid in a single trench. Dawlish insisted that it be deeper than five feet, even though it must be scooped out with whatever lay to hand. Cloths covered the faces, and then a layer of stones. Dawlish knew the burial service from memory – he had read it too often, and it was never easy – but the fact that O'Rourke had been a Catholic was a complication. Each Sunday, while Dawlish had conducted the Navy's traditional weekly service on deck aft, the dead man had led prayers for *Leonidas's* two dozen Catholics at the bows. Dawlish knew that there was another of the persuasion present among his men this night, a seaman, Walsh, a Liverpool Irishman. He took him aside, asked if he himself might want to pray for O'Rourke.

"Not me, sir. He'd have liked you to do it yourself, sir. He never talked of differences." Walsh brushed his eyes. "He was a good man."

It was over in five minutes, the words heartfelt, if hurried. Gloom hung over the men as they returned to their duties, leaving a single bluejacket to supervise the porters filling the trench, then dragging branches to and fro across it to hide its outline.

*

242

Sunrise at last. The two marines were already on their way back to fetch Nguza, a single mouthful in each water bottle. The slaves were stirring, still dazed and bewildered. The captive slavers – abject in their chains and nakedness – were glancing fearfully towards the seamen and marines guarding them, sensing their contempt, dreading what might yet be in store.

Lutz appeared. His fury had abated and he was politely correct, if not apologetic. He extended his hand and Dawlish took it.

"I too had men to bury, captain. Three. The wounded man died in the night."

"And now, what now, doctor?" Dawlish had already guessed what the answer would be.

"I'm departing now, Captain Dawlish." No mention of hanging nor of further retribution. Defeat had been accepted, if not admitted. "And I'm taking enough porters to carry my share of the ivory." He paused, as if waiting for Dawlish to object, and when he did not, pointed to the two long rows of tusks, sorted and re-arranged during the night. "They're equal in value as far as possible. The choice is yours."

If it was an olive branch, Dawlish was not accepting it. "Take whichever you want, doctor. And where are you going then?"

"To Bagamoyo."

The small settlement on the coast, opposite Zanzibar. At least three hundred miles, but Lutz spoke with casual confidence. Nothing that this arrogant, driven and – yes – courageous man could say would surprise Dawlish now.

"I wish you a safe journey, Doctor Lutz."

"And I you, Captain Dawlish."

And so they parted.

*

The ivory was worth thousands, more likely tens of thousands, but even had it been possible to transport it easily, Dawlish wanted no part of it. Its cost in human lives exceeded any monetary value, however great, and he loathed touching even a single tusk. It had one use now, to punish the man who had unleashed such suffering to bring it here.

The captives – Achmed himself among them – were set to dragging dry brush to make a pyre in the middle of the track. The bluejackets supervising them had found discarded whips and did not hesitate to use them. Dawlish did not object. Further back, the freed slaves were being formed into a column. More had straggled back during the night and the total was almost a hundred and seventy by now. The prospects for any who were still lost would be grim, but there was no time available to search for them. Not with some fifteen miles of waterless trudge ahead.

The heap of brush grew. A marine demonstrated to a half-dozen porters how to destroy a rifle, catching it by the muzzle, swinging it in a long arc to smash the butt against the ground and shatter the stock. Now they set to doing the same, throwing the broken Chassepots on to the heap of wood, their bandoliers of ammunition following, and the clothing that had been stripped from the prisoners.

Now for the ivory.

Dawlish pushed through the captives, found Achmed. He too had been carrying brush and he was exhausted, tottering on his feet, his withered torso striped with weals, some bloody. All fury, all defiance had left him and yet the sight evoked no compassion. Dawlish jerked his head towards the tusks and Achmed understood. He stumbled towards them, the chain that linked his ankles dragging.

"That's far enough." Dawlish had guessed that the man must know some English. He pointed to the first tusk – the longest, well over six feet, and by Lutz's selection the most valuable of all. "Pick it up."

Achmed understood, saw that it was beyond his strength. He looked appealingly towards his fellow captives, many chained, all avoiding his gaze, all humiliated by their nakedness, fearful of the bayonets surrounding them.

"Pick it up, I said."

Achmed lifted the tusk perhaps six inches before his strength failed. He staggered forward as he dropped it. He looked up, eyes begging for reprieve, found none.

It took five minutes for him to drag it to the pyre, as much again to haul it to the top, collapsing there, panting when he finally succeeded. He was pulled off, dumped on the ground beside it and ignored as the other prisoners were set to piling the remaining ivory there also.

The last tusk was laid on the jumbled heap. The prisoners, all but Achmed, were driven down the track and abandoned there, gestures telling them they were free to go. Towards the coast, towards Mtwara. Achmed was jerked to his feet and a burning branch of thorn was thrust into his hand.

No words, no need for them. Achmed saw what was wanted of him, had no will to resist. He hobbled forward, shackles clinking, and drove the makeshift torch into the dry brush. He turned away as the flames caught, saw Dawlish point towards the prisoners plodding down the track. He was free to join them.

Retribution.

And now time to get this broken old man's victims to sanctuary.

*

The pyre was a mile behind, all but burned out by now, its smoke just thin tendrils drifting above the scrub, occasional crackles telling of the last ammunition consuming itself. The shambling pace was set by the slowest of the slaves. Exhausted by the previous day's march, shocked into almost catatonic stupor by the attack, mourning the loss of companions – perhaps even family – who had fled and disappeared, above all tormented by thirst, they had accepted what must seem a change of ownership with absolute docility. Dawlish had placed men at the head and tail of the straggling column, others to range up and down alongside. He had considered taking some of the porters to help carry the weakest but decided against it. They were virtually free men, Achmed's paid labour, and they should not know where the rescued slaves were headed.

An hour passed. Several slaves had collapsed already, were being helped forward by others, arms draped around their necks, slowing the pace still further. A halt was used to hack down branches to make rough hurdles on which to drag them. The last water had been consumed and more collapses must be expected in the coming hours. Somehow the slaves were induced to get moving again. Dawlish knew that he was close to his own limits – his head was aching, his vision blurring, his thirst a rage. His men could be no better, but his state and theirs were as nothing compared with that of the emaciated wretches they were herding – the inescapable word, however unpalatable. Deaths would be inevitable in the coming hours.

And as the sun soared higher, those deaths did come. They had left the track now, were threading between the thickets scattered over the increasingly rough ground. A woman, plodding along without previous need of support, suddenly fell, had only the slightest pulse as she was carried into shade, was dead five minutes later. Dawlish was moved by her loss. Skeletal, breasts withered, open sores on her legs, weals on her back, dimmed eyes that might have witnessed the death of her children, she must have had a will of iron to have survived hundreds of miles of suffering only to die so close to deliverance. Time only to scrape a shallow trench, to cover with stones and a scattering of earth, to blot out acceptance that some scavenger might be worrying her body within hours.

An hour later another died, a man whom a marine had been half-carrying, and soon yet another – the bloody weals around his neck told that he had been freed from a forked branch a few hours before. Most of Dawlish's men were supporting weakened slaves now. Well before noon it was clear that the march could not be continued without a long break in shadow. More would die during it, but they would die with a modicum of comfort, lapsing into torpid death in the shade. Few indeed might be able to stagger to their feet thereafter.

Everything depended now upon the relief the two marines had been sent to find.

*

Dawlish, hidden at the edge of a thicket, was fighting to resist drowsiness as he kept the country just traversed under observation. Half of his men were sleeping, the remainder on watch like himself.

246

A silent admission of failure troubled him. Achmed Ibn Hamed's career and prestige were at an end, and the supply of slaves that Imker had relied upon was now cut off, a major and perhaps final blow dealt to slaving expeditions between Mtwara and the unknown lands to the west.

But the cost had been high, too high, not just the men whom he had led to their deaths but the missing slaves – upwards of a hundred at least – who were now wandering disconsolately somewhere in the bush, a prey to hunger and thirst, to human and animal predators. And more of those who had been rescued were likely to be dead within the day. The thought nagged him that they might have been better off – more likely to be alive, if nothing else – if there had been no ambush, no liberation.

Leigh appeared. He had been watching on the far side of the thicket.

"There's movement, sir. But they're not our people."

Dawlish followed him at a crouch to a small gulley that afforded a good view southward. The ground was rolling, seamed with small ravines, dotted with light scrub. Ross too had been alerted.

"They're lost in a dip there." He pointed. It was some four hundred yards distant. "Twenty or thirty of them, moving fast."

"Not ours?"

"I don't think so. But in some sort of uniform. A bit like Doctor Lutz's people."

Now a drooping flag was rising above the edge of the dip, followed by red caps, black faces beneath. Then dusty jackets that might have been black or grey, crossed with bandoliers. Rifles slung on shoulders, the pace fast, as fast as Lutz's askaris had maintained, dust spurting from their steady tread. Three dozen at the least, and at their head a European in a uniform that must have started as white, a pith helmet on his head. For all that he was portly, he was pounding resolutely forward.

Dawlish knew him, had seen him in stubborn action in Ashanti, had admired him later as a dogged pursuer of slaver dhows off Zanzibar some seven years before, a man Topcliffe had said would never have accommodated to fleet service, but ideal to recruit and train a small army for Zanzibar's sultan.

Brigadier-General Lloyd Mathews had arrived.

247

# Chapter 24

They brought water, no more than was in their canteens, but even that much was enough to save lives. And they brought Nguza, escorted by Gibson and Foster – the two marines looked by now too exhausted even to stand. Nguza moved among the freed slaves, hope on his face that he might find some link to his lost homeland, that some at least would speak his language. It seemed that none did, but with some there was slight commonality of vocabulary and structure that allowed limited communication. He was clearly urging cooperation, pointing towards the pathetic haven to the south where he and his companions had survived. There was nothing to fear from their rescuers, he appeared to be telling them, and he was leading some forward to touch the marines who had brought him here, to show that they were not devils.

For Dawlish and Mathews there was time for no pleasantries other than a handshake.

"Your Mr. Wainwright is following," Mathews said. "Forty porters with him, several of your men, food enough. More water too – your fellows told me how badly you're situated. I thought it better to press ahead to meet you."

He had a greater air of confidence about him now than Dawlish had remembered. It was something more than the bold self-reliance and aggression Mathews had radiated as a junior officer, rather the assurance of a man who knew that he could inspire and lead large numbers, could prevail regardless of obstacles.

"You were delayed." Dawlish tried not to make it sound like an accusation.

"It was a bloody business at Malindi. It took longer than I'd hoped. And getting up the Rovuma was a nightmare. Your Commander Jarvis on the *Ibis* helped all he could but the river level's low. But we're here at last. The sultan's flag is flying at Nanguruwe, and it won't be coming down."

Dawlish scanned the report that Jarvis had sent with Mathews. No sign of Imker's gunboat. The landed sixty-eight pounder was in position on a palm-log mat. Its crew was being rotated on a twenty-four hour basis to reduce exposure to fever, likely to be less on the vessel moored in midstream, away from the swamp's miasma, than among the mangrove. Despite all rigid observance of quinine-wine discipline, five men were down with malaria. There must inevitably be more.

Mathews' askaris were as impressive as Lutz's, some of them Arab or Somali but the majority African. "Slaves too, a lot of them," he said. "Freed at Zanzibar on condition that they'd enter service with me. They were no different to start with than those you've brought with you now. With good feeding and strict training, they learn fast and make damn good soldiers."

Begrimed as they were, that was the impression they gave, their red pillbox caps and dark tunics worn with an air of jauntiness, their rifles spotlessly cleaned and oiled. And Mathews commanded some twelve hundred like them in total, even if he still had only a handful here, and was authorised by Sultan Barghash to recruit yet more.

But the first priority was getting the slaves moving again. Without Nguza it might have been impossible and, even then, the trek through the afternoon's heat was painfully slow. The fittest stumbled on in a daze, the weaker were supported hands laid over shoulders, those unable to walk were dragged on hurdles. Three more died. The sun was setting before the camp in the hollow was reached.

And Wainwright and his porters had already arrived.

Salvation.

*

Two weeks passed, Christmas and New Year with them, celebrated frugally and with forced jollity. Horne volunteered to come over to Nanguruwe from his mission to conduct a service. He could not be refused, but his fifty-minute sermon did little to raise spirits.

Nanguruwe was an armed camp by now, garrisoned by Mathew's force. The fittest of the rescued slaves had been put to work on strengthening the defences. The remainder were still back at the camp in the hollow where Nguza and his fugitive companions had built their shelters. There had been no further deaths for some days and soon they

249

too would be fit enough to be brought to Nanguruwe. A handful of freed slaves had elected to remain there with Nguza – he seemed to have gained an ascendancy over them and they were now communicating effectively in a rapidly-evolving pidgin. Mathews was establishing a small garrison at this point also, the first of a ring of defended outposts that would block inland expansion of the Sultan of Mtwara's domain. Another post was being established at the site of the devastated German mission, and yet another at Horne's own settlement at Kitaya.

Mathews' interview with Nanguruwe's Chief Kikuwa had been short and brutally efficient, leaving no doubt as to which authority now prevailed. Listening to Wainwright's whispered translations, Dawlish remained silent, his role explained as support – as an ally – of the Zanzibari sultan whose sovereign domain this now was. The yellow, red, white and green horizontal stripes of the sultan's flag already drooped over the village and allegiance to it must be absolute. The destruction of Achmed's column and the capture of his slaves had served notice, Mathews said, that any recalcitrance would be mercilessly punished.

Kikuwa made only one effort to protest, addressing Mathews directly, alarmed enough to bypass the custom of answering through his spokesman.

"He says that he has a treaty with Lutz," Wainwright translated for Dawlish's benefit. "He says that Achmed – with whom he says he cooperated with only under duress – could not have been defeated without Lutz. And that Lutz had promised to bring more men here in the future. Not just askaris, but Europeans, heavily armed Europeans. He fears what Lutz will do when he returns."

Mathews snapped a reply that sounded like an order. Kikuwa sent a messenger scurrying from the hut.

"He's trying to play us for fools." Mathews turned to Dawlish. "He knows damn well that we're here to stay but he'll try to use Lutz's name to wheedle whatever advantage from us that he can."

The messenger returned. He was carrying the gilt-framed lithograph of Kaiser Wilhelm and the long tin tube that held Lutz's treaty. Ignoring Kikuwa, Mathews gestured to the boy to hand him the tube. He took it but he waved away the offer of the portrait, then shook out the rolled paper and pulled it straight.

Kikuwa was alarmed, was looking appealingly towards Dawlish, but found no sympathy. He began to speak, but Mathews cut him off by ripping the paper down the centre into two halves. He doubled them, tore again, did so once more, then flung the scraps on the ground and trod on them. There was no need for Wainwright to translate Mathews' words. The import was clear. This treaty isn't worth the paper it's written on. Lutz won't be showing his face here again.

And then the non-negotiable demands.

An oath of loyalty to Sultan Barghash of Zanzibar to be sworn on a Bible, on a Quran and on local fetishes. A food levy for the sultan's troops. Labour for construction of a track from the German mission – the landing point for men and supplies in the future. More labour when called for. Provision of vegetable plots for the liberated slaves and sites on which they could build huts. Acceptance of any mission that the Reverend Joshua Horne would re-establish here and a grant of cleared ground to support it. And, in return, protection from slavers – a boon that Kikuwa clearly did not appreciate. He, and Nanguruwe, had done well from providing porters, food and a resting place for Achmed's caravans.

"He can like it or lump it," Mathews said to Dawlish. "It makes no damn difference. We're here to stay."

And not just here. Mathews had already set his sights on Mtama, the large village close to the ambush site. Lutz had signed a treaty there also, and its chief must soon be disabused of any idea of its worth. A garrison would be established there, and in time, others like it, extending northwards at intervals to Bagamoyo. Previous signature of a treaty with Lutz would be a guarantee of an early visit from one of Mathews' columns.

Dawlish was eager now to withdraw his force. Several men were down with fever – more would surely follow – and fear of his own recurring malaria attacking unexpectedly lurked at the back of his mind. Mathews was well in control and another two hundred of his men were making painful progress up the Rovuma to supplement those he already had here.

The more that Dawlish saw of the small army Mathews had created, the more he was impressed. Except for a single Sikh, the few officers were British – discharged sergeants who had served in India and who had been granted the sultan's commission, and a captain from a county regiment who was evasive about his reasons for having ended up here. Discipline was harsh – floggings were frequent– and the training was relentless, but the troops seemed contented with the status that allowed them to lord it over the villagers. A handful of the younger and stronger liberated slaves had already been conscripted, language difficulties notwithstanding. Any slaver who might fall into their hands might expect scant pity.

Relations with Mathews were cordial but it was clear that he too wanted the naval brigade gone and no other authority present here. He was dismissive about Horne and sceptical about missionaries.

"They stir things up without thinking where they'll lead," he said. "They start what they're incapable of finishing and, often as not, people die as a consequence. Like that fellow of Horne's you mentioned. Buckwell, wasn't it? And those Germans in their so-called abbey."

"Careful," Dawlish said. The truth was brutal. "Horne's vital to you. I wouldn't have been sent here had he not existed. As long as he's here, and better still if his mission is thriving under your protection, Sultan Barghash will be guaranteed Britain's full support."

Horne might not express it like that, but he knew it also.

Dawlish, his wounded arm painful but healing, followed the now-familiar paths to Sali, at the head of the Chidya lake, then on by canoe to the mission itself, to take his farewell. He had already sent some sixty liberated slaves ahead, including women. Mathews had sent a dozen askaris with them to establish a permanent defensive presence there. Though not an immediate concern, the pathway through the bush was to be expanded to a track.

"The hand of God was upon you, Captain Dawlish." Horne greeted him when he stepped out of the canoe. "He strengthened your arm, even as he strengthened that of Saul when he went forth to smite the

252

Amalekites. And you've brought grist for our mill, souls for the saving, benighted wretches to whom the Gospel could never otherwise have been made known."

Those benighted wretches – bewildered too – were already clearing land for vegetable plots and erecting huts.

"So, the German brothers are working with them?" Dawlish was surprised to see them doing so. One – Albert, the Alsatian – was demonstrating how to dig with a spade and the other, Friedrich, was plastering mud on a wall of wattle.

Horne looked uncomfortable, like a man admitting to an embarrassing lapse.

"They don't preach their errors here and they give their labour gladly. Though not for much longer."

"They're leaving?"

"They want to go back to their old mission. To start it again."

It sounded like an impossible aspiration.

"If they do, that'll be protected too," Dawlish said. He would see to that, the only way he could honour von Hohenfels' memory. He half-expected Horne to protest, but he was surprised.

"They're labourers in the vineyard too, captain, erroneous as they are. I won't hold aloof from them."

Horne had new hopes for his own mission too. Mr. Miller's nerve had been restored by the recent news and would be left in charge of the existing settlement on the river. Horne himself would move to Nanguruwe, pick up the work of the martyred Mr. Buckwell – it was easy to imagine him being described as such in missionary journals – and expand activities there. Chief Kikuwa's backsliding would soon be redressed and baptisms would be common among the liberated slaves settled there.

Dawlish sought out the two monks. He spoke to Albert in French.

"What will you live on when you go back?" he asked.

"The vegetable plots will still be there. We'll have enough." The prospect did not seem to worry the Alsatian. "There are walls still standing. It won't be hard to make a shelter. And I understand that you will have people there?"

253

"Not mine, not British. Troops of the Sultan of Zanzibar. They'll be landing supplies there and there'll be some there permanently. You'll have their protection."

"We'll have our labour to offer them if we have need of something – medicines, tools, small items," Albert said. "I'm a carpenter. The jetty will need repair."

Dawlish had not imagined the abbey being reoccupied but now the facilities that von Hohenfels' community had built there were being restored by Mathew's troops and several were already in use.

"I'll see that you're paid rent for the jetty and for any warehouses that need be constructed," Dawlish said. He hesitated to mention it, but he wondered how two men alone could hold out for long, even with faith and hope to sustain them.

Albert must have sensed it. "Others will come, captain," he said. "Not just a new abbot, but men like Friedrich and me also. Men with skills."

"Is there any way I can help you now, brother?"

"It will be enough if you carry a letter to Zanzibar. And if you could forward it to Germany." Albert paused, as if ashamed. "We've got no money to pay for postage and…"

A sudden memory of the chanted Vespers in the torch-lit church, the tranquillity of the moment, the brief release from that sense of evil that had lingered since the *Lady Emmeline*. What was so apologetically requested was laughably trivial by comparison.

"Not just postage, Brother Albert. You're welcome to whatever else you need."

He dismissed their thanks, shook hands, and left them. Theirs would not be the only letter he was being asked to bring. Horne's had something else to accompany it, a thin wadge wrapped in oilcloth.

"A pamphlet," he said. "A memorial to our martyred brothers."

"And to my people also, Mr. Horne?" Six bodies in a single trench, two more buried in a riverside grave downstream.

"Even such men may have their crowns of glory, captain, drunk and profane and debauched though some may have been in life. They too are remembered in my writing."

A hundred-thousand copies, at the least, Dawlish thought, entire congregations in halls and chapels reduced to tears, contributions flooding in, new volunteers stepping forward to share in the work, half-literate innocents like Joyce and his wife, aspiring translators like Dalton, driven visionaries like Buckwell and Horne himself. And the future of the Bethel Mission bought by direct British intervention and protected by a client state of Britain. The sanctimonious and astute old man in Downing Street could not have asked for more.

Dawlish was not sorry to make his farewell. He hoped he would never see this place again, nor Horne either. They walked together to the lakeshore where a canoe waited to take him back down the Chidya Lake.

As he passed the decrepit buildings and the ramshackle church, the row of graves where Horne had already reserved his own place, the African village and the vegetable patches where there was no sense of bustle or of happy gossip, Dawlish wondered if this had indeed been worth so much sacrifice. It was better, without doubt, than what Achmed represented, better than Chief Kikuwa's capricious rule, better than the tawdry deals Lutz offered, but there must be more, far more than this, to be aspired to.

And he did not know what that could be.

*

The landed bluejackets and marines were moving back down the river day by day, the descent as difficult now as the ascent had been, for whole stretches had become so shallow that boats had to be dragged across where they had floated previously. After transferring men to *Ibis,* the emptied craft toiled back upriver again to bring yet more back. Rather than wait at the German mission, Dawlish marched the last contingent along the northern bank to meet them, slow going, but still a gain of time. With them came thirty of Mathews' askaris. The ex-Royal Artillery sergeant who commanded them, now a lieutenant in Zanzibari service, was confident that with two days' instruction from the *Ibis's* gunners, and constant drilling by himself thereafter, they would be well capable of taking over *Ibis's* landed sixty-eight pounder. It would be kept in position

255

for now, hidden by mangrove, but Dawlish had little expectation that they would need to face Imker's gunboat.

For he himself was going to seek that vessel out and destroy her, wherever she might be. He wanted that satisfaction.

Chapter 25

There was little joy in coming aboard the *Ibis*, even though Dawlish's arrival with the last of the landed party heralded her departure from a location and duty that her crew had come to loathe. Awareness of empty hammocks, enervation of bodies debilitated by fever, exhaustion by marching and wading and hauling of those who had come through otherwise unscathed, all combined to cast a pall of depression over the gunvessel. There had at least been the challenge, and the fleeting sense of triumph, for those who had gone upriver. For those who had remained on *Ibis* however the time had been of monotonous routine, overlain by fear of illness.

Jarvis – surly, just short of insubordinate, when he welcomed Dawlish back on board – had felt it, and resented it, most of all. The words were unspoken, but he clearly regarded himself as cheated of the opportunity to share in whatever glory there had been in the fighting ashore. It might have been his last chance of redeeming the reputation he had lost in Borneo. Dawlish could imagine him pacing the decks in long sweltering days and long humid nights and making repeated visits to the landed sixty-eight, in an agony of frustrated hope that Imker's gunboat might at last reappear and afford him personal satisfaction. It was better to leave him to his anger and resentment, to ignore what were close to provocations, to keep relations formally correct, to avoid an explosion of passion that could only be mutually harmful.

Depression had settled on Dawlish also, fight it though he might, while showing no sign of it to officers or crew. It was worst in the night, when the nagging ache of his healing arm kept him from sleep. The enormity and ubiquity of evil, the weakness of goodness confronting it, still troubled him. His expedition would be termed a victory in Horne's pamphlet, would perhaps be hailed as such in the newspapers, would

256

probably merit a pious note of thanks from Downing Street, might possibly earn further advancement through Topcliffe.

Yet to himself it represented only failure.

Horne's mission had been saved, Sultan Barghash's authority asserted, ruin and humiliation inflicted on a brutal slaver. But the cost had been high. Had his expedition never thrust upriver, then Buckwell and Dalton, Abbot Albrecht and his brothers, a half-dozen of his own men – he mourned O'Rourke especially – would still be alive. Horne's mission could still have retained its precarious, if not now-assured, hold.

Hard as it was to admit it, Dawlish knew that the single outright success that could have justified the venture had eluded him. An hour's earlier arrival of his whole force would have allowed a perfect ambush that would have ensured almost instant annihilation of Achmed's guards and rounding up of all the slaves. Instead, in the running battle that had developed, half of the captives had dispersed in panicked flight into the unfamiliar countryside, there to die of hunger and thirst, or to wander aimlessly until enslaved again.

His ambition alone, his willingness to undertake what other men might avoid with an easy conscience, had brought this about. Whether from *Leonidas* or from *Ibis*, his men had given him all the loyalty and courage – and more – that he could ever have wished for. But he sensed now that their respect was tinged with caution, which at worst might grow into fear, of a leader who might spend lives too freely. Flag rank could almost certainly be his within the next decade. He had craved it since his uncle's reminiscences of Navarino and Sidon had enthralled him as a boy. But the price was high.

Doubt – that insidious enemy – gnawed hungrily. He longed for Florence's cheerful optimism, for her indomitability in the face of any obstacle or hazard, but in the long letter he was now writing for her he could never mention his concerns. She would sense them, and assuage them, when at last they would be reunited.

And until then, hold firm.

\*

Even the Rovuma's main channel was dangerously shallow in places as *Ibis* dropped seawards on a high tide, a whaler sounding a cable's length ahead, her own leadsman casting and chanting. The depth never exceeded five fathoms and the keel once brushed silt beneath. But at last the channel widened, the mangrove fell away, and the ocean's vast blue horizon lay ahead.

*Leonidas* was found five miles offshore, south of Mikindani Bay. She was ghosting under sail alone, only the slightest wisp of smoke confirming that one at least of her boilers was at harbour pressure, even if the engine itself stood idle. The endless cruising back and forth along the coast must have been even more stultifying than the *Ibis's* vigil on the river and yet when Dawlish went aboard he found that Edgerton seemed to have enjoyed the monotony of his temporary command. The smooth purity of the holystoned deck, the gleam of the brasswork and the brightness of the soap-washed paintwork told of his delight in routine.

And now, to *Leonidas* also, the news came of hammocks that would remain unoccupied, of the empty place at the wardroom table that had been O'Rourke's.

"Any movement into or out of Mtwara?" Dawlish was back in his own cabin to hear Edgerton's report.

The commander shifted uncomfortably in his chair. He already knew of the engagement with Imker's gunboat and of the massacre at the German mission. The sailing cutter that Dawlish had sent to Zanzibar with his report to Kirk had encountered *Leonidas* and had passed the news.

"That gunboat," Edgerton hesitated, like a man about to admit some secret shame. "She's back at Mtwara."

Dawlish felt anger rise within him but strove not to show it. Imker's craft must have emerged from the delta through that side-channel she was last seen entering and must have hugged the coast to regain Mikindani Bay. *Leonidas* – Edgerton – should have detected her. One salvo from the cruiser's Armstrongs would have dismembered her.

"One day no sign of her, but the next morning she was back at her anchorage." Edgerton broke the long silence. He was avoiding Dawlish's glance. "She must have crept close inshore in the night – there was no moon. God knows from where she came and it must have been all but suicidal to have navigated so near the shore in darkness. And…" His voice trailed off.

"She's in Mtwara now?" Dawlish asked.

"She hasn't moved since she got back. And she won't, not without being detected. Each night I'm sending a cutter under sail to lie close off the mouth of the bay. No lights, but carrying flares. If there's movement then it'll be reported. That gunboat won't get out a second time." A hint of pleading in Edgerton's tone.

Dawlish ignored it, recognised too that the ultimate blame was his own. He had known Edgerton's limitations, his aversion to initiative, but he had still trusted him enough to maintain a steady blockade. He had overestimated the man's capabilities and this was the result.

"We'll take a closer look at the anchorage, Commander Edgerton," he said. "I'd like to see that gunboat again."

An hour later, *Leonidas* was creeping slowly across the mouth of Mikindani Bay. Dawlish, as when he had first seen Mtwara, was again at the foretop with Wainwright.

"She's been moved," Purdon, the gunnery lieutenant, was with them also. He had the telescope, was sweeping it slowly. "The last time we came in this close she was anchored in the middle of the bay."

Which was where Dawlish had hoped to find her. He imagined Purdon dropping a half-dozen six-inch shells on a sitting duck and blowing her – and with luck, her master too – to fragments.

"Let me see." Dawlish took the telescope.

The bay was empty but for a score of dhows moored close inshore. Beyond them lay the vast mass of Fort Manuel and a long, dense, cluster of buildings lying between it and the foreshore. And there, moored alongside a quay lay Imker's gunboat.

Dawlish passed the glass to Wainwright. "What's behind her? Between her and the fort?"

"The town. The market, houses, slave pens, a few mosques – you can see the minarets. I know it well." Wainwright paused, had clearly guessed what Dawlish had been thinking, then said. "Over ten thousand people. Not all of them like Achmed or Imker. Women and children too."

"Lieutenant Purdon? Could you hit her with an opening shot?" Dawlish feared the answer, could guess it already.

"I couldn't guarantee it, sir. Only if it were point blank."

Even one overshot, one shell falling in the maze of lanes and houses just beyond the gunboat could kill dozens. Behind her, they might be, but those buildings and their occupants were as strong a defence for the gunboat as if a solid wall of masonry shielded her. And to come in close, to blast her at point-blank range at the quay, or to board and burn her, would necessitate manoeuvring *Leonidas* in unknown water, with every chance of grounding.

A long silence as Dawlish scanned the fort and town and gunboat again. There had been loss enough already on this venture, he thought, and Mtwara was cut off from the hinterland by Mathews' force – there had been that much success. He remembered Kirk's words, that once such isolation had been achieved then Mtwara would be Zanzibar's in time, that at least three of Sultan Saif's half-brothers there would be glad to succeed him – by lethal means, no doubt – and to swear allegiance as vassals of Zanzibar.

The capture of the *Lady Emmeline* had ended Imker's ambitions for steam-powered slave trading. All that remained now was that single gunboat. Her destruction might bring personal satisfaction, the death of Imker himself even more, but that would not merit further exposure, further loss, further letters to bereaved parents and bereft wives.

Better to leave *Leonidas* here on blockade for now, Dawlish thought and to return himself to Zanzibar with *Ibis*. A consultation with Kirk and an exchange of telegrams with London should bring this entire enterprise to a close.

Unless Imker's gunboat emerged.

"Mr. Purdon," Dawlish said before they descended. "You may have some practice yet. Commander Edgerton will have my orders to engage that gunboat should she venture into the centre of the bay. I trust that you'll see to the matter."

"With relish, sir," Purdon said. "With relish".

*

The pristine white hull moored in the Zanzibar anchorage was unmistakable as *Ibis* nudged past the dhows there.

SMS *Hildegarde* lay where she had lain before, and with every indication that she might have been here for some days, boats lying along her mooring boom, painting cradles slung over her sides. The sight did not bode well. The German corvette should have been in the Maldives or in the Celebes by now, the savants she carried plumbing the ocean depths for new forms of life or classifying plants and insects ashore on remote islands. There must be a reason why her scientific circumnavigation had been interrupted, her track reversed.

As *Ibis* steamed slowly past, Dawlish recognised Fregattenkapitän Kaunitz standing at *Hildegarde's* bridge-wing, hand raised in salute. He returned the greeting with mixed apprehension and pleasure, concerned by what this vessel's return might signify, yet pleased to see again a man whom he had liked. He wondered for a moment if he should be the first this time to extend a dinner invitation – relations had been relaxed before, and information could surely be gleaned as the wine flowed and the port was passed. But no, better to make no approach until he had spoken to Kirk.

The consul was not waiting by the harbour steps, but he had sent an escort of six of the sultan's guards, commanded by a Baluchi sergeant who spoke tolerable English. Dawlish passed with them through the familiar streets to the consulate. Kirk greeted him at the door and ushered him into his office.

"I trust that I can congratulate you, captain?"

"Not just me, Kirk. My crews, and Mathews and his people."

Kirk was concerned by the massacre of the German mission.

"I went to the German consul – Stieglitz, a decent fellow – when I received your report of it," he said. "He went pale when I gave him the news. He didn't know much about the place. He's a merchant dealing in cloves and his consulship is honorary. Then I handed him the letter that you had forwarded on behalf of this fellow Lutz. He read it while I watched and when he did he went paler still."

"What did he say about Lutz?"

"He said he had heard of him, but didn't know much about his activities, and certainly nothing about treaties. He said he hadn't dealt with him and I can all but believe him."

"A decent fellow, you said?"

"Stieglitz? Yes. And he was genuinely confounded," Kirk said. "He'd never dealt with anything much more than commercial disputes and he didn't know what to do next. I advised him to telegraph Berlin."

"And that's why the *Hildegarde* is back?"

"In time, Dawlish. We'll get to it in due time. Tell me first all that happened."

It sounded so easy when it was summarised. The consolidation of the base at Nanguruwe, the attack on Achmed's column, the arrival of Mathew's force, the hemming in of the Mtwara sultanate on the landward side, the assurance of the security of Horne's mission. And that of another mission also, even if was depleted for now.

"The two German monks whom Horne succoured are going back there," Dawlish said. "They're determined to rebuild it and they've every expectation that others will join them from Germany. They asked me to forward a letter and I agreed."

"Not good." Kirk frowned. "No matter how damn innocuous it sounds, this means a continued German presence, even if Lutz's treaties are dead letters now. While these monks are here there'll always be a reason for Germany to meddle, even if we get over this next business and sort out Mtwara for once and for all."

"Next business, Dr. Kirk?" Dawlish suddenly felt sick with apprehension. "I thought we'd settled Mtwara? That the place would wither on the vine? That you'd see to it that some half-brother of its sultan would make short work of him and submit to Zanzibar?"

"It's gone beyond that." Kirk sounded weary. "Chancellor Bismarck may not give a damn about missionaries but the massacre is being seen as an afront to imperial honour. Germany wants more than just an apology. It's a damned shame that you let that scoundrel Achmed go,

Dawlish. If you'd shot or hanged him there'd be no talk of further punitive expeditions. But he's back in Mtwara now, and the sultan there won't give him up, and the Germans will be satisfied with nothing less than blood."

"Is that why the *Hildegarde* is here?"

"When she put in to re-coal at Madras there was a telegram awaiting her and ordering her to return to Zanzibar. London warned me of it before she reached here. And, though there was nothing public yet, more German ships were to follow – a significant force, two more corvettes like the *Hildegarde*, and a transport carrying a half-battalion of troops. God knows how anybody in London could have found out such details."

"There must be sources that you and I could never know about," Dawlish said innocently. He could imagine Topcliffe reading coded telegrams from a dozen informants, dismissing some, poring over others.

And then the full implications hit him.

"A force that powerful could take and hold Mtwara," he said.

He was back in that Pall Mall club with Topcliffe. Britain might someday want East Africa. *But not just yet. For now, it's enough for us that nobody else does. Nobody whoever.* The death of Albrecht von Hohenfels and his brothers would provide chivalrous justification for seizure of a foothold, a first addition of colonial glory to the prestige of the young German Empire.

Kirk killed that unwelcome vision.

"Thank God for the telegraph," he said. "The line must have been all but burned up by the traffic that followed. I argued that Britain had guaranteed Zanzibari sovereignty and that Mtwara was essentially a vassal state in revolt. I proposed that Zanzibari forces – with British support – could more quickly restore order and exact full retribution in Mtwara, and that German participation would be appreciated"

"British meaning *Leonidas* and *Ibis*, and German meaning *Hildegarde*?"

"And Zanzibari meaning Mathews' people," Kirk said. "Most of them are up the Rovuma with him but there are enough back here to make a respectable contribution."

263

"And was your proposal accepted?"

Fort Manuel loomed in Dawlish's mind, vast, thick-walled, virtually impregnable if defended with even a modicum of skill. And Imker was there, resourceful and desperate, knowing that a noose might await him for his involvement with the *Lady Emmeline*.

"My proposal? It took almost a week and the telegraph cable must have been damn nearly burned out," Kirk said, "but sane counsels prevailed in the end. On the German side as well as ours, I believe."

It made sense. Bismarck was no enthusiast for colonies, Topcliffe had said, and the Crown Prince had little appetite for adventures abroad either, even if his own son, Wilhelm, was greedy for them. And Crown Prince Friedrich's wife was Britain's Princess Royal. Familial as well as diplomatic skills would have been brought into play.

"Does Kaunitz know about this?"

"I've met him. He knows that you're to lead the venture, Dawlish. He seemed relieved by that, though I imagine he would never admit it. He's hoping to see you as soon as possible to start joint planning."

"My people will have to bear the brunt of it." Dawlish felt no joy in the prospect. "The *Hildegarde's* virtually unarmed. She can't contribute much. And as for her landing seamen, I doubt if even one of her crew has ever see a shot fired in anger."

I've lost men enough, too many. I'm damned if I'm going to lose more if I can help it. If the Germans want their glory and their revenge then let the *Hildegarde* carry her fair share of losses.

He did not say it, never would openly, but the consul seemed to sense his lack of enthusiasm.

"There's a telegram here for you," Kirk said. "A long one, coded."

The sender could be guessed.

"Do you have Dickens here?" Dawlish saw Kirk's surprise. "Collected works maybe. Or even *Bleak House* on its own?"

"Yes. Yes, my wife is a devotee. But I don't see…"

"Let me have it please, Dr. Kirk," Dawlish did not mention that he had a copy on *Leonidas* but he needed one immediately. "*Bleak House*, paper and pencil, and a room to myself for an hour. We can talk again thereafter."

*

Dawlish began work in Kirk's own vacated office. *Bleak House* lay to his side, open to the eighth chapter. Dickens' sombre masterpiece was Topcliffe's choice for source of keys for encrypting longer messages. Earlier messages had used up most of the first paragraph's six-letter or longer words, with no letter repeats, that qualified them as keys. Now Dawlish underlined the remainder – BRIGHT, PLACES, SOFTER, SHADOW, COMPATIBLE and OUTSIDES – enough to start with, one for each single sentence. He wrote each of them in to the first squares of five-row, five-column Playfair tables, then filled the remaining spaces with the rest of the letters of the alphabet, allocating I and J to a single square.

He was adept – and fast – in encrypting and breaking Playfairs but doing so always brought sadness. His uncle Ralph had taught him when, as a boy, he had lived with the consumptive and prematurely-retired naval officer during what proved to be the last months of his life. It had been a game between them, his uncle even faster then than he now was himself. Over a quarter-century later he still missed his mother's kindly brother who had shown such calm fortitude in the face of slow debilitating death and who had made him his legal heir.

It took less than a half hour, fifteen sentences that demanded keys from Dickens' next paragraph also, and when he scanned them Dawlish could all but hear Topcliffe's own chill voice enunciating an unambiguous demand.

No mere restoration of order, no simple 'butcher and bolt' punitive expedition. Rather a diplomatic triumph that would simultaneously buttress the pride and reputation of Imperial Germany and yet block any hope young Prince Wilhelm might have of a future foothold in East Africa.

It was time to discuss details with Kirk.

# Chapter 26

Kirk had held back a surprise.

"Lutz is here in Zanzibar," he said.

"Since when?"

"Five days ago. He crossed by dhow from Bagamoyo. He's lodging with the consul, Stieglitz. And I'm informed that he's been received on the *Hildegarde* – apparently with some acclaim. As if he were Germany's own David Livingstone."

"Did he come alone?" Impossible to imagine Lutz's askaris being welcome in Zanzibar.

"He left his escort on the mainland but he brought enough ivory to make him rich for life. But he's in no hurry to return to Germany to spend it."

"Stieglitz told you that?"

"He came to see me yesterday and told me that Lutz has more official standing than we thought. More than Stieglitz knew either. It seems that Lutz has held an army-reserve commission for over a decade. A lieutenancy – it dated from his days in university. It's not unusual in Germany apparently. But now confirmation of promotion has been wired through – to colonel."

"Three ranks at a single step?" Dawlish was amazed. "That's unheard of."

"More than that. Significant. And there's more. Stieglitz came around again this morning to tell me that he'd received another telegram. From Berlin, the Foreign Ministry. He's to present it to Sultan Barghash as a request to attach Lutz – and his askaris – to the Mtwara expedition. He wanted to know if I would advise His Highness to accept."

"I damn well hope not," Dawlish said.

"I'd have hoped that myself if there hadn't been yet another telegram this morning," Kirk said. "For me, from London. Lutz's involvement had been raised there also – a confidential approach by the German ambassador, apparently. There must have been some horse-trading. The telegram's unequivocal. I'm directed to advise the sultan to accept."

No further argument possible.

Lutz would join the expedition.

*

Kirk liked the idea of an informal dinner with Kaunitz.

"But not on the *Ibis*," he said. "No matter how you phrase the invitation, he's likely to arrive in full uniform and expect full honours, and be all the more unlikely then to drop his guard. It would be better at my residence."

Dawlish saw the sense of it, but it took three drafts of the short note of invitation before they felt content with it.

Dr. Kirk recalled with pleasure the botanising expeditions when *Hildegarde* was last in port and looked forward to hearing news of the findings of her scientists while in the Seychelles. Mrs. Kirk would be delighted to welcome Fregattenkapitän Kaunitz, though domestic obligations would regrettably prevent her from joining the gentlemen at dinner. Captain Dawlish of the Royal Navy had also been invited.

And since the occasion was to be private and informal, a renewal of valued friendship, it was suggested that Fregattenkapitän Kaunitz might find it more comfortable, like the other guest, to come in civilian clothing.

No reference in the note to Mtwara, to Lutz, or to impending joint action. A Baluchi sergeant was sent to deliver it.

The only civilian suit that Dawlish had brought to sea was on *Leonidas* but Kirk was roughly of the same build and willing to assist. Even if the shirt collar was too tight, and the freshly-ironed jacket also, Dawlish felt adequately presentable when he viewed himself in the long mirror in the bedroom placed at his disposal. He felt put to shame however when Kaunitz arrived – informal or not, a half-dozen seamen of parade-ground smartness had escorted him and would wait outside. In mufti Kaunitz might be, but it was exquisite, the suit's linen blindingly white, the creases ironed to knife-edge sharpness, the gleaming patent leather shoes worth a month's salary, the cream Panama perfection itself, the silver-topped ebony cane a thing of beauty. The fiction was to be upheld that Dawlish had arrived only minutes earlier and he stood back as Kaunitz snapped to attention before a surprised Mrs. Kirk, bowed stiffly, kissed her hand and introduced himself by his full title. She excused herself after few minutes small-talk and left the gentlemen together.

The next hour was slow and difficult – drinks, followed by the first courses of a dinner that was might seem splendid in Zanzibar but which seemed inappropriately frugal for a guest of such elegance. Kaunitz was as little as ease as Dawlish himself, despite all Kirk's efforts to keep the conversation going. He clearly knew that there was more to the occasion than discussion of marine organisms or botanic curiosities and he seemed in an agony of indecision whether he himself must broach the real subject.

It suddenly occurred to Dawlish that Kaunitz was out of his depth – a sailor, not a diplomat, a conscientious officer who felt all but overwhelmed by the uncertainties confronting him. For that, Dawlish liked him all the more, for he felt something of it himself. He was several times about to break the long silences and mention Mtwara, but each time Kirk seemed to sense it and by the slightest inclination of the head indicated patience.

Wait – leave it to Kaunitz.

And at last, over brandy and cigars, the German officer steeled himself enough to say, "I am looking forward to cooperating with Captain Dawlish."

"It will be an honour to work closely with the Imperial German Navy, Fregattenkapitän Kaunitz."

Dawlish meant it. Even only partly armed as she was, the *Hildegarde*, her crew and her officers had impressed. The memory of the ineffective Prussian gunboats off the Danish coast in '64 had been cancelled out.

Kaunitz forced a laugh. "I understand that English officers are not permitted to mention ladies or religion or politics after dinner."

"There's only one Englishman here," Kirk said. "I'm a Scot, so if you and Captain Dawlish raise any such topic I won't take offence." He turned to Dawlish. "Perhaps you might tell us about your doings up the

Rovuma recently. Fregattenkapitän Kaunitz might find it as interesting as I would."

As he told the story, Dawlish realised that even if a fellow countryman had not been present, Albrecht von Hohenfels would have stood at its centre, not just for what he had done, but for what he had been.

"He died well." It was not easy to tell the final details. "As bravely as on any battlefield. I think he would have regarded it as such."

A long silence.

"A good death," Kaunitz was clearly moved. "An officer's. Noble. We might all be grateful for as much."

It was less painful to speak of Lutz.

Kaunitz had already met him and had been impressed by his exploits. "A man of the new Germany," he said. "A patriot, a scholar and a man of action. And those men he trained, captain, even if Africans, they too were effective?"

"Splendid soldiers. Their only defect was that there were too few of them." Dawlish hoped that he sounded ignorant of Stieglitz's approach to the sultan. "With more, Doktor Lutz could have made a valuable contribution to our joint expedition against Mtwara."

"But Oberst Doktor Lutz will be invaluable even without more such men," Kaunitz said.

"Oberst?" The word was new to Dawlish.

"Colonel, you would say. He will accompany me on the *Hildegarde* as adviser. He knows these lands and their people's ways like few others."

"I've no doubt he'll be invaluable," Kirk flashed a glance at Dawlish.

"Invaluable," Dawlish said. "Very welcome."

"I will treasure his advice," Kaunitz said. "Just as I will yours, Captain Dawlish."

"I'd like to commence fixing details of the expedition," Dawlish said. "I suggest that —"

"I agree." Kaunitz was ahead of him. "As soon as possible. I understand that you know this place, captain. This Mtwara. And that it is a hard nut to crack." He seemed proud of the colloquialism but there was a hint of uncertainty in his tone.

"A show of force might have been enough." Kirk was launching into the argument he had rehearsed with Dawlish. "Three warships and the threat of a landing if necessary. But with this wretched man Imker at the sultan's side I doubt if it will go so easily. If they retreat into Fort Manuel they could hold out for months. Your guns, Captain Dawlish, or yours, Fregattenkapitän Kaunitz, effective and well-served as they may be, might make no great impression on its walls in all that time."

"For months, you say?" Kaunitz was frowning.

"Not a prospect that Britain would welcome," Kirk said. "Germany either, I imagine. Humiliating. Damn humiliating."

Kaunitz said nothing but looked sobered. Britain could survive a measure of humiliation, and frequently did, but it was another matter for the recently-fledged German Empire. At this moment Kaunitz was its most prominent representative. And a potential scapegoat.

"I've seen the place," Dawlish said. "Dr. Kirk is right. It could be damn humiliating. Guns alone won't do it. We'll need to storm it and carry it at the point of the bayonet. We'll have to blast our way in through a gate or go in over the walls."

He paused, uncomfortable within himself for what he was hoping to bring about, to spread the inevitable casualties more widely, lessen his own people's, ensure that the German crew took their share.

"To be frank with you, Fregattenkapitän Kaunitz, I doubt there are men enough on my ships to undertake storming it with any great hope of success. But with your contribution, with *Hildegarde's*, with every man you can muster, it may just be possible."

"The Imperial German Navy won't hold back." Kaunitz's voice conveyed pride as well as determination.

"You've suggested that I know Mtwara, captain," Dawlish said. "I don't. I've seen it from a masthead and I've studied it through a glass. That's not enough. Not if we're going to storm that fort." The memory of an ill-planned assault on Chinese fortifications, his first experience of combat – as a thirteen-year old boy – had made him swear to himself never to commit men so carelessly. "We know the layout. Mr.

Wainwright, Dr. Kirk's associate, has been inside. He has sketched it for us. But that's not enough either. The problem isn't the interior. It's getting into the fort at all. And for that we need to know much more about it."

"How, Captain Dawlish?"

"By the only way that's worth a damn. By going ashore there to see for ourselves, Fregattenkapitän Kaunitz. You and I together."

*

Dawlish would allow *Ibis* only a single day in port, but that one day was unavoidable. The gunvessel had been almost continuously at sea – or up the Rovuma – since leaving Singapore some three months previously. The rigging, boiler and engine all needed attention, more than time available allowed, and only the most urgent demands could be addressed. The crew too needed rest they could not have, for the weeks up the Rovuma had taken a heavy toll. Even the men who had not endured bouts of fever looked worn. Now even the meagre reward of leave ashore at Zanzibar was to be denied them. They were at least spared the brute effort of taking coal on board, for labour was cheap here, and the sacks were lugged from a lighter by the supplier's African workers, some of whom might well be slaves. The black dust billowing from the bunker hatches cast a dark film over the deck, guns and men, demanding yet more effort to wash it clean afterwards. *Ibis* was Jarvis's and he drove the work relentlessly and efficiently. It might have needed another week to bring her to the gleaming standard a Queen's ship merited, but by nightfall she was ready in the essentials for what lay ahead.

At Kaunitz's invitation, Dawlish spent much of the day aboard the *Hildegarde*. She was a warship again. Her scientists had been left behind at Madras, and their most valuable specimens and equipment offloaded with them. The orders telegraphed from Berlin had been explicit – decisive action and absolute success expected. *Hildegarde's* passage from Madras to Zanzibar had been entirely under steam, freeing crew from duties aloft, and intensive arms training had been conducted daily on deck. Kaunitz was rightly proud of the demonstration of cutlass drill he laid on for Dawlish and, even though the *Hildegarde* carried no marines, her seamen seemed more than competent with the bayonet. Their equipment too was first-rate, most of all their superb Mauser rifles. What impressed most however were the men themselves, their unmistakable devotion to excellence, their solidity and their air of serious, indeed dour, determination, so much at variance with the more carefree willingness of the British seaman. Young this Imperial Navy might be, but her men seemed proud to serve in it and dedicated to the same grim efficiency by which the German Armies had demolished the French Empire in a few months little over a decade before.

But the *Hildegarde* was deficient in one respect and Kaunitz knew it.

"She has mountings for ten guns." Regret in his voice. "We carry only two."

With all mounted, she would have been a formidable complement to *Leonidas*, even though her weapons were four-inch calibre to the cruiser's six. With just the two she now carried, broadside positioned on either side and unable to bear ahead, only one could be brought into action at a time. But that problem could be solved.

"One gun can be moved over to the opposite side," Kaunitz said. "We'll need a lighter to assist. The mounting is as heavy as the barrel, but it can be done."

Dawlish was glad of it. "The Krupps are fine weapons," he said. "A fast rate of fire, and accurate, very accurate."

*And I know.* That morning in the Poti anchorage, a Turkish gunboat's Krupps disembowelling helpless Russian steamers, strewing the calm water with wreckage and drowning men. And again, at Gelendzhik, no less a massacre. But never to be spoken of…

"Accuracy, Fregattenkapitän Kaunitz, that's what will be needed to cover our boats as they go ashore. And afterwards, land targets that may demand pinpoint precision. It'll be up to our signallers then as much as to our gunners."

They parted. Dawlish went ashore to the consulate. Kirk too had been busy and had just returned from the palace, to where he had brought Wainwright.

"Congratulate the new ambassador," he said.

Wainwright had been given papers accrediting him as representative of His Highness, Sultan Barghash of Zanzibar. He also carried a letter, beautifully calligraphed in Arabic and rather more plainly scripted in English, and addressed to Sultan Saif Ibn Rahman of Mtwara. Nine-tenths were taken up with assurances of respect, admiration for virtues and prayers for good health and manifold blessings.

The real import was reserved for the few sentences – the demands – at the end. Instant acceptance of Barghash's suzerainty, an oath of loyalty to him to be sworn by Mtwara's sultan, immediate surrender of one Willem Imker and of one Achmed Ibn Hamed.

No ifs, buts or maybes.

"It'll be rejected out of hand, of course," Kirk said. "But that won't matter, will it, Captain Dawlish?"

"Not if Mr. Wainwright can drag out the discussion as long as possible."

"I can complement and flatter like the best." Wainwright said. "Arabic's the ideal tongue for it. They'll be surprised by my elevation – the last time I was inside the fort I was pleading for a few hundred dollars of delayed payment and thinking about my five percent commission. I managed it well enough. This time, I should be able to string the matter out for an hour at least, two maybe."

"You're sure they'll recognise a white flag?" Dawlish said.

Everything would hang on that. And not just for Wainwright alone.

"They'll give us that much."

"And we'll take the rest."

Easily said. It was the doing that promised to be harder.

*

*Ibis* would slip out to sea at sunrise. Dawlish allowed himself two hours before sleep to write to Florence, the last of the numbered letters which would be sent with the mail-packet leaving for Aden in two days' time, the first step towards a breakfast table in a Southsea villa. He had already written about what had transpired upriver. He had been less than explicit as regards the butchery at the German Mission and the battle with the slavers, and its aftermath, but he knew that she would guess that it had been worse than he reported. She had seen horrors enough when the broken Turkish forces, and the pathetic columns of refugees with them, had retreated before the Russians through a savage Balkan winter. She had herself killed – once, in self-defence – and in Cuba she had been wounded as she had shielded a sick man on a stretcher. She had no illusions as to humanity's benevolence and she recognised, like him, that good intentions without the strength to back them were futile. And yet he marvelled that this harsh truth had never oppressed her as it had him. Her resolution in the face of threat was no less strong than that which he had been trained to, yet in her case it had come naturally, and there was a cheerful optimism in it that he lacked himself.

On sandbanks, in a launch's tiny cockpit, in huts and on hard bare ground, he had scribbled in pencil the dozen other numbered letters to her that still awaited transmission. But he had not allowed himself to think of her, except in the abstract, lest care for her and sense of absence unman him. But this humid night, in the cabin set at his disposal on *Ibis*, with sweat dripping down to blot the paper, awareness of her came to him strongly, not just of the times of shared danger and of shared ecstasy, but of the joy of just being together, of amused tolerances of each other's mannerisms, of quiet contented silences, of admiration of what each had become. Memory came too of that dreadful miscarriage, the nightmare of bloody sheets and pain that had made her ever more precious to him, and the impossibility of further children that she endured with such fortitude.

It shamed him to remember that her status – she had once been a lady's maid – had at first held him back from letting himself love her. Her gaiety, no less than her love, had infected him – he recognised his own tendency to gloom and pessimism – and he had often half-joked that he had never really laughed until he had married her. He had once wondered why Hope should have been ranked with Faith and Charity as cardinal virtues but it had been Florence who had shown him Hope's meaning. Not foolish expectation that took no account of realities, but rather acceptance of them and of the action they demanded. And recognition too that failure in a just cause was victory in itself.

Aware that this could be a last letter, he wondered how much of this he should write to her, in gratitude, tonight. He made two attempts and tore both up as mawkish. Enough to say that some offensive action was still anticipated before heading homewards – within a month, he hoped. Better that she should imagine him calm and confident and to hint at his pride – and there was some – in the saving of Horne's mission and the defeat of Achmed and the partial liberation of his slaves. Better not to refer to the consciousness of evil that still hung heavy on him and better too, as always, not to allude to the possibility of death ahead.

And best of all, to tell her that he loved her.

Chapter 27

*Ibis* slipped out to sea just after dawn and headed south-south-west to parallel the mainland's coast at a steady ten knots. Kaunitz had boarded, alone, just before departure. Every detail of the gunvessel's management interested him – "We have still so much to learn from the Royal Navy," he told Dawlish. His manner was so frank that even Jarvis did not tire of his questions. Kaunitz had been delighted by the masquerade that Dawlish had proposed and he had already established an easy familiarity with Wainwright, quizzing him not only about Mtwara and Fort Manuel but also about his scientific background.

"That gentleman is not enough valued in Britain," he told Dawlish as they shared cigars that afternoon. "In Germany he would be honoured, would have funding for his researches, might be invited to join an expedition such as *Hildegarde's*. But instead, if he is to pursue his vocation, he must survive here by any menial way he can."

It was an opportunity.

Dawlish shrugged, hoped to make his probe sound casual.

"There's nothing menial about what he's been doing now. And your Doktor Lutz – I find him just as impressive a scholar – also seems to have little official support for his explorations."

"The good doctor is a free soul, content to make his own way. But he's a patriot. He's been glad to volunteer his support. It will no doubt be valuable." There was something in Kaunitz's tone that indicated distaste, a clear hint too that the subject should be dropped.

Dawlish took it.

"I'm not looking forward to tonight's sacrifice." He tried to laugh as he said it.

Yet, make light of it as he tried, the moment was difficult when it came. In the mirror above the cabin's washstand he saw reflected the same neatly bearded face he had known for almost twenty years, shot now, like his black hair, with the first streaks of grey, even the first flecks of white. It was the style that so many officers now affected that it was almost a uniform in itself. It was the only image Florence had of him and it was the way, whitened fully, that he hoped to look when death would at last claim him. The countenance he had last seen bare had been all but a boy's, still unaware of the world's full tragedy, for all that he had already glimpsed something of it in China and in the West Indies and in Denmark. It had been a face then that had not yet realised its depth and inescapability of that tragedy. That had come later.

He was unaccustomed to shaving but he did not want it done for him. His wounded arm – healing well, though with a feeling of painful tightness – was of little help. He nicked himself several times, tiny wounds that bled surprisingly. As he stripped the beard away, the face that was gradually revealed was one that he had not expected. The coin-sized scar on his left cheek, which the beard had never fully disguised, showed more livid than he expected as the paler skin was exposed. The crow's feet, price of a quarter century's exposure to sun and its reflection on water, and to wind and rain and spray on endless watches, seemed suddenly more pronounced, the eyes themselves more sunken.

His appearance surprised, even shocked, him and he doubted that even Florence would have recognised him. His dignity seemed gone and the bleeding nicks made him look like an ordinary seaman who had emerged from a drunken tavern-brawl ashore. But that was all to the good for what was now intended. For there were two men in Mtwara who would never forget his usual face, never forgive either. The chance of encountering them would be low but he still feared recognition.

Willem Imker and Achmed Ibn Hamed.

*Leonidas* was still ghosting back and forth off Mikindani Bay. Edgerton came across to *Ibis* – he looked shocked by Dawlish's altered appearance but was too courteous to remark on it. He had nothing to report, no movements out of Mtwara, nothing but the dull monotony of blockade duty that must by now be driving spirits more ardent that his to extremes of frustration. He expressed no alarm at the prospect of the action now considered, when Dawlish told him of it, but he did not welcome it either, unlike both Jarvis and Kaunitz. Edgerton's ambitions would be well satisfied by a comfortable shore appointment until the end of his service and he had no need of a desperate feat of arms that could redeem Jarvis's career or boost Kaunitz's.

But it had been no different off Korea, Dawlish remembered. He had relied on Edgerton then for his solid competence, his unswerving willingness to carry out an order to the letter, a safe pair of hands in which the care of the cruiser might temporarily be left. Precise ship-handling would be expected of Edgerton in the coming venture, and he would deliver it, but until then he must provide more however. What was wanted most of *Leonidas* was her men, and not only those who had been up the Rovuma, but every man not needed on deck and to tend the engines and to serve the six-inch Armstrongs. No matter how much they had already given, yet more would be demanded. The routine of polishing and painting and holystoning that so satisfied Edgerton must be replaced by ever more relentless rifle and cutlass and bayonet exercise. And as for the guns, Dawlish had confidence in Purdon. He had proved himself in Paraguay and off Korea.

And tomorrow the gunnery lieutenant could study his future targets at close quarters.

*

A whaler would have been sufficient to carry the four who mattered – Wainwright and Dawlish, Kaunitz and Purdon – but *Ibis's* twenty-five foot cutter was more suited for deception. It required an eight-man crew, among whom all but Wainwright would pull an oar, all clad like common seamen and intermingled with the other rowers. The craft had been swung out, ready for dropping, as the gunvessel crawled towards Mikindani Bay an hour after sunrise, leaving *Leonidas* astern two miles offshore.

Dawlish was aware of the suppressed laughter and nudges among the gunvessel's crew as he emerged on deck in a seaman's duck shirt and trousers, his bare face shielded by a sennet hat. Purdon and Kaunitz were similarly attired and, like half the members of the boat-crew, they were equipped for landing, armed with Sniders, shod with boots and with their calves encased in freshly whitened canvas gaiters. Kaunitz had agonised over the donning of a foreign uniform and fear of ridicule. Now, he alone looked uncomfortable and self-conscious. Dawlish had insisted that, from the moment they came on deck, they should play their roles as common seamen to the letter, be subject to the cutter-coxswain's orders, salute Lieutenant Maddox, who would be in ostensible command, and speak only when spoken to. Wainwright, in an immaculate linen suit lent by Kirk, acted with a degree of feigned arrogance that befitted a sultan's accredited representative.

*Ibis* pushed on into the almost circular bay and hove to at its centre, bows headed north. A scarce two miles distant, Fort Manuel loomed massively over the town. Thousands of eyes there must be focussed on her, for *Leonidas* had never ventured so close inshore. Now, to draw attention of any who might still not be aware of her, one of the gunvessel's remaining sixty-eight pounders, that mounted to starboard, and pointing harmlessly towards the open sea, fired a single blank charge. The message was clear. No hostile intent.

The cutter had been swung out over the port side, prepared for dropping, crew at their places, oars passed, ready for tossing when the craft would touch the water and push away. Dawlish could sense the tension around him – the men had been warned of the necessity to behave as if he and three others, one a foreigner, were not sitting among them in disguise. Wainwright was with Maddox in the sternsheets, concern, fear even, on his face for what must now follow. They sat on either side of the coxswain, Fuller, an older, grizzled man.

Five minutes passed, and then the sixty-eight spoke again, its boom reverberating across the bay. All but a few of the small fishing craft that had dotted it had scurried for land. Imker's gunboat was tied up at the quay on the town's frontage and Dawlish felt sick as he fancied that he detected movement around the Krupp mounted on her foredeck. *Ibis* was well within its range and had nothing capable of useful reply – her main weapon, powerful though it was, lacked the breech-loader's accuracy at this distance. It had been a gamble to bring *Ibis* in this close, but one that conveyed no hostile intent, and it was based on Dawlish's confidence that any opening fire from the Krupp would almost certainly overshoot or undershoot. Though stationary now, *Ibis's* boiler was at full pressure and a single telegraphed command from bridge to engine room would send her racing back seawards in aim-defeating zig-zags.

Another five minutes and still the Krupp, though apparently manned, remained silent. Dawlish, grasping his oar, looked up from the cutter towards Jarvis on the bridge-wing above, saw the enquiry on his face, and nodded. *Drop the cutter.*

A steady rhythm drove the craft shorewards. At a word from Maddox, a seaman stood up in the bows and began to sweep a large white flag, a towel on a boathook, slowly back and forth. With his back to the shore, and intent on keeping time with the other rowers, Dawlish longed to turn to look forward. Instead he could only see the apprehension on Maddox's and Wainwright's faces as the coxswain lightly adjusted the tiller to maintain course towards the stone steps at the midpoint of the quay. The wound on Dawlish's arm was virtually healed but the act of rowing was more painful than he had anticipated even though Fuller, the coxswain, had been instructed to maintain only a slow rhythm.

Five minutes passed and the cutter must by now have entered well within rifle-range. Silence still reigned. The white flag was still sweeping steadily, the oars' beat regular, hope rising that no crashing volley might meet them, that the offer to parley was being accepted. The craft was passing a moored dhow now, and then another, dark faces above the bulwarks watching in curiosity.

279

Their crews and owners must hate us, Dawlish thought, imprisoned in this bay for weeks by the white cruiser patrolling outside.

Yet more dhows now, clustered close to shore, the cutter threading her way between them, sight of *Ibis* lost behind their dark hulls.

Suddenly, a hail.

"What do you want here?"

The words English, but heavily accented, the voice Dutch, Dawlish guessed, but coarser than Imker's.

Maddox called "Hold water!" and lurched to his feet as the craft slowed. He shouted the response that had been agreed, that a plenipotentiary of Sultan Barghash wished to land. The Royal Navy was escorting him as a courtesy. His message was for Sultan Saif's ears only.

Now a long and fruitless exchange – no authority to let anybody come ashore, whatever they might call themselves. They'd have to wait for somebody to come and if they didn't like it they could go back where they came from. No further word – the Dutchman seemed to have gone elsewhere.

Dawlish, bent over his oar to shield his face, glanced up and caught Maddox's eye. Maddox, spoke quietly to the coxswain. The cutter was drifting slightly and a few nudges of the tiller turned her enough for Dawlish to see the quay. Imker's gunboat lay against it fifty yards to the right, smaller craft moored in between. The steps descending to the water here were of weathered stone, probably laid under Portuguese supervision three centuries and more before. The buildings beyond were as squalid as those on the Zanzibar frontage but what the eye was drawn to was the lowering bulk of the fort behind, more immense, more imposing – and perhaps even more impregnable too – than it had ever appeared from seaward.

Curious onlookers were looking down from the quay but they scurried away as a dozen armed men appeared. In their uniforms they looked not unlike Mathews' people, the same mix of Africans and Somalis, commanded by what might be a Baluchi. But the young man they escorted was clearly an Arab, and his robes and head-dress and the dagger at his belt looked rich. He halted at the top of the steps and when he spoke it was in Arabic. His tone was not necessarily welcoming, but not outrightly hostile either.

Wainwright was on his feet, a hand on Maddox's shoulder to steady himself as the cutter rocked gently. He was calm, clearly courteous in his speech, and the slight smattering of Arabic terms that Dawlish knew told him that the ritual exchange of meaningless courtesies had commenced.

The reply, when it came, seemed no different. There was an impression of both men having known each other before, that there might have been some degree of amity in their earlier dealings, that perhaps – best of all – the other might have benefitted from the commercial dealings in which Wainwright had been involved. Minutes passed and by then, courtesies observed, a dialogue had been established relating to the visit itself. Wainwright motioned to the official-looking briefcase he had borrowed from Kirk – the crest on it was worn, but it still gave some dignity – and he must be explaining that what it contained could be confided only to Sultan Saif in person.

More discussion, then indication from tone and gesture of some degree of agreement.

"His Excellency Ibrahim Ibn Rahman is Sultan Saif's younger brother." Wainwright spoke to Maddox loudly enough that Dawlish would hear. "He is in charge of port dues. He has been gracious enough to offer to conduct me to His Highness and to arrange an audience."

From the formal language used, Dawlish guessed that this Ibrahim must understand some English, perhaps even be fluent.

Now the exchange seemed to grow more difficult and Dawlish suspected that the most critical point, the need for an escort, was now at issue. Wainwright was pressing politely but persistently but Ibrahim's answers either began or ended with a slight click of his tongue, with a short backwards jerk of his head, the gesture, not necessarily discourteous, for an emphatic "No!" But Wainwright still returned to the argument, patiently and courteously, and gesturing to the rifles lying, conspicuously untouched, along the centre of the thwarts. And then, apparently suddenly, there seemed to be a resolution, Ibrahim smiling and tilting his head sideways – clear agreement.

281

"His Excellency consents to an escort." Wainwright caught Dawlish's eye as he spoke loudly to Maddox. "He recognises that protocol demands it, God be thanked. But only four men and under an officer's command. For an envoy's dignity only. Rifles may be carried, but unloaded. No other ammunition. And no bayonets."

Lambs to the slaughter, Dawlish thought. Naked into Hell. Madness. But too far now to turn back.

Then Wainwright said one word, just loud enough for Dawlish to hear.

"Hospitality."

And that word said it all. Once accepted as a guest, safety was guaranteed until departure. No obligation in Arabic culture could be stronger, no other could earn greater contempt through violation. Kaunitz, sitting with his oar sternwards of Dawlish, had looked back to him with alarm mixed with incomprehension on his face. Dawlish closed his eyes, a gesture that Wainwright and Maddox too could see.

*Accept. Accept with grace and with confidence.*

The cutter moved towards the steps and the white flag's boathook pulled it close enough for Maddox to step ashore. He jerked his head towards Dawlish, Kaunitz and Wainwright, and to the seaman, Staunton, who had proved so reliable in the attack on the slaver column. Bayonets and ammunition-bandoliers laid aside in the craft, and the rifles' bolts ostentatiously pulled back to reveal empty chambers, they followed Maddox up the steps. He drew them up there like a miniature guard of honour and called them to the salute as Wainwright's head and shoulders appeared. Kaunitz's handling of his rifle was clumsy – the German saluting drill must be slightly different – but the sultan's brother, watching with his own guard drawn up raggedly behind him, did not appear to notice.

Dawlish's heart was thumping, fear gnawing, as the procession commenced, half of the Mtwara guard in front, half at the rear. Sandwiched between them was Wainwright – with Ibrahim by his side and talking without apparent rancour – and Maddox's small escort. Recognition was unlikely, Dawlish told himself. Other than Imker and Achmed there could be nobody here who might recognise him, and the clean-shaven face was an added disguise, but he nevertheless found it an effort not to bend his head to hide himself under the sennet hat's broad brim. Purdon was marching on his right, Kaunitz and Staunton following, all in step behind Maddox. They passed along the open quay for a hundred yards – leftwards, away from Imker's gunboat. What would normally have been a scene of loading and of offloading, of jostling and of shouting, of hurrying porters and heavily-loaded donkeys, was now all but empty of activity. *Leonidas's* blockade had bitten deeply.

They turned, rightwards, into a broad street, two and even three-storied houses, many of stone and with screened wooden balconies at higher levels, passages between giving a glimpse of inner courtyards. There was the usual scattering of stalls, and of stores open at the front, displays of foodstuffs, brightly coloured spices, cotton fabrics printed with garish designs in some far-off Lancashire mill, cheap hardware that might have come from Birmingham – or Germany. And everywhere the slight smell of sewage.

It was like Zanzibar as Dawlish remembered it almost a decade earlier, before Sultan Barghash's intermittent efforts at modernisation had begun to make some impact. There was the same mix of Arab and African, with smaller numbers of Somalis and Baluchis, the sight of cheerfully uncovered black women at stark variance with the shrouded anonymity of so many of their Muslim sisters.

A small crowd was gathering to watch the procession – several shouted insults or spat as Wainwright and his escort were spotted – and a troop of urchins was following alongside. The street was curving slightly, its end not yet in sight, but the fort's walls loomed like a dark precipice above the houses. Dawlish forced himself not to look too closely at it as he marched – better to wait until nearer – and his attention was for now focussed on the street and how effective an approach it might offer a landed force.

A crossroads now and a turn to the right into a narrower street, more squalid than before, a liquid, better not guessed at, flowing between the cobbles underfoot. The courtyard of a large mosque lay on the left, a single minaret soaring above it, one that had been clearly identifiable from the bay as the highest in Mtwara. As they marched on, the stench

283

grew denser, more repulsive – and wholly unmistakable – even before the passage led into a huge open square.

The slave pens there were larger than those at Nanguruwe, substantially fenced, three large ones for men and a fourth for women. A few slaves were standing or trudging about listlessly – the occupants of one of the men's pens were shackled, trailing chains that linked their ankles to a row of piles driven into the ground – but the majority were sitting or lying in the shade afforded by open-sided palm-thatch shelters built against the fences, too low to stand up in. Several barracks lay behind, a few of stone but most of wattle and daub, many of them looking as if they had been thrown up recently.

There must be up to a thousand people in these pens, Dawlish realised, more than would usually be retained here, for the cutting off of coastal trade had halted the normal turn-over. The smell, and the clouds of loudly buzzing flies, confirmed that nothing had been done to cater for the waste of these greater numbers and that the enclosures were little better than cess pits. The guards along the fences, armed with rifles and whips, a mix of Arabs and others like those that which had guarded Achmed's caravan, were fewer than might have been expected. Those they watched were too far sunk in lassitude and apathy to consider – or even imagine – escape. It hurt to wonder if among them were some of those who had fled into the brush after the attack on Achmed's column and who had been rounded up since.

Along the edge of the pens now and on between stone houses and warehouses beyond and into a labyrinth of streets that were mere alleyways, onlookers shrinking back against the walls to let them past.

Dawlish was memorising the turns, fixing images in his mind – here market stalls, there a mosque with a minaret that seemed disproportionately tall, and further on a well where women were filling water jars. The others with him had been ordered to be equally sharp-eyed for even Wainwright, despite having been here before, had found it difficult to sketch a map of this maze. Afterwards, back on *Ibis*, the first task would be to share observations and prepare one.

And then one more turn, and what they had come to see lay directly ahead – Fort Manuel.

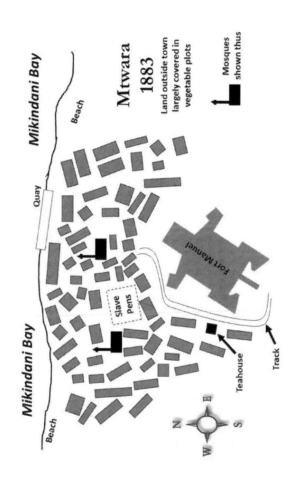

Mikindani Bay

Beach

Quay

Mikindani Bay

Beach

Mtwara
1883

Land outside town
largely covered in
vegetable plots

Mosques
shown thus

Fort Manuel

Slave
Pens

Teahouse

Track

N E S W

# Chapter 28

Fort Manuel had been built on a steep, rocky, bluff. An open strip of ground sloped gently up to its base and separated it from the town's buildings. It had been burned bare – recently apparently, for only the scantiest traces of green had yet thrust back through the charred earth. This was the face that the fortress presented to the sea, at its centre a massive, flat-fronted square fortification, a citadel that jutted out from the walls stretching to either side from its rear corners. The crenellations at the top were pointed, like bishops' mitres, and a few canon-muzzles protruded between them. Given their height, they would once have dominated the bay and shoreline but now they were antiquated relics which had reportedly not been fired in living memory. It was rifle fire that concerned Dawlish most – and he remembered the splendid Chassepots he had seen the slavers carry – for this jutting citadel allowed flanking fire along the walls extending from it. Diamond-shaped bastions thrust out at the extremities of these walls to allow sweeping of their bases not just along this front face but on those, as yet unseen, along the fort's flanks.

The small column was moving rightwards, parallel to the seaward face. Dawlish felt his initial apprehension fade as he marched – he was as anonymous as any bluejacket might have looked and whatever interest the group would arouse would be concentrated on the splendidly attired Wainwright. Heads had appeared above the walls but Dawlish's attention was focussed on the structure itself. Nowhere were the walls lower than twenty feet, inclined at five or six degrees to the vertical, the outer surface of the stone blocks smooth, unbroken at any point by a door or opening.

And that was Dawlish's disappointment, for he had hoped for some small entrance, perhaps even as tiny as a postern gate, on which *Leonidas's* guns could bear to batter an entry for a storming party. But there was nothing, only blank stone on which Purdon's six-inch Armstrongs could make little more impact than sixteenth-century culverins. The Portuguese engineers who had laid out the fortress had been intent on protection from attack by sea or from forces landed directly from it. They had built well with coral stone and lime mortar – Fort Manuel had successfully repelled two assaults by the Dutch when they had challenged Portugal's control of the spice-trade. Only starvation and a three-year siege had later allowed Arab occupation when Lisbon's power had waned. Now, with the ground below it scoured clean by burning – and that might well show Imker's hand – an approach along here, much less an assault, could only be suicidal if riflemen were positioned between the crenellations.

The track curved to the left, around the rightmost bastion, and led now along the wall behind. This wall too was set back so that it could be swept by fire not just from this bastion alone but from another, fifty yards distant. Here too Dawlish could see no opening. He could sense the unease of Kaunitz and Purdon also as they stole quick glances at the walls, already coming to the same conclusion as he had done, that naval gunfire would avail little here. Only when the track swept around to reveal the fort's landward side could a point of entry be seen, seemingly the only one. Flanked by sharp bastions, surmounted by what was all but a castle in its own right, was a single gate, the stonework above it carved with what must be the Portuguese royal arms. The bluff was steepest along this side – an all but vertical rock outcrop – and a long narrow ramp, supported on three arches, essentially a steeply-inclined bridge, led up from the track to the guarded portal.

Dawlish felt despair welling inside him. Shielded from the bay by the fort's entire mass, no naval gunfire could be directed here. Assault up that slender ramp looked to be the only feasible way in. If there were sufficient defenders, no matter how inexpert they might be, the musketry they could pour down on attackers would be murderous. The slightest shake of the head confirmed that Kaunitz had realised the same. He must now be confronting the full horror of the fact that the die had been cast, that national honour had been committed, that an assault, however desperate, however suicidal, was unavoidable. The only hope could now be that Fort Manuel lacked men to defend it. And even that hope was vain, for Dawlish heard a small, cold internal voice telling him that less than a hundred men could hold this position with ease against any force that he and Kaunitz could launch against it.

There were guards at the base of the ramp, loosely-turbaned Somalis, long, lithe and thin-faced, Baluchis also, all well-equipped with Chassepots, crossed bandoliers. Their feet were shod in sandals but their khaki uniforms had pretensions to smartness. Sultan Saif clearly aspired to Mtwara possessing a force comparable to that which Mathews had trained for Zanzibar. As the column approached they moved into a single blocking wall.

Ibrahim turned, called on his escort to halt, said something to Wainwright – he was too far off for Dawlish to discern the words, but there seemed to be anger as well as embarrassment in his tone. He walked forward alone but before he had reached the guards a figure in a white European-style uniform with brass buttons and rings on his sleeves was emerging through the gateway and striding down the ramp.

Imker.

He bellowed and the guards parted to let him through. He stood before them, waiting for Ibrahim to come near, a smirk of assured superiority on his face. Dawlish felt fear, doubt too that his barefaced disguise could withstand this man's scrutiny if he drew close. His whole demeanour advertised his confidence in the power of his position here, satisfaction that even the sultan's younger brother must approach him like a supplicant.

Even at this distance it was clear that Imker was dominating the discussion, snapping questions that Ibrahim was answering volubly, and apparently to little avail. A curt nod, almost dismissive, indicated at last that he had consented to something. Ibrahim turned away and walked back. He was fighting to keep his face composed and his fists were clenched. He spoke to Wainwright – an impression of embarrassment and apology in his manner. Wainwright was smiling, seemed understanding and to be making light of it, before he called Maddox forward, spoke to him briefly.

Maddox returned.

"Mr. Wainwright will be entering alone," he said. His tone indicated that he was finding it difficult to maintain the pretence of commanding his commander. He was looking Dawlish in the eye, seeking approval. The slightest nod told him to continue. "We're to wait over there." He pointed to a what looked like a tree-shaded tea house among the buildings beyond the open strip.

Ibrahim and Wainwright had moved up the ramp behind Imker, and had disappeared into the gatehouse. The Baluchi in charge of Ibrahim's escort introduced himself to Maddox in perfect English as Lieutenant Ramzi Khalid, late Havildar Major, 29th Bombay Infantry, and indicated politely that they must wait at the tea house. Refreshments would be provided.

They sat outside, welcoming the shade. Maddox, as befitted an officer, took a place apart from the three mock seamen and one actual. Khalid was solicitude itself, ordering mint tea for them, then seating himself with Maddox, one officer with another. There were several other customers, Arabs, one smoking a waterpipe, but after the first quizzical looks they appeared to take no further interest. Better, nonetheless, to maintain absolute caution.

Staunton, the genuine seaman, looked ill at ease with the disguised officers. Fearful that his stiffness might draw attention, Dawlish asked him, "Have you a pipe with you? And baccy?"

He had.

"Then light up. Look like you're enjoying it. I damn well wish I'd brought some myself."

Kaunitz and Purdon were silent and looking too intently towards the walls, searching glumly for what they knew by now they would not find, their glances returning repeatedly to that narrow ramp, that potential place of slaughter. From where they now sat two faces of the fort were visible, the landward face, with its gateway and its threat of failure and carnage, and that which ran out towards the frontage, with bastions at either end. That to seaward was closer to the bay.

Dawlish had spotted something.

Hope rose – a chance, the very slightest chance – but he suppressed it until he could be more sure.

"Tell me something, Purdon," he hissed. "Anything. About yourself, about your family. Make us laugh, any story. Laugh yourself as you tell it." He looked to Kaunitz – who looked bemused – and to Staunton. "Laugh loudly with him when he does."

Purdon seemed to have caught his drift and launched into a long story about his father, a country doctor, falling from his horse into a ford. It seemed endless, and devoid of all humour, but as Purdon rambled on with forced hilarity Dawlish was looking towards the seaward bastion. There, on its inner side, in the sharp angle where its flank met the side wall, something like a dark jagged crack ran down all the way from the crenellations above to the rock beneath.

"– and when the gypsy and his wife hauled the old chap out, the woman said…" Purdon was forcing himself to laugh and Staunton was guffawing loudly. Kaunitz, still bewildered, was trying to join in the impression of devil-may-care seamen ashore in a foreign port and determined to enjoy themselves whether the locals resented their presence or not.

As the laughter faded Dawlish leaned forward and said in an undertone, "On the left. That bastion. Look carefully. Now, Purdon, keep talking."

He tried to look amused by the account of the thick snow that had slid off a steep roof and had half-buried Purdon when he was a boy but his glance kept flicking back toward what must be a crack. There seemed to be a slight dip in what should have been the unbroken horizontal line of the wall's top – there had been subsidence there at some time. Purdon too seemed to have seen it and after his tale reached a less than hilarious conclusion, though the others were laughing anyway, he inclined his head to Dawlish and said quietly "It's a crack. And look below it."

Staunton had now risen to the challenge, was telling of a night ashore at Malta and of an escapade that had been comical if not seemly, while Dawlish focussed on the rock below the wall.

There was a definite fissure that ran from the wall's base in a long zig-zag, a well-established bush emerging from it halfway down. It could only have resulted from some long-forgotten earth tremor but there was no doubt that, even though it had not been catastrophic, there had been weakening of the foundation. Clumps of vegetation protruded from small cracks in the rock below the bastion itself, but it was difficult to see how extensive, or how deep, they were.

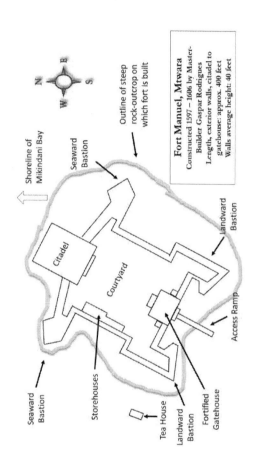

N E S W

Shoreline of
Mikindani Bay

Seaward
Bastion

Outline of steep
rock-outcrop on
which fort is built

Citadel

Courtyard

Landward
Bastion

Access Ramp

Seaward
Bastion

Storehouses

Tea House

Landward
Bastion

Fortified
Gatehouse

**Fort Manuel, Mtwara**
Constructed 1597 – 1606 by Master-
Builder Gaspar Rodrigues
Length, exterior walls, citadel to
gatehouse: approx. 400 feet
Walls average height: 40 feet

291

Staunton's story had reached its disgraceful climax, the cover of the laughter allowing Kaunitz's attention too to be drawn also to the fissures.

Purdon had recognised the same promise as did Dawlish.

"We could give it all we have," he whispered, "full broadsides, again and again. Our magazines are full."

And so it went for a half-hour or longer, feigned conviviality, frustration rising the while because it was impossible to learn more without closer inspection. For that, there would be only a fleeting opportunity, a minute or so of observation, when they would march back to the quay. From his seat Dawlish could see Maddox involved in desultory conversation with the Baluchi officer and hoped that he was probing for information about the number of defenders. Maddox had impressed as stolidly reliable, rather than quick-witted, and Dawlish feared that his probing might be unsubtle enough to alert the caution of a seasoned old campaigner like ex-Havildar Major Khalid. Maddox would be lucky to elicit anything of value.

\*

Wainwright's visit lasted much shorter than the two hours he had hoped for, his appearance with Imker and Ibrahim at the gate bringing Maddox and the escort hurrying back to the base of the ramp. Waiting with his empty rifle held at the salute, Dawlish saw that Imker's dismissal of the two men was peremptory, no handshake for Wainwright or hand held to heart for Ibrahim. He was stamping back into the fort – the danger of recognition gone now – even as they began to descend the ramp. The line of guards at its bottom parted to let them through. Ibrahim's face was grim, his teeth clenched in what could only be suppressed rage, but Wainwright's was impassive. Only when he reached the escort did he glance for an instant towards Dawlish, catch his eye and smile faintly.

As expected. Proposal rejected, as it had been intended to be.

The only reason for it had been to facilitate this reconnaissance and now the best must be made of what remained of it.

Ibrahim remained by Wainwright's side and the escort trailed behind. As it wound back along the base of the bluff, Dawlish's eyes,

Purdon's and Kaunitz's too, were locked on the great crack that ran down in the inner angle of the bastion to the rock below. It was deep there and it fanned out, a lacework of fissures that extended, some small, some gaping, many half-obscured by foliage, out towards the bastion's pointed tip. The temptation to glance back as that corner was turned was dangerous, but irresistible. Heart thumping with elation, Dawlish saw that tracery of cracks extended also through the rock below the bastion's seaward-facing side. And, better still, the merest trace of a crack there snaked up between the blocks of the fortification's stonework towards the top of the wall. At another point there had been a minor rockfall, all but hidden by bushes.

Eyes front again, Dawlish hissed, "Look back!" to Purdon and sensed the gunner's joy as he too saw what he himself had seen.

Back now past the misery of the slave pens, past the stalls and wells, past the mosque with the high minaret, though the maze of alleys, through the wide street leading to the quayside. From here only the tops of the fort's walls could be discerned and the town's jumble of buildings shielded the bluff that supported it from view. Purdon had spoken of broadsides but it would be more difficult than that, much more difficult...

The quay was as lifeless as before, though beyond the steps there seemed to be some activity at Imker's gunboat. Ibrahim and Wainwright stopped at the top of the steps and the local escort fell back. Maddox led Dawlish and the others forward, brought them to the salute, and at a nod from Wainwright they descended to the cutter below. Its crew were shaking themselves from their torpor – they had sat in the sun patiently, if not comfortably, for over two hours – but their faces registered relief that the group had returned safely, that they would be back on *Ibis* in ten minutes. Dawlish and the others boarded and again took their places at the oars. Maddox followed and sat in the sternsheets.

Wainwright and Ibrahim were shaking hands at the top of the steps, the one fulsome in his thanks, the other still clearly upset. The lot of a sultan's junior half-brother was in an unenviable one – Dawlish had once known two and fate had not been kind to either. Imker had shown today that he himself was clearly the sultan's favourite – perhaps as much an *eminence grise* here as Kirk was in Zanzibar – and he had not hesitated to advertise Ibrahim's marginalisation to others.

The cutter had been manoeuvred to lie with its transom touching the bottom step, ready for Wainwright to step in, only the boat-hook's grasp detaining it. He spoke a last quiet word with Ibrahim and descended, boarded and seated himself. The oars were out now, blades poised just above the water. A thrust of the boat-hook was driving it out as Fuller, the coxswain, called "Give way together!"

Intent on his oar and beginning the stroke, Dawlish was leaning forward, a glow of relief and satisfaction flushing through him – the risk, well calculated, had paid off – when suddenly there was a flurry and a cry on the steps. Ibrahim, robe snatched up to free his legs, was rushing down, two at a time, and calling "Wait!"

Wainwright was looking back and up, Maddox too, both paralysed by surprise. It flashed on Dawlish's mind that this man's worth was incalculable, that he could be the key to Mtwara.

Dawlish seized the moment, half-rose from the thwart, and shouted "Back water!" It was the voice of command, no longer a humble seaman's, and the rowers responded, killing the cutter's sluggish forward surge and driving the stern back to the steps. Now Ibrahim was leaping, landing unhandily, was grabbed and hauled down by Maddox and the coxswain.

"Give way together!" Dawlish bellowed.

The cutter leaped forward.

"Back to *Ibis*! Fast!" Dawlish called to Maddox.

The crew had realised the urgency, were pulling hard, and at the top of the steps the mercenary officer Khalid was gaping as if dumbstruck, the remainder of the escort he commanded running up to join him. Then realisation dawned and he shouted, the words incomprehensible but the intent clear, as the men around him fumbled to bring up their rifles. Ibrahim's store of courage had been used up in his rush and now he was cowering on the boards at Wainwright's feet. The coxswain, Fuller, was pushing the tiller over to head for the cover of the nearest moored dhow and Maddox was pushing rounds into the revolver that he had been forced to carry empty when ashore.

Dawlish had never rowed so hard as this, nor any other on the cutter either – no fiercely-contested fleet regatta could compare – and a line of men from the erstwhile escort was stringing out along the quayside and raising weapons. Khalid had snatched a rifle from one of them and was dropping to one knee in approved British style, steadying his elbow on his other as he took aim.

Time stood still, all will concentrated on one purpose only, to maintain the rhythm of the strokes. The quay was receding, the nearest dhow – unseen by the rowers, its hull a shield, salvation – could be only yards ahead, the coxswain's gaze locked on it as he nudged the tiller over. Maddox – stupidly, for his objective should be escape alone – had turned to face astern. He was half-kneeling, half-distracted by Ibrahim grovelling below him, was calling on Wainwright to steady him, was raising his revolver –

And he died.

Khalid, ex-29th Bombay Infantry, put a bullet straight through Maddox's chest, blood exploding from his back as he collapsed on to Wainwright. But Fuller, the coxswain, was keeping his nerve, flinging the tiller far over so that the cutter curved under a dhow's stern, a useless ripple of fire sounding astern as it swept into cover. It ran for yards only in the hull's lee, then arced out again to run between the flock of anchored dhows ahead. Wainwright, scarlet-spattered and shocked, pulled himself from under Maddox's body and called "He's dead!"

"Fuller!" Dawlish, still pulling, shouted to the coxswain "*Ibis*! Nothing else!"

The cutter weaved onwards between the dhows – surprised faces glimpsed looking down, then hastily withdrawn below bulwarks. The worst lay ahead, the long stretch of open water still to be crossed to reach the *Ibis*. As the craft slid past the last of the moored craft the full extent of the quay was revealed, Imker's gunboat too, and at that instant flame blasted from the Krupp on her foredeck and billowing smoke engulfed it. The sharp report was almost instantaneous and a long plume of spray tore across the cutter's heading, some twenty yards before her.

"Keep pulling!" Dawlish bellowed, and to Fuller "Zig-zag!"

A well-drilled crew – Imker would have settled for nothing less – could have that Krupp reloaded in under a minute, re-aimed in little more. Given its range, not just this cutter but *Ibis* too was at its mercy. The rowers' rhythm was furious now as the open craft surged in a sinuous course towards the bay's centre.

"Good old *Ibis*!" Fuller shouted. "She'll not let us down. Pull hard, lads! Pull!"

Dawlish was forcing himself not to look towards the gunboat at the quay, not to imagine the crew there slipping another round into the Krupp's smoking breech, the block sliding shut behind it, the gun-layer spinning the handwheel to hold the cutter in his sights – no need to worry about elevation, for the trajectory would be flat at this near point-blank range.

Then the sharp crack, every head in the cutter drawn over involuntarily to glimpse the rolling smoke, a line of spray streaking towards them as the shell skimmed the water, seconds that seemed like aeons. And then reprieve, relief inexpressible, hearts singing in the realisation that the foam showering down on them was from the round's passage only feet astern.

"Pull! Pull!" Fuller was sending the cutter arcing away to starboard. "It's *Ibis*, lads!" he yelled. "She's coming! She's not leaving us!"

Suddenly a flicker of movement in the corner of Dawlish's right eye – and there was the gunvessel herself, driving forward with white foam at her bow, a leadsman in the chains just above calling the depth, smoke and sparks vomiting from her funnel, screw churning and wake boiling astern. On her bridge Jarvis turned for the briefest instant towards the cutter and saluted.

And something yet better, figures in the foretop, two, and a Gatling visible between them, the loader crouching by the Broadwell ammunition-hopper, the gunner swinging the barrel-stack shoreward.

*Ibis* was heeling in a turn to port to lay herself between the cutter and the shore – all but suicidal, for her unarmoured flank was worth little more against a Krupp shell than a sheet of pasteboard, and her one-fifty pounder did not possess accuracy enough to menace Imker's craft.

But her Gatling did.

It barked into life, four, six rounds, a pause, six more – the gunner was taking no chances of a jam – and then another pause, another burst. The crew were scurrying from the Krupp – impossible to see if any had been hit, but that did not matter, only that the weapon itself was standing forlorn and silent.

Jarvis had taken his vessel at speed into unknown waters and had gambled everything on the skill and reliability of the leadsman to avoid grounding, but now caution was bringing *Ibis* around to head seaward, to parallel the cutter's path, to draw closer still.

A messenger line was thrown and caught. It drew a heavier line behind and the cutter was dragged over against the gunvessel's flank. The craft leaped and plunged as *Ibis* raced towards the open sea and as the exhausted crew clambered up a Jacob's ladder. Maddox's body was hauled up, and Wainwright and Ibrahim followed. Dawlish waited until last – this was Jarvis's moment of glory and he should be left to savour it to the full. The Krupp, manned again, sounded one more time, but the aim was badly off, its shell throwing up a plume fifty yards off the port quarter.

Fortune had smiled.

## Chapter 29

Zanzibar.

Eight days of preparation, of planning, of victualing, of coaling and of training. Eight days of frustration, of unforeseen problems, of inadequacies discovered and of solutions improvised. Eight days of hope of bloodless success, of chilling acceptance of what the reality might be, of unadmitted fear of abject failure, of dread of unqualified defeat

*Ibis* had remained on station off Mtwara to maintain the blockade, venturing further seawards only briefly before *Leonidas* left her to bury Maddox. Jarvis had conducted the service and Dawlish had added a few words that felt so trite in the face of loss. Even before the canvas-wrapped body slipped overboard from beneath the union flag, gloom had replaced the euphoria that the crew had felt when *Ibis* had so daringly rescued the cutter from Mikindani Bay. There had been death enough already and now, though the crew knew nothing of the plans, continued patrol off Mtwara told them that there might not yet be an end to it.

Kaunitz accompanied Dawlish to Zanzibar on *Leonidas*, as did Wainwright and Ibrahim Ibn Rahman. The Mtwara sultan's half-brother – a relationship so often inimical to fraternal trust – had regained his dignity since he had cowered on the bottom-boards and Dawlish yielded possession of his own cabin to him.

"It's worth the inconvenience," Wainwright had urged. "Kirk will see that he's a godsend. He'll want to install him as Barghash's catspaw once the place is taken."

And already Ibrahim was proving his worth by the information he provided, helped by the fact that he had a strong preference for spirits despite praying ostentatiously several times a day. Mtwara's sultan had three hundred mercenaries in service, he revealed, recruited and trained by Imker himself. Guards employed by slavers could add half as many again. Imker had arrived almost two years before. Berate the Dutchman as he now might do, it had been Ibrahim who had seen first merit in Imker's proposal to ship slaves by steamer and to create an armed force that in the sultan's own name could take control of those lands far inland now dominated by the slavers' columns. Ibrahim had recommended the scheme to the sultan – half a woman, he called him, and a slave to opium – and had gained his support. Within months, Imker had gained ascendancy over Sultan Saif and had marginalised Ibrahim completely. Now it was time for revenge.

Kirk, when Dawlish arrived in Zanzibar, endorsed Wainwright's view.

"A scoundrel," he said, "but he's the cleverest as well as the most unscrupulous of all the Mtwara half-brothers. Most of them came here at one time or another to get Barghash's support but it was impossible to take any of them seriously. But Ibrahim's a sly one – he stayed close to the sultan, played the loyal brother, and feathered his own nest while he waited for a chance to push a pillow over his face. But now that Imker's in Mtwara, he knows there's no future for him."

Dawlish had no desire to be involved in the dealings with Ibrahim – he saw a squalor in them that dishonoured the memory of O'Rourke and Maddox and the other dead. He shared little of Kirk's satisfaction when, two days later, the consul confirmed that Ibrahim had pledged his loyalty to Sultan Barghash, that once installed as Sultan of Mtwara he would rule as a faithful vassal of Zanzibar.

Once installed...

The words assumed so much, as if capture of a fortress that had proved impregnable in the past, and was probably little less so today, was a mere formality. Kirk's exchange of telegrams with London, those he showed Dawlish, had confirmed the desirability – a weak word that, capable of multiple interpretations in the event of failure – of capture of Mtwara and the necessity for full cooperation with the German forces involved. There was full confidence in Captain Dawlish's judgement.

Dawlish sent his own coded telegram to Topcliffe, not disguising the likely cost in life. The answer was unambiguous, *"Adopt whatever measures you may consider necessary."*

Cooperation with Kaunitz was an obligation, but it was also a pleasure, his suggestions pragmatic, his criticisms fair and usually valid, his dedication total. Consolidation of what was now known about Fort Manuel – Wainwright's knowledge of its interior, Ibrahim's information on numbers and weapons, Purdon's and Kaunitz's and Dawlish's own observations – was the starting point for planning the assault.

Several options were evaluated, each with a glimmer of promise until the weight of the attacking force was thrown into the balance, and then there was but one that remained. Details could be argued but the overall plan was always the same. And, even for that, the numbers available for the assault might well be insufficient. *Leonidas* and *Ibis* between them could contribute a hundred and thirty-five officers and men, *Hildegarde* another hundred. Mathews, when he arrived back from up the Rovuma, would command a hundred of his men drawn from the Zanzibar garrison itself. Lutz – introduced by Kaunitz as Oberst Doktor Lutz – could not be excluded from the meetings. Other than his local knowledge he had nothing to contribute but his dozen or so remaining askaris who had been brought across from Bagamoyo.

Dawlish kept back his concern over numbers even from Kaunitz. He agonised over how many he could safely take from *Leonidas* if she were to be still delicately handled and her guns – her vital guns – were to be expertly served. The ratio of attackers to defenders was close to one-to-one, might be worth perhaps half as much again when superior training was taken into account, but conventional wisdom advocated three-to-one as a minimum.

Only one factor could tip the scales, and on that he was gambling.

It would be essential to get the attacking force ashore as fast as possible but the three warships between them did not carry enough boats to allow it to be done in a single wave. There were pulling boats aplenty at Zanzibar however, property of merchants, some large enough to carry two or three dozen men. Five were requisitioned, not without protest. Leigh was assigned to erecting a stiff-leg crane on a flat-topped lighter for hoisting and lowering them, and seamen from *Leonidas* were set to training men from Mathew's force in rowing. The cruiser herself would tow the lighter. The small tramp that had previously been chartered to take Mathews' force up the Rovuma was now available to carry his men to Mtwara. Provisions were no less a concern and Wainwright, familiar with Zanzibar's merchants and traders – Indians, Gujaratis, for the most part – proved invaluable in securing not just quantity, but quality, at a cost that Kirk was prepared to countenance.

Training was relentless, not just the boat-pulling, but the manner of fast exiting from them, practised at a remote beach, and the relentless bayonet and cutlass drills, and the rifle practice for both British and Germans on a range laid out ashore. The men might grumble among themselves of exhaustion and of banning of shore leave, but when they stormed Mtwara their improved chance of survival would make that a price worth paying. Driven relentlessly by Latham, *Leonidas's* commissioned engineer, grimy artificers and stokers and trimmers slaved in the boiler and engine rooms to clean grates and fire-tubes, to adjust glands and packings, to tighten flanges and to re-lap suspect bearings, to grease and to lubricate, to restore the cruiser's motive power to the same peak of efficiency that had previously carried her from Portsmouth to Hong Kong in unprecedented time.

Rigging of temporary lifting tackle allowed the four-inch weapon on *Hildegarde's* starboard side to be lowered into a lighter, the mounting and the barrel separately. They were brought around to port, then hoisted for location on the sternmost of the empty gun positions. The task demanded a combination of brute strength and delicacy. A Royal Navy crew could not have managed it more efficiently, Dawlish admitted to himself. Efficiency seemed characteristic of everything undertaken on the German ship. Kaunitz, impressed by *Leonidas's* weapons, requested, with some hesitation, that Purdon might come across to *Hildegarde* to share experience with her own gunners. Like the Japanese, whose navy had also been created so recently, the Germans were eager to learn.

"They're keen, damn keen, sir," Purdon reported to Dawlish. "Not bad chaps either. They can't wait to fire in anger – this navy of theirs hasn't done so yet. They don't like it that they haven't more guns, though they won't admit it – they're embarrassed by the empty mountings. But for all that I'd prefer guns with interrupted screws to sliding blocks, they're likely to give a good account of themselves."

"And their signalling?" Everything would depend on that, no less than it would for *Leonidas*.

"Adequate, sir. It needs to be better."

There was no need to emphasise that to Kaunitz. It was enough that he had witnessed the speed of exchange of flag-semaphoring between *Leonidas's* signallers on shore and their counterparts on the vessel herself. Fast as it was, it was still subject to constant practice. The German captain had drawn his own conclusion and *Hildegarde's* signallers were following suit.

And with time running out, Dawlish hoped that would be enough.

*

Departure imminent.

A last meeting ashore with Kirk, confidential and political, with Wainwright also present, but not Kaunitz or Lutz. Mathews joined them, having arrived three days before and externally the fiction must be maintained that he was overall expedition commander, to whom Dawlish and Kaunitz were providing support. His actual role would be command of the Zanzibari contingent. Wainwright was especially charged with care of Ibrahim, not just to preserve his life and see him proclaimed in Mtwara, but to remind him of his new-found loyalty, if necessary with a pistol to his head.

Then a last conference on *Leonidas,* tactical, not political. Slowed by the need for translations, British and German officers saw their roles explained on large drawings of Mikindani Bay and Mtwara's labyrinth of streets, and of Fort Manuel itself, its interior as well as its walls and bastions. Dawlish recognised the same solemnity he had witnessed at similar conferences before, awareness that the game was deadly serious, that there was no turning back, that any individual failure might compromise the entire venture, that wounding and death were probabilities. O'Rourke's absence lent intensity to the questions asked by *Leonidas's* officers when Dawlish called for them. The Germans, none of whom had seen action before, were even more meticulous in seeking clarification once Kaunitz had emphasised that queries did not imply insubordination.

Afterwards, toasts to the Queen-Empress and to the Kaiser, to success, to eternal friendship and fellowship. Handshakes, assurances, disguised fears, boats stroking back to the *Hildegarde* through the darkness.

Last letters sent ashore, the knowledge sobering that they might be read when the telegraph might already have alerted the addressees that they had been bereaved.

Last lingering doubts, dismissed as luxuries impermissible now that battle was imminent.

And last of all, dawn departure.

\*

The flotilla steamed down the coast in line ahead, *Hildegarde* leading – Dawlish had suggested flipping a coin to decide the honour. *Leonidas* followed, the boat-laden lighter straining on tow astern. In her wake, the squalid little tramp carrying Mathews' Zanzibari troops was struggling to maintain the eight knots that set the overall speed. The seas were calm, giving perhaps too much time to all, and to Dawlish perhaps more than most, for brooding on what might lie ahead.

He wondered whether the Reverend Joshua Horne, or Abbot Albrecht von Hohenfels, could have imagined what their well-meant, unworldly – and yes, naïve – aspirations had set afoot, whether they had ever despaired in the face of the immensity of the world's evil. A week since, the sight of the slaves confined like cattle in Mtwara's pens had restoked Dawlish's own awareness of it. And now, to combat that evil – and not because of what it was, but for national prestige – some men still healthy, still breathing, eating, sleeping on these ships would almost certainly die.

It was close to sunset on the second day when *Ibis* was sighted, still continuing her slow to-and-fro crawl across the broad mouth of Mikindani Bay. The three newcomers hove to a mile further out, fully visible from Mtwara town and Fort Manuel above it, no white flags this time, no indication of a desire to parlay. The sea was mirror-calm, the moon almost full and there was light aplenty to begin lowering of the boats, transfer of stores, checking of personal kit and weapons.

Jarvis came across to *Leonidas* for last instructions.

"Imker's gunboat?" Dawlish asked.

She was his first concern, must be Purdon's first target, to be smothered by a half-dozen six-inch shells as *Leonidas* moved shorewards at first light.

"She hasn't moved. She's still at the quayside."

"Still moored?" Dawlish had expected Imker to have shifted her to a location that would allow manoeuvre and a few desperate shots at any incoming force before abandoning her.

"It may be a blind," Jarvis said. "Imker does nothing without a reason. He knows he's safe from us where he's tied up, that we can't risk ranging shots landing in the town behind the gunboat."

"You think he's going to slip out of the bay in darkness?"

"Would you not try, Captain Dawlish?"

"I don't know. With the fort to retreat to, and believing that storming would cost too much, I might hope to negotiate a deal."

"And won't we? Isn't that why Wainwright's here with that fellow Ibrahim?"

"No," Dawlish said. "He's here to make him sultan. So are we."

"So what if the gunboat doesn't leave the quay?"

"We'll have to accept the risk of Purdon's ranging shots." The thought was horrifying.

"Am I permitted to go ashore this time?"

Jarvis spoke as if he had half-convinced himself that he would again be denied the opportunity. He was surly in his relief when Dawlish confirmed that he would lead *Ibis's* contingent personally, scarcely more thankful when his exact role was detailed. Dawlish did not mention Imker's name again, but did not need to.

For Jarvis, the morrow's assault would be personal.

*

By three o'clock, daylight still two hours away, the steam launches were in the water, their boilers stoked, pressure rising, smoke drifting from their brightly-polished funnels. The boats that they would tow to shore astern of them still lay along the sides of the three warships. Stores had been loaded in them and the bluejackets and marines would board in another hour. *Leonidas's* pinnace, largest of the small steam-craft, lay alongside the tramp and was assigned to towing the heavy harbour-boats requisitioned at Zanzibar. Shells and charges had been brought up from the magazines and were stacked by the guns of all three warships.

There was little Dawlish could do now but watch, direction of *Leonidas's* activity being smoothly managed by Edgerton, the few queries referred to himself easily resolved. The work was progressing equally satisfactorily on the other vessels.

"Deck there!"

The lookout's call from the darkness at the foretop was unexpected, what was shouted down thereafter inconclusive. Something was happening in the harbour, what exactly, uncertain.

Dawlish went aloft.

The moon, to the west, showed the land as a dark streak, Mtwara identifiable only by a few stationary pinpricks of light and by the black outline of Fort Manuel. The unrippled waters of the bay were a weak silver. A glance, even before Dawlish took the night-glass from the lookout, told that they were empty. It was towards the quay that the man was pointing. Weak lights bobbed there, briefly exposed, never for more than a minute, then dying suddenly.

"It started about five minutes ago, sir. I wasn't sure at first, they're so dim..."

Dawlish cut off the lookout. "Call for Commander Edgerton to come up.".

He was focussing now on the shapes at the quay, dark against the slightly lighter dark behind. At this distance – some three miles – it would be hard to pick out much detail even in daylight, but as his eye adjusted he fancied that he could make out the dhows moored close inshore. They had not moved. He shifted his focus ever so slightly to seek the bulk of Imker's gunboat. She seemed to be at the exact location where he had last seen her tied up. And it was there that the lights were winking briefly, there and strung out on the quay behind, and in what seemed to be one of the streets leading to the harbour. The glows were dim to the point of near-invisibility and they danced slightly, appearing and disappearing irregularly.

Edgerton appeared, slightly winded, and took the glass, was as mystified as Dawlish.

Then, unexpectedly, for seconds only, there was fortuitous quietness on *Leonidas*, the slightest interval between voices of command, the noise of creaking hoists, of boats rubbing against the hull, all sounds of activity accidentally and coincidentally paused. In that fleeting moment a sound carried across the still waters from the town, human voices, a dull murmur broken by shouts, then all lost as activity on the cruiser drowned them out again.

It was enough.

Dawlish had the glass again and now the flickers made sense, lamps revealed and obscured and revealed irregularly again, their rays interrupted by the movement of bodies. Understanding – horror – dawned, even as his mind wanted to deny it.

"The slaves," he said. "They're loading the slaves on board. Here," – he thrust the glass to Edgerton – "tell me if it can be that."

Edgerton watched for half a minute and he too recognised it for what it was. "They're hostages." Revulsion in his voice. "Like a shield. We can't..." Words failed.

Because the Krupp, that single weapon, deadly accurate at less than two miles and firing on an almost horizontal trajectory, could doom every boat of the landing force long before they could reach shore. Dawlish had steeled himself to accept responsibility for the casualties that Purdon's two ranging shots falling in the town might inflict. They would all but guarantee a direct hit with the third and with those which would follow. They would disembowel the gunboat, silence the Krupp, with luck might kill or incapacitate Imker himself, and with him Mtwara's will to resist...

And kill wretches by the dozen who had survived a trail of misery across half a continent. Some at least might be shackled to the masts – the man who had massacred a village in Borneo, and who had conceived of slave-shipment by steam, would not shrink from that. Others, women too, would be packed around them. A single shell exploding among them would cause carnage...

That Krupp breech-loader, the superbly cast, machined and rifled product of the most accomplished gunmakers in Europe, was as well protected as if shielded by armour plate. It set at naught the power of the guns outnumbering her on the warships in the bay, made a massacre of innocents the price of proceeding with the landing...

*Adopt whatever measures you may consider necessary.*

Topcliffe's authorisation was a carte blanche in name only. The pious groups which had prevailed on Gladstone to send succour to Horne's mission, who wanted to know nothing of the brutalities of impossible choices, would demand a victim if success was bought by a conscious decision to open fire on hostage slaves. That victim would be Dawlish himself. He could already imagine the accusations – callousness, bad planning, impetuosity, disregard for sanctity of life. Another Jarvis.

306

But, both London and Berlin demanded Mtwara's capture...

"What now, sir?" Edgerton's relief was palpable that the decision was not his.

The Armstrongs and Gatlings and Hales Rockets were of no value now. All that remained was the hazardous option that had been the navy's last, and most desperate, resort for three centuries.

*Boarding.*

## Chapter 30

The whaler disappeared into the darkness, oars muffled and double banked, Corporal Shand in the bows, Lieutenant Ross at the tiller. All fifteen occupants, officers and bluejackets and marines alike, were armed with rifles, cutlasses and as many revolvers – ideal for the sort of work ahead – as *Leonidas* could provide. One carried a sledge hammer and had a wooden cylinder slung over his back.

Dawlish watched from the port bridge-wing, smoking a cigar and masking his apprehension with a show of nonchalance. On the decks below him men were now lining up prior to boarding the boats that would carry them ashore – there had been no change to that schedule. The Armstrong crews were at their stations and the searchlight that had been hoisted to the foretop was in position, its gutta-percha insulated cable snaking down to disappear through a hatch to the dynamo in the engine room. Electric power was already available – tests below deck had confirmed it – but the order for throwing the switch to initiate the white-hot arc was reserved for Dawlish himself.

The waiting was intolerable and he would have preferred to be in that whaler himself. Fear gnawed within him that too much was being asked of Ross, that too much would depend on his success or failure. Kaunitz, Jarvis and Mathews had been informed by hand-carried notes of what was intended. They must not be surprised, neither should they react to it. It was better that they concentrate on the agreed preparations, that men be loaded into their boats in the next half-hour, that the move shorewards commence as the sky lightened. For, if Ross should fail, the landing would proceed exactly as planned, if necessary at the cost of

307

Purdon's Armstrongs blasting Imker's gunboat and all on board her to atoms, slaver and slave alike.

And such a decision, however unavoidable, would cost Dawlish his future quiet of conscience no less than his career.

Long minutes dragged, twenty, thirty, and he was grateful for the distraction offered by the few items referred to him for decision. The landing parties had dropped into the boats by now. The steam pinnace and launches were drawing them away in strings from the side of *Leonidas* and the other ships to loiter, rocking gently, a half-cable seaward of them.

"Ross must be close now." Edgerton, no less tense, was standing beside Dawlish.

There was no way of knowing. The whaler had headed in the darkness towards the shore a mile or more to the left of Mtwara, should have crawled along it, had obviously not been detected. It could not now be far off the small beach, some four hundred yards from the quay's end, where Ross would bring his men ashore.

"Yes," Dawlish said. "He must be close."

He moved to the steering position, nodded to the quartermaster, stood by the telegraph, Edgerton following.

The shoreline was still dark, though the bobbing lights were fewer. It was likely that all the slaves had been crowded aboard the gunboat by now, that Imker and his people would be smugly satisfied with the surprise they could unveil at sunrise.

Five minutes more, dreading the unexpected bark of gunfire, knowing that, with daybreak a little over an hour ahead, the friendly darkness was a waning asset.

And then decision.

"Carry on, Commander Edgerton."

No room for deviation from the immediate plan. Ross would be depending on absolute adherence to the steps that Dawlish had dictated at the hastily convened ten-minute conference before the whaler had departed.

Edgerton put his hand on the telegraph, signalled for dead-slow ahead. A pause, then the screws bit, and *Leonidas* nudged forward. High in the foretop, Blythe, the searchlight operator, would be searching for

Imker's gunboat, eye to night glass. So too Purdon, standing with the crew of the foremost six-inch on the port side, its mounting on a sponson allowing fire directly ahead. In the coming minutes, only this one gun would be brought into action.

Four cables advance, water gurgling slowly along the cruiser's flank with hardly a wave. Ross's party had to be ashore by now, must be moving from cover to cover along the foreshore, might even now be lurking in shadows at the end of the quay and waiting for …

"Searchlight! Ready?"

"Ready, sir!" Blythe's call from the foretop answered Dawlish's.

"Mr. Purdon! Ready?"

"Ready! Aye ready, Sir!"

Dawlish pushed the handle of the electric knife-switch forward over a full half-circle. Sparks fizzled at the foretop and instants later a white-hot arc was trembling between carbon rods within the searchlight's short cylinder. A frigid beam lanced ahead and cast a long, bright ellipse on the dark waters short of the shoreline. Now, as *Leonidas* still crawled forward, Blythe was spinning the light's geared elevation-handle, raising the beam until it struck the shore – low buildings, somewhere to the right of the quay – and then edging it across until it lit up the first of the moored dhows. A brief glimpse of a few figures rising in surprise from behind bulwarks, dropping again with shielding arms thrown across their eyes as the beam swept slowly on and lost them.

And there was the gunboat, hull, masts and yards stark, as if ice-encrusted, against the shadows behind. The searchlight's disc moved slowly from stem to stern – and there were the dropped bulwarks exposing the six-inch Krupp and behind them, and further aft, a dark mass that seemed to heave and shudder in the probing glare, that was lost again as the beam passed on.

*Leonidas* was now creeping to starboard to increase the arc available to the Armstrong in the port forward sponson. The searchlight's beam swung back along the gunboat's flank – the pulsating mass on its deck was composed, all too clearly, of packed slaves cowering and wailing before this new terror. Carried forward by the cruiser's wide turn, the beam ran on, lost the gunboat, transfixed the dhows again. Blythe swept it back to find its quarry.

He found it, and he held it. Surely nobody on that gunboat could imagine any other danger than the craft seeking them from the bay, nor could any imagine Ross's force moving forward – it must be close now – along the quay…

"Mr. Purdon! Your gun!"

A flaming tongue blasting from the Armstrong's muzzle, and the crack of her report, and the weapon and its crew engulfed by its rolling yellow smoke. The range was two miles at the most, and the shell's protectory was an almost flat parabola, and Purdon's challenge was to drop it well short of the gunboat, close enough to terrify and draw attention, far enough away to avoid destruction. From the bridge Dawlish saw a racing streak of spray rise up perhaps a thousand yards from the target and tear towards it for another hundred, icy white in the searchlight's unwavering beam. The plume lasted seconds only – seconds that must have seemed no less a lifetime for those who watched from the gunboat than it did for Dawlish himself – and then it dropped and died.

"Searchlight out!" Dawlish called to warn Blythe as he pulled the knife-switch open.

The light was suddenly gone and darkness shrouded the cruiser as Edgerton rang for half-revolutions and as the helm was thrown over to bring her into a tight turn. If Imker was on that gunboat, if he was holding his nerve and hoping to get his Krupp into action, then his target had already disappeared. Below him, Dawlish heard the clang of the Armstrong's breechblock, the gun-captain's call that it was again ready for firing, Purdon's acknowledgement. Ross should be storming across from the quay at this moment, while all on board the gunboat were still shocked and dazzled. The only sound now heard above the swish of waters alongside was of distant though prolonged screaming, wailing rather, hundreds of throats crying out in fear.

*Leonidas's* circle was three-quarters complete. The telegraph rang for dead-slow but the cruiser's momentum held her in the turn as the speed diminished.

"Searchlight! Ready!"

"Ready, sir!"

Dawlish ground the switch's handle forward again and the light blazed into life, reached out, swept along the line of dhows at the quay, caught and held the gunboat.

"Yours, Mr. Purdon!"

Once more the Armstrong's bark, the streak of spume sprinting shorewards, the final collapse, all velocity spent, but this time less than a cable's length distant from the gunboat. A moment's silence, and then the terrified screaming rising again. Caught in the beam – there were no colours there but brilliant white and deepest black – were figures hurling themselves in frenzied terror into the water.

Then, sharp above the sound of misery, the unmistakable crackle of rifle fire, the longed-for announcement that Ross was mounting his assault from the quayside. Half his men would be giving covering fire, the remainder thrusting forward with bayonets to board and clear a path towards the Krupp. And then there would be the melee, cutlasses and revolvers hacking and blasting at any who showed opposition, orders clear that nobody, slaver or even slave, would be allowed to impede possession of the weapon.

Now *Leonidas* was dropping a second whaler, crewed by rowers and coxswain alone, and it raced toward the gunboat to take off the attackers. The cruiser was all but stationary now, the only contribution she could make to keep the gunboat bathed in light. Dawlish watched in a disguised agony of helplessness and through his binoculars could make out nothing but a mob around the Krupp. The diversion had proved perfect, and surprise at the onslaught from the shore must have been absolute. Had the gunboat's crew alone been on board, then the vessel would surely have been carried by now. Against Ross's assault however, the slaves were as much a human shield for Imker's people as they were against the guns of the warships offshore. Shots still crackled – impossible to judge from which side – and the bodies surged to and fro, yet more now leaping overboard in panic.

It might have lasted three minutes, certainly not more than four. A space was cleared around the Krupp, bodies crumpled about it, an outward facing ring of marines' bayonets now fencing it. Dawlish's heart sang as he saw Ross look towards *Leonidas* and raise his rifle in triumph while behind him the marine who had carried the wooden cylinder was hammering it deep into the Krupp's barrel. A section of spare spar had been hastily pared down, before setting out, to little more than six-inches diameter. Now it emasculated the weapon.

The whaler from *Leonidas* drew alongside the gunboat. Ross's party dropped into it, himself last of all. It pushed off and stroked away between the wretches struggling in the water. Lost in the darkness as Dawlish shut off the searchlight, it bumped alongside the cruiser a few minutes later.

Ross bounded to the bridge.

"Damn well done!" Dawlish met him at the top of the ladder. "And Imker? The Dutchman? Was he there?"

"I don't know, sir. Several Europeans there, Lascars too. We must have seen off half-a-dozen of 'em. When they saw we had the best of it they went over the side."

"Our people?"

"Only a few bruises." Ross paused. His elation at success and survival was ebbing. "It was hell there, sir," he said. "Those slaves. Women too. God knows how many of them were there, how many dead either, trampled and..." His voice trailed off.

Dawlish guessed that not all of the blood on the young marine lieutenant's bayonet had belonged to slavers. However unavoidable, he would carry that memory to his grave.

But, whatever the cost, the way was now clear.

The sky was lightening in the east. In a quarter-hour the landing would commence as planned.

*

The die was cast as the sun leaped over the eastern horizon like an incandescent ball.

A single rocket soared from *Leonidas,* the agreed signal.

Dawlish watched in silence from the bridge, Wainwright by him. His heart was thumping and he was forcing calm on his features, hoping to radiate a confidence he did not feel, resisting the urge to comment or interfere. *Leonidas* was to be entrusted to Edgerton in the coming hours and under his terse directions the cruiser was already moving shorewards at dead-slow towards her planned position. Four cables to starboard the *Hildegarde* was moving towards the bay's western extremity. Astern of them, the strings of open boats had begun their own advance, straining on the pinnace and launches' lines, while others were beating forward under oars.

*Ibis* passed ahead of *Leonidas* at half-revolutions, foam churning under her counter, Jarvis in full uniform on her bridge, brass buttons flashing in the sunlight. Her bows were headed directly towards the quay. The gunboat there was all but deserted, the slaves that had thronged her now fled ashore, but several figures were clustered around the spiked Krupp, poking into its barrel to dislodge the plug. They scurried away at the sight of *Ibis's* approach, hurrying on to the quay and losing themselves among the buildings behind. There had been other movement there too, uniformed men from the sultan's guard flitting from cover to cover, how many it was impossible to guess.

Edgerton moved closer to Dawlish.

"About now, captain?" A hint of desire for the decision to be another's rather than his own.

Dawlish glanced towards Fort Manuel's massive walls and bastions looming above the town.

"About four-thousand yards, I'd estimate." His eyes had shifted to the two minarets rising high over the roofs close to the slave pens. "Yes, commander. Now."

Edgerton was competent to do the rest.

"Our friend Ibrahim," Dawlish said to Wainwright. "Is His Highness awake?"

Mtwara's would-be sultan had drunk too much the night before and had been carried to bed. Distasteful as it might be, it was best not to deny him the brandy he demanded, for refusal made him belligerent.

"I've poured black coffee down his throat," Wainwright said. "It made little difference. The steward is trying to get him dressed now."

"He'll be carried ashore in a blanket if needs be."

Dawlish had enough of this petulant sot, would be glad to be rid of him. But for now he was needed, and ideally – and however briefly – on the throne of Mtwara.

*Leonidas* had swung to starboard, momentum dying as her engines stilled. She was parallel to the shore as the anchor that had been rigged above the stern was dropped. Its cable paid out, tautened, as the vessel drifted forward, and then a bow anchor fell also. Seamen at the forward capstan began to draw the cable in. The holding was good and now, anchored fore and aft, the cruiser lay broadside on to Mtwara, a secure gun-platform on a sea of mirror-calmness. A half-mile ahead, *Hildegarde* was executing a similar manoeuvre – smartly so, Dawlish noted. From her he could see her launch chugging towards the town's most distant extremity, where the buildings petered out in a fringe of palms along the beach, with five boats trailing on tows astern. Four carried *Hildegarde's* landing party and among them was Lutz and his few askaris. He had been insistent during the planning conference – to the point of discourtesy to Kaunitz – that he should be with the first ashore. In the last craft in the string, the fifth, were the eight men from *Leonidas* who were bringing her seven-pounder field gun ashore with the Germans.

A leadsman in her bows, bulwarks dropped to reveal her one-fifty on its turntable, *Ibis* had turned to creep parallel to the shore, two cables from it. Two minutes more would take her to the end of the quay. Ineffective rifle fire – wasted shots – were crackling from the low buildings there. Jarvis was resisting the temptation to return fire. He was intent on another target, one that must delight him.

*Leonidas's* steam pinnace steamed past her mother, five packed boats in tow. Her launch was following with another three and, a little further beyond, the oar-propelled craft carrying Mathew's force. All were driving towards the area just to the left of the quay, a sloping beach, a scattering of fishing craft drawn up along it, only a sparse line of houses there, the last of the town proper, cultivated fields beyond.

A crash as *Ibis's* main weapon blasted into life.

Deprived of a target when a bend in the Rovuma had cheated her of an earlier opportunity to bring Imker's gunboat under fire, the seven-inch was at last getting satisfaction. The 150-pound shell – explosive, not solid shot – tore into the wooden hull, an irregular rupture in its flank visible for an instant before a scarlet fireball erupted within. The mainmast thrashed, its stays and shrouds parting and lashing like whips, then toppled forward. Smoke billowed from the ruptured deck, flames flickering through it. The blaze grew – the tarred rigging had taken light – and the inferno was spreading to the shattered planking. Now another explosion, and another, on the foredeck this time, as flames engulfed the ready-use charges for the abandoned Krupp. But *Ibis* was well past by now, her broadside-mounted six-inch muzzle-loader aft smashing a moored dhow and then the seven-inch speaking again, its shell's detonation blowing a second dhow into fragments. If defenders had lurked among the moored shipping then they had miscalculated.

The pinnace and the launch had cast their towed strings loose by now and the individual boats were beating over the last half-cable's length to shore in ragged line-abreast and under oars alone. The Zanzibaris, unhandy rowers for all their hurried training, were following in a second wave. *Ibis* had turned, was steaming back on her previous track. The fire on the gunboat had leaped across to a dhow moored to the quay directly aft of her. But Jarvis had no eyes for these doomed vessels, his attention drawn to what might have been defenders among the buildings beyond. The seven-inch one-fifty had been pivoted around to bear to starboard, another massive shell had been rammed down its bore, and the gun captain was raising the elevation. Another roar, a bright flash against a large whitewashed structure, then rolling smoke and cascading debris as a whole wall collapsed to disclose rooms within.

Dawlish steadied his telescope on the bridge rail. Back from the waterfront, in that broad street he had marched up in disguise ten days before, people were milling, not defenders, but residents driven by panic from their dwellings, tumbling and jostling as they surged towards imagined safety. He swung the glass leftwards towards the beach, just beyond the quay's end, towards which the boats were stroking. Rifle fire was barking from the straggle of squalid huts and houses there –

315

somebody had stiffened the resolve of the briefly-spotted uniformed defenders as they moved from cover to cover and the men in the pulling craft could only be helpless targets. But Jarvis had seen the danger – something like this had been foreseen and *Ibis's* duty was to deal with it – and his muzzle-loaders, ideal for such work, were pounding shells into these buildings as fast as his gun-crews could reload.

And all this time the guns of *Leonidas* and *Hildegarde*, the potent, deadly-accurate breech-loaders, stood silent, awaiting only a command to call them into life, each with its numbered crew in their positions about it, ready-use reloads in racks behind, other men detailed to hoist more from the magazines below. For now, they could only wait. Their time would come.

Beyond the far end of Mtwara the German boats had reached the beach – no opposition there, where none had been considered likely – and seamen had dropped into the water to drag the bows up on the sand. Now men were leaping down, forming hurriedly into small groups, then moving inland through vegetable patches dotted with small huts with a clear impression of disciplined purpose. The Imperial German Navy was going to war – if this could be dignified as war – for the first time and Kaunitz had ordered that all, officers and ratings alike, would do so immaculately uniformed in tropical white. Dawlish fancied that he held him for a moment in his telescope's disc, striding forward with a brown-clad figure, certainly Lutz, by his side, before being lost behind vegetation. *Leonidas's* field gun was being manhandled ashore and would soon follow them.

*Leonidas's* boats were now grounding on their beach also, men from the first rushing forward at Ross's command to occupy the huts so recently demolished by *Ibis*. A cloud of dust overhung them but there was no opposition – the Mtwara forces there had fallen back. With this flank secure, the remainder of the boats, those carrying Mathews and his men, were also running in safely.

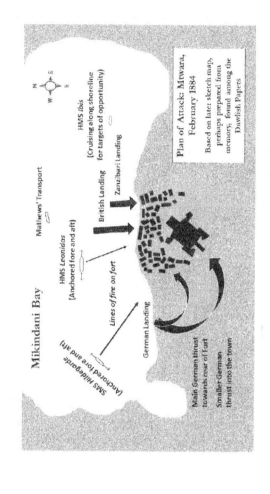

Plan of Attack: Mtwara, February 1884

Based on later sketch map, perhaps prepared from memory, found among the Dawlish Papers

Mikindani Bay

SMS *Hildegarde*
(Anchored fore and aft)

HMS *Leonidas*
(Anchored fore and aft)

Mathews' Transport

HMS *Ibis*
(Cruising along shoreline for targets of opportunity)

Lines of fire on fort

British Landing

Zanzibari Landing

German Landing

Main German thrust towards rear of fort

Smaller German thrust into the town

317

The assault force was ashore, one wing, British and Zanzibari, on the east, advancing along the quay prior to pushing into the town itself while the other, German, a mile distant to the west, was skirting around Mtwara's edge to head for the fort's inner face. Except for one small German party that would break away from the main group. They had an objective inside the town, a critical one.

Dawlish snapped his telescope shut. The landing had gone as well as had been hoped and he could do no more here. He turned to Edgerton.

"As decided, commander." He held out his hand. "She's yours now."

"You can depend on us. Good luck, sir." Edgerton's grip was firm.

"Mr. Purdon!" Dawlish called down to the forward six-inch, felt a surge of affection as he saw the eager face turned towards him. Whether with the *Toad's* ponderous nine-inch muzzle-loader on the Rio San Joaquin, or with these same Armstrongs off Korea, the young gunnery officer had never failed him. Now he was again wagering his life – and his career – on Purdon's expertise. No need for words, just a single nod, and that returned.

Confidence, respect, pride, affection.

He turned and glanced aft. The crews of the other four weapons mounted along the side were looking up. Names and faces familiar no less from defaulters' parades than from shared service in the Yellow Sea. No words for them either, only his hand rising in salute, theirs acknowledging.

Wainwright had been standing a little apart.

"It's time to rouse His Highness," Dawlish said. "Time for him to earn his throne."

Five minutes later the drink-befuddled sultan-apparent was slumped beside Wainwright in the sternsheets of Dawlish's gig as it beat towards the quay. Dawlish himself stood in the bows, glad to be more than an onlooker, fearful that he was pushing his luck to the limit, disguising that concern with an air of confidence, pushing aside as a luxury a fleeting thought of Florence.

For he knew that the worst was yet to come.

And for that, he must lead from the front.

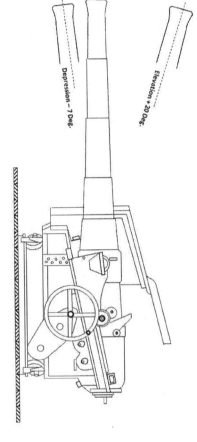

# Armstrong 6-inch Breech-loading Rifle
## on Vavasseur Slide & Turntable Mounting 1880
### As mounted on HMS *Leonidas* 1882
(Note that Shield is shown cut-away for clarity)

Weight: 81 cwt (4 tons)
Barrel length: 156 inches
Shell Types: 80 pounds Palliser Armour-piercing, Shrapnel, Common Shell

Depression – 7 Deg.

Elevation + 20 Deg.

## Chapter 31

Foxley was waiting at the top of the steps down which Ibrahim had made his undignified escape. Now he made an equally undignified return, stumbling, and half-carried by a seaman.

"It's going well, sir," *Leonidas's* navigator was commanding the fourth of the groups ashore on this side of Mtwara, thirty men who were to act as a rear-guard and reserve. "The scoundrels have fled into the town."

Other than two crumpled khaki-clad bodies, the quay area was deserted. The buildings behind had been shattered by *Ibis's* cannonade. Rifle fire sounded from somewhere beyond, brief and irregular, never more than a half-dozen shots at a time. It might be wishful thinking, but it sounded like a half-hearted retreat by the defenders.

"Any word from Mr. Ross?" Dawlish asked.

None yet. Ross's force was headed for the slave-pens. Nor from Leigh either, who should be pushing along the alleyways to Ross's right. But Mathews has sent a message back – the broad street leading in from the waterfront was secure and the bulk of his Zanzibaris had branched off from it to follow Ross. Small patrols had been left to pass back and forth through the alleys and lanes to ensure that nobody left their dwelling.

The ramparts were all that Dawlish could see of the fort from here. There was briefly-glimpsed movement behind the crenellations, but it was impossible to tell how many men were there. Whoever was in command – and it might well be Imker – must know that the town could not be held, that he should pull all he had back into the fortress, sit it out in confidence of its impregnability as Portuguese and Arab defenders had before, and hope to parlay terms.

Up that broad street now. A few bodies scattered there, most in the khaki of Imker's Mtwari guard, but several civilians too, blood patches shockingly red on white robes, dogs already hovering near. The houses to either side were shuttered, doors barred, and fearful eyes must be watching from within. Each main intersection had its own small guard of Mathews' Zanzibaris who grinned in confirmation that all was quiet here, that the main forces had headed rightwards into the labyrinth of alleyways. Dawlish remembered the route he had followed previously – Wainwright was by his side and confirming that they were on course, the high minaret that soared above the roofs before them their point of reference. The rifle fire ahead was dying but other, fainter, fire was sounding from far beyond, Kaunitz's people meeting their first opposition.

A Zanzibari soldier crouched by a wounded comrade confirmed that Mathews had branched off here to concentrate his force in the part of town opposite the citadel at the middle of the fort's seaward-facing wall. Dawlish's group pressed straight onwards toward the minaret. Two uniformed Mtwaris lay in grotesque postures around the next corner and one more twenty yards beyond. Smoke and flames billowed from a substantial whitewashed house at the corner at the end of the next alley. Several men – stupid rather than heroic – must have made a stand there and been driven out by the blaze. If they had expected quarter, then they had been mistaken, for they had been finished with the bayonet.

Another lane, more shuttered houses, an unseen child crying disconsolately within and a woman trying to calm it, everywhere the impression of suppressed terror behind blank walls. More Zanzibari wounded, none too serious, and – Thank God! – no sign of British casualties.

They reached the mosque, its courtyard guarded by a half-dozen bluejackets, no sign of it having been defended, nor of its significance having been recognised by the town's defenders. Twenty or so Mtwari prisoners, some uniformed, some robed, squatted in one corner, hands on bowed heads, cowering before the four Zanzibari troops guarding them with fixed bayonets.

The leading hand in charge touched his hat. "Mr. Leigh is up there, sir." He jerked his head towards the minaret.

"Lunt and Canavan too?" The yeoman of signals and the seaman most proficient in flag semaphoring.

They were.

Another *Leonidas* arrived, sweat-soaked, panting.

"Mr. Ross's compliments, sir. An' he says that he's in position."

That would be beyond the slave pens, following orders not to push further forward for now.

"Wait here," Dawlish said to Wainwright. "And him," – disgust stopped him using Ibrahim's name as he gestured towards the mosque door – "Get him into shade there. Don't leave him." He turned to Foxley. "Go forward and join Ross. There are men enough here already. Report to Commander Jarvis when he gets there."

Up the spiral steps in the minaret's interior. Leigh met him on the small circular balcony encircling the top. There was barely enough room for four men and there would be even less when Canavan got to work.

"It's ideal, sir" Leigh said, "We can't see inside, but there's a good view of the bastion." The minaret's top was on a level with the base of the fort's wall, the distance to it some eight hundred yards.

Dawlish took the telescope that Lunt, the yeoman, handed him. He knelt, steadied it on the parapet, focussed. He might have missed it if he had not known where to look, but the fine tracery of cracks in the rock beneath the rightmost bastion seemed close enough to touch. He turned, looked out across the bay, saw the white hulls of *Leonidas* and *Hildegarde* broadside on.

"We've got contact with 'em," Leigh said. "We've signalled. *Leonidas* acknowledged."

Flat roofs stretched from here towards the great open space occupied by the slave pens. They were empty now – any wretches not driven from them to the gunboat in the early hours must be confined in the huts along the perimeter. The pens lay directly on the line of fire between the anchored ships and the bastion. With luck, any undershoots would land harmlessly on empty ground. Mathews' force should be concentrated to the left by now, the British contingents to the right, a gap of some two hundred yards between them, a thin line of houses filling it. The track that ran around the base of the fortress walls lay just beyond.

Sounds of shouted protest, of screams and wailing, washed from the houses. Mathews' Zanzibaris were hammering on doors, evicting the occupants – it would be impossible to convince them that it was for their own safety – and driving them to take shelter with neighbours outside the line of imminent fire. Brief glimpses of the white duck of British uniforms and the khaki of the Zanzibaris showed that men had already been positioned on roofs to watch for any movement from the fort. Occasional rifle-shots told of some last resistance around the other minaret, that beyond the pens. Then the last reports, and after it an all but absolute silence, eerie and ominous. Dawlish had a sense of an entire town frozen in fear, breath held in knowledge that this could be a respite only, that more violence was to come. And beyond, the great brooding fortress gravid with quiet menace.

"Over there, sir!" Leigh pointed to the right of the bastion.

A mile distant, where the town thinned and the cultivated fields began, two compact white-clad groups were moving forward, *Leonidas's* field-gun detachment following. Dawlish took the glass and saw three figures out in front, one most certainly Kaunitz, and the other Lutz, with a seaman between and carrying an imperial ensign proudly aloft. They had skirted the town successfully, had driven back any opposition met, and were now heading for a position directly in line with the ramp leading to the gate on the fort's inner face. The advance was as planned, and yet Dawlish felt uneasy. There was an impression of foolhardy confidence about the execution of the movement, of vainglory and theatricality even, of an apparent scorn for a stealthier approach in smaller groups, of making insufficient use of cover. He hoped that Kaunitz would resist the temptation to take position too far forward. A skilled marksman with a Chassepot – and there must be hundreds of such rifles atop the walls of Fort Manuel – could kill at over four-hundred yards.

"Beg pardon, sir." Lunt again. "Them Germans has that other tower."

And there they were, an officer and two seamen on the balcony of the second, lower, minaret, three hundred yards beyond the pens. Several more seamen must be positioned below to defend the courtyard. This small group detached from Kaunitz's main force had thrust successfully towards the mosque. What small opposition they had encountered must have been in the alleyways and the precious minaret did not appear to have been defended. Now one of the German seamen was standing on the parapet, his comrade grasping him about the knees, as he semaphored towards *Hildegarde*. The officer with them – Dawlish recognised him as a young lieutenant – had turned this way and was saluting. From that tower's vantage too, the fort's bastion could be held in observation, not just the outer side visible to Dawlish at this moment, but its inner face also, and the sharp angle where it met the side wall.

Where the great crack had initiated.

"Call a man up here," Dawlish said to Leigh.

He pulled out a notebook, scribbled two messages in pencil, one for Ross, the other for Mathews, notifications of what was imminent. A seaman arrived, took the papers, and was gone.

Out on the bay the British cruiser and the German corvette lay in dead-calm, white hulls and ochre funnels reflected mirror-like on the still waters, taut moorings slanting like thin threads fore and aft, no hint of the fury to be unleashed. The *Ibis* had finished her last sweep along the shore to blast any residual opposition there that never came and she was all but stationary opposite the quay. Her antiquated muzzle-loaders were of no value now. A boat had drawn alongside to take off her gun-crews and all seamen who could be spared – small numbers might yet be needed to tip the balance. Laden, carrying Jarvis also, the craft drew away and stroked towards the landing steps. *Ibis* turned away and headed to take station, in safety, just seawards of *Leonidas* and *Hildegarde*.

"A signal for *Leonidas*," Dawlish said to Lunt. No need for heroics, no mention of England's expectation. *"Your guns."*

Not to be outdone by the German on the smaller minaret, Canavan climbed on to the parapet, balanced there while Lunt held his legs, and shook out his flags. He was fast, very fast, the cloth cracking as his arms semaphored the words. Dawlish had focussed his glass on the cruiser, could see the signaller's counterpart acknowledging from the bridge-wing, Edgerton leaning over to shout to Purdon at the weapon near the bows, the gunnery officer responding and in turn calling to the gun-crew. This was the moment they had waited for. Their platform was as steady as any ship could be and the fort's bastion was squarely in their sights. Only the elevation was a matter of judgement, the ideal angle to be found only by trial and error, adjusting in minute steps as the barrel heated with successive rounds

Long seconds – time enough for gnawing fear of miscalculation – and then, in what still seemed absolute silence, an orange flash close to *Leonidas's* bow, and an instant later rolling grey smoke engulfing her.

Dawlish swung his glass towards the bastion. He was counting mentally, five, six, seven seconds, and then the Armstrong's sharp report drove past and he knew that the shell – six-inch, one hundred pounds – was following on its low trajectory. An instant later a flash somewhere far behind, the bastion's top. Even before the sound of detonation reached him, he recognised that the shell had fallen far beyond, perhaps even beyond the fort itself. Purdon had taking no chances of hitting the town with his opening shot.

"Signal *Down one hundred*," Dawlish said.

Canavan's flags whipped.

*Leonidas* acknowledged. The second shell should be in the breech now and Purdon himself would be winding down the elevation, guessing just how far to deviate from the range table now that the barrel had begun to heat.

The second shot. Once more the agonising wait for the wave of sound and the flash and the report of detonation. And once more an overshoot. Better that than the shell falling short, plunging into alleyways and houses, slaughtering terrified innocents still within.

"*Down fifty.*"

Another overshoot. Down another fifty. An overshoot again.

The fifth shot and this time the sound of detonation sharper, contained within the fortress walls, blasting skywards from within the courtyard, smoke following. Dawlish's heart leapt. The shell must have grazed across the top of the bastion, must have dropped enough to hit the inner face of the fort's most distant wall, perhaps even the gateway itself. For one mad moment he thought of ordering continued firing on this elevation, to drop more shells inside to break nerve and sow despair among the all-but unseen defenders, but reason told him that the shot was lucky, that not one in another ten would achieve the same. Better to stick with the plan.

*"Down fifty."*

And this time, success.

A flash some ten feet below the bastion's top, the boom of detonation, flying stone chips, the wall obscured with smoke. As it cleared, a round disc that might have been a yard across was visible on the stone, its surface scoured a lighter grey than the surrounding area. A hundred hits like this, might do no more than scar the wall, could blast no breach, but that was not important. It was the tracery of cracks and fissures that counted, how they might withstand repeated tremors.

"Signal *Spot on. Repeat. Three rounds.*"

The first and third impacted, both within ten feet of that shallow bowl already blasted, though the second was an overshot. The first of *Leonidas's* portside guns had the range – good enough as long as each hit could be reported back so that elevation-handwheels might be crept forward or back by infinitesimally small degrees. Time now to register the next gun, the second from the bow. It hit with its third round and its fifth, then its sixth. It in turn fell silent as the next weapons, the third and fourth, and the fifth on the sponsoned mounting close to the stern, also got the range. It took over an hour and in that time sixteen hits had been scored, most of the light-grey craters pocking the wall within an irregular patch eight or ten yards across and extending down from the crenellations to the wall's base. But – best of all – three shells had beaten into the rock outcrop beneath. No sign yet of any fissure opening, no hint of a shudder of the massive wall, but that, Dawlish comforted himself, would be to hope for too much too soon.

*Leonidas* fell silent. A flag soared up her signal halliard from the bridge, notification to *Hildegarde* that it was now her turn to register her two guns. The burden on her gunnery officer must be all but intolerable, an awareness that the honour of Germany's recently-born navy was at stake, her national prestige itself, and that his weapon-crews must not disgrace themselves in the eyes of critical allies.

Beyond the town, among the fields and groves inland of the fort, there was no sign of the German landing force. It had gone to ground behind cover, as it should, sheltered in whatever shadow might be found from the merciless pre-noon sun. There would be parched throats there, stern water-discipline enforced, officers and men who had never experienced combat brooding on their untried courage, each with his doubts unshared, praying silently that it would be adequate when, inevitably, it would be called for. Somewhere there too would be *Leonidas's* seven-pounder on its field carriage, ready to be rushed forward to effective range when needed. Its crew – all had been with it when it had been used to deadly effect in Korea – would be affecting casual insouciance in the presence of their German allies.

Dawlish felt his throat burning, suggested to Leigh that he might allow his men a mouthful from their water bottles, took a swig from his own. He surveyed the fort's walls. There were men atop them, some in khaki, others in loose white robes, and but they were visible for an instant only as they passed at a crouch between the crenellations. None had been spotted on the bastion since its pounding had begun. The black cannon barrels jutting out along the walls were antiques, unfired perhaps for a century or more – no danger there – but determined men up there with rifles could yet wreak havoc.

He turned his glass again towards the *Hildegarde* as her first report reverberated. An overshoot – no shame in that. A flash of sunlight on the field glasses of the German lieutenant on the other minaret before he turned to the signaller, barked something, and then the message was semaphored to the corvette. Her second shot was also over but the third fell short, too short, blasting a dust-filled plume from a flat roof beyond the slave pens, in the gap between Mathews' and Ross's men, revealing a half-collapsed house as it cleared. The occupants should have been driven from it previously but from this distance there was no way of knowing.

It took seven rounds, but at last *Hildegarde's* first Krupp had the range, and three more pounded into the angle between bastion and wall – impossible for Dawlish to see it, but the rising smoke was confirmation – before it fell silent. The second weapon registered in shorter time, driving a shell into its target on its fourth shot.

Now the moment to unleash the full anger of the guns. A brief exchange of signals, then fire rippled along *Leonidas's* flank, bow to stern in succession. The time between the reports was set only by the need for the signaller to report each hit or miss, for the gunners to make their minute adjustments. Dawlish must soon leave Leigh on his high perch with his signallers, leaving to the young officer the duty of observation, but he waited first to see more than a dozen of the cruiser's shells beat into the wall and the outcrop beneath. The *Hildegarde* too had also settled down to a steady firing rhythm.

Between both ships, an average six of every ten rounds fired were hitting their target. Most of the others were overshots and one exploded in the fortress courtyard. The bastion was half hidden by smoke and stone-chip sprays but as yet there was no hint of structural weakness. But no matter how thick, how strong, the walls might be, it must be terrifying to be inside Fort Manuel, to feel the reverberation of each landing shot, to fear the havoc wrought by a shell exploding in the open courtyard within.

Had it been up to the opium-addicted Sultan Saif alone, Dawlish suspected that a white flag might have been run up already. That it was not, indicated that it was Imker who was in real command, that he still had the ascendency over his mercenaries to stiffen their resolve to resist, that he hoped that the walls might endure longer than the attacking ships' magazines.

One last look – confirmation that the Germans were still shooting well, that their liaison between observer and ship was as faultless as that of his own people. Dawlish shook Leigh's hand, complimented Lunt and Canavan – the latter must be close to collapse and had wisely stepped down from the parapet to semaphore no less effectively from behind it. He descended the tightly winding stair. Inside the mosque he found Wainwright and a comatose Ibrahim.

"We're going forward," he said. "Get him to his feet."

"Is there...?" Wainwright hesitated to finish the question. He had heard the gunfire and knew how much was being gambled on its success.

"No. Nothing yet. They're hitting, but the bastion's still there." Dawlish suppressed his own growing concern. Neither ship had limitless magazines.

Ibrahim had slept through the cannonade so far but he was frightened now that he was awake and did not want to leave the mosque.

329

Dawlish marvelled that Wainwright had the patience to cajole him into departing, a seaman steadying him and hurrying him forward.

Dawlish had his revolver out as they moved through the deserted alleyways towards the slave pens, then along their edge. Ross had posted men here to guard his rear and one now led the small party to the far side, across the line of fire and on to the fringe of single-storey stone houses and low huts beyond, cringing involuntarily as each shell screamed over. The rock-outcrop and the fortress walls, towering above the roofs and less than four-hundred yards distant, were all but obscured by smoke.

Ross came to meet them. Most of his men were sheltering in shadow in an alleyway, bayonets fixed, an air of suppressed fear and excitement about them. A smaller number were occupying a house forward that gave a clear view of the bastion. Recently arrived from the *Ibis*, Jarvis was commanding his own contingent, with Foxley's now subordinated to him, as planned. They were in a sheltered lane further to the right and, in a large courtyard close by, several were busy assembling a rocket-launching frame, two boxes of nine-pound Hale projectiles open beside it. Jarvis exuded a sense of elation, knew that he and his ship had performed faultlessly so far, was clearly thirsting for what should come. Not just action. Opportunity. To settle a score, to redeem a stalled career. He asked Dawlish to step aside into a shaded corner, out of other earshot.

"Commander Jarvis?"

"Have you reconsidered, sir?" A hint of resentment in Jarvis's tone. "I'd be proud to lead the first wave. It would mean so much and…"

Dawlish felt impatience. This had been argued before and had been settled, if not to Jarvis's satisfaction.

"I need you to command the reserve." Dawlish wanted cold calculation as well as fury when the time came. Personal scores could distort judgement. "And if I myself should fall then you …"

"So, it's settled then, captain, is it? Nothing's changed?" Almost a snarl, wholly insubordinate. "Still the reserve, sir?"

"It's settled, Commander Jarvis. Still the reserve. Nothing's changed"

Dawlish turned away. His conversation with Ross was easier.

"How long do you think this will last, sir? It still looks solid." The marine lieutenant pointed towards the bastion, looked worried. He too must be concerned by the emptying magazines.

"It'll fall," Dawlish said. "It'll fall. Depend on it. And without much warning. The men are ready for it?"

"Their blood's up. It was easy coming through the town and hard to hold them back. But the longer they've got to wait and the longer they've got to think about it, the less confident they'll be."

And Mathews had the same concern when Dawlish was guided to him – another fear-chilled passage under the warships' line of fire. The Zanzibari troops were also sheltering in a lane, grinning and smiling to Dawlish as he passed, clearly flushed with delight by their success so far, some arguing over what were clearly looted goods.

"They've had their head," Mathews said, "but it's been easy, damn easy." He paused, as if about to admit a shame. "Some of them like killing – really like it – and most were looking forward to sacking this whole damn town. But they hadn't reckoned on..." he glanced towards the smoke-wreathed bastion "... on that. It hasn't sunk in yet. And the longer they've got to think about it the worse it'll be."

It was past midday now, the shuttered town an oven, the smell of sewage strong, flies a torment, throats dry, resolution sapping, fear rising. And still the relentless smashing of the shells continued, the Germans' detonations sharper than the deeper blasts of *Leonidas's* as they scourged the wall. Dawlish went forward with Mathews to a house on the town's edge now occupied by a dozen Somalis from the Zanzibari force. A scant hundred yards of open ground between this house and the rock outcrop. They could see the bastion through a haze of acrid smoke. Small shards of stone pattered on nearby roofs.

Dawlish took Mathew's proffered field-glasses, focussed them on the wall to trace the cracks whose pattern was by now etched upon his mind like a familiar map. He concentrated on finding the minor rockfall he had noted when he had marched past as a common seaman. And yes! There it was, half-obscured by tendrils of drifting smoke, then lost briefly as another shell burst above it.

331

He moved his disc of sight slowly upwards, seeking the crack – the narrow crack – that had snaked up from there between the wall's great blocks to the crenellations high above. The smoke cleared, for an instant only, but in that brief moment he saw what might have been another crack opening, racing out to the right like a living thing, still moving as it was lost again in the dust-laden cloud that came swirling back. Heart thumping now, Dawlish waited for the next impact. A German shell blasted in the angle between bastion and wall – impossible to see the point of impact from here – but there was another fissure there and hope that…

*Leonidas's* next shell exploded at the point where wall and outcrop met, chips showering out from the flame-lit smoke. As the reverberations of the detonations died, there was another sound.

A low rumble.

An agony of uncertainty in the long seconds – in the eternity – before smoke cleared.

And as it did, two, three, four new fissures were reaching out like branches from either side of the main crack. Another rumble – and yes! – the wall was shuddering and a stone block, then two, three, then a shower, cascaded down, carrying with them fifteen or twenty feet of crenelated parapet. It crashed down, was lost in the churning dust. The cloud thinned to reveal a jagged vee-shaped gap, its point a dozen feet above the rock outcrop's top, the fallen masonry rising like a part-conical ramp half-way up to it. Another rumble, another shudder, but not another fall.

Not yet.

"Have your men stand to," Dawlish said to Mathews. "And follow close, very close, when the time comes."

As *Leonidas's* next shell struck – with no further visible impact on the bastion – Dawlish started back to rejoin his own bluejackets and marines.

Their time might just be at hand.

## Chapter 32

Ross had brought his men forward to mass in an alleyway leading directly to the track running around the rock outcrop. Marines to lead, bluejackets to follow. Silence among them, fears unspoken, a few lips moving in silent prayer, the sobering confrontation with mortality that men awaiting an assault had faced through all ages.

Dawlish stood with Ross at the alley's end and watched the bastion's torment. Even here the smoke and dust all but blotted out the view. Far back, atop the minaret, Leigh must have observed the initial wall collapse, must have realised that a last brutal impetus was needed, must on his own initiative have signalled for fire without intermission for correction. *Leonidas's* salvos were all but a continuous roar, two or three or even four weapons firing at once, most shells hitting – no undershoots, Thank God! A few more blocks were dislodging and tumbling down through the smoke and dust.

A few, but not enough. Dawlish was in mental agony now. A quick estimate told him that perhaps ten percent of *Leonidas's* stock of shells remained. The Germans must surely be in no better state. And when the Armstrongs and the Krupps fell silent there would be no alternative but to –

A blast greater than any yet, two shells, by some unlikely chance, smashing simultaneously into the bastion's nearer face, and an instant later a round from *Hildegarde* detonating in the corner beyond.

Then a long growl from within the rolling murk, and it grew louder and continued. Dawlish could feel tremors beneath his feet. He willed the great rumble to intensify, felt his heart leap as more stone blocks drove from the choking fog and bounced, like so many children's balls, across the track below. He was fingering the whistle on a lanyard around his neck, not a bosun's trilling article but one powerful enough to be heard at the limits of a sports field. He was longing for, and fearing, the moment for its piercing call. He turned to Ross.

"Ready for it?"

"The sooner the better, sir."

And at that instant a deep roar, the smoke and dust themselves driven back as the bastion seemed to shake itself, wounded but still somehow standing, as if clutching on to its long existence. Blocks were falling in a continuous cascade, not only close to the great notch that had been gouged before, but from along the entire parapet. A ramp of fallen stone was forming, and growing, at the base of the supporting outcrop. But now that outcrop itself was starting to collapse, new fissures darting out from old. A twenty or thirty-yard length of wall to the right of the notch was falling in its entirety, intact, cohesive for one last brief instant before it dissolved into a raging torrent of rubble.

The final downfall was more complete than Dawlish might have dared imagine. What remained of the bastion – the great stone arrowhead that was now all but severed from the adjoining walls – was arcing outwards as the outcrop beneath disintegrated. The tremors of its crash shuddered through the alley where Dawlish stood transfixed, cracking walls and flowing on into the town behind, and still the masonry tumbled down, hidden by the swirling dust.

Leigh must have seen it from his minaret, the German officer from his, and both must have signalled for firing to cease for there were no more shell impacts, nor any needed. Mathews to the left, Jarvis, champing on the bit to the right, would have seen it too, would be waiting for the whistle's shriek. And over a mile away, sheltering in the fields beyond the fort's landward face, Kaunitz and Lutz would know that their moment too was almost on them.

The roar lessened – smaller, shorter rumbles now, last sections of weakened masonry yielding, last small avalanches, last rubble settling – and then a silence, a dreadful, frightening silence as only the cloud remained to shroud the bastion's shattered corpse. That thick fog now masked whether an assault was even now practicable – everything depended on how high the ramp formed by the fallen masonry extended up the outcrop, how near to the bottom of the breach.

Dawlish put the whistle to his lips, gave three short blasts.

*Stand by.*

The mist was thinning, brief glimpses of the shattered wall, of a chaos of fallen stone, obscured once more, another section revealed, then hidden again. And shouting from beyond it, not of panic, not of despair, but the sharp bark of orders, of discipline asserted, of drilled men rushing to obey commands. Commands of a renegade Dutchman and slaver who knew that, even if a white flag were to be run up this instant, nothing would save him from a noose. Commands of a man who had nothing to lose by continued defiance, who knew that a repulse – a very bloody repulse – was still possible. Every moment the assault was delayed played into that man's hands.

Decision.

A long blast on the whistle, then Dawlish raced towards the murk, his revolver still in his unbuttoned holster, both hands free for the climb ahead. Behind him he heard Ross calling his men to follow, then the sound of pounding feet. Over to the right, Hale rockets were soaring in quick succession from Jarvis's force to plunge down into the fort's courtyard. Dawlish heard their blasts as the choking cloud enveloped him – he had reached the track, was crossing it, knew that the outcrop was only yards ahead. He saw the first scree and boulders that had rolled this far and he weaved between them. He could hear Ross's people close behind, swearing as some stumbled in the mist, Corporal Shand's bellows to keep up the pace.

The sloping base of the fallen rock was before him now, a jumble of dressed stone blocks from the broken wall and of jagged fragments ripped from the outcrop. It was steep and the footing was bad – after a few upright steps he had to drop on all fours, toes scrabbling for a hold, hands reaching for an anchor above to drag himself upwards. The dust was thinning as he climbed – he glimpsed Shand scrambling past, rifle slung across his back, then Ross also, and he could hear the remainder close behind.

The walls must be intact to either side of this devastation, and on them men with rifles, waiting for the first attackers to appear. He clambered on, breath rasping, saw a shape loom ahead, and then a hand outstretched – Ross's. He grasped it gratefully, was hauled up, shook it free, and together they blundered on and up.

Another long whistle blast screamed to the left – Mathews was launching his men forward to join the climb. They yelled as they came

335

on, battle cries from a half-dozen tribes and races. The first rifle fire rippled now from the fort above, lashing into them before they too drove into what was now a thinning haze.

The last of the Hale rockets had dropped like fiery comets into the fort's unseen interior, but now there was another sound from far beyond, a single report, sharp, puny even, the unmistakable crack of *Leonidas's* seven-pounder field gun. As the column of dust and smoke had blasted skywards, as the defenders' attention was riveted on the fallen bastion, Kaunitz would have ordered it forward. Lined up along the access ramp on the landward face, the small weapon would be blasting towards the great iron-studded gate itself, the German bluejackets and Lutz's askaris waiting impatiently for their own order to advance.

Shouting ahead, brief cheering, more rifle fire, and then, suddenly, the last wisps cleared. Dawlish saw that he was only yards from the top of the slope. It was more than a breach – rather a long ridge of tumbled masonry sloping down to the right where the bastion had stood so proud while on the left a section of intact wall towered like a cliff above it. Further back leftwards was the citadel's massive square fortification, five or six storeys high. Within it, as Wainwright had reported, was a labyrinth of rooms, the sultan's personal quarters and harem, the treasury and a central hall. On its roof, on the wall that jutted from it and that ended so abruptly, men in khaki had clustered and were shooting down. Yet, even so, the assault was flowing past across the breach's crest and down the slope on the far side, into the fort's interior.

Dawlish stumbled behind the attackers – he had his revolver out now. He saw a stricken seaman in his path, could spare no time or pity, had eyes only for defenders gathering at the base of the inner slope, men already half-stunned by the rockets, shrinking back as Ross's men drove at them with bayonet and cutlass. The urge to join this attack was strong, but a rational internal voice told him that he must hang back, retain control, impose order on the melee developing. Chips flew off a block to his left – a rifleman above had him in his sights – and he darted to take shelter behind piled rubble. The first of Mathews' men were arriving at the crest, then the brigadier general himself, puffing and winded, but undaunted.

"There!" Dawlish pointed down the slope and to the left, along the bottom of the wall and towards the great square citadel. "Get up those steps!"

He could see three sets, wide stone stairways, one close, men in khaki at its top, but on the distant wall there were two more sets, leading to the two most distant bastions. Whatever guards had been posted on them had descended into the courtyard to meet the storming force and for now there was an opportunity – one that could not last – to get up on to the parapet and work back towards the citadel to clear the riflemen atop it.

Mathews made no answer but launched himself forward, yelling in Swahili for his men to follow. They surged down the slope – they were massed too closely and many were falling under the hail of fire from above – but they still drove on, were now in the courtyard, thrusting along the flank of the Arabs and mercenary guards who were falling back from the stabbing bayonets and hacking cutlasses of Ross's men. Beyond the advancing line of seamen and marines was the inner face of the gatehouse, the gate itself hidden by the tunnel that extended from it beneath this other great defence. Now that gatehouse looked unguarded, as if those stationed atop it had also descended to join the fray in the courtyard. From beyond it, unseen, *Leonidas's* tiny field gun was barking as fast as its gunners could swab and load and fire and swab again.

The defenders in the courtyard broke, dashing to the right, towards the line of linked single and double storey buildings of solid stone, guardhouses, storerooms and kitchens, built against the inner wall, each a possible small fortress in itself. They left their dead and wounded, but one figure stood firm as they streamed past, pistol in right hand, sword in left, uniform caked grey with dust, face begrimed, blood running down one cheek – Imker.

Two marines rushed towards him, bayonets levelled, but he did not flinch. Revolver extended at arm's length, he fired as calmly as if on a range, smashing down his first attacker, swinging towards the other, thumbing back the hammer, firing again, but missing as the marine's nerve failed and he swerved. The last of Imker's men had rushed past him, and now he turned and sprinted after them. A heavy door swung

337

to as he disappeared inside a storehouse. Rifle muzzles now sprung from a dozen narrow openings in the building's face, well placed to sweep the centre of the courtyard.

Ross was yelling to his men to head for the undefended stairway leading to the most distant bastion, that diagonally across the courtyard, and the first were bounding up. To their left, Mathew's Zanzibaris had been repulsed by the riflemen above the first steps they had attempted, but a handful now had mounted the stairs further on. They raced back along the parapet towards the citadel, some struck down to become a barrier their comrades must stumble across. Mathews himself, at the top of the steps, was urging more on to follow.

Ross's people were on top of the far bastion now and were dropping to one knee, pushing new rounds into their Snider breeches, opening fire on the khaki-clad figures on the citadel's roof, each man settling into the steady rhythm practised so often. Lashed by their hail, the resistance on the roof was faltering, heads dropping from sight into cover. Now Mathew's fierce levies had cleared the parapet, were nearing the citadel itself, their advance blocked from Dawlish's view by its mass.

Time to commit the reserve.

He looked back – the dust had cleared and it seemed impossible now that he or any other could have struggled up that ramp of debris. Beyond it, at the houses on the town's edge, he saw that Jarvis had brought his men into the open – wilfully, stupidly, for he had been ordered to remain under cover, but anger and impatience must have overcome him. Time now to commit them. Dawlish blasted on his whistle, saw the force come surging towards the rubble, Jarvis in the lead.

Sudden cheering made Dawlish spin around. Down in the courtyard white-jacketed seamen – Germans – were flooding from the tunnel beneath the gatehouse. They had stormed up the access ramp, their path cleared by the seven-pounder, the thick gate shattered. Caught in the flank by fire from the storehouses to the left, now occupied by Imker and his mercenaries, the Germans pulled back into the tunnel's cover. Two still bodies were left behind, a third, wounded, dragged back by two heroes who dashed out to his aid.

Covered by Ross's steady fire, the Zanzibaris had gained the citadel's roof. A furious struggle was raging there – slashing, hacking, stabbing, a few shots – and khaki bodies were being hurled down, screaming, to crash into the courtyard or down on to the outcrop outside. Individual Germans were slipping from the tunnel, braving the fire of Imker's unseen men in the storehouse to rush the few yards to gather in the angle of the gatehouse's further wall before storming up the steps there. They appeared at on the structure's deserted roof, six or eight of them with an officer, all chosen as marksmen, Dawlish guessed, for they were now opening carefully aimed rifle fire on the apertures in the storehouse wall. The battle on the walls and citadel roof was petering out in babbled pleas that ended with a scream or with hands raised in surrender.

"Half of 'em will be in my service a week from now," Mathews had predicted. "They'll know what side their bread's buttered on once they've been bested."

So it was now proving, Imker's mercenaries throwing down their weapons before Mathews' mercenaries, men drawn from the same varied stock, turning their coats in the moment of defeat. But down below them the courtyard was empty – and untenable, because of Imker's fire – of anything other than the bodies and wounded littering it.

Jarvis scrambled up beside Dawlish, Foxley following, the men panting up behind relieved and bemused that their ascent had been unopposed.

"All finished, sir? All done?" Jarvis's voice was bitter with sarcasm. "Just the mopping up left for me, eh?"

Dawlish ignored the slight. "There!" He gestured towards the buildings on the right. "Imker's in there."

"Is he, by God!" A savage smile.

"He's got thirty or forty men. Work down along the wall – hug it. Get under those openings and pour in all the fire you can."

As Jarvis led his men down, Dawlish saw three other figures toiling up the outer slope towards him. Wainwright and a seaman were on either side of Ibrahim, half-dragging him. But the citadel where the drunkard must find his throne was still holding out, for Mathews could be seen on its roof now, signalling that he had possession of it, but that it was

339

impossible to penetrate from there into the floors below. But there must be a door opening to the parapet, blocked as it might now be.

"And the main door's down there," Wainwright, panting, had taken in the situation. "You can't see it from here." He was pointing towards the side wall of the citadel. The door must be just beyond, giving access from the courtyard.

"Any other?" Dawlish said.

"I'm not sure. If there is, then it's on the far side. Probably a very small one."

The steady volleys that the Germans were pouring on Imker's refuge had been joined by Ross's people lying down on the opposite parapet and firing across the courtyard. Some rounds at least must be entering and the fire from inside was slackening. Jarvis's men had reached the bottom of the rubble slope and were starting to edge along the wall towards the entrance of the storehouse.

They had reached the nearer end of the building and were inching forward as voices yelled at them from the gatehouse to fall back. A figure had dashed from the tunnel-mouth – Kaunitz, in his still-spotless white uniform, sword in hand, scorning the new burst of rifle fire rippling from the storehouse. Behind him rushed a knot of German and British seamen dragging the nine-pounder by its trail. They swung it around to point it towards the storehouse door, swung it back slightly for better alignment – Bealson, the gun-captain, was unhurried, deliberate. Then he called to the others to stand clear, rose at a crouch to the side of the carriage and jerked the lanyard. The weapon leaped back across the cobbles as flame blasted from it – there was nothing to restrain the trail – and at the point-blank range its shell could not miss.

Smoke, flame and splinters belched from the doorway – it must be worse still within. Jarvis had started forward again, he and his men flattened against the wall, a group of five shooting into the first aperture encountered – little wider than an arrow-slit – while the remainder leapfrogged them at a crouch to the next, and the next. As they neared the smoking doorway it appeared that all resistance had ceased on the ground floor. Whoever survived within had retreated to the level above and were still resisting, heads and rifles briefly thrust out to fire down unhandily and ineffectually on the seamen crouching below. Several Germans were down, but now, with the *Leonidas* gun-crew, their comrades were swinging the nine-pounder around to aim directly for the citadel's door.

Kaunitz was standing calmly by it as it was charged and rammed, was calling to his men above the gatehouse, then back to those sheltering unseen in the tunnel. In a minute or less the field-gun – *Leonidas's* field gun – would be smashing an entrance to the citadel for the German assault.

Ibrahim had taken shelter behind a stone block on the slope's outer side, just below the crest. This was his moment, hesitate to seize it though he might.

Dawlish pointed to him as he turned to Wainwright. "Bring him with us."

Down now into the courtyard, boots slithering on the rubble, Ibrahim dragged like a rag doll. They paused in the angle between citadel and wall. The would-be sultan was wholly passive, could barely comprehend what was happening about him, his eyes dilated, lost in a private world of opium and alcohol.

*My men are dying for this creature!* A voice screamed inside Dawlish, but to Wainwright and the escorting seaman he said "Follow me and take him with us! Be fast!"

Jarvis could look after Imker's trapped force and what mattered now was the citadel. No defensive fire echoed from it but the assault's prize lay within. Dawlish edged to its corner.

"Ross!" He shouted towards the far bastion. "Get your men down!"

Much as he liked Kaunitz, he needed his own people to be first in, for that honour to be for *Leonidas*, for *Ibis*. He sprinted across the courtyard, glimpsed to his left the citadel's great iron-bound and studded entrance door, to his right the field gun bearing on it, the German seamen massed in the tunnel behind it, ready to storm forward. Behind him he could hear Wainwright and the seaman, dragging Ibrahim between them. He met Ross at the bottom of the bastion steps. Behind him men were lugging down a long black object streaked with rust.

"Look there, sir!" Ross pointed to the side of the citadel that had been hidden from Dawlish's view before. A small door nestled there and, on the parapet twenty feet above, Mathews and his men were clustered at another door like it, striking it with great reverberating blows. Corporal Shand and a half-dozen marines came hurrying forward with a small and ancient cannon barrel carried between them on slings stripped from their rifles – the same sort of battering ram as being used by Mathews' men.

Dawlish stood back as Shand's marines began to pound the door, the others waiting behind to rush in when it failed. But it was stronger than any might have thought, blackened wood hewn three centuries before and seasoned to iron strength, thick metal bars criss-crossing it. It shuddered under each swing of the improvised ram, but it was still holding.

Wainwright had been inside the citadel before.

"Where does this lead?" Dawlish pointed to the door.

"I don't know. I didn't come in this way. But this ground-floor's a labyrinth."

"Would Ibrahim know?"

"He's past knowing. Useless. We just need to keep moving upwards when we get in. The audience hall's on the next floor up – I've been there. The sultan's chambers are higher still."

The citadel's great door was proving no less strong. The nine-pounder barked, its exploding shell tearing a shower of splinters from it. Kaunitz's sword was raised, the seamen behind him ready to charge as it would slice down, but as the smoke cleared there was no sign of a breach and the blade stayed raised. To one side of the tunnel mouth Dawlish saw Lutz, sunlight flashing off his round spectacles, a pistol in his hand, his askaris ranged behind him. The tiny field gun was being dragged back to be aligned again on the door, another charge and shell rammed through its muzzle.

Shand's men had a rhythm in their swing now as the antique cannon beat into the side door. It was starting to splinter, but the iron straps were still holding firm. Ross and his remaining men were clustered behind in an agony of impatience and frustration, a round in each breech,

342

blood already drying on their bayonets. On the parapet above Mathews' mercenaries were cheering, their repeated blows beginning to tell at last, the last barrier between them and the citadel's interior starting to yield.

Again the nine-pounder's report, flame and splinters blasting out from the main doorway, again Kaunitz's raised sword still held aloft as the smoke cleared, again no breach, no charge.

Then a rending sound as the marines' cannon barrel smashed again into the door before them. It was buckling inwards, a small jagged gap opening between the iron straps, yet still the bolts anchoring it inside were holding. The men swinging the ram had tired and others took their places. The hammering continued, each new blow widening the rupture and driving the door inwards a little further.

Now the third shell hit the main door, and this time Kaunitz's sword was sweeping down as the smoke cleared to reveal a breach. The German seamen boiled from the gatehouse tunnel in a compact mass, cheering as they came, and to the left Lutz and his askaris were already ahead of them, streaking across the courtyard with levelled bayonets.

Another crash, this time the door wrenched from its frame as the ram's last blows sheared its restraining bolts.

"Stand aside!" Ross yelled and the marines threw themselves against the wall to either side to shelter from a blast of gunfire from within that never came. Now they in their turn edged around the frame to shoot in, a dozen rounds that drew no response.

"In!"

Shand was at the front as they rushed in, shouting back that the passageway beyond was deserted. Dawlish and Ross were close behind, temporarily half-blinded by the transition from bright sunlight to unlit shadow, Wainwright with them as guide, Ibrahim being hurried in the rear by his seaman minder. Down a deserted corridor, an open door ahead, an empty room with desks and cupboards that might have been an office, light streaming in from a narrow window high in its wall, then through it to another – still no sign of life. From somewhere to the left came the sounds of other rushing feet, of shouting, of the Germans now also inside and blundering through the dark maze.

Another passage ahead, dim light from somewhere beyond revealing steps there. Halfway down it a single figure in a white robe emerged from a door at one side, arms raised, babbling what might be surrender, but a marine's bayonet impaled him and he fell with a scream that died abruptly with him. Up the steps, a blank wall ahead, passages extending to the left – dark there – and to the right, where sunlight streamed through an opening in the wall at the end.

"This way! I recognise it!" Wainwright pointing rightwards.

Half-way along, steps on the left, a closed door at their top, but one flimsy enough to yield as shoulders were thrown against it. Another room, large, deserted, lit by shafts of sunlight, layered rugs and carpets springy on the floor underfoot, low tables, brass trays with tiny cups, divans covered in faded silk and strewn with cushions, an air of dingy splendour, a heavy smell of opium.

And an open door beyond, a loud, hectoring voice ringing through it and further beyond the low sound of the German advance drawing near.

That voice was familiar, evoked memory of it rising almost to a scream on that distant track after the attack on the slavers' column. Dawlish, pushed forward to the door.

The audience chamber lay before him, three bodies slumped unmoving on the carpeted floor, red stains extending around them, one a silk-clad old man recognisable as Achmed Ibn Hamed. A low dais at the further end. A figure cowered on a throne there, his rich robe stained down the front with vomit, his turban awry, his shaking noticeable even from this distance, his eyes dilated. Sultan Saif of Mtwara was no more impressive than his half-brother Ibrahim. But it was not on him that Dawlish's gaze was fixed, but on the man standing over him with a smile of triumph on his face, a dozen askaris surrounding him.

Lutz.

## Chapter 33

"Welcome, Captain Dawlish."

A voice shrill with satisfaction and triumph.

Lutz was holding a sheet of thick paper like one once glimpsed in Nanguruwe, though smaller and stained, and severely creased. Three solid columns of print and a title block above. In his other hand Lutz held a silver pen case – Dawlish recognised the type from his Turkish service – with a small receptacle for ink at one end. The pen itself was still grasped in Saif's hand, black drops falling from it on to his befouled robe.

"Doktor Lutz," Dawlish stepped forward, "what is the –"

"Step back, captain. You've no further business here." Then Lutz spoke in Swahili and his askaris moved to flank him, swinging their bayonets down to waist level as they did.

Ross anticipated Dawlish's command. The marines moved to either side of him, a continuous line, their own bayonets arcing down.

"This is nonsense, Lutz, damn nonsense." Dawlish felt his anger rising. He walked forward slowly until the first of the askari bayonets all but touched his chest. "This is nothing that we agreed."

"His Highness, Sultan Saif, has accepted the protection of Kaiser Wilhelm." Lutz raised the document

Dawlish was close enough to see the banner at the top, not the name of the *Die Bremen und Oldenburg Ostafrikanische Handelsgesellschaft* but something much more impressive, heavy Gothic type surmounted by a coat of arms a black, red-taloned eagle on a yellow ground, a shield with a smaller eagle on its breast.

"You see the signatures, Captain Dawlish?" Lutz pointed to two in the bottom right-hand corner, both sealed with red wax. "You recognise the signature of His Imperial Majesty Wilhelm? And that of Fürst von Bismarck? And you don't understand Arabic, captain, then your lackey Wainwright will identify this third one as that of Sultan Saif."

A commotion at a door to the side, Kaunitz bursting in, sword in hand, two officers and several men behind. He stopped suddenly, bewildered by the tableau before him.

"You've known about this, Fregattenkapitän Kaunitz, haven't you?" Dawlish's fury was bitter with disappointment. He had admired this man, had trusted him as if one of his own.

"About what? I don't understand. What is this?" Kaunitz advanced towards Lutz, spoke in rapid German, his face flushing in anger as he heard the reply.

Lutz was calm, his smile a smirk, but Kaunitz's voice was rising. Dawlish spoke no German but amid the impassioned flow of language he heard the word *Ehre* repeated again and again. Kaunitz gestured several times towards Dawlish but each time he quickly looked away again as if ashamed to meet his gaze.

Lutz was reaching inside his tunic, was pulling out another folded paper, a corner wet with sweat. He looked at Dawlish, pointedly ignoring Kaunitz.

"My authority, Captain Dawlish. And if you doubt it, then the good Fregattenkapitän can translate it for you."

Kaunitz snatched it from his hand, unfolded it, disclosing as he did another eagle on a yellow ground, florid signatures, red seals. Colour drained from his face as he read. He turned to Dawlish.

"I didn't know. I couldn't have." Kaunitz stretched out the paper. "I swear on my honour that I knew nothing of this."

Dawlish saw the heading *Wir Wilhelm*, scanned the Gothic type beneath, made out the words *Oberst Doktor Eitel-Heinrich Lutz*.

"What does it mean?" Dawlish was as shocked as Kaunitz.

"He has authority. He speaks for –"

"For the *Deutsches Reich*, for the German Empire!" Lutz was close to screaming. "With full accreditation to enter into treaties on the Reich's behalf. As I have just done – as the Reich has just done – with this fine gentleman." He pointed to the whimpering figure crouched on the throne. "A sovereign ruler who has accepted the Reich's protection and its right to represent him in all dealings with foreign states."

"Damn your nonsense!" Dawlish snapped. "Damn your bloody nonsense, Lutz." He turned to Kaunitz. "Why are you tolerating this? Can't you restrain this madman?"

Kaunitz was shaking his head. His face was even paler now, the hint of tears welling in his eyes.

"*Eine Schande!*" he hissed towards Lutz. "*Eine Verletzung der Ehre! Eine Schande!*"

Lutz ignored him, spoke in English to Dawlish. "You have six hours to remove your people from Mtwara, captain. And ..." He pulled out his watch, made a show of looking at it, of nodding, as if calculating, "... and you have precisely fourteen and a half hours to get your ships out of this harbour. Tomorrow, six o'clock. Fregattenkapitän Kaunitz will be directed to take appropriate action should you not comply."

Wainwright was close behind and was explaining the situation in an angry undertone to an outraged Mathews, who had just burst in. Dawlish could feel their fury, knew that it was of no avail, motioned to them to be silent.

And time stood still.

*A man who's prepared to take decisions on the spot,* Topcliffe had said.

That's why I'm here.

But this situation now – the senile kaiser's signature, the chancellor's – was at variance with the perception the admiral had shared in the library of that London club.

*Bismarck's no enthusiast for colonies. And the Crown Prince has little appetite for adventures abroad either.*

Yet something had changed. There was no telegraph here, no way of seeking advice, and Dawlish knew that any decision of his could be disowned. Kaunitz was a soul in agony but, if ordered to by Lutz, might be obliged to open fire in a hopeless duel with *Leonidas* and *Ibis*. And what would follow that would not stop with Mtwara.

A confusion of possibilities swirled in Dawlish's mind, but two ideas dominated.

Boldness and Caution.

*Don't step back. Don't provoke.*

And, at last – it might have been a half-minute, might have been a century – a decision.

"British and Zanzibari forces will occupy this building," Dawlish ignored Lutz, spoke directly to Kaunitz. "Your people can occupy the gatehouse. The courtyard's neutral ground."

"Kaunitz!" Lutz screamed.

But the German captain was ignoring him, was looking at Dawlish, something like understanding, like fellow-feeling, dawning.

347

"HMS *Ibis* will remain at anchor in the bay," Dawlish said. "I guarantee that she will fire no first shot on the *Hildegarde*. You have my word of honour as an officer for that."

Kaunitz smiled. "*Hildegarde's* magazines will have been emptied by the bombardment, Captain Dawlish. Wholly and absolutely. The *Ibis* will have nothing to fear. But the *Leonidas*?"

"Zanzibar," Dawlish dropped his voice. "The telegraph's there. Others can sort out this mess. It's neither yours nor mine, Kaunitz. And I trust that your crew – damn good fellows, all of them – will hold the gatehouse?"

A nod and a glance laden with contempt towards Lutz. "And the courtyard neutral ground, Captain Dawlish. A sensible solution."

"Kaunitz! Kaunitz!" Lutz shouted. "*Dafür wirst Du bezahlen! Du denkst das wird nicht ungestraft bleiben?*"

But the German captain strode forward, pushed aside the bayonets of the askaris standing by Lutz and put his face close to his. What he said was inaudible but it left Lutz looking chastened as well as furious. He shouted a command towards his askaris. They stood back.

Kaunitz reached out his hand, and Dawlish took it. No words, but sense of something that went far beyond respect or personal liking, something of shared caste, perhaps even of brotherhood. Then they saluted and Kaunitz wheeled about and left.

Only Lutz and his askaris remained, and behind them the cringing Sultan of Mtwara.

"You can take him with you to the gatehouse, Doktor Lutz," Dawlish jerked his head towards Saif. "And this gentleman will be remaining here." He pointed to Ibrahim. "If you've anything to say to him you'll need to speak first with Mr. Wainwright and Brigadier General Mathews. They'll remain in Mtwara."

Lutz snarled something incomprehensible – and no doubt uncomplimentary – in German and then to his askaris in Swahili. Dawlish was pleased to see that Lutz was trembling as he and they trooped out. His own knees were weak now, heart thumping, blood racing, mouth dry.

It was a truce.

But not a resolution.

*

There had been a truce of a sort in the courtyard also.

Forty or more disarmed Mtwara mercenaries squatted along the wall of the storehouse where Imker had taken refuge, their hands on their heads, fearful of the bayonets of the bluejackets penning them there.

Jarvis advanced to meet Dawlish. He seemed deflated, his fury and resentment dissipated.

"They shoved out a white flag," he said. "They saw that it was up with them."

"Imker?"

A pause, then Jarvis said "He's dead." He looked away.

"Did these people murder him?" Hard to imagine him yielding under a white flag.

"He killed himself." A pause. "He shot himself."

"Where's he now?"

"In there." Jarvis indicated the storehouse.

Sudden cool as they passed into the stone building. A large space, ivory stacked along one wall, several bodies – mercenaries – frozen in grotesque poses of agony, blood pooling about them. Dawlish and Jarvis stepped back to make way for four bluejackets who were lugging out a man on a blanket – a Somali, by his looks, his shoulder a shattered ruin of blood and shockingly white bone. "You'll be fine, mate, you'll be fine," one of the seamen was repeating without conviction.

Steps ahead, another body sprawled on them. No sign of easy surrender.

"You stormed the place, Commander?"

"They broke." Hesitation "We forced them back up here. That's when they saw it was hopeless. That's when they gave up. We let them out one by one, took their weapons."

"Imker agreed?"

Again hesitation. "He must have done. He must have wanted them to save themselves. He must have felt that he owed it to them."

"He didn't come out himself?"

A shake of the head. "I went in for him."

"And he'd shot himself?"

"He'd shot himself."

"Show me."

He was in a corner in the furthermost room, sitting on the floor, one leg outstretched, the other doubled beneath him, as if he had slipped down from the great spatter of blood – and worse – on the wall above, a long smear marking his slide down. A revolver lay by his side. His head was slumped forward, a huge exit wound at its back.

Dawlish forced himself to take hold of the hair above the forehead, to push the head gently towards the wall. Then, horrified, he dropped it, let it fall forward again.

Little remained of the face but a scarlet crater below the eyes – the terrible staring eyes, frozen in anger and hatred and fear.

Long silence.

Dawlish had known suicide several times before – inevitable in the navy. Slashed throats, hanging, suspect disappearances overboard. But when a man had put a pistol to his head it had always been in his mouth, or to his temple. Never to the centre of the face, never this.

He stood back, appalled as much as by what he suspected as by the reality itself.

"He... he must have heard me coming," A hint of pleading in Jarvis's voice. Of pleading to himself. "But then I heard the shot and ..."

"Was anybody with you?" Dawlish was facing him now and Jarvis was avoiding looking him in the face.

"Nobody. I pressed on by myself... I had to, the men were busy."

"And you found him like this?"

"I found him like this." Jarvis own head hanging now, as if some great weight was pressing down on him, as if he knew already that it always would.

Nothing to be gained by pressing the matter further, better to know nothing more.

"There was nobody else here, was there, Commander Jarvis?"

"Nobody else." Still not meeting Dawlish's eyes.

"You'll see to it that he gets a decent burial, commander?" Dawlish said. "And we'll need to talk with Wainwright and Mathews about what happens now. You'll be staying here with the *Ibis* for some time."

Out in the courtyard they reckoned the butcher's bill. Cheaper than feared, four dead from *Leonidas*, three from *Ibis*. Two Germans dead, but a half-dozen of Mathews' people. Eleven men badly wounded, two of them likely to die. Tadley had already set up a treatment post jointly with his brother surgeon from the *Hildegarde*. They had already completed two amputations. No more than five of Imker's Mtwari mercenaries wounded but many, upwards of forty, dead. There had been little mercy.

The fury had burned itself out and everywhere there was near-silence, broken only by long moaning and sudden screams that all pretended they did not hear. Shock and exhaustion had replaced jubilation, surprise at survival too, and unspoken gratitude that courage, which might have been doubted beforehand, had not failed. Dusty, thirsty and weary, there was little to distinguish British from German as they shared tobacco or lapsed into sleep in the shade.

And Dawlish was most heart-sick of all.

Whatever he had sought to achieve in this mission – so simple a goal to start, how elusive, how impossible to define thereafter – it had not been achieved.

But there was still Zanzibar.

And the telegraph.

## Chapter 34

"Lutz must have had that draft treaty for months," Dawlish said. "Long before this business."

The afternoon air was heavy in the high-ceilinged consular office, scarcely disturbed by the creaking punkah. Outside the open mesh-covered windows, beyond the union flag drooping so limply on its pole, Zanzibar baked in the merciless glare and shipping lay mirrored on the glass-calm harbour. Even the sight of *Leonidas* at anchor, her crew swarming over her to chip and paint and polish and scrub, could not raise Dawlish's spirits.

351

"They had us for fools," Kirk was bitter.

They had been studying the copy of the treaty that Stieglitz, the German consul, had brought to Kirk.

"How much did he know?" Dawlish asked.

Kirk shrugged. "Nothing. He's cock-a-hoop about it though, sees great scope for German trade, but for all his self-importance he seems only to have passed sealed packages to Lutz."

"You're sure that Kaunitz knew nothing of it?" Still that nagging doubt, the fear that friendship and regard could have masked deceit.

"They had him for a fool as well."

And '*they*' were not all in Berlin. An immediate response from London to the telegram that Kirk had despatched, when Dawlish had arrived with the news from Mtwara, had confirmed British acceptance. The substance must have been known of beforehand, had perhaps emerged from covert negotiations.

"It's been drawn up by a master," Kirk swept his hand over the third, English, column of text, next to the Arabic and German. "Thirty-one clauses, every damn one of them unexceptionable, most of them lifted from our own treaty with Zanzibar."

Not just unexceptionable, but noble. Immediate outlawing of slave trading outside Mtwara's borders. Commitment to gradual abolition within them, with compensation for owners, and immediate freedom for all newborns. All cases involving Europeans or Americans to be tried by consular court. Representation of Mtwara by the German Empire in all external matters, diplomatic, military and commercial. Provision for advisors on educational, economic, medical and agronomic improvement.

And protection for missionaries of all denominations.

"Horne won't like this," Dawlish said. "He wanted us, nobody else."

"He'll like it when he knows the details," Kirk said. "There's separate provision specifically for his mission. Generous even. The People's William will have no problem getting acceptance by his chapelgoers."

The devastated mission that the two surviving German brothers hoped to raise from its ashes would flourish too, Dawlish thought. He wondered how long Horne's fraternal feelings would survive.

Then – appallingly – a thought that had not struck him before. The memory of a conversation as the early sun had burned away the last wisps of the night's mist on the Rovuma.

"A Doktor Lutz," Albrecht von Hohenfels had said. "He renders to Caesar – or rather to the Kaiser – and we render to God."

The massacre at that monastery had been convenient for Lutz. A quiet word with the slavers at Nanguruwe would have been enough, not even a direct word but a message passed through Chief Kikuwa and a few hundred Maria Theresia dollars changing hands. Any suspicions of connivance would have been set at naught by fervid participation in the attack on Achmed's column. Once German blood had been spilled, German blood had to be avenged, no matter that the victims themselves would not have wished for it.

Had Berlin been party to that? Most probably not. Lutz was his own man, his own messiah, driven at any cost to others, or to himself, to establish a German foothold in Africa. Others might want the same but might shrink from the means that he embraced without hesitation.

But it had been convenient.

Dawlish recoiled from the thought. Better not to know for sure, better, as with Jarvis's final encounter with Imker, not to enquire too deeply. The temptation to despair in the face of evil's universality and strength had never yet lain so heavily upon him.

He had sought clarification from Topcliffe by telegraph. One word. *"Why?"*

And the reply scarcely longer.

*"Raison d'etat."*

Reason of state. Words that could justify anything, or everything. No argument. A decision that takes account of the world as it is, not as it might be hoped to be.

Ibrahim was back in Zanzibar now, an inconvenient pensioner of the sultan and likely to be dead of his addictions within a year. Mathews' troops were being withdrawn from Mtwara and the *Ibis* would carry the last of them when she left. Jarvis and Kaunitz had cooperated easily and had conducted a joint burial service for British and German dead. Dawlish had already commended Jarvis in his exchange of telegrams with the Admiralty. There was every reason why the embarrassments of his service in Borneo should no longer prejudice his career.

Dawlish's own command of *Leonidas* was all but at an end. He had confirmation of what Topcliffe had hinted in that Pall Mall club library. She was to join the Mediterranean Fleet and Dawlish would hand her over at Malta and proceed to London thereafter. No mention of his next assignment. He was craving for the quiet haven of love and joy that Florence was to him. Whatever lay ahead, they would at least have a few months together, the European tour he had promised her, quiet evenings in the villa at Southsea, the sounds of her piano in another room as he sat with a book, laughter shared across the breakfast table as she read some bizarre newspaper item out loud.

He longed urgently for the cleanliness of the open sea, to leave behind so much horror, so much confusion and betrayal, so much sacrifice. A stop for coaling at Aden, a fast run through the Red Sea's steam-bath and the Canal beyond, another four days to Malta. A week, ten days there at most to complete hand-over and then home. He could foresee searching interrogation by Topcliffe, who would determine what he must, and must not, say in interviews with ministers and Foreign Office officials. He would slave over long reports too, no detail unimportant, reports to be consigned to fire-proof safes and never to be seen by more than a dozen eyes.

But until Malta he would turn his mind from that, would glory in his last weeks' command of *Leonidas*, enjoy her slim white hull cleaving the waters, deck throbbing faintly underfoot, pistons flailing, screws churning, cutlass and bayonet practice on deck, Purdon's guns exercised with pride justified by their smashing of Fort Manuel.

And write letters to the families of the dead.

The worst duty of all.

\*

The *Hildegarde* slipped into Zanzibar the day before *Leonidas* departed. Salutes were exchanged and crews lined both decks to cheer each other. No time for formal dinners but Dawlish – in full uniform, and pleased that his beard had by now grown back – went across, was piped on board with full ceremony, joined Kaunitz in his personal quarters. The conversation was guarded, the compliments on each other's crew's performance stilted. A boundary had been crossed since they had sailed together from here so recently. No matter how much personal regard persisted – and Dawlish recognised it in Kaunitz, unspoken though it was, as he did in himself – a gulf had opened between them, each privy to events that could never be acknowledged.

It was an uncomfortable half-hour. The excellence of Kaunitz's Elbtal wine was praised with forced enthusiasm. Best wishes for the continuation of *Hildegarde's* circumnavigation – she was to pick up the scientists she had left at Madras and would continue the expedition as previously planned. Equally warm wishes for *Leonidas's* run to Malta and for Dawlish's next appointment. Compliments to be presented to each other's wives. Hopes of future meetings. Nothing of politics.

Until…

"What did you whisper to Lutz in Mtwara?" Dawlish had to ask the question, however much he shrank from it.

Kaunitz waved his hand slightly. "I'm a Prussian junker, Captain Dawlish. That brings some entitlements as well as obligations, some valuable contacts also." No need to say more.

Almost time to leave, but first the real purpose of this meeting.

"An unofficial request, Fregattenkapitän Kaunitz. From me personally. That you'll take charge of something that does justice to the memory of a brave man. Of other brave men with him."

"An honour, Captain Dawlish."

"It's waiting in my gig. If a man could be sent for it?"

It was a chest, specially fabricated by *Leonidas's* carpenter, functional in design and elegant in execution, corners dovetailed and brass-bound, wood smooth and polished.

Dawlish laid his hand on it. "It's a legacy," he said. "One that I know you will see reaches those who'll most value it."

He threw the lid open.

Seven ash-smeared ledgers.

Matthew's Gospel.

# The End

Below you will find a personal message from Antoine Vanner and a historical note on the background to *Britannia's Mission*. Note that this book ends with Captain Nicholas Dawlish anticipating a fast return to Britain, via Malta, in HMS *Leonidas*. How that hope proved to be vain is told in the opening chapters of the next volume in chronological order, *Britannia's Gamble*.

## A message from Antoine Vanner

I'd be most grateful if you were to submit a brief review of this book to Amazon.com or Amazon.co.uk. If you're reading on Kindle you'll be asked after this to rate the book by clicking on up to five stars. Such feedback is of incalculable importance to independent authors and will encourage me to keep chronicling the lives of Nicholas and Florence Dawlish.

If you'd like to leave a review, whether reading in Hard Copy or Kindle, then please go to the *"Britannia's Mission"* page on Amazon. Scroll down from the top and under the heading of "Customer Reviews" you'll see a big button that says "Write a customer review" – click that and you're ready to get into action. A sentence or two is enough, essentially what you'd tell a friend or family member about the book, but you may of course want to write more (and I'd be happy if you did!).

You can learn more about Nicholas Dawlish and his world on my website dawlishchronicles.com and you may like to follow my weekly blog on dawlishchronicles.com/dawlish-blog in which articles appear that are based on my researches, but not used directly in my books. They range through the 1700 to 1930 period.

By subscribing to my mailing list you will receive updates on my continuing writing as well as occasional free short-stories about the life of Nicholas Dawlish. Click on: bit.ly/2iaLzL7

## Historical Note

The *raison d'etat* referred to by Admiral Sir Richard Topcliffe regarding acceptance of a German Protectorate in East Africa was almost certainly the result of secret discussions with Germany in advance of the Berlin Conference of 1884. "The Scramble for Africa", in which European nations contended to claim large portions of the continent for themselves, was already in full swing. Though a late convert to the idea of overseas colonies, the German Chancellor, Otto von Bismarck, pressed for a meeting between the main players so as to provide a legal and diplomatic framework for establishing territorial boundaries.

Though confidential negotiations between several nations almost certainly took place beforehand, and secret deals made, the conference itself did not begin until November 1884. A total of twelve European nations attended, plus the United States and the Ottoman Empire. Agreement of a "Principle of Effective Occupation", which allowed colonial powers to expand into Africa's interior from bases already established on the coast, was to be the underpinning of a division of the continent between Britain, France, Belgium, Portugal, Spain and Italy in the coming decades. No Africans were consulted and only Ethiopia remained independent in the long term, and Zanzibar and Morocco in the shorter. None of them had been invited to the conference.

The onshore area of what is the present Republic of Tanzania became in due course the German colony of Tanganyika. Zanzibar maintained its nominal independence until 1890, when a formal British protectorate was established. Germany assented to this protectorate in return for Britain ceding to Germany the fortified island of Heligoland in the North Sea. Since Heligoland lay close to the North German ports and the entrance to the Kiel Canal, one of the great "What Ifs" of history is what the consequences could have been of Britain retaining it. Though great in area – almost a third greater than Germany itself, and rich in cash-crop potential, Tanganyika did not see large scale German settlement – little over 800 farmers and planters by 1914. Tanganyika was however to be the scene of one of the most extraordinary campaigns of World War One when a force of some 3,500 German troops and some 12,000 African askaris and porters held out for four years against British and Empire forces. Led by the brilliant General Paul von Lettow-Vorbeck (1870-1964), cut off by British blockade from supplies from Germany, this small army held out against forces three times larger. It was still on the offensive when the war ended in 1918 and it submitted to an armistice three days later than German forces in Europe.

The Sultanate of Zanzibar endured as a British protectorate until it became an independent country in 1963. The sultan was deposed soon after, an episode that led to massacres and, finally, to incorporation in the independent Republic of Tanzania.

The indomitable Lloyd Mathews (1850-1901) remained in Zanzibari service, fighting several impressive campaigns with minimal forces. In 1891, by now knighted, he was appointed First Minister. In 1896 he played a key role in "The Shortest War in History" – some thirty-eight minutes – when a dispute arose over succession to the sultanate. In the aftermath he realized his ambition of abolishing slavery in Zanzibar and its possessions. He died of malaria in 1901.

John Kirk (1832 - 1922) was to be the last survivor of the heroic age of African exploration. Starting as a medical doctor, accompanying David Livingstone on his expeditions in the 1860s, establishing himself as a botanist and zoologist of note, he played a crucial diplomatic role in Zanzibar until 1887. He continued thereafter to take an important part in African affairs, both commercial and political, in areas as diverse as Nigeria and Uganda, and he represented Britain in international efforts to eliminate the slave trade. Though deservedly knighted for these activities, he was possibly most proud of his scientific work. This was honoured by his name being given to a species of monkey known as Kirk's Red Colobus *(Procolobus kirkii)*, a species of lizard *(Agama kirkii)* and a limbless amphibian named Kirk's Caecilian *(Scolecomorphus kirkii)*.

Naval Brigades – forces composed of landed seamen and marines – were a feature of the Royal Navy in the late-19th and early 20th Centuries. They might be as small as a few dozen men drawn from a single ship, up to a thousand or more contributed by entire squadrons. Their service often took them far inland and facility with blocks and tackles proved a boon for moving equipment in difficult conditions. They fought in major conflicts such as the Crimean War, the Indian Mutiny, the Abyssinia and Ashanti campaigns, the Zulu War, the Egyptian campaign of 1882 and in those in the Sudan in 1884-85 and 1898, the Benin Expedition of 1897 and the Boxer Rising, as well as in many smaller deployments. The "Landed Field Gun" that could be carried in pieces across every obstacle became emblematic of such brigades and its memory lives on in competitions still organized by the Royal Navy. The largest "brigade" of all was not indeed a brigade, but rather an entire division, the 63rd (Royal Naval) Division, a brainchild of Winston Churchill, which fought with distinction at Antwerp in 1914, at Gallipoli in 1915-16 and on the Western Front 1916-18.

Christian missionaries of every denomination had a massive impact on values and beliefs in Sub-Saharan Africa in the late nineteenth and early twentieth centuries, an impact that is still important today. Selfless, indomitable, sometimes naïve but always heroic, often to the point of madness, they were responsible for the fastest and largest mass-conversion in history. Anyone familiar with Africa today cannot but be impressed by the exuberance and sincerity of the Christianity that flourishes there in so many forms and how integral it is in community life. It is touching also to see how often the memory of missionaries long dead is still revered there.

Many missionary societies were active in the fight against the Indian Ocean slave trade and were tireless in pressing European governments for its suppression, the lead being given by David Livingstone himself. Judged by today's standards, the missionaries are frequently misunderstood, and on occasion caricatured to the point of ridicule, but they left a legacy not only in the field of religious belief but in medical care, education and raised awareness of the value of human life. Whether poorly educated, like so many of the men and women from humble backgrounds who volunteered to meet challenges they could barely imagine beforehand, or representatives of better-funded undertakings by well-established religious bodies, they cheerfully accepted the risk of death by violence or disease and the certainty of long years of privation or loneliness. As regards Tanganyika it is interesting to note that missionary work was undertaken from the 1880s by German monks and nuns of the Benedictine Congregation of St. Ottilien, several of whom were martyred in 1889. More were murdered in 1905 when their mission was destroyed during the so-called Maji-Maji rising against German rule. German Lutheran missionary activity was similarly energetic and Lutheranism remains a force in Tanzania today despite the ending of formal German government presence at the end of World War One.

And the slave trade itself? Though finally suppressed in the North and South Atlantic, and in the Indian Ocean, by the late nineteenth century, this curse lives on in other forms today, sometimes even on our own doorsteps in developed countries. Our outrage against it, and our resolve to combat it wherever it flourishes, should be no less strong than that of our Victorian forebears.

Old Salt Press is an independent press catering to those who love books about ships and the sea. We are an association of writers working together to produce the very best of nautical and maritime fiction and non-fiction. We invite you to join us as we go down to the sea in books.

Our writers are Rick Spillman, Joan Druett, Linda Collison, V. E. Ulett, Alaric Bond and Antoine Vanner, all of whom write fiction. Joan Druett, in addition to her novels, also writes meticulously researched maritime history.

Visit oldsaltpress.com/about-old-salt-press

Made in the USA
San Bernardino, CA
30 March 2019